HOLDING OUT

a novel

ANNE O. FAULK

SIMON & SCHUSTER

Simon & Schuster
Rockefeller Center
1230 Avenue of the Americas
New York, NY 10020

Simon & Schuster and colophon are registered trademarks
of Simon & Schuster Inc.

Designed by Jeanette Olender
Manufactured in the United States of America

10 9 8 7 6 5 4 3 2 1

Library of Congress Cataloging-in-Publication Data
Faulk, Anne O.
Holding out: a novel / Anne O. Faulk.
p. cm.
I. Title.
PS3556.A916H65   1998
813'.54—dc21   97-35638   CIP
ISBN 0-684-84671-3

TO HAMILTON WITH LOVE,

AND FOR BIGGIE AND PAPA

HOLDING OUT

Chapter 1

I think I should start this off by saying that I am the last person on earth you would expect to end up a political prisoner. Except maybe Burl Ives, and I think he might be dead. I mean I am hardly the type. I'm much more likely to be compared to Madonna than Mandela. At least I *was* before all this happened.

I've been in a lot of places and fantasized about being in a lot of others, but I certainly never dreamed I'd end up in the Hardwick Women's Correctional Facility. Granted, I have my own trailer, which we call "Tara," and I'm allowed "special privileges," but let no one believe that these gifts flow from the benevolence of the great state of Georgia. They are both for the benefit and convenience of the national news media and a political concession to the thousands of people who come here regularly and chant my name at the gates.

They say that some people are born great, some people achieve greatness and some people have greatness thrust upon them. I am clearly in the third category, and at this point I'd like to thrust it right back.

I certainly wasn't born great. I grew up the third and invisible child of five, the "brain" in a family that valued only athletic achievement. For all the hoopla about my looks, I wasn't considered the beauty in my family. That honor went first to my older sister Gigi, who was even briefly a runway model, then to my baby sister Bobbie, who waddled through junior high and metamorphosed in her sophomore year into a teen queen.

I was a bored and uninspired student at Miss Porter's until I was asked to leave on May 2nd, in my junior year. My crime was substituting Marvin Gaye's "Let's Get It On" for the traditional May Day processional on the school's loudspeaker. The audience loved it, but the May Queen, whose father was on the board of trustees, was not amused. So, I finished my secondary school career at Girls Preparatory School. The yearbook at GPS doesn't list me in the Senior Honors section, although I was the president of the SSDS (the Secret Senior Drinking Society) as well as the holder of the record for the most classes skipped in a year (205).

I went to the University of Virginia, where I became engaged my freshman year to a boy whose family I had fallen in love with. We married my sophomore year, and I had Razz my senior year. The marriage was low-grade misery, but when I became a mother, I vowed that Razz would have a happy home with his original mommy and daddy. Then, four years later, when most of my friends were marrying for the first time, I just gave up and got a divorce.

As for achieving greatness, I can say that I've aspired to a lot of things, but I don't know that greatness would have even made the short list.

I've aspired to be a wonderful mother, something that surely doesn't fit my image, but anyone who knows me at all knows it has been my number one priority since that afternoon sixteen years ago when John Ransom Fontaine was delivered, absolutely livid, at University Hospital in Augusta, Georgia.

I have aspired to be a loyal friend, a fearsome enemy and an accomplished lover, and I think that anyone who has known me in any one or more of the aforementioned capacities would likely tell you that I've been successful. I have also aspired to things where I've been an abject failure. I aspired to be a good and dutiful wife and was unable to pull it off. I aspired to be a great athlete and never overtook mediocrity. I also aspired to never cause my family and friends pain. The last three months have been a veritable monument to *that* failure.

If I aspired to anything resembling greatness, it's that I always wanted to live a giant life, full of passion and adventure, love and achievement, a life unsullied by fear or regrets for what I almost did or almost was. I certainly did not aspire to the kind of "greatness" that some in the movement now ascribe to me.

Three months ago no one knew who I was, now I'm one of the most famous people in America. I think I must have appeared on the cover of every magazine in the country with the exception of *Popular Mechanics* and *Opera News*. My sister Gigi is keeping a scrapbook, and the damn thing must weigh twenty pounds. On Sundays she brings it, with all the new things she's collected, and reads the articles to me as we marvel at the sheer creativity of the press. I mean, where do these people *get* this stuff?

Gigi's favorite, back toward the very beginning, was the cover of *New York* magazine. The photo must have been taken at the Met premiere of *Turandot*, and I'm wearing a low-cut dress and laughing. The caption reads "This woman may have caused the end of civilization as we know it . . . and she thinks it's funny."

Maybe I'm just touchy but I thought that seemed a tad hysterical.

Razz's favorite is the quote, "This century has seen some real trouble-makers—Adolf Hitler, Idi Amin, Saddam Hussein—but they must be considered rank amateurs compared to Lauren Fontaine." And this wasn't from some religious monthly, this was from the *Wall Street Journal*, for God's sake! And it wasn't even on the editorial page—this was supposedly an unbiased "journalistic" story on the movement.

This "thing," as my mother would say, has made people forget themselves. My mother, however, has *not* forgotten herself. She doesn't visit, though she calls twice a week. She's gone from being thrilled at my fame to mortified that, as she puts it, I've "ended up in jail." I have tried on several occasions to explain to her the difference between being a political prisoner and a criminal, but it makes no difference—she's as embarrassed in front of her bridge friends as if I'd been convicted of knocking over 7-Elevens.

Gigi comes every day. It's an hour commute each way, and she's only missed twice, and knowing that she's coming is one of the things that keeps me sane. It's not that I don't have plenty of visitors, but Gigi's the one who can make me laugh. She has a wonderful sense of the absurd, and some days she can even make me think of this as an unexpected adventure instead of a hideous nightmare.

Razz is taking this pretty well, I think. "As well as can be expected" is the phrase he uses, because he knows it just slays me. I talk to him every day for as long as he feels like talking. Sometimes that's two hours and sometimes two minutes. When I came here, I hired an old friend of mine to be his bodyguard. Razz acts as if this is a horrible imposition but is secretly thrilled to be the first kid on his block to have one.

I think this has been harder on Razz than anybody. After all, he's the age where he doesn't want any attention called to himself, where a normal parent is a terrible burden, much less one who's regularly on the nightly news.

It is, I have to say, by far the hardest part for me—to be separated from him and to know that he's in pain is more horrible than I can describe. Late at night it sneaks up on me and sits in this room like a fog of sadness. Missing him and knowing that he's suffering and not being able to comfort him is a wound as hot and deep as a dog bite. We talk about the difficulties together, but out of kindness neither of us elaborates, and every night I pray that we'll both be OK.

Prison has very little to recommend it. It's a dreadful experience, especially if, like me, you don't enjoy the company of criminals. Not that this is my first experience with them, since I spent several years working on Wall Street. It's just that the ones here can't even talk about why Negril is more fun than St. Barts, or why *Rigoletto* is a better opera than *La Traviata*.

Similarly, I am at a loss to debate why it is more effective to "cut" a girl who has moved in on your pimp than just to get her into a "lock" and break off her teeth on the curb. Funny, but this sort of lively discussion surpasses my realm of experience.

What's worse than the people and the lack of freedom and the horrors of prison, most of which I've been mercifully spared, is the stupefying sameness of every day. I've always wallowed happily in the chaos of my life—a Rubik's Cube of people and activities. But prison is the tedium of repeated movements, like walking endlessly around in a circle. I have an almost constant sense of déjà vu.

In prison the most basic pleasures are surrendered, even things like jogging. I've jogged for years, but running in a prison yard is simply not a prudent thing to do. All of the guards are male, the meanest kind of no-neck rednecks, and they carry large automatic weapons. Watching them watch me makes me feel like a ten-point buck on opening day of hunting season.

So now exercise consists of working out with old Jane Fonda tapes on the VCR or dancing nonstop through the entire tape of *Little Richard Live at the O.K. Club.* This, I might add, is harder than you'd think.

The mornings are taken up talking on the phone, either with interviews or with the movement leaders. There is enormous tension in the ranks, and I spend a part of every day trying to hold things together. When I started this you could never have convinced me that it would last for more than a couple of weeks max. Anyway, it gets harder and harder to control, but I guess that's the natural progression for this sort of thing.

The afternoons are taken up with visitors, reporters, or friends. My sweetheart comes frequently, and we are even offered conjugal privileges. "Fat chance," is my only comment. I'm quite sure that Tara is bugged, and even if it weren't—well, it would hardly be kosher. I must admit though that I think about it almost constantly.

I also entertain my fair share of visiting dignitaries, politicians, etc. I try very hard to be uniformly passionate, articulate and charming, but sometimes it's like dancing nonstop through the entire Little Richard tape—harder than you'd think.

I never make appointments after 2:30, so by the time Gigi gets here I'm finished with my guests. I've even been known to escort startled politicians to the door at the stroke of 4:00. I am happy to be hospitable; I guess that's the Southerner in me. But my time with Gigi is a treasure I guard jealously, like a woman with a married lover.

She arrives at 4:00 and we make drinks and I tell her about my day and she tells me about the outside world. We give each other advice, we strategize and sometimes we even laugh. Gigi and I have two things that keep us incredibly close: the billion reference points that allow us to communicate in verbal shorthand, and an identical sense of humor. We can say more to each other with three words than other people can express in twenty minutes, and we can drive each other into hysterics over something that outsiders might find only marginally amusing.

Every afternoon we cook together, trying out recipes, just the way we did as teenagers. Then, visiting hours over, I eat alone and she drives home to make dinner for her new husband, the fabulous Tom Patterson.

I used to play basketball in the evening with the other women, until it became a problem. So many of the inmates think of me as a hero. They want to touch my hand and encourage me and tell me their stories, and I've always tried to listen and let them know that I'd heard them, and I'd hug them when they cried, because I know everybody needs that. But it became fairly evident that I had become the "object of affection" for several of these women, and I can't decide which made me more uncomfortable, the ones who'd write me love letters and make me presents, or the ones who'd call out their romantic and sexual intentions like dockworkers. I mean, regardless of what I started or how I'm viewed by the male population of the world, I have always been a lover of men.

Exclusively, totally, purely, a girl who likes boys.

Chapter 2

The whole thing started on June 18th. That's the day that the Congress found Larry Underwood faultless in the death of his wife. Like so many other modern outrages, it began with a grisly headline and ended with a miscarriage of justice. At times it literally seemed pieced together from old headlines. Though it was often described as the Clarence Thomas hearings meets the O.J. Simpson trial, its focus wasn't a mere nominee to the Supreme Court but its chief justice, and its catalyst wasn't a murder but a suicide. The suicide of Mrs. Underwood, to be exact.

Actually, it really all began on April Fools' Day. That was when a neighbor found the body. I was as stunned as everyone else by the news that one of America's best loved and most admired women would kill herself, but it certainly never occurred to me that her death would change my life forever.

I followed the case with the same growing horror and disbelief as the rest of the country. Which is to say that I scoured every article and watched every second of the TV coverage of the unfolding investigation. And I was just as certain as everyone else that, while he technically may not have killed her, Chief Justice Lawrence Caine Underwood III was one hundred percent responsible for the death of his wife.

So I was every bit as stunned as the next person when Underwood declined the President's call for his resignation. And while it was the discovery of Larry Underwood's glee in causing his wife's suffering that made him repulsive to every woman in America, it was his arrogant refusal to go gracefully that made him the most hated man in this country's history.

Though a lot of people would claim the honor, I'm sure I was the happiest person around when Congress was called into session to impeach the bastard.

There was nothing memorable about that Tuesday morning, nothing that would have given warning about what was to come. I remember Gigi dropped by the office with donuts, and we had this conversation about how I hadn't been involved with anyone since the polo player, unless you count Slick, which I don't and who's a whole separate story anyway, and how things at my office seemed to be humming along without the obligatory weekly crisis and how I was sure my life was finally getting simple.

By early afternoon I was on the StairMaster at my club, working my tail off, or at least trying to, and watching CNN. My right shoe was tied too tightly, and the tongue was digging into the top of my foot. I'd been on the machine for about forty minutes and was looking down to see how much longer I had and how many calories I'd burned.

It was one of those moments that you remember perfectly, like when Kennedy was shot or the *Challenger* exploded. The shock brings the moment into sharp focus and fixes it forever in your memory. You live big chunks of your life in a blur, but at times like those your brain takes one hideous snapshot so that you can forever remember the horror in flawless detail. Agony on Kodachrome.

I was looking down at the controls, trying to decide whether to get off and retie my shoe, so I didn't see the TV screen—I just heard the words of the woman announcer: "Today, in a stunning verdict that came after less than a day of testimony, Congress found Chief Justice Lawrence Caine Underwood III innocent of all charges of spousal abuse stemming from the suicide of his wife and declined to impeach him."

I don't remember what she said next; I was so stunned, I couldn't think. I don't know how long I stood like that, for I had gotten off the StairMaster. I turned to get other reactions, to speak to someone, to share the icy outrage, but there was no one there. The clock said 1:27, and it was as if I were the only person in the world who knew, as if the news were a terrible burden that I would be responsible for revealing.

Then I realized that it was not an annunciation but just another of the day's news stories. I walked, shivering, through the dressing room and collected my clothes. I didn't shower, and I didn't change. I just drove back to my office and surprised my assistant, Sherry, who was trying to scrape one more bite of frozen yogurt from the bottom of her cup. "What's the matter? What's wrong? Has something happened?" She stopped with a spoonful halfway to her mouth.

I guess it was obvious from the look on my face and the fact that while my clothes are often cutting-edge fashion, I've never appeared in the office wearing a sapphire blue leotard.

"Are you OK?" She put the spoonful back in the cup uneaten.

"No, I'm not OK, but thanks for asking."

"What happened?"

I shook my head. "They did it. They let him off."

She stared at me with her mouth open. "That's not possible." Then she smiled to lure a confession that I was, of course, only kidding. I wasn't. Her face fell. "Are you sure?"

"I just heard it on the news."

"Goddammit!" She slammed her fist on the desk, spilling the spoonful of yogurt on the counter. It was the first time in all the years that I'd known her that I'd ever heard Sherry swear, and it startled me. We looked at each other for a long time.

I shook my head. "I just can't believe this. Can you believe this?" But I didn't stop for an answer. "I can't get over it. I'm going to my office and I don't want to be disturbed."

I sat and finally loosened my shoe and rubbed the top of my foot, which by now was totally numb. Then I began to call my friends. They would feel the same way I did. I don't think there was a woman in America who didn't despise Lawrence Underwood and think he deserved to be in prison or worse.

No one was available. I left a message on Gigi's answering machine, with Betsy's secretary, on Kate's voice mail. I even called Jo Lewis, but she was on vacation.

I finally gave up and attempted to get some work done. I kept trying to listen to the tape of a conversation between one of our traders and a client. All trading rooms have voice-activated recorders on the phones, so if there are misunderstandings or an order is misplaced, there is a taped record of it. A client was claiming that he had placed an order for 40,000 shares of IBM and the trader claimed that it was for 30,000 shares. As the managing partner of Sterling White's Atlanta office, it's one of my jobs to settle client-trader disputes, so I played the tape, rewinding it several times. But it was no use; I couldn't concentrate. I turned the machine off and just stared out the window.

I know it's been out of vogue for years to be a feminist. I hear young women saying, "No, I'm not a feminist, but I do believe that a woman should get equal pay for equal work and have all the same opportunities as men and be treated fairly . . ." I always wonder what in the hell they think feminism is if not that. It irritates me that they enjoy the rights and expectations and dismiss the women who won them.

Well, it may be as out of favor as communism, but I'm a feminist. I believe in the sisterhood of women. Although to be honest, I find this much easier to subscribe to in theory than in practice. Groups of women scare me, for I've seen firsthand that women are capable of extraordinary cruelty. I learned it young and have seen it exhibited every time I've forgotten and ventured into their midst. This doesn't mean that I don't feel strongly about women's rights, it just means that I like to do it from a safe distance.

So I sat looking out the window, not focusing on the view but thinking of the message today's verdict sent to men: if you're powerful enough, you can do anything you want, and that included beating your wife to a pulp on a regular basis. This wasn't like the O.J. Simpson verdict; it couldn't be explained as a race thing. It was *gender*. It was powerful men protecting a powerful man for political reasons, and its ramifications were sickening. I was trying to imagine what it would mean to women.

There was a knock on the door and I heard it open. Sherry's tentative voice came through the crack. "I know you don't want to be disturbed, but on the radio it says that there's going to be a march in Washington on Sunday."

I looked up.

"They want two million women to show up. They want it to be twice as big as any march in history."

"Call Ali Wolverton's secretary and tell her I'm coming and I want to help." I didn't even think, I just said it. When Sherry closed the door, I was left trying to imagine what the march would be like. I'd never done anything remotely like it, never been agitated enough about anything politically or socially to do more than develop a strong opinion. I was wondering where two million people would possibly fit in the Washington Mall when it dawned on me that it meant one thing for certain —Port-O-Lets. Though it may sound weird, I have a giant case of Port-O-Letaphobia, and the idea of them is frequently enough to deter me from outdoor activities involving large crowds. That thought made me even angrier. I left my office and stood at Sherry's desk. She was still on the phone.

"What's the problem?" I asked.

"Hold on a second," she said into the phone, then looked up at me. "You're not going to like this, but there are no seats, not even coach, on either Friday or Saturday. The airlines are already swamped with people trying to get to Washington for the march."

Sherry was tapping one long crimson fingernail on the desk. She always does that when she tells me bad news. I started to say forget it when a memory crawled up the back of my neck. "Well, what about Amtrak?"

"What about Amtrak?" She repeated into the phone. We waited. She looked up triumphantly and stopped tapping. "No seats for Saturday, but there's one seat available Friday night. Hold on." She was listening. "It's not a sleeper. The train leaves here at 6:30 Friday night and arrives in Washington at 8:20 Saturday morning."

"I'll take it."

I left the office as soon as the market closed and I'd checked the firm's positions—won big in equities, lost bigger in bonds. The news came on the car radio as I was turning onto our street, and I was so busy cursing and changing channels that I almost ran into my neighbor's Ferrari. No one was home when I arrived. Elizabeth was in class and Razz was still at baseball. I poured half a tumbler of Glenlivet, put in an

Aretha Franklin CD, and sat in a hot bath until I was wrinkled, half drunk and only livid.

My friends began to call around 5:30. Each conversation began with where we were when we heard. Betsy hadn't gone back to the office but had heard on the car radio while stuck in traffic; Kate had heard it from one of the women in her group, and they had spent the whole hour discussing their feelings about it. Gigi had heard at the salon while getting highlights. Gigi was by far the angriest.

"It makes me so goddamn mad!"

"I know. Me too. I was pissed off when Clarence Thomas was confirmed, and I was *furious* when O.J. Simpson got off, but those were nothing compared to this. I would personally like to kill that evil bastard with my own hands." I made a fist at the thought of it.

"Yeah? Well, get at the back of the line. I'd like to deliver my own verdict—with a baseball bat. I just can't believe they think they can get away with this."

"They think they can get away with it because they always do. There'll be a furious outcry for a few weeks, then things will die down. That's always the way it works."

"I don't know. This has made women madder than anything I've ever seen. Did you see tonight's paper? It has a giant picture of Larry Underwood's face when the House announced its vote, and over it the headline 'This One Really Beats All.' "

"It's just inconceivable. But guess what? I'm going to the march in Washington."

"You're kidding."

"I'm not."

"I'll go with you," she announced.

"You can't. I got the last seat on the train and all the flights are booked."

"Oh. Well, I couldn't really go anyway. I'm having a dinner party for Tom's boss and his wife. But I'm counting on you to go up there and make those creeps really sorry."

"Speaking of Tom, what does he say?" Tom was Gigi's second husband. They had been married for about a year and a half, and she was happier than I'd ever seen her. Her first marriage had been a nightmare, and Gigi attended to this one like the mother of a premature infant.

"He really didn't have a chance to tell me. I simply bit off his head the minute he walked in the door. Then I had to apologize. I told him, I'm just mad because you're a man. And he said he was confused because he thought that's why I married him." She laughed. "What does Slick say?"

"I haven't talked to him, and he's smart enough not to call."

"Poor Slick," she said. "He'll get it from you and from her."

"Her" was Slick's wife, Annie. Slick once said that the way God punished men for having affairs was to make them live through two PMS episodes every month. Not only does Slick feel the effects of PMS twenty-four times a year, he gets a double dose whenever a new outrage against women occurs, because Annie and I not only share Slick, we share the same views on women's issues.

Now I've never met Annie in person, of course, but Slick says that if we met under different circumstances, we'd be great pals. He is mistaken. I detest her. Part of it is simple: I'd be hard pressed both to like her and to justify borrowing, without permission, something as personal as her husband. But it's much more complicated than that. She's never had to struggle for anything; everything has simply been handed to her. I know what Annie thinks her problems are, and I find them stupid and petty. She has no idea how tough it is or how tough it makes you to fight every day to make sure that what you receive bears some resemblance to what you've earned.

Another reason why I hate Annie is because she discarded Slick like old garbage, then when she discovered that he'd found someone who thought he was a treasure, she decided she had to have him back. I have to confess, the enormity of my loathing is due not to the fact that she wanted him back so much as the fact that she *got* him.

I turned on the cold water. "If he gets it from both of us, it serves him right," I said. "Even though I know he's on our side. He always is. He's probably one of about sixteen men on earth who deserve to live."

"Yeah, honey, that's the truth." Gigi loves Slick. She had been both skeptical and hostile when we first fell in love. "Just what you need, some married asshole," she'd moaned, but over the years she changed her mind. By the time we split up for good, she'd become his greatest advocate.

There was a long silence, then she said in a voice soaked in sadness, "You know, I've been thinking about Sofia all day."

"I know, sweetie. I have too."

I'd skipped the second grade so Gigi and I were in the same class in school, and her best friend was Sofia Noury. In the spring of our senior year, Sofia turned up pregnant. The second week of May, Gigi started getting late-night phone calls from Sofia, which was not terribly un-usual. What was strange was that she would take the phone into the bathroom and close the door.

I had assumed the calls were about Travis. Sofia had dated Travis Lee for about two months before spring break. I'd been very skeptical about their romance because Travis had a bad reputation for using girls. He was incredibly handsome, and Sofia had had a crush on him since junior high. She was giddy about his attention, but two days after spring break was over, he dropped her and asked Happy Baker to the senior dance.

The calls had continued for several nights before I confronted Gigi, who told me that Sofia was pregnant. Gigi said that Sofia was hysterical, and we went to her house the next day after school because she called in sick for the second day in a row.

Her mother had died when Sofia was a baby, leaving her at the mercy of her father, a wealthy man with both the hooded eyes and the personality of a pit viper. He was suspicious of all of her friends. He was always calling, checking up on her whenever she was at our house, which was most of the time. He would have made a top-notch stalker. She never talked about it, but it was obvious she was terrified of him, and for good reason. Gigi had told me why Sofia dressed and undressed in a bathroom stall for gym, and it had nothing to do with modesty.

The only time Gigi would ever go to their house was when she knew Mr. Noury wouldn't be home. I'd never even been closer than the curb in front of the mansion, where we'd pick Sofia up or drop her off. But that second day in a row that she missed school, I went in.

The maid answered the door, and Gigi led me down the long hallway.

I'll never forget walking into Sofia's room and seeing her in her night-gown, face white, eyes dead, rocking from side to side, chanting, "My father will kill me, my father will kill me."

Gigi held her and we tried everything we could think of to calm her down, but she was inconsolable. She wouldn't consider abortion nor would she allow us to stay with her while she told her father, a suggestion I offered but certainly didn't relish. No, she said, she was going to tell her father alone and she would call us after she did.

She didn't call the next day, and Gigi was afraid to call her house. That weekend, Gigi was like an animal in a cage, pacing around our room, asking a hundred times what I thought she should do.

Monday, Sofia still wasn't back at school, and during lunch the headmaster came on the cafeteria intercom and asked *all the seniors* to come to chapel at the beginning of the next period. Rumors flew around the lunch tables, and everyone was speculating on whether they were going to make National Honor Society announcements or declare another crackdown on girls who smoked in uniform. When we had all filed in and settled down, I was sitting in the front row between Jaynie Roberts and Bethy Robinson.

It was another of those moments burned into memory. The headmaster stood at the pulpit and the senior teachers were in the back of the room and they were very quiet and several of them had been crying and he began, "Girls, I am so saddened . . ."

And I knew and I began to get up, to look for Gigi, and by the time he got to "your classmate," I was standing, turning and I saw her behind me three rows back and our eyes found each other's and her hands flew to her mouth, and I heard "a terrible accident, a tragedy," and I was moving in slow motion. I was trying to get to her to cover her ears so she wouldn't hear, so she wouldn't know. I came around the pew, and he said, "fell down the marble steps" and I felt the reaction as ninety pairs of lungs sucked involuntarily, in unison, mass shock, and I was on my way and our eyes never left each other's, and I was holding her. I was holding her tightly, and she had the look of someone whose windpipe is blocked. Her anguish was too enormous to escape, and I held on while she pitched and then finally sobbed, and the headmaster was praying and no one was listening. We were crying. The girls who hadn't been close to Sofia held and comforted those who had. The headmaster called off the afternoon's classes and Gigi and I went straight to the police station and told them what we knew. They were very polite and concerned and thanked us for coming. We might as well have been reporting an alien picnic.

I remember the memorial service. The entire senior class showed up, and we all sat together. I sat on the aisle, holding Gigi's hand, pulling Kleenex from a little plastic packet and handing them to her. If I sat straight I could see Sofia's father, rigid in the front pew, and if I turned in my seat I could see Travis Lee one row behind me on the other side of the aisle. I alternated all through the service, focusing the white hot glow of my loathing on one and then the other. I didn't hear a word the priest said; I was too busy hating the two men who had killed my sister's best friend.

"So, anyway, I'm going to Washington, for Sofia . . . and Lynn Underwood."

"For all of us."

"Yeah, for all of us. Anyway, I'd better go. I'm supposed to be at a dinner party at Hank's," I said. "Although, I'd prefer to stay home and stick a fork in my eye."

"How come?"

"I'm just not in the mood. He's got some new flame he wants me to meet, and I just don't feel like playing spectator to someone else's romance. Of course, that's the closest I'll probably ever come to love, so I guess I should just be grateful . . ."

"Lauren, don't say that."

"Well, it's true. I've been in love exactly twice—once with a man who didn't even have the wit to stay alive."

She didn't say anything for a long minute. Any mention of Frank is still, even after twelve years, a showstopper. He was my fiancé, who died in a freak skiing accident three weeks before our wedding.

She sighed. "Oh, Lauren." Then the line I'd heard a million times: "You're going to find somebody wonderful. I just know it."

"I am not. I'm never going to find anybody who doesn't end up saying, 'Thanks for the fun, but you're a little more than I bargained for.' "

"You found Slick and he thought you were the greatest thing since the cut in the capital gains tax. He still does."

"Yeah, but where is he now? Back with his stupid wife. When it came down to deciding, he chose her because she was manageable and I wasn't. "

"That's not true and you know it. He chose her because they had twenty-some-odd years of history, not because there was one single thing wrong with you. Shake it off, Lauren."

"Yeah, yeah." I sighed and began to drain the water from the tub. "Besides, I'm going to be late as it is. Call you tomorrow."

It was ten till seven when I got out of the tub and toweled off. I dressed in an off-the-shoulder, very fitted white crepe dinner dress. I put my hair up in a French twist and was looking for my white sandal high heels when Razz got home. "Hi, sweetheart, how was baseball?"

"It was OK. Where are you going all whomped up?" He was three-quarters in the pantry, trying to pull a Coke from the plastic necklace that held a six-pack.

"I'm going to a dinner party at your godfather's house." I was poking my ear with a pearl drop, trying to insert it without benefit of a mirror.

"Hey, Mom, didya hear about the creeps in Congress letting off that Supreme creep? What a pisser! Are you just out of your mind?"

"Berserk," I admitted.

"Yeah, I know how you get about that kind of stuff. Well, what am I supposed to eat while Elizabeth's at school and you're sashaying around Hank's in that tight dress?"

"Chinese from the takeout, in the fridge. Do you think it's too tight?" I was trying to see myself in the glass door of the microwave.

"Nah, not too tight, but I wouldn't make any sudden moves or parts of you might come flying out."

I shot him a look.

"Just kiddin', you look OK. Is there somebody there you're trying to put the make on?"

"Not that I know of, but if I appeared at Hank's looking really grungy, then I'd be sure to meet Mr. Right."

"Yeah." Razz leaned out of the pantry and cut his eyes at me. "But if you met Mr. Right at Hank's, he probably wouldn't be studying you."

"What's that supposed to mean?"

"Just that if he's at Hank's, he's probably Mr. Right looking for Mr. Right, not Mr. Right looking for Miss Right or Mrs. Right or whatever."

"Well, you're probably right." I laughed, walked over, and kissed him on the shoulder. "I love you. You're my favorite thing in the whole world."

"Back at ya, Ma," he said and gave me an affectionate bump, his equivalent of a hug.

"Oh, by the way—I'm going out of town Friday."

"Where are you goin'?" He was rummaging in the utensil drawer for no apparent reason.

"I'm going to march in Washington."

"Whoa, you're getting kind of militant in your old age, aren't you?"

"Not as a general rule, but this is big-time important, babe. What happened today is an atrocity, and I couldn't think much of myself if I didn't stand up and say, 'No, this just will not do!' "

He drained the last of the Coke. "Makes sense. Do you want me to go with ya?"

I studied him, inflated with love and pride. "God, I'd love for you to, but I got the very last seat on the train. Thanks for asking, it means a lot to me." I drew myself up and took a deep breath. "I've got to run. I'm late."

"Have fun and tell Hank hey."

Edward Anson Williams, known to his closest friends as Hank, is a baritone who sings at the Met, Santa Fe, San Francisco, Teatro alla Scala, Vienna Staatsoper, the National Opera of Australia and Oper Berlin.

A lot of knowledgeable people say that if he wanted, Hank could be opera's greatest superstar, with all the fame and glory that entails. I know it's true; but the fact of the matter is that Hank is no longer interested in fame and glory. He had both and was absolutely miserable. Besides, Hank inherited something in the nine-figure range when his

grandfather died, so he doesn't exactly need the money. Now he says he
sings only because God gave him both the voice and the obligation to
use it.

But he's a star all right, and you can tell before he ever opens his
mouth. He appears to have just dropped down from Mount Olympus
—broad shoulders and a wide chest, a small waist and long legs. He has
wavy blond hair, high cheekbones, silver-green eyes, a chiseled nose
and a ripe mouth with a pouty lower lip. He looks like a Greek god,
but it's that platinum voice that's made him so sought after. There's
not a general manager of any major opera company in the world who
wouldn't set himself on fire if it would score points with Hank.

He also happens to be one of my dearest friends. I met him the third
week of my freshman year in prep school, when he came to visit his
twin sister, Ali, who was my roommate. We've nursed each other
through countless crises and romances, which for us are usually the
same thing. And if you tried to total up all of his and all of mine, you'd
need one of those Hewlett-Packard calculators that you have to take a
class at Wharton to learn how to operate.

Even our careers have been weirdly parallel. He started out in the
chorus of a regional opera when I was working as a credit analyst at a
bank. He got the job as a cover, or understudy, in Richmond right after
I got mine as a brokerage trainee, and he made his debut as a principal
singer at the Met two months before I made partner.

After all those wonderful years of flying closer and closer to the sun,
we even managed to melt our wings and come crashing to earth at
about the same time, he with booze and me with depression. He's the
great constant in my life, and if things had been different, we'd have
surely been lovers. Actually, I'm one of the few people I know, man or
woman, who hasn't done the deed with Hank. He won't let go of the
rope, which is Razz's expression for he swings both ways.

Anyway, Hank sings about six months a year and travels two or three
more, and when he's home, he throws these incredible dinner parties.
Everybody in Atlanta wants to get invited; it's like this big social coup.
Hank's parties have caused more love affairs, blind items in the gossip
columns, friendships, fights and betrayals than you can shake a baton
at. The reason that they are so phenomenally eventful is that he plots

them out like operas. Grand Drama is always the dessert course at Hank's dinner parties.

I drove up the long driveway to Hank's mansion, a three-story Italian villa built in the twenties. The design, the stonework and the surrounding gardens have made it one of the most photographed homes in the state. Despite the fact that Hank lives down the street from us, I was now half an hour late, and the curtain had already gone up.

Chapter 3

I could hear the laughter and the music when Hank opened the door. He has a butler, but he always answers the door himself. Regardless of how many guests he has, Hank always greets each one, to gauge and adjust moods, to prepare his guests like a veteran stage manager. A guest in an unpleasant mood would have as much chance getting into one of Hank's parties as a singer at the Met would have of wearing a costume from *La Bohème* in a performance of *Madama Butterfly*.

"Hi, little baby!" A kiss, lightly but directly on the lips. "Don't you look killer!"

"Thanks, it's my last-of-the-vestal-virgins dress."

He laughed. "Well, my dear, when those vestal virgins find out you've stolen it, they're going to be plenty mad!"

"Did you hear about the decision?"

"Have I heard about it? My dear, I have just spent two hours on the phone with my sister, listening to her gnash her teeth about this exact subject. She says that you're coming to Washington to become a soldier for the revolution." He said it as if he thought I'd laugh and admit the joke.

"Hank, listen," I warned. "This thing has made me crazy. I don't know if I'll be very good company tonight."

He pulled me close and kissed me on the forehead. "Just try to put it out of your mind. You are going to have a fabulous time tonight. Have you talked to Jo about it?"

"Not yet, she's in the Hamptons till Monday."

Jo Lewis had been my therapist in New York. Joltin' Jo Lewis, Slick calls her, and she is to the couch what her more famous namesake was to the ring. Her insights come with the same soul-jarring force, and her softly spoken observations are as devastating when one lacks courage and only wants to shadowbox with the truth. My friends often ask what Jo thinks, partly because I quote her all the time, and partly because when things get to me, I call her and get an over-the-phone tune-up.

"You still taking your medicine?" That's his standard line to me. Mine to him is, "Have you been to a meeting?" We speak the code of the damaged.

"Of course I'm taking my medicine, but I've been crazed ever since I heard about the decision."

"Just remember, my love," he whispered, "one day at a time. Besides, I have a very special surprise just for you." The smile was back.

"So, where's the amour du jour?" I asked and kissed his cheek.

"He's in the living room. And be nice," he said.

That was my clue that Hank's dream date was no mental powerhouse. The absolute last thing in the world I needed was to have to feign fascination in the mental meanderings of some himbo. I made a face of extreme displeasure.

"You can do this. Now come meet everyone," he said and led me around the corner. The room was ablaze with white candles. Hank has a fabulous collection of antique candlesticks and candelabras, and he puts them all out for parties. There were also huge bowls of white flowers—lilies and orchids and huge French tulips. Ella Fitzgerald was singing Cole Porter. The first people he introduced me to were Maestro and Mrs. some German name I can't remember. He was a famous conductor from Vienna, and she was his very gorgeous, very Italian wife. He was old-world courtly, even with her, and she was easily twenty years his junior. It was interesting to watch them, because she was smoldering all over the place and he never took his hands off her, though they had been married long enough to have two sons in boarding school. She was the archetypal Latin bombshell, and I thought I remembered Hank having an affair with her seven or eight years ago.

Then he introduced me to his date, who was about twenty-nine, divinely handsome and obviously besotted with Hank. With him the expected, "So nice to meet you and how do you know Hank?" sufficed.

"Oh, my gosh," he said. "We were fixed up by mutual friends, and it was just like introducing cat hair to a black sweater."

"What a lovely sentiment." I laughed and cut my eyes at Hank, who did not even have the good judgment to be embarrassed. Oh, Lord, I thought, I cannot cope with this.

Hank would never be overtly affectionate with a man in public, but I detected enough electricity between these two to power the World Trade Center. Struggling to make conversation with Mr. Cat Hair, I said, "Hank says he has a surprise for me. Do you know what it is?"

"I do know," he purred, "and if you don't want it, I sure do."

Hank interrupted, putting his hand on my shoulder. "Darling, meet Will Oemig and Brenda Mickel." I started to say something, but I was caught off guard by how beautiful they were. Malibu Barbie and her suntanned friend. She was tall and slender with long blond hair and tilted blue eyes. I had heard about him. He was, of course, dark and handsome, but surprisingly young for a museum director.

Hank was still behind me. "Brenda is a visiting lecturer here at Emory. She's an expert on Greek mythology."

"What a wonderful coincidence," I challenged. "I'm an expert on geek mythology. I can tell you stories about geeks that would curl your hair."

She laughed. "Oh, really. Well, I could tell you stories about Greeks that would straighten yours!"

"Oh, yeah, well, if you could tell me a story that would color it, then I'd be impressed."

"Well, maybe just a little story for highlights, there in the front."

I laughed and felt my emotional load lighten. Will was laughing, watching her out of the corner of his eye. I turned to him. "Will, I hear great things about your museum. I can't wait to see your new addition."

His voice was like Courvoisier. "I'd love to show it to you anytime." But he was looking at her. I remember thinking to myself, "Jesus, this is going to be a long night, here on Noah's Ark on Valentine's Day."

The room was golden with candlelight, and over Brenda's shoulder moved a shadow on the wall, and next to it Jake Ward was standing. Standing there with a glass of red wine in his hand, my favorite writer since I can't even remember, national icon, winner of the Pulitzer Prize, legendary womanizer, literary lion. In real life, standing there against Hank's wall.

Not only was he my favorite writer, he was my all-time hero—a man of conscience and heart and courage. As a young political science student, he had fought against America's involvement in the Vietnam War. I still get chills whenever I see the famous photo of him facing off against the National Guard soldiers on the steps of Columbia's administration building. One defiant student, arms folded, standing a step above a dozen armed men.

As a result of taking on Lyndon Johnson's military machine at the age of nineteen, he emerged an international celebrity, part political commander, part Cajun sex symbol. His exploits continued to be newsworthy; he was right back in world headlines when he went to Poland to work with Lech Walesa in the infancy of the Solidarity movement. I knew that he had battled throat cancer about eight years ago and dealt with it like he had all the other battles in his life, never losing his sense of humor or his swagger. He was still a swashbuckler at forty-eight.

He looked just like the photographs on his book jackets—thick black hair, silver at the temples, covering the tops of his ears and brushing the back of his collar. It was parted on the side and showed all of his high forehead. The shape of his face was broad and masculine, his jaw firm and square. He was much bigger than I would have guessed from his pictures, but it seemed appropriate. Jake Ward was simply larger than life.

He was dressed in a shawl-collar tuxedo that emphasized his broad shoulders, a shirt with a very subtle white-on-white pattern, lapis studs and cuff links and patent leather slippers. Understated, elegant and expensive. I would have been impressed even if I hadn't known who he was.

His complexion was rough; he had a five o'clock shadow and his skin was crosshatched at the temples and under his eyes with deep laugh marks. The lines on his weathered face seemed like hieroglyphics, symbols that, with time and care, could be decoded, revealing the passions and wisdom of a great heart.

Thick eyebrows and star-burst eyelashes framed heavy-lidded eyes the color of an old saddle. His nose was flared at the tip and looked like it might once have been broken, and his mouth—well, there is only one word to describe his mouth . . . carnal.

He was watching me, amused—obviously tickled, as if someone had told him a dirty joke. I would have sworn that he was chuckling, but no sound was coming out, and his eyes held mine and I was having a mild case of coronary arrhythmia.

Ella was singing, "Birds do it, bees do it . . ." There were voices around me and flickering golden light and neither one of us had broken the gaze. I was vaguely aware of a hand on my back. Hank's.

"Well, little baby, I see you've found your surprise," he whispered. Then: "Jake, I want you to meet my favorite woman in the world, Lauren Fontaine. Lauren, this is Jake Ward."

"I'm so glad to meet you." I stuck out my hand and he kissed it and knocked all clever repartee from the shelf in my brain where I keep it. "I've long admired your work."

"The pleasure is mine," he said, his voice deep and gravelly. "I like your dress."

"It's her vestal virgin dress." Hank laughed.

"Oh." He looked at me, arching one of those magnificent eyebrows. "Are you a virgin?"

"Not since Nikita Khrushchev was making headlines," Hank replied, sotto voce.

"Why, yes, I am." Absolutely straight-faced, ignoring Hank.

Jake laughed. He was looking at me just like the polo player used to look at the ponies he was thinking of buying. I could tell that he liked what he saw but didn't want to let on and drive up the price. I was practically waiting for him to ask Hank if he could ride me for a day or two before he made up his mind.

"Lovely," he said to Hank, and at that moment, Hank's butler, Walter, announced dinner was ready. We walked into the dining room and found our seats. Hank had placed me, as always, on his right. Jake held the chair for me, then sat down at my right. The black lacquer walls shone velvet in the candlelight, and their tips of fire rose, stretched and fluttered sideways.

Walter appeared at my side. I took the roast beef, deep pink in the dim light, served myself; then without hesitating, I served Jake. Walter, who was straining to hold the massive silver tray, pretended not to notice the breach of etiquette. Jake smiled, slightly surprised. The butler, leaning slightly backwards to balance the weight of the tray, took a step back, and moved on. Jake leaned toward me, and I could feel the whisper of his breath. "Are you always so accommodating?"

"Only the first time," I said and cringed at the way it sounded.

He smiled, picked up his wineglass and held it, expectantly. I picked up my glass, and he touched his to mine. The candlelight sparkled in his eyes. "Well, then, here's to the first time."

"To the first time," I said and smiled.

The conductor's wife put her hand on Jake's arm, he turned to her and I turned to Hank, my face filled with wonder. When Walter had served the asparagus and the wild rice salad, Hank stood. "To my wonderful friends and all that they represent, welcome." He turned to Will and Brenda and the maestro, who were seated on his left, and raised his glass, "To art and history and music." Nodding to his date at the end of the table, "To chemistry." He came to the conductor's wife, "To beauty." He looked at Jake and toasted, "To passion," then he smiled, clinked his goblet against mine, "To courage."

We all raised our glasses until they met in a tinkling, and drank. Then Jake leaned close. "Why is 'courage' the word that sums you up?"

I shrugged. "I've been given lots of opportunities to develop that particular characteristic."

"Really? By whom?"

"God."

"Should I call you Job?"

I laughed.

"No, seriously," he said. "Why do you think God's been picking on you?"

I laughed again. "I have no idea. Maybe I annoy him."

"I bet you don't," he whispered. "Let me tell you the way I see it. I have a picture of God as a loving and gentle and generous parent. Because He loves us so much, He's always presenting us with wonderful presents: love affairs and interesting work; Cuban cigars and sunlight on leaves; Michelangelo's sculpture. He gives us all these terrific things, but by far His greatest gifts are the things He teaches us. I think those lessons are kisses from God, and I really believe that the best ones are reserved for the courageous. He has lessons for the timid and the fearful but the really good ones, He reserves for the brave."

I smiled and recited my favorite verse: " 'Courage is the price that life exacts for granting peace. / The soul that knows it not knows no release / From little things; / Knows not the livid loneliness of fear, / Nor mountain heights where bitter joy can hear / The sound of wings.' "

"That's lovely." He smiled.

"Isn't it?" I said. "Amelia Earhart."

"It feels like a benediction," he said and looked away.

I took a breath and ventured a confession. "Actually, courage is one of the things I pray for. I think it's the greatest of all virtues and the single common denominator in all great lives."

By now he'd crossed his arms and was resting them on the polished white fabric between our plates. "And you want a great life?"

I thought about it. "Yeah, I want a great life," I said.

The dinner conversation went on without us. Hank and Brenda were happily chatting, and I was trying to evaluate whether Jake Ward was also feeling the incredible connection I was. Could this be happening? I pushed back my hair and tilted my head. "And why is 'passion' the word that sums you up?"

He leaned in closer. "Passion lies at the bottom of all of us, down the slippery anchor chain to the base of who we are, the real, the shameful, the furious. It's born in the screaming, moaning, frenzied core of us. Most people learn early that it's a dangerous thing, best kept in check. By the end of adolescence, certainly by the end of early adulthood, they've successfully eradicated passion. I guess I'm just a slow learner."

"Don't feel bad." I grinned. "I never got the knack of it either."

"I guessed that," he said and picked up his fork.

I picked up my glass and took a long sip of wine. "What else should I know about you?"

He took a bite of asparagus. "In what category?"

"Let's see. I'll take Regrets for $200."

"I never had kids. I would have loved to be a daddy," he said. "Now one for you—childhood heroes."

"Jimmy Hoffa."

He pretended to choke. "You're kidding."

"I'm not either. I used to watch the evening news with my father, and Hoffa was always on trial for something—looting the pension fund, jury tampering, bumping off people."

"Oh, yeah. I always look for that in a hero," he said, and moved his chair away.

"No, wait." I laughed and pulled him back. "That's not why he was my hero. He was my hero because he was so tough nobody dared mess with him. What about you—childhood heroes?"

"Joe DiMaggio."

" 'Cause he was such a great hitter?" I took a bite.

"Because he married Marilyn Monroe. Favorite place?"

"Rome. Favorite name for a place?"

"Pascagoula, Mississippi. Invisible playmates?"

"Now—or when I was a child?"

He laughed. "When you were a child."

"Slam Bishop. Yours?"

"Shockamumu."

"Shockamumu?"

"He was a wild jungle boy from Borneo." He rolled his eyes as if he couldn't believe my not knowing.

"Sorry. First love?"

"Kate Brock. First lover?"

"Ned Mobley. Age you lost your virginity."

"Thirteen. Most erogenous zone?" he shot back.

"My ears," I admitted and blushed.

A long moment of silence. "I'll remember that," he promised.

My heart was pounding, and I had the urge to get up and run. I put my fork down. So did he. "Happiest moment," I demanded, trying to regain my bearings.

"Does right now count?" He hesitated, then put his hand on mine.

"It could," I said and turned my hand, palm up, and we sat there in the middle of one of Hank's swank soirees, holding hands and smiling like idiots while everyone else ate dinner. I was holding hands with this man whom I'd admired for a lifetime and known for less than an hour, and my heart was pounding against my chest like a furious neighbor.

Walter came around again, and Jake was still holding my hand, and Hank and the maestro started in on this story about a production they had worked on together in Budapest, volleying all these hilarious accents, and I was, of course, watching Jake out of the corner of my eye. He took seconds of everything. I probably shouldn't admit this, but I always notice three things about an attractive man: the size of his hands, the way he dances and his appetite. I couldn't help it—I found myself trying to remember all the things I'd heard about his physical gifts.

Anyway, at about this point I tried to snare a glance, but he'd scooted his chair back and I didn't want to be obvious so instead I joined the conversation. It now centered on a comparison of the decor at Graceland and the Met's new production of *Aïda*, which sounds pretty dull, but it was one of those nights where every comment is clever, and the lines get better and better until you think that maybe Noël Coward or Dorothy Parker wrote the whole dialogue and everybody's just acting it out.

I remember that the famous conductor had a tiny piece of asparagus stuck between his teeth, and I was relieved because I figured the law of averages meant I didn't have any stuck between mine. I also remember that a couple of times I said something funny, and Jake threw back his head and roared. Older men do that when they find you attractive. They laugh at your comments like you're the wittiest person in the free world.

Walter reappeared, this time with strawberry glacé, and Hank put his hand on the back of my chair. "In addition to her current duties as mother and pillar of the financial community, Lauren is about to undertake a new endeavor."

I looked at him quizzically; I had no idea what he was talking about.

He laughed. "Have you already forgotten your plans for the march in Washington?"

"Oh. No, I haven't forgotten," I said, sorry that he'd brought it up once I'd finally stopped thinking about it. "I'm leaving Friday to go to Washington and participate in the demonstration march," I announced to the faces around the table.

"Have you ever marched before?" Brenda asked. "I wouldn't know the first thing about what to do."

I shook my head. "I'll be staying with Hank's sister, Ali. Ali Wolverton," I repeated for effect. "She's an old hand when it comes to things like this."

No one batted an eyelash at the drop of that well-known name.

"My sister is very committed to women's issues." Hank stated the obvious for the benefit of either his foreign guests or his idiot date. "She's the head of the political science department at Georgetown and a powerful voice in the women's movement. She's been around forever, and she's trusted by all its factions."

"Lauren, what faction are you?" Will asked, putting his fork down.

"I'm not any faction. I've never done anything like this, but I just don't feel like I can sit by while a man who tortured his wife, to the point that she would rather die than have to live with him, continues to be chief justice of the Supreme Court. I'm not the activist type, but this is where I draw the line. Not that I have any idea what we'll accomplish, but I still have to go." I shrugged. "I just have to go."

The maestro started waving his fork toward me. "I'm afraid my wife and I have not followed this trial that has all you Americans so upset."

I took a deep breath. "Well, it began with a short note that Mrs. Lawrence Underwood III jotted just before she washed down about six weeks' worth of Seconal with a Diet Coke. I think her exact words were, 'I cannot tolerate the abuse any longer.' "

Jake leaned over his plate. "And for those who found that ambiguous, records showed that she had made something like eight separate hospital visits over the last decade, each to a different local emergency room, for such common household injuries as a concussion, a fractured sternum and a severely bruised kidney."

"There was an inquiry after her death, and that's when all the hospital records turned up," I said. "But the police said there was nothing they could really charge Underwood with since A: she'd clearly died at her own hand, and B: nobody could prove that her husband was the one who was beating her."

Jake nodded. "There was enough proof, however, to convince the American people that he was the one responsible, and the President called for his resignation. When he refused, the President called for impeachment hearings. Chief Justice Underwood went in front of the

House of Representatives today, and in spite of overwhelming evidence, they found him innocent after only a few hours of testimony."

I summed it up. "So now we have a wife batterer to preside over the highest Court in the land."

"My goodness," the maestro announced, his heavy brows eclipsing his gray eyes. "That is terrible."

Brenda fluttered her hands as she searched for words. "This is such a horror to women, partly because Lynn Underwood was revered for her work with abused children, and partly because her husband is obviously a monster. But what's so unbelievable is that not only did he get away with what he did, but that he should then be allowed to preside as the most powerful judge in America." Her hands were shaking at the thought. "The idea that this man will continue to interpret our laws, that he will decide anything that affects women, feels like a personal blow to each of us."

"That's exactly it," I said, pointing to Brenda. "It feels personal, and it's unleashed an almost primal fury in women that I don't think anyone understands yet."

We were back in the living room. Someone had shut the windows, and the fire tips had settled and were resting on the stalagmites of white wax. Walter was serving coffee and liqueurs, when Will patted the sofa softly, considering a thought, and offered, "Why don't we all drive over to the museum. It's a perfect night, and it's not far." His face was eager as a first grader's. "Our new wing is finished; the premier exhibit is almost up, but no one has seen it yet. It won't be open to the public until next month. Come on, I'll give you a midnight tour."

"Oh, yes, it would be lovely," said the conductor's wife. I could tell Hank and Brenda wanted to go. Jake looked at me and asked, "Are you interested?"

"I think you know I am," I murmured, leaning in to let him smell my perfume.

"Well, it's all settled." Will grinned and stood up. The decision made, we rose almost in unison and slipped out of the golden cocoon and into the night. In Hank's driveway, unsure of logistics and etiquette, I stood quietly and heard the chick-chick of a lawn sprinkler nearby and the

crunch of dress shoes on the gravel. I looked up to send a silent prayer
of thanks and saw that the stars were freshly polished for a new season.
I was filled with the perfect happiness that is a mix of expectation and
infatuation and champagne.

Jake appeared at my side and claimed my hand as if it had belonged
to him for years. I could feel the perspiration between my breasts and
was grateful for the breeze cool-washing my skin.

He opened the passenger door to his 1964 gray Jaguar, shining in the
moonlight like a South Seas pearl. I tried to get in gracefully, but the
seats rested almost on the ground, and as I slid in, my dress rose
noticeably. I lifted up slightly and tried to pull the hem down, but I was
practically supine. I refused to look up, and he just stood there looking
down at me with the door open and his big hand resting on the top of
the window.

I could feel my face redden. "What are you doing?" I demanded.

"Just admiring the view." He laughed.

"Fuck you," I whispered.

"Maybe later," he said.

I stuck out my tongue in response.

"For a virgin, you sure are anxious," he whispered and closed the
door carefully. He slipped into the driver's seat, started the car and eased
it down the driveway. Our midnight caravan was waiting, and we drove
in hot silence.

He's too cocky, too damn sure that he can get whatever he wants, I
thought, and I certainly haven't helped. *I think you know I am.* Jesus,
what a stupid thing to say.

I was sucking on a ball of self-revulsion when he turned on the radio
and the invisible honey of the Four Tops oozed into the car. I watched
him in the light from the dashboard, and he seemed so happy that I
completely forgot about being miserable, and we slipped through the
darkness. The car smelled just like him, masculine and mysterious. I
was melting into the seat, wishing that our destination were a thousand
miles away, when the cars in front of us slowed and, one by one, turned
into the museum driveway.

We pulled into a space. I opened the door myself and was out before
he had time to turn off the ignition, a feat not unnoteworthy. By the

time we walked to the entrance, Will had dispatched the security guard, and everyone was waiting for us. We walked through a huge rotunda, our footsteps echoing on the marble. No one spoke. It was, as if by agreement, the silence of midnight intruders. At the right of the rotunda, Will led us through a large doorway.

The spotlights were in place, so it was easy to see where there were exhibit pieces missing. Two empty pedestals waited, and several lights shone on nothing but the gray floor.

Will was talking about the museum's architect when I noticed that Jake wasn't with us. I looked around and saw him standing in the corner, a half step inside a pool of light, in front of a large stone figure. His black-and-silver hair, his raised face, and the front of his dinner jacket were illuminated.

"What a magnificent work," Hank announced.

"And a nice sculpture too," I whispered.

"Will," Jake boomed, "she's beautiful. Who is she?"

The figure was that of a woman. She stood, breasts bared, with a broken sword at her feet. One cheekbone and the side of her nose had crumbled or been sheared off; clearly, she hadn't been sculpted yesterday. She was smiling. It was the first thing you noticed. On this two-thousand-year-old face was the smile of the powerful, a heavyweight-champion's smile, a dictator's smile, Jake Ward's smile.

We had gathered with Jake. "Lysistrata . . ." Will began, but Brenda's voice picked it up, ". . . which means 'she who disbands armies.' "

At first I was afraid that I was the only one who didn't know Lysistrata, and I had no intention of showcasing my ignorance in front of Jake, who, I figured, certainly did know. Fortunately, the conductor's wife saved me. "I don't know of this story. Could perhaps you tell it?"

Brenda smiled shyly and looked at Will, to be sure he didn't want to be the one to tell the story, but he was obviously delighted to relinquish the spotlight to her and literally stepped back into the shadow.

"Well," she began, "the play *Lysistrata* was written about 411 B.C. by a man named Aristophanes. It takes place during the Peloponnesian Wars—between Athens and Sparta. The war had dragged on for a long time. Athens had suffered serious defeats, and morale was very low, so

Lysistrata called together the Council of Women. These women were the wives of the senators and the generals from Sparta, Athens, Boeotia and Corinth."

I was watching Jake watch Brenda, and I was sick because I didn't know any fancy Greek stories; maybe when she was finished I could stand in the spotlight and wow everybody with a pithy dissertation on financial derivatives. Maybe we could have a little grown-up show-and-tell.

Brenda was twisting her hair with one hand and smiling, a little hesitant to go on. "Well, the women were tired of the war, tired of losing their sons and brothers and having their husbands always in battle, and Lysistrata had a plan. She told all the women that they should use their power to end the war. She said that they should refuse to make love with their husbands until the husbands made peace."

"Ah," chuckled Jake, "the original make love, not war."

"Exactly." Brenda smiled like a substitute teacher telling a story to seventh graders.

"God, this is great." I was loving the story. "So what happened?"

"Well, the women agreed. Their plan was to perfume themselves and dress beautifully and entice their husbands, but refuse to be touched. In the second act the women take over the acropolis. The magistrate orders the policemen to arrest Lysistrata, but the women attack the policemen, and they back off. Then Lysistrata gives this speech about how the women are going to save Greece because they have common sense and the men don't."

"Well, I guess some things haven't changed in over two thousand years," I blurted. Jake turned around and looked at me with one eyebrow raised. Suddenly, I didn't care what he thought, I was right there in the acropolis with those Greek women. "Good for you, Lysistrata. Give 'em hell, honey!"

Brenda hesitated. She looked at Will and waited for me to shut up. "Well, things didn't go smoothly because the women kept breaking their vow of celibacy."

Jake turned to me and smirked as if he had personally seduced each and every one.

"Lysistrata doesn't give up, though. She encourages and berates the women until they return to the acropolis. About this time, a herald comes from Sparta."

"Harold who?" asked Mr. Cat Hair.

I rolled my eyes at Hank, who pretended not to notice.

"A herald in those days was like an ambassador," explained Brenda. "So a herald from Sparta comes, hoping to make peace. He tells the Athenian magistrate that the Spartan women are also holding out and that the Spartan men are desperate."

I was looking pointedly at Jake, who was pointedly avoiding catching my eye.

"The magistrate tells the Athenian men about the conspiracy, in which all the Greek women are involved. The men quickly arrange a peace settlement, and they have a big party. Lysistrata speaks out about war, and then the men take their wives home."

"This is such a great story." I was laughing. "Jake, don't you think that was a great story?"

"Yes, Lauren, that was a great story." He was humoring me, but his eyes were twinkling, and I could tell that he was amused by how much I liked it. "Well, boys and girls, it's almost one o'clock and I have to be up early. Thank you, Will, for the tour; Brenda, for your 'Ode to a Grecian Urge'; and Hank, for the wonderful evening." He turned to me, "May I drive you back to your car?"

"Yes, thanks." I kissed Hank and whispered in his ear. "I love you. I really like the surprise, and I'll call you in the morning." We said the rest of our good-byes, and this time I was excruciatingly careful getting into the car.

We had just pulled out of the parking lot when the news came on. "This is Dianne Lindsey, with WNBC's news on the hour. The day's top news story is the House of Representatives' refusal to impeach Supreme Court Chief Justice Lawrence Underwood. Reactions from women's organizations range from stunned disbelief to outrage. The National Organization for Women and other feminist groups have called for a march on Washington this Sunday. Organizers expect over two million participants, making it the largest demonstration ever in the country's capital. The Reverend Savannah Moran calls this one of the blackest days ever in this country's history."

"He cannot get away with this," I murmured. Then I realized where I was and looked up. "That's why I have to go to Washington. I just have to do something."

He was watching me, waiting.

I laughed. "You probably think I'm a lunatic."

"Lauren, I know what it's like to feel that strongly about something." He was looking through the windshield, now, far past the field of vision. "It's what got my Cajun ass almost killed in 1968."

I didn't know what to say. I had read his book on the antiwar movement, and it had taken my breath away and won him virtually every major literary award that year. He caught the look of uncertainty on my face and mistook it for confusion. He reached over and patted my hand. "It's OK. I know that was before your time."

I didn't say anything. He stopped patting and just let his big hand rest on mine. His fingers were thick and his nails were broad and I spread my fingers slightly and his slipped between mine and curled them into a source of happy electricity, and the silence felt like a bed on a rainy Sunday night, warm and comfortable and safe.

But I couldn't stand it—it felt so dishonest not to tell him. "It wasn't before my time," I blurted. "I was madly in love with you from the time I was seven until I was eleven."

He burst out laughing. "Well," he said, blushing. "Why didn't you tell me."

"I didn't know how to get in touch with you," I said, anguished for my eleven-year-old self. Then I realized that he'd meant why didn't I tell him earlier in the evening, and I turned bright red, and rushed on. "I saw you on the news and I thought you were the bravest, most honorable, most heroic thing I'd ever seen. I used to fantasize about you all the time. You know that famous picture of you and the National Guardsmen that was on the cover of *Life* magazine?" He nodded. "Well, I kept it under my bed and um, I probably shouldn't tell you this." I was really embarrassed now, but he was holding my hand and I had already come this far and there was no graceful way out. "I used your picture, to, um."

"I'm honored." He lifted my hand and kissed it. "I can think of no lovelier compliment."

We were both silent for a moment, then I said, "I've always wondered what it must feel like to be famous so young."

He let go of my hand and scratched his eyebrow with his thumb. "Fame is difficult. But fame at an early age is particularly tough because you become a symbol before you become a person. I was created in the media for one act of passion. In 1968, I was against this country's involvement in Southeast Asia and I felt strongly about it—but it didn't represent to me the sum of who I was or even of what I believed. And yet I became the symbol for that belief and it became *who I was* to the whole world. I couldn't articulate it at the time, but it felt false. And that's why, when I was older and wanted to get involved again with a cause I thought was really important, I went halfway around the world to do it."

"You thought you could do the Solidarity thing without attracting attention?"

"Sure. When we started, it was nothing but a bunch of guys in the shipyards of Gdansk. No one had any idea what would happen. By the time the world media showed up in Poland, I was old enough and experienced enough to know who I was.

"I could read about the Jake Ward that I was reported to be and know what was true and what wasn't. Fame has been one of my lessons from God. I have a lot of gratitude for the opportunities that fame gave me, but the price has sometimes been exorbitant. I wouldn't wish it on anyone I cared about."

By now we were back at Hank's. Jake came around to my side and held out his hand for me.

"Is it all right if I call you?" he asked when we were standing in the driveway.

"I'd love for you to." I was looking in my purse for a card. "This is my office number. They always know where to find me."

The security lights on the corner of the house shone from behind him as he looked down at the card. He could have slipped it in his jacket and I would have thought nothing of it, but he didn't. He reached in his coat pocket and pulled out his glasses, put them on slowly, and I can't explain why, but I think that's the moment I really fell in love with him. I know it sounds weird, but I was so touched that he would take the trouble to actually read it. He looked down, his beautiful silver-touched hair backlit by the lights, his massive shoulders bent so that he could focus on the words. He was leaning on the front of my car with his legs spread. I was a step away from him and could not breathe, and he looked up and smiled. " 'Lauren Fontaine, Managing Partner.' That's nice . . . managing partner."

He slipped the card in his pocket, reached out and pulled me to him. My feet moved only a half step and I came falling into him and his hand came around the small of my back and he smelled like expensive cigars and cedar chips and he kissed me. Not the kiss I was expecting, but the softest whisper of a kiss, so soft I could feel his whiskers more than his mouth. I looked at him for a moment and kissed him back, as tenderly and even softer. He touched the curve of my jaw with his hand and brushed his lips across the corner of my mouth so gently that he barely made contact. Then he moaned. And I was shaking and neither one of us was going to give in and be the one who lost control. My heart was flying at him, but my chest was in the way, and I was taking his pulse through my dress.

Suddenly, he put his hands on my hips, and set me back a step to study my face. "Trouble," he said to himself as he slipped from between me and my car and opened the driver's door. I slid in. "Buckle up and drive safe."

He closed the door and backed up a few steps. He was watching me, and I felt a flash of panic, not sure if I remembered how to start the car. After a moment, it came to me. I winked and drove away.

Razz was asleep when I got home. I sat at the head of his bed, in the dark, stroking his hair and listening to him breathe. He opened his eyes briefly, mumbled something I couldn't make out and smiled. We have a tacit agreement. During the day, I try to limit the hugs and kisses that are such a burden to an adolescent, and he allows me to heap affection on him as long as it's night and he's unconscious.

The antique clock on my bedside table said 1:22 when I finally slipped, exhausted, between the sheets. I turned out the light, and in the dark I could see him. Coffee-colored eyes, soft bad-boy mouth, broad shoulders. Jake, Jake Ward, Jake and Lauren, Lauren Ward. Would he call me? Where would he take me on our first date? What would he be like in bed? Would he and Razz like each other? Should we have a big wedding, or just a few close friends?

My brain was slipping on the sweet syrup of sleep, I was falling and I remember one thing: the very last word in my mind before I went under was not Jake, it was Lysistrata.

Chapter 4

Friday morning, we had just finished breakfast on the patio, surrounded by the irises, jonquils and azaleas that decorate the new grass and the pristine sky of our backyard. Once again the newspaper was full of stories about the Underwood decision. There were four articles on the front page alone. The headline story was an interview with Jerry Dixon, an emergency room doctor who had treated Lynn Underwood for a dislocated shoulder and a concussion in December 1995. He told the reporter that she had told him that her husband was responsible for her injuries and that he would kill her if she reported him to the police. He said that he'd sent a sworn affidavit to that effect to the Congress as soon as impeachment hearings were announced and that he was never contacted.

The second article was about how the Secret Service was having to add agents to the detail protecting Chief Justice Underwood because of the thousands of death threats he'd received since Tuesday's decision.

The third focused on the politics of the decision and blamed House conservatives for the swift and amazing verdict. It broke down the acquittal votes by party affiliation and highlighted what everyone already knew—the decision was simply the refusal of the House leadership to put the President in the position of naming a new justice to the Supreme Court. It was a rocket booster for my blood pressure.

The last was yet another article that chronicled the amazing life of Lawrence Underwood. It was a story everybody in the country had heard a million times, about how young Larry grew up in a Philadelphia ghetto, that his father had abandoned Larry and his mother when he was six and that his mother had been brutally murdered when Larry was twelve. We all knew how he had been the one to find her and how a newspaper story about his ordeal had touched an elderly couple, who'd adopted Larry and enrolled him at a prestigious prep school; how Larry had excelled and won a scholarship to Harvard Law School and graduated with honors. I couldn't read more than the first couple of paragraphs. I had to put the paper down and force a couple of deep breaths.

My son was trying to decide whether the dollop of pear preserves that he had dropped in his lap warranted changing his khakis. Just looking at him calms me. After sixteen years, I still can't get over how gorgeous he is—thick chestnut hair, chiseled features and a baby's rosy-cheeked complexion. By far, the most extraordinary thing about him, though, is his eyes. They're the most unusual color I've ever seen. As a matter of fact, the only other pair in existence belong to his father. There's not even a name for the color; they'd be called hazel if they were green and brown, but they're blue and brown. And they change constantly. I first noticed it when he was tiny; when he was happy they were sapphire blue and when he was troubled they would turn bronze, then slate. If he was frightened or in pain they looked almost aubergine. I always tease him about having mood rings for eyes.

They were the color of blue smoke as he stood up, examined the spot of jam and its location and excused himself. I was left trying to identify the feeling I'd woken up with. It had started out as vague as the fragment of a memory, but it was full blown now, a sensation I recognized but couldn't put in context, like someone you know whose name escapes you.

The door behind me swung open and Elizabeth rumbled out to clear the dishes.

"Where's that boy?" she demanded, picking up the monogrammed linen napkin from his chair. "His ride will be here in a minute."

"Changing his clothes." I was smiling, I knew exactly what was coming.

"Changing his clothes! Lord, he hadn't had 'em on ten minutes. Between feeding that child and ironing his clothes, I hadn't got two spare minutes to do what I need to in this house much less study. No wonder I made a B− on my final."

"I know it, Miss E., what do you think we ought to do, put him up for adoption?"

"Shoot, nobody fool enough to take him," she declared. She picked up his plate and disappeared back into the house.

I took a sip of coffee and it was cold. I started to call her, when she reappeared with the coffeepot. The thin arc of black juice filled the cup, and the steam clouded the silver surface. "He call last night?"

"Not that I remember."

"That you remember?" She snorted. "Girl, you ought to *remember* who you're talkin' to."

I have no secrets from Elizabeth. I think it was Madame Cornuel who said that no man is a hero to his valet, and I would add that no woman is a mystery to her housekeeper. Especially a housekeeper like Elizabeth, who is confidante, collaborator and coconspirator.

Elizabeth had come to work for me right after the divorce, when Razz was four. We had gone through seven housekeepers in five weeks. The agency I had hired had sent us a bunch of real charmers: the Colombian who couldn't speak English, the woman whose body odor was so severe I had to breathe through my mouth when she was in the same room, the bimbo who showed up obviously stoned, and last but not least, the creature who, at the end of her first day, presented me with a son whose fingernails had been painted and whose hair had been curled and pulled into a little grosgrain ribbon. I don't remember my exact reaction that afternoon, but I do seem to recall that she threatened to press charges. After that I had a little chat with the owner of the agency about all kinds of interesting topics, like the weather and the Better Business Bureau, and the next day, Elizabeth arrived. She was quite a sight, 260 pounds in a scarlet pantsuit, cocoa-colored velveteen skin, eyes like mica and the most glorious smile I have ever seen on a human. She and Razz took one look at each other and fell in love.

Elizabeth picked up the crystal water pitcher. She'd sensed the disappointment in my voice. "Honey, you go look in the mirror at your movie-star gorgeous self. Look at that gold hair and those big old blue eyes. Look at that pretty magnolia-petal skin and that little Cupid's-bow mouth. Then while you're at it, take a look at that Miss Centerfold shape you got and tell me that old goat's gonna forget you."

"Thanks, Miss E., but Jake hasn't called, and it's been three days."

"That's all right, he will. Serves you right though," she said. "You never should have got rid of that polo player. He was the prettiest man I ever laid an eye on, and sweet too."

"You know, I think we've been through this before," I reminded her. Razz reappeared, having not only changed his pants but his shirt as well. To appease Elizabeth, he began to help clear the table, picked up my plate and examined my face for a long moment.

"Mom, what's wrong?"

"I'm having the weirdest feeling," I explained. "It started this morning, even before I was completely awake." Both of them were watching me. The sensation was coming up from awareness to definition. It was preparation, instinctive preparation. "It feels like . . . the moment before impact. The instant before something happens that you know is coming but you're powerless to stop." Very slowly, I began to wrap words around it. "The moment before impact, like right before a plane touches down or the instant before a kiss or the second before you get hit in the stomach. That's what this feels like, like something's about to happen and I don't know what it is, but it's like I'm preparing for it."

Elizabeth eased into Razz's chair and looked at me, worried. "Miss L., I think you're having a premonition."

"Ma, I think you're having a nervous breakdown!" said Razz, who was patting my shoulder in mock solicitousness. He leaned over and said in a loud whisper, "I'm sure it's nothing that shock therapy can't cure."

I grabbed his wrist, "I'm tired of you sassing me, you little brat. I'm going to whip your butt. Miss E., bring me a switch!"

They both laughed at the thought. First off, Razz is six feet tall, 170 pounds, with a farm boy's build, and is unlikely to get his butt whipped by anyone, least of all by a 125-pound woman. And secondly, it's been at least seven years since I last spanked him.

A horn sounded and he swung down for a kiss.

"Be good, mind Elizabeth. I'll call you from Washington. . . . Razz, I love you."

"Love you too, Mom. Have fun at the march, but don't get arrested or do anything that'll embarrass me."

"I'll try not to," I said, but he was gone, the sound of the back door exploding.

Elizabeth was still watching me. "Maybe that feeling's trying to tell you not to go marching with all those people. You know you got no business going up there." Her eyes were defiant, which I knew meant that she was frightened.

"What's the deal? Three days ago you were delighted that I was going. As I recall, your exact words were: 'Go on up there and jerk a knot in their heads.' "

The morning after Hank's dinner party, I had told her about both Jake and the story of Lysistrata. She'd laughed. Then I had told her about my plans to go to the march.

She'd been all for it. "Oooh, girl, go on up there and tell those men they had better find a way to fix what they've done, because we're not standing for this shit. Not for one minute are we standing for this." But now she said, "Well, maybe I've changed my mind."

"What's the matter, Elizabeth?" I was genuinely baffled.

"This family's had a lifetime of troubles, but we've got a good life now . . . and I just don't want you messing it up."

Then I knew exactly what she was afraid of. The first years after the divorce, we had no money. I was working as a credit analyst at a bank, which I detested and which just barely paid our expenses. We rented a tiny little house with almost no yard in a marginal part of town. It was dark and musty and had shag carpet and appliances from the sixties.

When Razz was almost six, he got sick. He started having diarrhea one morning, and I took him to the doctor who said not to worry. So I didn't, but the diarrhea didn't stop and the doctor couldn't figure out why, so I took Razz to another doctor who gave him some medicine and the diarrhea still didn't stop and he was losing weight he couldn't afford to lose and his father was too busy drinking to be any help and I was so scared I thought I would die.

Elizabeth saved both our lives. She was there while I went to work every day so that we'd have insurance. She moved in so that she could be there in the middle of the night, to relieve me. She was even there when I didn't have the money to pay her and for a long time when I could only pay her part of her salary because I was trying to keep Emory Hospital from throwing me into debtors' prison for the money I owed them.

While she was nursing Razz back to health, she discovered her real calling, and when Razz started junior high, she started college. Now she's in nursing school, and we've got it worked out so that she and Razz will graduate at the same time.

I could certainly understand that she didn't want my being a revolutionary to ruin her dream of being an RN, which depends in part on my ability to pay for her school. My ability to pay for her school comes from the fact that I'm no longer working as a credit analyst and living in a tiny rented house with shag carpet and appliances from the sixties.

That's because everything changed when Razz was seven and I got a job at Goldman Sachs. It was as if Ed McMahon had shown up on our doorstep with one of those giant checks from Publishers Clearing House.

I had hoped to be trained as a bond trader for several months and sent back to the South, but the top brass at Goldman had other plans for me. I was assigned the equity trading desk in New York. Not knowing any better, I signed a one-year lease on an apartment in the city. Razz was mesmerized by Manhattan, but Elizabeth was miserable from the first day. I know if she hadn't loved us so much, she never would have stayed, but she did.

As soon as our year's lease was up, I moved us to Connecticut. I was beginning to make a lot of money, and the house was beautiful, the yard lovely and the neighborhood posh, but Elizabeth desperately wanted to be back in the South. Like a large, black Alice in Wonderland, she was never at ease in a place where the customs, the food and the speech were so alien to her. It wouldn't have been so bad, but she just could not tolerate cold, and the long winters tormented her. So when I was recruited three years later by headhunters for the job of managing partner of the Atlanta office of Sterling White, I jumped at it, not just because the money they offered could only be described as obscene, but because I wanted to repay Elizabeth's many acts of love with one of my own.

I was trying to think of something to say and I looked in her eyes. She looked away, and I reached over and took her hand. "Elizabeth, please don't worry. I have no intention of messing anything up for this family. First of all, I'm going to be one of two million people in this march."

"Yeah, and *I* bet none of those other two million folks have got as much to lose as you or paid as much to get what they've got as you." Elizabeth had seen up close what it cost me to make the journey from Goldman Sachs bond trainee to Sterling White managing partner.

I'd come to Wall Street when highly compensated women were as rare as pterodactyls, where the disgusting remarks, repulsive propositions and rampant discrimination were as much a part of the day as the opening bell. Every day, I ignored or fought off what would now be slam-dunk sexual harassment cases.

It was bad enough for my female peers in the other departments, but my assignment was the hands-down worst. That's because while investment banking and corporate finance have always been the realm of the suave and the educated, the trading floor has always been the last bastion of the crude and the Neanderthal. It's a place where balls are worshipped, where they are scratched and rearranged and spoken of, literally or figuratively, with a reverence usually reserved for deities. They're every bit as much a requirement for the job as brains . . . and every bit as important.

Trading is the ultimate boys club, and it was made clear to me from the beginning that it was a club where I was not, and never would be, welcome. In addition to the crime of being female, I was one of the youngest traders around, so the old boys at the other firms assumed that I'd be an easy mark. And I was, in more instances than I'd like to admit. As a matter of fact, I was cheated so often in my first months on the job that I almost quit, for the good of Goldman Sachs. Except that I knew it was my one big chance, and I wasn't going to let anything or anybody take it away from me.

So I got smart fast. I studied the markets and learned how to measure and treat risk and I even started acting at work like I had my own three-piece set. I got used to fighting, and I even got good at it. Anyway, I arrived a small-town innocent, and left the toughest thing ever to walk in high heels. I even earned Wall Street's highest and most prestigious designation—big swinging dick. Despite the fact that it didn't exactly jibe with my perception of my femininity, it was a title I prized.

As Slick always says, "If it were easy, everyone would do it." But what

I do is not easy. Controlling the mix of colossal egos and dizzying amounts of money requires you to balance being fair with being fearsome, and the stress of it is indescribable. And no one knows that better than my friend Elizabeth, who witnessed the years of poverty-induced insomnia and who knows that I don't sleep all that much better now.

I didn't want to talk about it. "Miss E., I'm sure there are going to be plenty of people there who have as much to lose as I do. And we have a hell of a lot more to lose by not doing anything and letting Larry Underwood get away with this. Besides, there's no way anyone can do anything to hurt us just because I go to this thing. This is the land of the free, remember?"

Her look alleged that I was either purposely lying or pitifully stupid. Now I was annoyed. I put my hands on my hips. "Elizabeth, I'm not going to debate this with you. I am going to march in Washington because there are men who'll continue to get away with killing women in this country until we do more than just sit in our offices and kitchens and bitch about how terrible it is. It's only going to stop if we make it stop, if we really start yelling about it. You know, 'I am woman, hear me roar, in numbers too big to ignore . . .' "

"Just don't roar yourself into trouble!"

I rolled my eyes to irritate her and smiled because I could tell I'd succeeded.

"Time for you to go," she announced, wanting the last word, then picked up my cup and saucer to be certain I wouldn't linger.

I started to protest but looked at my watch and saw that she was right, threw my suitcase and hanging bag in the car and gave her a hug.

It was 8:30 A.M. when I arrived at the office. The firm occupies the forty-seventh floor of one of the city's glass skyscrapers, and I was standing at the enormous window, watching dark clouds gather over the southern horizon. There was a knock on the door and I heard it open. Sherry stuck her head in. "Mr. Moriarty on line two."

Sometimes he calls during the day or after the market closes, but the

8:45 A.M. call is a ritual. Regardless of what time I get to the office, the day really begins when Sherry announces, "Mr. Moriarty on line two," and I hear the deep, patrician voice of my boss.

I turned and picked up the nearest phone on the trading desk.

"Good morning, Lauren."

"Hi, Slick."

To the employees of the firm it's Mr. Moriarty, to the other managing directors it's J.T. and to the press it's always *the aristocratic* John Tarleton Moriarty IV. To me, it's simply Slick, a loving but irreverent reference to the way he wears his hair.

"You all set to ride the freedom train? To lock arms with your down-trodden sisters and fight the tyranny of your oppressors?"

"Why, as a matter of fact, I am." I laughed.

"Good for you. I don't suppose you'd want to meet me for lunch Saturday before you man, or should I say woman, the barricades?"

"Where?"

"Anywhere you want to. We could have lunch at Two Quail or at my club. Lauren, I miss you so much. It's been too damned long."

Five months, two weeks, three days.

"I miss you too. Let me see what time my train arrives." I flipped through the itinerary on my desk. "I get to Washington at 9:33."

"How 'bout I pick you up at the station and we can spend some time together, then grab some lunch? Then I can take you to Ali's."

"Mmm. What exactly did you have in mind between 9:33 and lunch?" I asked as I slipped the itinerary in my pocketbook.

He laughed. "I didn't have anything in mind."

"You lie, Communist dog!!"

"All right, I lied. I do have something in mind. You and me in a suite at the Hay-Adams."

"No, no, a thousand times no. We swore we weren't ever going to do that again! Besides, I thought you were supposed to be in Europe."

"I don't leave till Sunday, and don't try to change the subject." Then he sighed. "Lauren, I miss you terribly. It's been five and a half months. I don't know how much longer I can keep this up."

"Honey, you've had it up the entire five years I've known you," I shot back, and he laughed. The backdrops of my memories of Slick were always either the office or the bedroom. Whenever I closed my eyes and thought of him, he either appeared in full Wall Street regalia, smooth as unblended scotch and just as intoxicating, or naked in my bed, his face and legs sleek with sweat, his almond-colored and almond-shaped eyes smiling and half closed, and the hair on his broad chest matted down to his slim hips and manhood. "Besides, I promised Jo that I was going to keep my self-induced traumas to a minimum this year. And you are never going to make your peace with this if you keep starting it up again."

"My conscience can fight my heart for just so long before it gives out and other more powerful instincts take over. Besides, you were the one who started back last time."

He was right, but if there's one thing I hate it's being blamed for something I'm guilty of. "I couldn't help it, and besides you're supposed to be the strong one, John Tarleton Morality."

"I'm not strong enough, I'm afraid. I love you. I can't help that," he said, then switched tactics. "Please let me make love to you on Saturday, then we'll each take a white chip and start again in Lovers Anonymous."

"That's what you said last time." Suddenly, I was remembering that last time. We'd gone about four and a half months without sleeping together and I was going through a rough spot and he had been so incredibly kind and loving that I just showed up in New York one Friday afternoon, called him from my room at the Park Lane and announced that I was holding a private fashion show of the season's most diaphanous negligees and did he want to come and see. He said he'd like to do both, though not necessarily in that order, and we spent the following four hours in bed. We spent the next day in full-fledged relapse and the next week with killer emotional hangovers. If there were such a thing as treatment centers for love junkies, we'd have both checked in. That's actually not a bad idea, come to think of it. If Betty Ford could have her own place, so could I . . . The Lauren Fontaine Center for Adults and Adulteresses.

Anyway, I had more than enough experience to know that the aftermath was always excruciating and occasionally even debilitating. "No. I won't live through that again. If this were just a fuck that would be one thing, but it's not, and I'm not willing to pay for hours of ecstasy with days of anguish."

"OK, I'm not gonna push, but I do miss you."

"I miss you too."

"Lauren."

"Huh?"

"I do love you."

"I know, sweetheart, but you know what Jo says: love is necessary but not sufficient; and unfortunately, our loving each other hasn't done much but make us both miserable."

There was a long silence and then he cleared his throat, but emotion clotted his honey voice. "Well, let's don't talk about that anymore. I've got your positions in front of me. It looks like Mr. Kovacevich's shorts are growing larger every day."

There was a part of me that wanted to tell him about meeting Jake, but it seemed both premature and unkind, so instead I said, "That's true in more ways than one, and I don't like it. Somebody's bound to drop rates, and if they do, Mr. Kovacevich will deservedly choke on his shorts," which translated meant that our head bond trader had bet on the bond market falling, and I was concerned that if one of the major banks lowered their lending rates, then the bond market would rise, leaving him with large losses.

"Have you spoken to him?" Slick asked.

"Twice, once Tuesday and once yesterday."

"I'll leave it in your beautiful hands. Lauren, have a terrific time in Washington. I'm real proud of you for going."

"Thanks. I'll tell you all about it when you get back."

"Good girl," he said and hung up.

I sat there for the longest time, sad and empty. I know I shouldn't say this, but I think that letting people fall in love with people who are already married is one of the meaner things that God does.

I walked a few feet to my glass office and was reading the third section of the *Journal* when the clerk brought in our position sheets. I use the big private office off the reception area to conduct personal business, private conversations with employees and meetings with both the CEOs and the heads of the large pension funds that are the firm's clients. But it's the much smaller office in the trading room, glass on all sides, where I spend most of my time. It's where I'm most comfortable.

I was studying our positions when our head equity trader, Arthur Munroe, stuck his handsome head in. "Hi, Lauren."

"Hey, babes. Which way do you think we'll swing today?"

He licked his finger and raised it up as if testing the direction of the wind. "Up, I think." Then he turned to me as if to make sure that I didn't know something he didn't. "What do you think?"

"I think probably up. I'm not sure though; I've got this very strange feeling. I woke up with it. It's kind of like something big is about to happen."

"Good or bad?" Traders put great store in intuition and he was suddenly serious.

"I can't tell, but it sure feels like something important." He was frowning and I suddenly felt annoyed with myself because I'd only succeeded in spreading my apprehension to Arthur, who would spread it to the other traders. If I was right about the market going up, I didn't want my traders hesitant and uneasy, so I tried to recover. "Look, I'm not exactly Dionne Warwick, and besides, maybe it's something great," I offered.

"What's great?" interrupted Vinnie Kovacevich, who filled the doorway.

"Nothing," said Arthur and walked to the door. Vinnie moved just enough to let him squeeze through. Vinnie is an enormous human being with an exaggerated sense of personal territory. He appears to be unaware, but knowing Vinnie, I'd bet it is intentional. He has these huge bulging eyes set in a head shaped vaguely like a football. With his olive skin and 270 pounds, he looks so much like a bullfrog that sometimes I expect him to unroll his tongue and zap some unsuspecting insect. Universally disliked, Vinnie had three primary hobbies: bingeing on indecent amounts of food, making repulsive body noises and abusing the trading assistants. He's gone through at least a dozen assistants that I can remember and seems genuinely happy when he's reduced some young woman to tears. "A slob, a sleaze and a pig" is what Sherry calls him, and I can't honestly disagree. I'd love to fire him, but he consistently makes the firm money, which unfortunately, in this business, is all that counts.

"Vinnie, I'm very concerned about your short positions. I can't imagine that the banks can go much longer without lowering their rates. They're just getting too much pressure from the Fed. You know I don't like to interfere, but you're way too exposed on this one. Hell, as it is, you've a $1.2 million loss, and this play just doesn't make sense. Don't be stubborn about this, Vinnie. Even J.T. is concerned, and the last thing either one of us needs is J.T. crawling all over us." As soon as I said it, I had a visual flash of J.T. crawling all over me. It made me want to call him back and tell him I'd changed my mind.

Vinnie looked at me and belched. With anyone else it would have been a show of gross disrespect, but with Vinnie it was just a normal show of gross. I was trying very hard to keep my cool, but I was furious that he had ignored my two previous warnings.

Still, requiring a trader to reverse or even reduce a position is very tricky business. It's a little like telling an artist what colors he may use. The compensation of professional traders is determined solely by how much money they make placing their bets in the market, using the firm's capital. Besides, it's a profession that requires the ability to believe that you are right when everyone else in the game thinks you are wrong. Even the bad traders are egomaniacs, and the good ones genuinely do believe that they are Masters of the Universe, a trait not exactly conducive to taking suggestions, much less orders.

In addition to the usual trader's megalomania, Vinnie still resented the fact that I was the managing partner, a job he had aspired to for years. When I was brought in to run the office, Vinnie had made his displeasure widely known in New York. "Some girl who doesn't know shit about managing an office or fuck about trading" was, I'm told, the refrain to his battle song.

Well, he was right about the fact that I had never run an office, but as far as not knowing about trading, that couldn't have been further from the truth, and he knew it. Fact is that I was one of the best-known traders on the street. Before you start thinking that I'm some big egomaniac myself, let me explain: when I arrived at Goldman Sachs' training school, it seemed like everyone there knew the story of how I had secured one of those coveted spots. I had neither an MBA from Harvard, nor a father who was chairman of a Fortune 500 company. I'd simply won it in a poker game.

One afternoon eleven years ago, Hank called, said one of the regulars for his Monday night poker game was out of town and would I substitute if he staked me a hundred dollars. I thought it might be a hoot, so I said yes. I had a wonderful time, hit a winning streak and by the end of the evening was up about twelve hundred dollars. I was about to call it a night when the partner in charge of the southeastern division for Goldman Sachs challenged me to a one-on-one game of five-card draw for a thousand bucks. I not only won that hand, but three successive double-or-nothing hands, the last with nothing more than a pair of eights. He had wanted to play one more time, and I called the bet. "You win, you get your sixteen grand back. I win and you give me a job, and I don't mean as some bozo's assistant, I mean as a trader." He laughed, said I had more balls than the Harlem Globetrotters and dealt the cards. Four minutes and three jacks later, I was Goldman's newest employee.

Once I finally got the hang of trading and the markets, I started coining money for the firm. Around the end of my second year, I got a real uneasy feeling about the markets. They rose steadily every day, even as the economic news was getting worse, and one day I sold all my long positions and opened a couple of huge shorts. Everybody thought I was crazy, and enough people were talking about the scope of my bet against the market, that a reporter at the *Wall Street Journal* heard about it and tracked me down. His story about me came out two days before the market imploded, and he did another story three days later about how I'd earned the firm a cool $58 million by the end of the closing bell on Black Monday. The next payday, the big boys surprised me with a little thank-you: a $500,000 bonus in my pay envelope.

See, what most people don't understand about being a trader is that even if you're good, you're wrong about as often as you're right. The only difference between the big winners and the big losers is knowing when to close out the trade—knowing when to go is every bit as important as knowing which way. Because the spotlight had shone on me at exactly the right moment, everyone started acting like I was Nostradamus or something. Nobody said a word about the literally hundreds of times I'd guessed wrong and gotten my head handed to me.

It even got to the point where financial journalists were writing articles about my "eerie prescience of the markets." The firm, of course, loved the hype, but I was absolutely mortified. I just wanted them to give me the money and shut up about it. I mean, the whole thing was so unbelievably stupid that, after all these years, I still cringe when the subject comes up.

I thought about what Jake said about being defined by one act and how false it felt. That's exactly what I'd experienced without being able to define it. He had articulated what I couldn't. What an amazingly perceptive guy and incredible kisser and why in the hell hadn't he called me?

Anyway, back to Vinnie. The simple fact is that Mr. Kovacevich was convinced that any woman privileged enough to work with him should be there solely to attend to his every need. He continued to stare at me until the opening bell rang. "OK, OK," he croaked, then turned and waddled out.

The markets began to shake in the first minutes. Chase Manhattan announced a half-point reduction in their lending rate at 10:15, and by 11:30 the bond market had broken into a dance. By midmorning, it had reached across to the stock market, and they were doing a jitterbug to the sky.

The traders sit at a long console stacked with pizzas and burgers and donut boxes, talking into headsets, studying the state-of-the-art computer screens and jabbing the flashing phone-line buttons. It always makes me think of what mission control would look like if NASA were taken over by overgrown fraternity boys with eating disorders.

Sherry paged me at about 2:00, and as I was walking back to my desk, a young stock trader jumped up on his chair, did a little butt-wiggling jig and screamed, "Boogie-woogie, baby, even the fat girls are dancing at this party!" Which translated means, "This is wonderful, colleagues, even the less-attractive stocks are being swept up in this bull market!" When he saw me, he turned as red as his suspenders and stepped down off his chair. I raised one eyebrow and kept walking.

I picked up the phone and stuck my finger in my other ear to block out the din. "Hello," I yelled.

"Lauren?" I couldn't make out the voice.

"Yes?"

"It's Jake." I heard it this time, and it had the same effect on me as if he'd slid his hand into my panties.

"Can you hold on a second? Let me close my door." He didn't say anything, so I set down the phone and pulled the door shut, trying to calm my heart, which was running around my chest like a gerbil in a new cage. "Jake, how are you?"

"Flawless."

I laughed, "Is that a promise?"

"Absolutely. Have I caught you at a bad time?"

"Not at all, I'm happy to hear your voice," I admitted. My hands had begun to perspire, and I was cradling the phone on my shoulder and looking at them.

"You're sweet," he said in a voice that felt like he was licking my ear. "And I'm happy to hear yours. Are you still planning to go to Washington?

"I am. As a matter of fact, I'm on the train tonight."

"Good. I've been asked by *Esquire* to do a piece on the aftermath of the Underwood impeachment hearings, so I'm going to be in Washington for the march myself. I wondered if I might buy you a cocktail tomorrow afternoon?"

I know it's silly, but I loved that he used old-fashioned words like "cocktail." He was such a grown-up, so 1940s elegant, the kind of guy you might expect to show up at your door in white tie and tails and sweep you off to El Morocco or something. "I think that would be divine."

"Well," Jake said, "I'm at the Four Seasons. Why don't you drop by around 5:00."

"Sounds great."

"Super. I look forward to seeing you and maybe picking your brain on the ramifications of the decision."

"Saturday at 5:00. See you then." I hung up, stung by his last words. Did he really want to see me or was he simply doing research? Suddenly,

I was more annoyed than excited. As I sat with my hand still on the receiver, I began to talk to him. "Jake Ward, you presumptuous asshole. If you think I'm going to be one of those women who fall all over themselves to give you anything you want, you've got another think coming." And with my resolve firmly in place, I stood up and walked back into the chaos.

I spent the next two and a half hours in the trading room. The feeling I'd woken with was still strong, and I kept checking the news wires, waiting for something extraordinary to happen. Both markets continued their steep climb, but nothing earth-shattering occurred.

I was back in my office at 4:30, when the clerks brought in the closing positions. We'd had a great day in equities, and I banged on the glass to get Arthur's attention. He was putting on his jacket and turned around at the sound. I gave him the thumbs up, and he winked.

When I flipped to the bond positions, I thought I'd have a stroke. Not only had we lost another $1.7 million, our short positions were larger than they had been at the start of the day. I was livid. Not only had Vinnie ignored my direction, but I'd promised Slick that I'd taken care of this. Added to that were the size of the loss and the uneasy feeling of the morning.

"Vinnie, what in God's name do you think you're doing?" I roared. Several traders stopped and turned. No one wanted to miss the chance to hear Vinnie get a verbal thrashing. "Christ, Chase has just lowered their rates, you've lost over $3 million and your short positions are larger than they were this morning, when I specifically told you to reduce them!!"

His face turned white at the public reprimand, and he began to yell, "I'm the fucking trader, it's my fucking ass on the fucking line and I don't care who the fuck likes it!" He was up in my face and I could smell the jalapeños on his breath. If I hadn't been so furious, I would have gagged.

"You're certainly right about that," I spat. "Your fucking ass *is* on the line, but so is mine, and you'd better do one of two things; pray to Almighty God that you are the most clairvoyant man on the face of the earth, or reverse your positions. Because if you're wrong, I'm going to be all over you like wet underwear. And if you're wrong and you don't at least hedge these positions, I'm going to make sure you end up as the goddamn night manager at Captain D's."

The people who had stopped to listen, now embarrassed, turned away and prepared to leave. I glanced down at my watch; it was nearly 5:00. I whirled away from him and walked out the door and down the long hall, my heart pounding. I jumped in my car and flew, zooming through yellow lights and anticipating green ones, pulled into Brookwood Station, slammed the Lexus into park, careened toward the lobby with all my gear, picked up my ticket for the 6:30 train at 6:28 and shot through the door and down the stairs. The porter was standing alone, fifty yards down the platform, and I was running as fast as I could.

"Slow down, slow down," he called, "we're not gonna leave you," but I could hear the engines revving. He helped me on the train, and it immediately began to move. I made my way through the cars and found my place. I remembered Sherry saying that the train was totally booked, so I was pleasantly surprised to find that the seat next to me was empty.

I didn't begin to relax until we rolled through the mountains of north Georgia. I like to ride the trains sometimes and always try to take ones that leave in the late afternoon. The last hour of golden light that bleeds red and disappears makes the ride through the darkness somehow magical. To board a train at night without the foreplay of dusk would be too abrupt, too hurried, not at all satisfying.

As I hit the recline button, my thoughts were of my confrontation with Vinnie, and although I was clearly within my authority to insist that he close or hedge the positions, I still felt a little guilty. I didn't like him, I didn't trust him and the thing about my ass being on the line was true, but Vinnie was a good trader, and being a good trader takes three things—the mathematical fluency necessary to calculate risk a few dozen times a minute, confidence or balls or ego, or whatever you want to call it, and instinct. Vinnie had an abundance of all three.

I hadn't honored Vinnie's instincts, and as I dropped one shoe to the floor, I cross-examined myself on how much of my reaction was influenced by Slick's unease about the trade. Although Slick was my boss and within his authority to question the position, he was not a trader and never had been.

Corporate guys swore that most traders had no class and traders claimed that most corporate types had no balls and each side begrudged the other the exorbitant sums of money they demanded. There were always fights about who deserved the lion's share of the firm's profits. But more emotional and more bitterly fought than simple money arguments were the battles about which side would control the executive committee and ultimately the firm's destiny.

At Sterling White, the corporate finance guys controlled the firm. Our chairman, Merrill Kennedy, had come up as an investment banker, as had Slick. And while Slick had earned the respect of the traders by going to bat for them when he thought they were right, Merrill hadn't and neither had the rest of the corporate crowd on the executive committee.

The more I thought about the situation, the more convinced I was that I had simply reacted to a bad guy who was a good trader with a bad trade.

With that settled, I stared out the window, and the conversations with Jake and Slick were repeated and rewound and repeated in my memory. James Cannon Ward and John Tarleton Moriarty were as different as catsup and caviar. Everything I know about Slick I've heard from his mouth as a friend and lover; everything I know about Jake I've read in the press over the years as a fan. Slick grew up in Greenwich, Connecticut, the only child in a fabulously wealthy family. His grandfather was the governor of Massachusetts and his father had started a little electronics company in the fifties that now ranks 236 on the Fortune 500 list. Jake grew up in Baton Rouge, Louisiana, the fourth of eight children in a family that was dirt poor. His grandfather was a farmer and his father had worked in the oil fields.

Slick had been educated at Lawrenceville and Princeton. Jake had gone to Saint Francis High School and Columbia. Slick had fought in Vietnam as a fighter pilot and had won both the Distinguished Service Medal and the Distinguished Flying Cross. He had been married for twenty-two years, and his sole marital indiscretion was me. Jake had fought against America's involvement in Vietnam, had been divorced for twenty years and according to the celebrity magazines, his romantic exploits were both legion and legendary.

Everything about them was different, everything, of course, but the effect each had on me. As I thought about them, I felt the beginnings of a killer headache. I decided that the only thing that would help was a "professional woman's cocktail," extra-strength Excedrin with a white wine chaser. I purchased the ingredients, knocked them back, then leaned my seat back as far as it would go and closed my eyes. I don't know how long I slept, but when I woke up, it was dark and she was there. Not a whisper above four feet eight inches, snow-white hair and mahogany skin. Very wrinkled, very old and very tiny, perched in the seat next to me, her feet not reaching halfway to the floor.

She seemed to have been waiting for me to wake up. I yawned, covering my mouth with my left hand, and shifted in my seat so that I could see her better. For a moment, we simply stared at each other, and then I remembered my manners and introduced myself. She offered her hand; palsied and miniature, it felt like holding a hummingbird.

"I'm pleased to make your acquaintance," she said, showing me a smile without teeth. "I'm Queen Esther."

I knew I had misheard her. "I'm sorry, I didn't hear you."

"Oh, yes you did. I'm Queen Esther," she repeated. Her bearing was dignified, but her eyes were mischievous, a combination that was simply enchanting. I couldn't decide if she was really some miniature monarch or if she was playing a trick on me. Either seemed possible.

"Is that your real name, or are you teasing me?"

"It's the name on my birth certificate. I am ninety-two years old and I was baptized Queen Esther Lawrence," she said with authority.

I couldn't hide my delight. "I'm so happy to know you. I've never met any royalty, and I certainly never expected to sit next to a queen on the train."

She was clearly enjoying the attention; her eyes squeezed shut and disappeared into the wrinkles on her face.

"Can I call you Queen or should I call you Your Majesty?"

Her eyes danced. "I think you may call me Your Highness." And she cackled with pleasure.

"Your Highness, it is. Now, is Your Highness going to Washington?"

She turned serious. "I ain't. Washington is a sinful place, full of folks who steal other people's money and tell lies."

"Oh, you mean the politicians?" I laughed.

"Yes'm, you know who I mean."

"Well, I'd have to say that you and I are in complete agreement on that. If not Washington, are you going to New York?"

"No'm, I ain't goin' to New York neither. I'm goin' to see my great-grandbaby. She's graduating from Princeton University."

"Wow, that's impressive. You must be so proud of her."

"Oooh, I am. She's a fine girl and smart too." Her face lit up and she dug into her ancient cloth purse and pulled out a photograph of a beautiful, laughing young woman.

I studied the picture. "She's lovely," I said. "I bet she's excited about having you come for her graduation."

"Oh, she don't know I'm coming," Her Highness said matter-of-factly.

"She doesn't know you're coming?"

"Nope. Just decided I was gonna surprise her."

Before I had a chance to express my concern, she fluttered her tiny hand. "Oh, and I got a brand-new hat for the ceremonies. You want to see it?" Her eyes glowed at the thought of showing me such a treasure.

"Absolutely," I assured her, and she pointed to the box above the seat. I retrieved it and handed it to her. She grinned at me, opened the top, delicately unfolded the tissue and pulled the hat out with the same flourish as a magician presenting a fluttering white dove. But this was no white dove, this was simply the purplest hat ever made. The color of a bishop's robes, it had a wide purple band with white polka dots and a spray of white paper flowers.

"Very snazzy! And just the right color for royalty."

She nodded at my good taste, then carefully returned the hat to the box, which I replaced on the overhead rack. "Now," she declared, pleased with all my responses, "that's enough talk 'bout me. Where you off to, all dressed up and looking so pretty?"

"I'm on my way to Washington."

"You got folks there?"

"No ma'am, I don't." I hesitated. I didn't know whether I should go into it, whether I'd upset or offend her, but I looked into her honest eyes and confessed. "I'm going to march in Washington against the men who are allowing Lawrence Underwood to continue to sit on the Supreme Court, knowing full well that he was responsible for his wife's death." I shrugged. "Although I'm not at all sure that marches do much good."

She considered this for a moment, rubbing her chin. "I think the marches used to make a difference, but there been too many of 'em over the years to get much attention now. I guess they just old hat."

"Maybe you're right, maybe they've got to have a new hat, just like you, Queen Esther."

"I know that's right. You young womens need you a new hat, just like Queen Esther." She smiled.

The conductor came through the darkened car, checking seats. We watched him pass, and then she turned to me, "I marched once, with Dr. King in Birmingham." Quietly, as if it were a lost memory, only just recalled. I stared at her. She began to unbutton her sleeve. "Got me a souvenir," she said simply, and pushed up the fabric. There were three overlapping crescent scars, thick and ancient, that began at her wrist and ended at her shoulder. I just looked at her. "Police dogs like to ate me up," she said.

I remembered the newsreels of the Birmingham march, and the pictures that flashed through my mind were so hideous that rage and adrenaline choked me. This tiny woman, who would have been in her sixties at Birmingham, this woman so magical and dignified, set upon by Bull Connor's German shepherds—it burned the backs of my eyes.

"I thinks that march made a difference. I don't mind this," she said quietly of the antique wounds. " 'Cause that made a difference."

"I think you're right, that one did make a difference."

She smiled, but it seemed that the memory had tired her. "Mmhm, I know that's right. Now, baby, you excuse me, but I'm not used to bein' up this late. I think I better take me a little snooze." She pointed to my reclining seat. "You help me do that?"

"Yes ma'am." I leaned over and pushed the button on her seat and she tilted backward, her little legs sticking straight out. Then I pressed the lever for the leg rest and nothing happened. I tried again, with no success. Finally, I got on my knees and tried to manually force the leg rest up. Frustrated, I moved into the aisle but still couldn't get the lever operable. Queen Esther looked like she was lying in a wheelbarrow.

"This is not gonna work, Your Highness. Let's swap seats."

"Oooh no, now, I can't take your seat."

"Oh yes you can. This leg rest is necessary for you but it's not for me, because my legs are so much longer. Besides, what good are you going to be to your great-granddaughter if you haven't gotten any sleep tonight? Come on now, we are swapping seats."

She looked up at me and I knew the great-granddaughter argument had won. She took the hand I offered, and I pulled her to her feet. We got situated in our respective seats and were quiet. It was totally dark, and the only sound was that of the train hurtling over the rails; I lay there, filled with admiration for this tiny old woman, and I just had to tell her.

"Queen Esther," I whispered. "Are you asleep?"

"No, baby, what you need?"

"Nothing, I just wanted to tell you something. I think that at ninety-two you're real brave to make this trip. It must be scary to do it alone."

There was silence. In the darkness, her hand found mine, and then her tiny voice, barely above a whisper. "Girl, every important journey is scary, and the big ones you usually take alone, but if you got faith in the Lord, you gonna find that He'll pack your bags with enough courage to get you where you need to go."

"I know that's right," I murmured and squeezed her hand gently. I held it until her breathing grew rhythmic and I knew that she was asleep.

I lay in the darkness for the longest time, thinking about her words. At the risk of sounding like one of those religious exhibitionists, I must report that this wonderful sense of calm came over me and I felt safer than I had in years. This was nice, especially in light of how pitifully uncomfortable I was physically. Lying in the seat with my legs dangling was both unnatural and unpleasant. Besides, the angle and the width of the seats made it impossible to lie on my side, which I have to do to sleep. And to top things off, the clothes I was wearing were bunching up in the strangest places. Chanel suits are wonderfully versatile, but they make very poor pajamas. All in all, it was like being wrapped in swaddling clothes and lying in a pet casket.

I stuck my watch under the tiny light over the window. It was 11:20 P.M. My only hope was to find the bar car, gulp two or three strong drinks, stagger back to my seat and pass out. This, of course, meant that I'd have a dead dog hangover in the morning, but I didn't care. I was really quite desperate.

I got up quietly, so as not to wake my friend, and made my way through the darkened train. I was worried that the bar car would be deserted and that I'd be a sitting duck for any lowlife or nutcase on the train. I decided I'd buy a couple of miniature bottles of scotch and a cup of ice and take them back to my seat.

As I pushed the gray steel door open, I was stunned. Not only was the bar car not deserted, it was packed. And as I stood looking for a place to sit, it hit me; there was not a single man in the place.

Chapter 5

"**M**en are only good for one thing."

"Yeah, honey—and damned few of them are good for that."

I was standing in line at the bar, semieavesdropping on the two women in front of me, although I didn't really count it as eavesdropping because they were talking so loud you couldn't help but overhear.

"You know it's the truth," the first woman said. "Single men aren't having sex anymore. The only guys that want to screw these days are married"—she paused for half a second—"to someone else."

"I can't believe you said that," said the woman in front of them, who had obviously been eavesdropping too. "I thought it was me, but I swear to God, none of the men I date can get it up!"

"That's so true," the second woman announced, as if she'd discovered a universal truth, making her the Galileo of sexual abstinence. "Either they can't or they don't want to. You know, ten years ago, everybody fucked and nobody dated; now everybody dates and nobody fucks!"

"All I know is, if I don't get some action soon, mine's gonna grow back together!" The first woman moaned.

I laughed. Since the polo player, I had gone out with several guys, none of whom seemed the least bit interested in sleeping with me. I must admit that I was relieved that this appeared to be a new social phenomenon and not a comment on what I had assumed was my dwindling attractiveness.

When it was my turn, I bought a scotch from the ancient bartender, who was still shaking his gray head over the previous conversation. I couldn't tell if he was disappointed in such sorry representation of his own sex or offended by such frank discussion by the opposite one.

The car was poorly lit, but as the train shimmied past the occasional light along the tracks, momentary brightness flowed from the first window, instantly to the second, to the third and backwards until it passed the last window and vanished.

At one table, a polished blonde in a designer jacket leaned forward to share a confidence, and five heads bowed momentarily to receive it. There was a second's hesitation, then the table exploded with laughter. Across the aisle, a handsome middle-aged matron listened with amusement as two college girls took turns telling a story.

The level of noise was startling. At first, I thought these women were talking so loudly to compete with the wailing of the steel rails, but as I listened I heard something else. These voices were more than loud, they were unself-conscious. Not the tentative voices that play down opinions to disapproving men, not the hesitant voices that expect to be interrupted by uninterested men; not the voices that sing the female anthem "I don't know" and its chorus "I'm not sure." These were full, sure voices.

As I stood in the aisle, it dawned on me that every woman in that bar car was talking about Larry or Lynn Underwood. They were all on their way to Washington for the march.

The train swayed, and I put my hand out to the back of the seat where a plump woman in her mid-fifties, wearing an orange caftan, was weeping her way through an obviously painful narrative. There was one empty table at the other end, and I walked toward it. I sat facing the length of the car, my head resting on the back wall, feeling the vibrations and the shifting of the train.

A woman at the next table was in midsentence. "Oh, sure. He had nothing to do with her injuries." Her voice was dipped in sarcasm vinaigrette. "The fact that he never took her to the emergency room proves nothing but that the creep had not one scrap of human decency."

She was still talking, but I faded away, hypnotized by the darkness and the movement of the train. Still looking out the window, I sensed someone standing at the table.

"Hello, ladies and gentlemen. We're Archie Bell and the Drells from Houston, Texas."

It was a voice from long ago, much too distinct to be a late-night memory. A grin stretched so far across my face that I could barely complete my part of the code phrase. "And we don't only sing, but we dance just as good as we walk." I turned slowly from the window, in case it wasn't really her, but it was and I was laughing with joy and amazement.

"Jinx 'Bad Act' Johnston!"

"Lauren Montague, live and in couture!"

"My God, I don't believe it's you." But it was. The same long, honey-blond hair, emerald eyes, deep-set in a wide face, and those unforgetta-ble cover-girl teeth.

"Believe it!" She held out her hands, and as fast as I could stand, we were hugging. I couldn't believe she was actually there. I had thought about her so often over the years, told so many Jinx Johnston stories, that sometimes I felt as if she were simply the harvest of my ripe imagination.

Jinx had lived across the hall from Ali and me in the freshman dorm during fall quarter of our freshman year. The daughter of an undertaker from Selma, Alabama, she was, at seventeen, the wildest person I had ever met; she drank martinis, had a vibrator she called "chain saw," gatored instead of shagged at fraternity parties, smoked Marlboros and marijuana and "bestowed her virginity" on at least five guys that I knew of.

"I can't believe it." She was shaking her head. I motioned her to sit down, and she slid into the seat opposite me. "If I had a dime for every time I told a story about you, I'd be a zillionaire. As a matter of fact, I was telling a story about you just the other day."

"Really? Which story?"

"The one about us and Professor Daly. Don't you remember?" I shook my head. "You don't remember the professor we had for philosophy?" I was still shaking my head. "Professor Daly was that fat little creep that fancied himself such a lady-killer. He tried to put the make on me the first week of class, and I told him in no uncertain terms that I wasn't in the slightest bit interested . . ."

"Oh, now I remember. After that he hated your guts, and he used to try to humiliate you in class all the time . . ."

"Exactly. That's the one." Now she was laughing, her eyes sparkling with glee. "But we taught him a lesson, didn't we?"

My memory was very vague; I shrugged my shoulders.

"Lauren, I can't believe you don't remember this! We typed up this ad that said something like 'Attention: all women who are current or past students of Professor Daly. If you have been pressured for sex by the professor, please send your account of the incident and any punishment you suffered as a result to this post office box.'"

"Oh yeah, now I remember . . . and we took it to his office and told him that if he gave you any more problems or if we heard of him bothering any other girl, we were gonna buy a full page in the school paper for it." I was shaking my head at the memory, and we were both laughing.

"And I'll never forget what you said to him as we left."

"What?"

"You said, 'Let this be a warning to you, shitlips, keep your little teeny weenie to yourself!'"

"I called him shitlips?" I must have picked that up from Ali, who specializes in inventive invectives.

"Yes ma'am, you did." She nodded, and we dissolved into laughter.

"God, it's been so long, Jinx. I have so many things to ask you that I don't even know where to start."

"Me neither. Oh, oh, oh, yes, I do. Do you still have Onan?"

"No, Onan's gone to that special prosecutor in the sky." Onan was my parrot, so named because he was always spilling his seed on the ground. He sat in a cage in our dorm room and screeched things like "Who's got the tapes?" and "I am not a crook" and "It's Haldeman's fault." Onan had learned to talk in 1974 and had stayed a very political bird.

"What about Tippi?" Tippi was Jinx's very funny, very Baptist roommate.

"You are gonna love this—she married an Episcopal priest."

"You're lying!"

"Honey, I wouldn't lie to you unless I was gonna get something out of it," she said and took a long swallow. "Do you ever see Ali?"

"All the time. She's doing well." I didn't go into detail because Jinx and Ali hadn't been friends since they both fell for Charlie Howe at a Kappa-KA social.

"What about Gigi?"

"Gigi's fine, still painting. She had a pretty tough time for a while: bad marriage, ugly divorce, but she's just gotten remarried, to an architect. He's a lovely man and she's really happy. I can't wait to tell her I saw you! And how are Edwin and Lilly?" While the rest of us had referred to our parents as Mama or Daddy, Jinx had called hers by their first names, a habit that had seemed fabulously grown-up to me at the time.

"Well, Lovely Lilly is the same; still growing prize-winning roses, still serving tomato aspic to her bridge club and still drinking Rebel Yell on the sly. Edwin's retired now. He's still sweet as he can be but, honey, his mind is gone. The doctors say it's Alzheimer's, but I think maybe sniffing formaldehyde all those years just pickled his brain." She waved her hand as if to dismiss the sadness of what she'd just said, and before I could say how sorry I was, she leaned across the table. "Now, sweetpea, tell me about you; the last thing I heard was that you married that cute guy from Augusta."

"Well, that turned out to be a very slow trip." I shook my head and laughed. "Talk about no ambition. He aspired to nothing more than to work for his grandpa's bank, get wall-eyed drunk every Saturday night and be invited to play Augusta National two or three times a year. It took about six months for me to realize that in order for the marriage to work, I was going to have to undergo a lobotomy—and we couldn't afford one on his salary. Anyway, I got pregnant on our first anniversary. That's the one thing that made it all worthwhile. My son, Razz. He's sixteen and in my humble, unbiased opinion, perfection incarnate."

"You have a son who's sixteen?" She shook her head in amazement. "God, how old were you when you had him?"

"Twenty. I had just turned nineteen when I married Teddy, the summer after our freshman year."

"Are you guys still married?"

"Lord no. We stayed married for four years after Razz was born. By that time, Teddy had discovered cocaine and I realized that I couldn't save him."

"Amicable divorce?"

I shook my head. "Very nasty divorce, big custody fight. The Fontaines have a lot of money and a lot of clout in Augusta, and they did everything they could to make sure that Teddy got custody of Razz. Teddy's father took the stand and swore under oath that Teddy did not have a drug problem. His mother got up and said what a devoted father he was. At that point, Teddy couldn't even take care of himself, much less a four-year-old." A shiver went through me at the thought.

"Their other big argument was that I was this twenty-three-year-old nobody who didn't have a pot to piss in. What they didn't count on was that I would take the two things I had asked for in the divorce, the wedding silver that had been a present from my family and the three-carat diamond-and-platinum engagement ring, sell them and hire the best custody lawyer in Atlanta. I won but our judge retired a couple of years later, so back to court we went. The second judge held for me too, but every couple of years the Fontaines would raise their ugly heads again, regaling the court with all that they could offer Razz."

"What a nightmare! Are they still trying to get custody?"

I shook my head. "Last time they took me to court was about five years ago. I haven't heard a peep since then."

"They've finally given you credit for being a good mother?" she offered.

I laughed. "There were two reasons why I'm sure they won't bother us again. The first is that Teddy's father had a stroke a few months after our last legal go-round and his mother has her hands full taking care of the old bastard," I said and drained the last of my drink.

"The second reason?"

"I think it finally occurred to the Fontaines that there is nothing I wouldn't do to keep my son safe."

She leaned in. "Does your son ever see or talk to his father?"

"Never. Fact is—I don't even know if he's still alive. Seems he graduated from powder cocaine to crack when it first hit the street. Poor Teddy, it was the first cutting-edge thing he'd ever done." It made me sad to even say his name. "Anyway, the last thing I heard was that he'd been in and out of a dozen treatment centers—that was, I don't know, maybe three years ago."

"Well, honey, I'm sorry you had to go through that, but you look like you're doing just fine now." She laughed. "You look like you just stepped off the cover of *Vogue*."

"Thanks. I didn't have time to change, came straight from work."

"Just what exactly do you do?"

"Same old stuff . . . righting the world's wrongs, keeping up with the Joneses, offending people who are only trying to help."

"No, seriously. There you sit in a Chanel suit, you've got to be doing something high-class."

"I run the Atlanta office of Sterling White."

"My God, Lauren, I'm impressed. I guess you understand high finance and the stock market and everything . . ."

"Yeah, they kind of like you to have some inkling of what's going on."

"Well, I'm impressed, but not surprised."

"Why, because I was such a math whiz in school?" I laughed. Jinx used to have to balance my checkbook for me.

"No, because I figured you'd pick a field where you didn't have to work with women."

"I work with women," I protested. The comment caught me off guard. I considered her point. Although I had never thought about it in exactly those terms, I had to admit there was truth in what she said.

"Yeah, but it's mostly men, isn't it?"

"Yeah, it's mostly men, but I have women friends."

"I'm sure." Jinx knew.

"I can't help it, Jinx. Most women give me the willies."

She nodded and looked away as if fascinated by the darkness outside the window. "It's not because of what happened with me and the Chi-Os, is it?"

"No. Absolutely not." As a college freshman I had been, to my absolute astonishment, rushed by several prestigious sororities. Ambivalent about joining but seduced by the idea of belonging to a sisterhood, I finally selected the Chi-Os.

I surprised myself by enjoying it and looked forward to the time I spent at the sorority house until one day in February a summons from the Morals Committee arrived at my dorm room. Stunned, I appeared at the designated time and was escorted into the living room, where there were five seniors sitting at a long folding table. I was told that "my sisters" were deeply concerned about my association with Jinx, who had, in case I didn't know, quite a bad reputation around campus.

I thanked them for their concern, took my pin off, tossed it to the president of the committee, called them several things that were both unchristian and unsisterly, turned on my heel and walked out of the house for the last time.

Jinx was afraid that my uneasiness around other women started in a college sorority living room, but the lesson that females are to be feared was taught me long before that. My ninth-grade year at boarding school was difficult and lonely. Not only was I younger than my classmates by a year, I was also pretty inept socially. While I had perfected my tennis skills with long hours at the backboard and on the court, they had honed their personal skills at Girl Scouts and slumber parties, and I was awkward where they were polished.

I drifted through most of the year on the fringes, but in March, I hit the social jackpot. The girl I lived with, a sweet but dull swimmer from Boston, had contracted mono and been sent home, and I was given Ali Williams as a roommate. Ali was one of the three most popular girls in our class. She was sleek and confident in the way that sought-after young girls are. I was anxious at first, afraid that she would find me stupid or offensive, but she didn't. After evening study hall we would burrow into our beds and I would regale her with stories of life on the tennis circuit and she would laugh; she would confide her secrets to me and I would swear to keep them safe. By May, I had my first best friend, and I felt like the luckiest person who ever lived. An unexpected dividend of this association was a newfound popularity with my class-mates, because my friendship with Ali made me an ex officio member of her group: the richest, prettiest, most admired girls in the ninth grade.

Ali acted as my advocate, constantly assuring them of my worth as a member of their glittering little group. They laughed at my jokes and stories and saved a place for me at their table, but I knew instinctively that none of them quite shared Ali's level of enthusiasm for my inclu-sion.

That was most apparent whenever it came time to choose guests for school holidays and vacations. They would pair up and giggle off to Aspen or Palm Beach or the Hamptons. Ali was always the first one to be snatched up to go someplace exotic and wonderful, and I was left lonely and jealous. But I loved Ali and was too grateful to her to spoil her pleasure by ever letting on how I felt. Actually, I refused to acknowledge to myself that I was hurt by or even aware of my exclusion. My heart knew that I was at the party on a borrowed invitation, but my brain would not entertain the thought. I concocted elaborate justifications to convince myself that it was sheer coincidence that I was never asked, and I would go home and spend my vacations bragging about my glamorous friends to Gigi and her pals.

The day was Tuesday, the first of October, my tenth-grade year. I remember the date because it was two weeks before my fifteenth birthday and I remember the day because Ali's grandmother had died that weekend. The funeral was on Monday afternoon and Ali was supposed to return to school Tuesday evening. The morning was crisp and glorious and I got a surprise A on a Latin test and I was happy. As the bell rang to end class, I felt something I had never felt before. First bewildered, then panicked, I rushed to an empty stall in the bathroom, threw my books on the floor, hiked up my uniform and pulled down my underpants. Blood. I didn't know what to do. I wished Ali were there. Like most girls, Ali had been menstruating since the sixth grade and treated it as a minor annoyance. I did the only thing I could think of; folded up a mass of toilet paper, placed it in my underwear and waddled out into the bathroom. Chassie Markham and Honey Grey were standing by the door, laughing. Chassie was a junior whose father had given enormous amounts of money to the school and Honey was one of our crowd. I tried to sound both experienced and nonchalant when I asked for a Kotex, but I must have used the wrong terminology or somehow given myself away, because Chassie asked with a combination of irritation and incredulity, "What is this, your first period or something?" My face turned beet red, and she rolled her eyes. "Kotex are gross, I only use Tampax." Honey didn't offer any help, but I eventually found an eighth grader who had one.

I can't explain how relieved I was. I had often worried that something was wrong with me, that I was a freak who lacked some essential female ingredient. I was so ashamed of my secret defect that only two people in the world knew of it—Gigi and Ali—and I couldn't wait to tell them that I was a woman, at least technically.

An hour and a half later, I was at lunch, listening to Mopsy Gregory imitate our pitiful old librarian, when I noticed Honey scanning the room. She seemed to find whoever she was looking for and nodded, and when she saw me looking at her, she smiled. Within a minute, several girls began to get up and walk to our table, then others noticed and followed and soon there were forty or fifty girls surrounding us. Miss Porter's had a wonderful tradition; when anyone had a personal, athletic or academic triumph she could expect to be serenaded by her friends at lunch with the customary "Congratulations," sung to the tune of "Happy Birthday." I began singing, looking around to see who was being honored, happy to celebrate whichever of my good friends had accomplished something else wonderful. Then I realized that everyone was singing to me.

For a second, I was baffled, then I looked at Honey and saw the look of excitement on her face. I realized with a bud of horror that bloomed like a black rose in time-lapse photography why they were singing to me. I was paralyzed with mortification, unable to move, able only to memorize the faces and the sound of that terrible choir. There were girls who knew the joke and then there were girls who'd obviously assumed that I had done something to celebrate . . . and it was easy to tell them apart.

I looked around at the girls at our table and I could see which group they fell into, and the elaborate fantasy that I had crocheted for myself of having these wonderful friends unraveled to nothing. I couldn't swallow, but a smile was frozen on my face as I rose and walked out of the cafeteria, followed by all those eyes. I felt like a thermos that had been dropped on a concrete driveway, unblemished on the surface and shattered inside.

Chassie had her back to the door and was recounting her contribution to my torment to two other juniors as I came out of the cafeteria, and they motioned for her to be quiet. She turned around, saw me and the humiliation in my blinking eyes and put her hand to her mouth. "Whoops!" she said and laughed. I remembered that. It was the last thing I told Ali when she returned and I sat on her bed and sobbed out the story to her.

And I remembered it eighteen months later to the day, as we sat with our class in the audience as the seniors were presented, on the fragrant front lawn, one by one, in their pastel gowns. Costumed eighth graders twisted the rainbow colors of the maypole, and Chassie Markham was presented to the faculty, family and friends of the student body as the May Queen of the graduating class. It's been twenty years and I can still recall the look of iced horror on her face as Marvin Gaye crooned over the loudspeaker, "I'm asking yooou, baby, to get it on with me."

I knew just how she felt in front of all those eyes and I turned to Ali and she knew immediately and we both, as if choreographed, put our hands to our mouths and said at the same time, "Whoops!"

As for Honey, the glittering excitement in her eyes came back to me, in perfect recall, when I saw a look so similar seven years later. That almost exact same look, coincidentally, in her own fiancé's eyes as I seduced him the afternoon he arrived in town for their wedding.

"Jinx, I was uneasy around women long before I got to college. I'm just a lot more comfortable around men."

"That's hardly surprising," she said.

"What do you mean?"

"It's all because of the way you look."

"Meaning what?"

"Simple, Lauren. Drop-dead gorgeous does two things. First thing it does is make you an enemy of women."

"But why, Jinx? I'm a damn good friend and—"

"Honey, you're missing the point. In their deepest hearts every woman I've ever known divides up the female population into four groups. First, there are her friends, whom she loves and trusts and relies on for advice and support and reality checks and the stuff that keeps us alive and functional."

I was nodding my head. It was exactly the way I felt about my friends.

"Second, there are safe women, women she considers out of the running because they're ugly or fat or old or of another race. She either trusts these women or ignores them, depending on circumstances. Third, there are all the other women in the world. These, she considers competition, to be watched and measured and feared. Then there's a special category for women she thinks of as superior to her—these are to be hated, punished or avoided."

"God, you're absolutely right," I said, "I do it too. I have this little voice in my head that plays one up, one down."

She cocked her head as if trying to hear it.

"You know—I meet another woman and Voncile says—"

"Huh?"

"The voice in my head, I call her Voncile."

She nodded, unfazed.

"Anyway, I meet another gal, and Voncile says, 'Well, she may be prettier, but you're twice as smart; or she's married to a fabulous guy, but you're a managing partner; or she's more successful, but you have bigger tits, or whatever.' " I hated Voncile, but I couldn't make her go away.

"Bingo!" She said, pointing at me to signify her agreement. "Every woman on earth has a Voncile, but on the flip side, it works just the opposite with men. For men the delineation is even simpler when it comes to women." I was waiting, concentrating. I wanted to understand. "As far as men are concerned, there are two kinds of women, women they want to fuck and women who are invisible."

"Hmm." I'd never thought about it that way.

"Lauren, I've watched them. I know what I'm talking about. And because you're one of the women men want to screw, they acknowledge and validate you in a way that women don't, and that's why you feel comfortable around them."

I shook my head. "But I'm not all that comfortable with men either. I get so sick of being hit on that I feel like I'm always on my guard so I put on this 'keep your distance' air. It's also why the only men I call friends are safe; either because they're ex-lovers or because they're gay. God, Jinx, sometimes I have these flashes of the future and see myself totally alone in the world, an old woman with long dark hairs on my upper lip, wearing heavy sweaters in July, living with a hundred cats and pots of African violets and old Captain and Tennille records." I have, over the years, sharpened my self-loathing skills to the point where I can sink myself in a millisecond.

"Besides, with a few notable exceptions, my experiences with other women are an unbroken string of disasters." I needed another drink. "That is all I'm going to say, I'm sick of talking about me. I want to know about you—but first, another drink. You stay here, I'll be back. Gin martini, four olives?"

She nodded. I went to the bar, bought the drinks and brought them back to the table. "Start with you and Charlie Howe."

"We got married," she said simply, and stopped. She took another long sip of her drink.

"God, he's such a dreamboat!"

"He was, wasn't he?" The past tense. I could feel my heart contract.

"Oh, Jinx, I'm so sorry, I had no idea." I couldn't think of another word to say, so I just reached across the table and took her hand.

"I know, honey, there was no way you could know. It's OK." But her grip told me that it was not.

"If you don't want to talk about it . . ."

"No, no, I'm OK." She swallowed the rest of her drink and took a deep breath. "Charlie and I got married two days after I graduated. It was one of those rare deals; the perfect marriage. We were madly in love, completely inseparable, blissfully happy and every year it just got better. We had a beautiful daughter named Caroline, she's nine . . . she looks just like Charlie. Those same gray-green eyes and high cheekbones . . ." Her gaze slid up the stainless-steel wall, and for a second she seemed as if she'd lost her place. Then, "Monday nights were Charlie and Caroline's special night. She'd get all dressed up and they'd go to Red Lobster for fried shrimp, then to Baskin-Robbins for ice cream."

She looked back at me and braced herself with a deep breath. "Six years ago, they were on their way home and a drunk driver crossed the median and hit them head-on. Charlie was killed instantly and Caroline's pelvis was crushed in the impact."

The memory of it seemed to keep her from breathing; then very slowly, she inhaled. "It was as awful as it sounds, and for the longest time, I was in a daze. An old friend of mine and Charlie's really rescued me. He just kind of took over, and I was so numb that I let him and the next thing I knew, he was telling me that he loved me and that he wanted to marry me and take care of us. I didn't love him, but he was so good with Caroline and so kind to me and I knew that I'd never have with anyone what I had with Charlie. So, I don't know, I just sort of let it happen."

She shrugged and stuck her fingers in her glass. "It was OK for a while, but after about a year, he decided that I'd had long enough to get over what had happened. He couldn't see why I didn't just 'get hold of myself.' But of course you can't just will yourself to stop hurting. It was weird, but it was like he started to take my grief as a personal affront, and to make a long story short, we got a divorce the week before our second anniversary." She fished out an olive and popped it in her mouth. "After the divorce, I had to go to work for the first time. I don't really have any special skills; I was just, you know, a housewife. Well, about the only thing I could do is be an administrative assistant, and I got this job at this company in town. I mean Bainbridge, Georgia, is not exactly the land of golden opportunity and I'm not exactly CEO material, but the pay was decent and the medical coverage was fantastic. A hundred percent coverage after the deductible," she said with something approaching awe.

She caught the unasked question on my face, "The doctors said that it would take four or five operations before Caroline could walk again, so you can imagine how important that was."

"Of course."

"Well, I'd been there about nine months, and at first everything was great, everybody was so supportive; I really loved it and for the first time in ages I didn't wake up in the middle of the night, worrying about money." She pulled out another olive and chewed it slowly. "Then I get this new supervisor, not really attractive but nice, mid-forties, married. Well, starting out, I couldn't have asked for a better boss; you know, he praised my work, gave me time off when Caroline was in the hospital, which was a lot. We kidded around, had a good time." She shrugged her shoulders. "Maybe we even flirted a little bit. One day, he took me out to lunch to thank me for the great work I'd been doing. We were having a nice time and I thanked him for being such a good friend to me and he said how much he admired my strength and blah, blah, blah, he thought I was so attractive and his marriage was so unhappy and what he'd really like—was to fuck me."

"Son of shitlips."

"Exactly."

"Goddamn it!" I slammed my fist against the wall. "This is the kind of stuff that just makes me wacko. OK, you're at lunch, he says he wants to do you and you say. . . ."

"I say that I'm very flattered and I think he's a lovely fellow, but that I don't sleep with married men or men that I work with."

"Then what happens?"

"He's the perfect gentleman . . . you know, he hopes that he hasn't offended me and of course I assure him that he hasn't and everything is peachy . . . until the next day." She fished out another olive. "Anyway, I go in to work thinking everything is going to be OK, and he calls me into his office."

"And . . . ?"

"And, honey, it was so cold in that room you could've hung meat. He says that he has been reviewing my records and don't I know that the company has strict policies on absenteeism and the fact that I've been out so much has clearly affected my work, which is only borderline acceptable." She laughed derisively. "This same work that he'd praised less than twenty-four hours before . . ."

"I cannot believe this."

"Neither could I. Then—you're gonna love this—he says that he has no intention of letting me manipulate him anymore. I'm either gonna put out or I'm gonna get out." She closed her eyes. "So I put out."

I reached across the table and took her hand again. She squeezed hard and so did I. Rage had me by the throat and shame had her and neither one of us could talk, we just looked at each other and shook our heads.

She was weeping now. "Lauren, I had to make sure that Caroline—"

"Jinx, I'm a mother. I understand."

"I should've tried to tell someone, but I was afraid, and this was long before Anita Hill. It went on for two and a half years and he was so horrible and abusive. He used to tell me what a slut I was and maybe he was—"

"The most evil piece of shit ever to walk the earth. Honey, this guy deserves to be Larry Underwood's cellmate in the sewers of hell and you have nothing to be ashamed of. You simply did what you had to do."

"Do you really think so?'"

"I know so."

"But haven't you ever been sexually harassed?"

"Sure, more times than I can count. But it's not the same thing, not even the same category."

"What do you mean."

"I mean if Razz's life or health were at stake, I'd blow the entire Mormon Tabernacle Choir, live on the *Today* show . . ."

She laughed.

"You know what I think is amazing?"

"What?"

"That between the two of us, we haven't written off the entire human race."

"*Au contraire,* my dear Lauren. I've written off the male gender and you've written off the female, so between us, we have indeed written off the entire human race."

"I don't know about you and men, but I haven't completely written off the women. Not really. It's just that identifying with and mingling are two different things. I care about women. It kills me for something bad to happen to a woman, even if I don't even know her." And then to prove my sincerity, I said, "As a matter of fact, I'm on my way to Washington for the march on the capitol."

She was grinning. "Well then, why, pray tell, are you on your way to mingle with what promises to be a fairly large group of women?"

"The Underwood debacle is the last straw—so I'm going to raise my voice with a couple of million or so of my sisters . . ." She was trying not to laugh. "What's so funny?"

"I'm just calculating the chances of you and me meeting after twenty years, on a train, on our way to a women's march. The odds must be about a billion to one."

"You're going to the march too?"

"You bet. After Caroline had her last and, thank God, final operation, I quit my job. By then, I was an absolute basket case. Talk about killer depressions, I could barely get out of bed. I ended up going to a therapist who has done a lot of work with sexual harassment and rape victims. She told me about depression being anger turned inward and how the rage I felt toward my ex-boss was going to kill me if I didn't deal with it and with him. So I confronted Caligula, reported him to top management and the EEOC and sent a letter to his wife. It was great; the depression lifted, and I felt powerful for the first time in my life. My therapist was really involved in the women's movement and she got me involved. I started working for the group she founded and ended up running it."

I laughed. "I must say that I'm amazed—the biggest man-killer I ever knew becomes an old-fashioned feminist."

Now it was her turn to laugh. "Feminist, yes. Old-fashioned—not by a long shot. We're pretty radical, I don't know if you've ever heard of us—WWW, stands for Wild Women Warriors." I shook my head. I didn't want to hurt her feelings, but it sounded to me like a tag team from World Federation Wrestling. "We're mostly women who are fed up with how little progress the movement has made in recent years. We're kind of a guerrilla faction. Anyway, I've been invited to meet in the morning with the leaders of other groups to talk about this latest debacle. I don't know any of the details, but I do know that the meeting starts early. Speaking of that, I've got to get to bed. It's late, late, late."

She was right. It was late. We hugged for the longest time and exchanged addresses and phone numbers and she was gone and I was left in the corner with two more swallows of scotch and I took one of them and watched the trees and the houses blur in the darkness.

I thought about what she said about my writing off half the human race. It sounded a lot like Jo, who always talks about my isolation from my entire gender. Well, I didn't like feeling this way, so I decided that I was going to start involving myself with women whenever I could. I watched the group in the middle of the car. They had been filling it with the sound of laughter since I arrived. I was just drunk enough to march myself over to their table. "Mind if I sit down?"

"Not at all," said a gorgeous woman with black hair and a white streak at the widow's peak. Obviously the ringleader, she had the look of someone who deals with life's difficulties by laughing at them. "Not if you'd like to join the jaws-of-life club." I was a little taken aback, but I took a slow sip of my drink and played along.

"I'm sure I'd be thrilled to join. But it's not like the Junior League, is it?" Teddy's mother had forced me to join the Augusta chapter of the Junior League. I hadn't lasted ten days.

"Oh, no, it's not like the Junior League!"

I sat down and looked around the table and everyone was smiling, about to let me in on the joke.

"Do you know what the jaws-of-life are?"

"I think so; aren't they those things they use to cut people out of cars after wrecks?"

"Yep, they can rip open steel or rubber or anything. . . . and when you become a member of the jaws-of-life club, we give you your very own set. Then anytime a man bugs you, you get your jaws-of-life, grab his head with them and—pop, no more problem." She made a gesture, showing me the technique.

I burst out laughing and she looked pleased. My mind turned a kaleidoscope of creeps; Vinnie Kovacevich and Bull Connor, Professor Daly and Jinx's boss.

"The only thing I'd worry about," I said, "is that mine couldn't stand up to the constant use!" They laughed. "This," I announced, looking around the table, "is clearly the militant faction here tonight."

"You've got that right. I'm Leslie. This," she nodded her head to the blonde with the designer jacket, "is Sally." The two of them seemed to be the spokeswomen for the group. She introduced the rest of the women and I introduced myself.

"We're the commandos in the war of the sexes and this," Sally announced, tapping the table with her drink, "is Command Central."

"It sounds like a revolution," I challenged.

"It is," Leslie said, "and Sunday's going to be our Fort Sumter!"

"Oh, really? What's your plan?"

"Well, we're thinking about overthrowing the government."

"Yeah," Sally agreed, "throw out all those jerks in Washington and take over."

"Like a palace coup," Leslie explained. "The Women's Revolution."

"I think in order to have a coup, you pretty much have to take over the military," I said.

"Yeah, in order to overthrow the government you have to have weapons . . . and unfortunately we don't have any weapons," Leslie said, as if this had just occurred to her.

All of a sudden it hit me. "But we do have weapons. As a matter of fact, each one of us has one."

"What are you talking about?"

"Have you all ever heard the story of Lysistrata?"

"Wait a minute," Sally said, putting up her hand as if to stop me. "Lysistrata? Isn't that the story of how the Roman women—"

"Greek," I corrected.

"Right, how the Greek women stopped their husbands from fighting some war by refusing to have sex with them until the war was over?"

"Exactly!" I said. "And as the story goes, the husbands found a way to stop the war pretty damn quick."

"Hmm. So you think we can take over the government that way?" Leslie asked.

"Sure, in the story, it's the wives of the generals and the senators. But why stop there? Maybe we could get all the wives in America to join our revolution."

"That's the answer!" Sally said. "We'll start a sex strike to take over the government." She was getting a little thick speeched. "How exactly are we going to do this?"

My head was a bit foggy now too. I shrugged. "I don't know. We'll figure that out later."

"OK." Leslie was convinced. "It shouldn't take us too long to bring them to their knees!"

"Turnabout being fair play, and all that," I giggled.

"This is genius!"

"You know the funny thing about this?" Sally asked. "It could actually work."

"Yeah, leave it to us to save the country, because we have the common sense and the men don't," I said, drunk by now on scotch and imagined power. But as soon as I said it, I had this weird feeling. Hadn't I heard that line somewhere before?

Chapter 6

My first thought as I oozed toward slow consciousness was that someone had very recently performed brain surgery on me and forgotten the anesthesia.

"Penn Station, Washington, D.C., coming up, Penn Station, two minutes, Washington, D.C.," the porter announced loudly, passing me on his way to the back of the car.

"Well, pleeease shut up about it," I begged under my breath and tried to sit up. Every muscle in my body wailed as I fumbled for my shoes. My feet were swollen, and the stiff leather of my new high heels pinched; I had a crick in my neck and a pulsing pain in my head. It was at least eighty degrees inside the train, and the air was stale and sour with the smell of forty unwashed bodies on a summer morning.

Queen Esther was curled on her side, snoring like a contented pet in a favorite chair. I had this urge to lean over and kiss her on the forehead, but I was afraid that she might wake up and then I'd be embarrassed, so I fished out my card, wrote, "Your Highness, I loved meeting you. Long may you reign," and slipped it into her hatbox. I gathered my things and stepped gingerly off the train into the cool darkness.

The redcap opposite me was singing softly but energetically to himself, his head jerking and hands pounding the handle of the baggage cart as if it were a set of bongos. The click of my heels echoing off the marble as I set off behind him seemed to be keeping time, making me an unwilling accompanist in this roving concert. I watched him suspiciously, wishing he would stop and certain anyone stimulated to such an extent must surely be so through pharmacological means.

We were standing outside in the shimmering heat of early morning, the calls of taxi drivers to one another floated through dust and diesel exhaust from a cluster of grimy silver buses and the flash of power ties hurrying into the terminal and the fade of dresses herding children out. I was cursing the light and the heat as I shaded my eyes, looking for Ali. The glare was too much, and I closed them. A minute later I heard the redcap gasp. We had been cast totally into shadow, and I knew without opening my eyes that either there had been a sudden eclipse of the sun or that Ali had sent Moore to fetch me.

Moore is a giant. He stands six feet eleven inches. Born in Barbados, he's as black as a Steinway grand and as wide as a Steelers lineman. He has an earring in his right ear and no left ear, and if you didn't know what a sweetheart he is, he'd scare the hell out of you.

I've known him since the day six years ago that he came to work for the Wolvertons—as a bodyguard. At the time, David had been working on an investigative series on the Colombian drug cartel, and he got a call one Friday night advising him that the FBI had reason to believe he might be in danger. They encouraged him to take extreme safety precautions. So he went first thing the next morning to the suggested security firm and arrived home at 2:00 that afternoon with Moore.

I happened to be in Washington at the time. The first thing Moore said he needed to do was get familiar with the house, so Ali and I gave him a tour. He was so shy and so uncomfortable, my heart just went out to him. I started making up silly, sinister stories about the neighbors until he relaxed, first smiling, then laughing this great baritone laugh. It was, as they say in the movies, the beginning of a beautiful friendship.

The Wolvertons were equally taken with him, especially when they discovered that Moore is practically a human encyclopedia. No exaggeration—during his years as a bodyguard, he had lived and spent every waking minute with people in every human endeavor: athletes, authors, arms dealers, bankers, bookies, borough presidents, CEOs, celebrities, doctors, despots. You name it—Moore has seen it up close and knows every detail of how it's done.

It immediately became Ali's mission to convince him to stay. Luckily for her, Moore was rethinking the concept of taking a bullet for one of the agency's clients—the majority of whom he disliked—in exchange for large amounts of money, of which he got only a fraction, the rest going to line the pockets of the owner of the agency, a man he detested.

It still took her six months of persuasion to get Moore from paid protector to permanent part of the family. Moore does everything for the Wolvertons, from helping David with sources and Ali with research, to being this planet's best seafood cook. And he's paid accordingly. I absolutely adore him, and if I didn't think Ali would kill me, I'd have hired him away years ago.

"Oh, Miss Lauren, such a treat for my soul to see you. I hope your trip was pleasant."

"It was actually pretty interesting, Moore, and I'd tell you about it, but my head hurts so bad I can't think."

"Not the flu, I hope."

"No, acute alcohol poisoning, I'm afraid."

"Ah, the demon rum." He let loose his great calypso laugh.

"Nope, the demon scotch," I said into my purse, where I was looking for money. "Moore, why am I so bad?"

"You're not bad, you just have a little refreshment on your trip and now it turn on you. No?" Moore is one of those truly rare people who is unfailingly supportive. When I do something bad, he tells me all the good reasons I had for doing whatever I did—or worse—and when I do something decent, he carries on like I'm Mother Teresa. He would be the first person I'd call if I ever, say, set fire to a home for the aged or needed someone to help me bury a body.

"Shall I dispatch this gentleman to buy you some aspirin?" He flashed the redcap a dazzling smile. The redcap had stopped singing and looked eager to perform any task that Moore might suggest.

"No thanks. I'll just wait till we get to the house. Moore, I'm so happy to see you!" I gave him a hug. His heavy-lidded black eyes and wide mouth displayed transparent pleasure, and he stowed my bags in the trunk, started the car and drove toward the Wolvertons'.

Moore and I usually talk each other's ears off, but my survival was questionable and wholly dependent on silence. I closed my eyes to visualize the poison jellyfish trapped inside my head, but then I started to feel carsick so I opened them and rested my head on the glass and looked into the windows of Volvos and minivans, at thirty-three-year-old suburban matrons talking to the tops of little blond heads, and thought about my friend Ali.

By the time I met Ali, in the ninth grade, she had traveled around the world twice. By the time we were freshmen in college, she spoke six languages, had interned a summer at the Carter White House and had the two things that proved she was a player: a Rolex and a Rolodex. It was that Rolodex that impressed me the most. Anybody can have an expensive watch, but an eighteen-year-old with several hundred phone numbers—that was real grown-up. I used to say that between Ali's sophistication and Jinx's street smarts, I felt like Gomer Pyle's girlfriend, Lou Ann Poovie. Anyway, Ali took advanced courses in political science as a freshman, claimed she was preparing to take over and run a small country. Only her closest friends knew how high her sights really were; she was preparing to be the first woman President of this one.

Unfortunately, Ali had one small problem that would keep her out of both the junta business and 1600 Pennsylvania Ave. She couldn't speak to large groups. She was fine with anything less than a hundred people, but over that, she'd freeze—paralysis of the vocal cords. She went to psychologists, speech therapists, public-speaking consultants—nothing helped. By the end of our freshman year she'd decided that her clout would come, not from speaking to the multitudes, but whispering in the ear of the powerful.

I've never known anyone as deliberate as Ali Williams Wolverton. She acquired contacts and credentials the way other girls acquired lipsticks and eye shadow, and "Don't Cry for Me, Argentina" became her theme song.

She was just as disciplined when it came to the people she dated. "Test-driving husbands," she called it. Occasionally she got involved with normal guys, but mostly she went out with princes and maharajas, an occasional Kennedy and every now and then a high-ranking diplomat. That's actually what brought her to Washington and Georgetown School of Foreign Service.

It wasn't until she got to Georgetown and became an associate professor that she found her real power in the form of the women's movement. She ascended like a rocket, so bright and well thought of that she became a tenured professor at the age of twenty-seven. She became the unofficial adviser to several of the major women's rights organizations, as well as a powerful influence on the next generation of political women.

Then she met David, got married, had Corinne and found that enviable balance of personal and professional life that all of us want. It's been a long journey with every step well planned, and I'm very proud of her success.

I caught Moore sneaking a glance in the rearview mirror and could see he wanted to talk. "So Moore, how are things on the romantic front?"

"Not a grand success, you know, but I keep hoping."

"What happened with the lady at the market?" Moore had had a crush on a Haitian cashier at the neighborhood market and had even taken me there so I could see her. She had once smiled at Moore and touched his hand, and upon that he had built an elaborate fantasy about their courtship and marriage. Like many people who are shy and have no experience with the opposite sex, he is wildly, unrealistically romantic.

"She doesn't work there anymore."

"Oh yeah? Did you get her number before she left?"

"No, I couldn't get the nerve to ask her, now she's gone." He sighed deeply, filling the car with dejection and misery.

I leaned forward to pat the starched white jacket that covered his enormous shoulders, "I'm really sorry, sweetheart. I know how disappointed you must be."

"I am. I want with all my heart to have someone to love, but all of the women are afraid of me because I'm a giant."

What could I say? "Moore, c'mon, it just takes one woman, remember?"

"Yes, dear one, so you always remind me. Tell me, how are your romantic prospects?"

"Well, I may have a nibble, a writer I just met." The hangover had weakened my defenses and made me susceptible to his gloom. "It probably won't work out though."

"Why do you say that?"

"'Because they never do. My romances never last more than about three months."

"I have observed that. Why do you think it is?" One great thing about

Moore is that he doesn't waste conversation denying the truth. I find that a very likable and time-saving trait.

"Well, I want a relationship, or at least I think I do, but then I only seem to respond to men with whom a relationship is damn near impossible. Either they live far away or they're married or both. I don't know what's wrong with me, Moore. I'm just scared that if I let anybody close enough, my whole self will come oozing out like the Incredible Blob and I won't be able to control it and the other person will be overwhelmed and run away and I won't be able to stuff myself back in."

He was nodding. "You and I, my friend, we have the same difficulty."

"Really?"

"Yes, I'm too big on the outside and you're too big on the inside."

It felt like a knife through my heart, but I leaned up and put my hand on his shoulder. "Well, Moore, I love you and I don't care what size you are."

I could see the corner of his mouth turn up as he put on his blinker and turned onto Littleton Avenue. Another minute and we pulled up in front of Ali and David's Georgetown mansion. I climbed the steps and was resting my face against the cool wood of the front door. Moore came up behind me, unlocked it and pushed it open, and I stepped into the foyer, which was flooded with morning sun.

White lilies and yellow roses bloomed in enormous crystal vases in each of the four niches, and the antique Austrian chandelier splintered the sun's rays, throwing off sparks of white and purple and chromium yellow on the icy white marble floor.

Around the corner came my best friend in the world, the stunning Charlotte Allison Williams Wolverton. Dark red hair shot with copper, thick and wavy and shoulder length; golden eyes with flecks of green; freckles, high cheekbones, a perfect nose and full lips in a face shaped like a valentine. She grinned, then gave me an appraising stare. "Cupcake, you look rough!"

I pressed the heel of my hand into my eye. "I feel rougher. I'll pay you four thousand dollars for some aspirin."

"Sold. Little hangover?"

"How'd you guess?"

"How'd I guess?" She wrinkled her nose. "You smell like the inside of a scotch bottle."

"Why, you flatterer!" I looked into the Chinese red dining room and noticed the stacks of gleaming silver, white damask napkins and gold-rimmed china set out on the mahogany table. A centerpiece of orchids sent white blooms floating across the black surface of the table like tiny clouds over still water. "Ali, are you having a party?"

"I thought I told you about it." I shook my head, then moaned at the crashing pain it brought. "It's a brunch for the heads of the organizations sponsoring the march. We have a lot to talk about, and I offered to host it here. It's not a party; it's a strategy meeting." We were in the living room, and she was rearranging the family photographs in their silver frames, her back to me. "We've got to decide what we're going to do and we have to decide today."

"Why today?" I asked, collapsing sideways onto the pale silver sofa.

She turned around, her belt buckle caught the light and the blocks of turquoise ran together in a ribbon of movement that made me dizzy. "Because the purpose of the march tomorrow is to ask women to unite in response to this outrage, and we have to decide today what the response should be."

"So who will be here?"

"The head of NOW," she said, and I nodded. "And of WAC, WHAM, POW, Riot Grrls . . ."

I had never heard of these organizations, and they sounded like comic-book fan clubs, which is exactly what she'd expect me to say, so I nodded as if in deep thought. "What about WWW—are they coming?"

She did a double take. "Lauren, you've really done your homework. I'm impressed."

"Well, don't be. I was just trying to fake you out. I've never heard of any of those groups, and they sound like comic-book fan clubs."

"How in the world did you know about WWW then?"

I told her about seeing Jinx and how she'd become the head of WWW, something Ali apparently didn't know. She rolled her eyes.

"What's with you?"

"I hardly think she's capable of looking out for the best interests of any woman but herself."

I squeezed the bridge of my nose to stop the throbbing. "Why do you say that?"

"You seem to have forgotten the facts about me and Jinx. She *was* one of my best friends. She stole my boyfriend and thought nothing of it. Remember those little details?"

"Yeah, I remember. I also remember that you'd had exactly three dates with Charlie Howe and that he pursued Jinx, not the other way around. I remember that she was just distraught about the whole thing and that she tried to talk to you about it and you wouldn't listen, you just shut her down. I would also like to point out this took place almost twenty years ago as well as the fact that the guy in question has gone to his final reward. Dead, deceased. That your husband is alive and hers is a cadaver. We're all trying to help here, and Jinx is my friend, so get off it."

I covered my eyes with a large powder-pink silk pillow with silver fringe but then I couldn't breathe so I tried putting it under my head. "Now, please explain to me what's going on with all these groups with bizarre names and why they're all coming here."

She sat down on the arm of the sofa closest to my feet, and I re-arranged the pillow so I didn't have to move my head to look at her. "Most are new organizations that were started by women in their twenties, the third generation of feminists. Very media savvy, very high energy and significantly more radical than the older organizations. The younger feminists have pretty much been doing their own thing, but because we're in crisis now, we need to be united. In order to be united, we need to involve everyone in our decision. So that's the idea of this brunch today—to bring together for the very first time every major women's organization, regardless of size or politics."

I sat up a little. "Sounds pretty interesting." The effort exhausted me, so I slowly lay back down.

"Yeah, it was my idea and I've been working like a maniac to make it happen and I'm happy that you're here, but you've got to pull yourself together," she said. " I haven't got time to baby-sit you."

"Excuse me. I don't recall asking to be baby-sat," I shot back and pulled myself to a standing position. "All I ask is a pound of aspirin and a shower. That is, if it doesn't put you out too much."

"I'm sorry." She jumped up. "It's just that I'm nervous as hell and I was counting on you to help me. I need to bounce some ideas off that big brain of yours."

"Surely you jest." I sighed. My brain felt like a BB rolling around in a boxcar.

"I don't jest. I'm sorry you feel bad, but this is the worst thing to happen to women in this country's history and I need you to be on top of your game, OK? I'm sorry, please forgive me, I'm a shrew."

"And a fishwife," I added.

She laughed. "And a fishwife. I'll get the aspirin, you get in the shower and I'll check on you in a bit. We've got less than two hours before everything starts—so hurry, 'cause I really want to get your thoughts . . ."

I had taken a quick shower and was lying on the four-poster bed in the guest room, a towel on my head and a royal blue silk bathrobe wrapped around the rest of me. It may sound ridiculous, but that bed is one of my favorite things in the world. It's an antique white four-poster and it has a little step next to it because it's so high and it has all these big white lace bed pillows and neck rolls with ribbons and fresh white sheets with melon-colored scalloped edges, and lying there always makes me feel like the princess from "The Princess and the Pea." Except that I was so tired you could have put a basketball between the mattresses and I probably wouldn't have noticed. A single knock on the door and Ali bounced in, carrying a hand-painted plate with three aspirins in one hand and a Bloody Mary in the other.

"Bless you, my child," I said gratefully, swallowed all three aspirin at once, drained half the drink and patted the white lace spread for her to join me. She kicked off her shoes, climbed up on the foot of the bed and sat cross-legged, facing me. I told her all about Queen Esther, which she loved.

"Amazing," she declared, absently fingering the lace. "Of course, the *most amazing* thing is that you actually came. I was stunned when I heard that you were going to be marching."

"I was more than a little surprised myself. The other day, Razz was teasing me about becoming militant in my old age, and you know, I really am. This stuff just—."

"I know, I know. I look at my sweet daughter and I just weep to think of how it's going to be for her. It is *so* depressing!" she wailed.

"Yeah, and we're not the only ones who feel this way. I've got to tell you about this conversation I had last night," and I recounted every word I could remember of my conversation in the bar car about Operation Lysistrata. She was listening intently. I was certain that at any second she'd start laughing or dismiss it as silly, and I was prepared to laugh with her about what a funny idea it was. But she didn't laugh, she didn't say anything, she just sat there looking at me intently. A minute passed and she hadn't said anything. Ali is one of those people who normally takes about half a second to grasp a concept, formulate an opinion and share it with you.

"What?" I asked.

"I'm thinking." She was still rubbing the lace on the coverlet, her coral-tipped fingers polishing the material.

"About?"

"About what you just told me."

"Fine. Well, while you're thinking, come in here so I can dry my hair," I ordered, and she followed me into the heavy air of the bathroom. Ali scooted the silver tray that held her grandmother's sterling brush set to the side and hopped up on the marble counter. I unwrapped the towel, ran my fingers through my hair and went back into the bedroom for my brush and hair dryer. "Tell me more about this brunch."

She lifted her arms and stretched like a Siamese cat. "There'll be about sixteen gals. Like I told you, it's really a strategy lunch. We have to develop a coherent plan on how to proceed." Now she was rotating her head slowly from side to side.

"What do you see as options?" I squeezed the red gel carefully onto my toothbrush and began to brush slowly so that I could still hear.

"We have basically two. We can start recall petitions for every congressman who voted to acquit, or we can try to force a revote in Congress with some sort of massive civil disobedience—a work stoppage or some type of boycott or something much more aggressive than we've ever attempted. That's why I think your conversation on the train is so interesting. It might be just what we need to show those assholes that we will not stand for this."

I spit the toothpaste in the sink. "Recalling all those cretins would take too long. I think we ought to reach down, put the squeeze on those fellows and not let go until they burn Larry Underwood at the stake."

She slid off the counter and took my face in her hands. "I know. I'm with you," she soothed. "We've got to fight back now while iron is hot."

I wiped the toothpaste off my chin. "Do you really think the Lysistrata idea has possibilities?" I was still surprised that she hadn't dismissed it as ridiculous.

"Actually, I do. It's just crazy enough to work." She grinned.

We were standing side by side, facing the mirror. I stopped applying mascara and pointed the wand at her reflection. "Yeah, it does have a kind of outrageous charm. Besides, it worked for those old Greek gals —it might just work for us."

She picked up a Q-tip and pointed it back at my reflection. "Absolutely. Just think about it. If American women, all of a sudden, got one big collective headache—I guarantee that would get some attention."

"Damn right! It's a response they couldn't ignore. And you know what else? I think it would really mobilize the good men. Think about it: this has happened in part because men who are horrified by this kind of thing haven't fought against it. Why? Because for the most part, it hasn't really impacted their lives. This would get their attention, too, and get them involved—and we need that."

"Exactly! This is a very nifty idea." She turned slowly from the mirror and looked at the actual me. "I'll bring it up and you sell it."

"Do you think I can talk 'em into it?"

"I think you could talk a hound off a meat truck."

"In that case, let's do it. And on the other subject . . . please be nice to Jinx when she gets here. OK?"

"OK, OK." She laughed. "Now get your ratty ass dressed."

I put on a black silk blouse and a pair of new tropical-weight black wool slacks. I rummaged through my suitcase for my black alligator flats, slid them on and went to find David or Corinne or Moore or anyone who might entertain me until curtain time.

I found David in his library, a large room paneled in burlwood and lit by the sun through the left wall, which is all glass and French doors and opens onto Ali's rose garden. On the right wall there's a fireplace with a stone mantel and over it a full-length oil portrait of Ali and Corinne. Set around the room, there are chocolate leather chairs and a deep caramel-colored sofa that can seat five people. And books. Shelves of books and stacks of books, antique books and books on antiques, books of short stories and books of tall tales, nonfiction and reference books and biographies, gardening books and books on war, books written by his friends and books about his friends, first editions and the latest novels. I knocked. He was sitting behind his tobacco brown marble desk, reading a volume on the history of Venice. He looked up, made a little sound of surprise and rose to greet me—six feet tall, gray hair, cobalt blue eyes, strong jaw and twenty-one years older than Ali and I. In spite of average features, his is a face made handsome by intelligence and kindness.

"Hello, Sunshine," he said and held out his arms.

"David, I'm so glad to see you!" I met him halfway across the room and we hugged for several long seconds. He smelled like late afternoon in deep woods, and I pulled away before I wanted to. I'd be less than truthful if I didn't admit to being a little attracted to David.

We were happily debating whether the government ought to regulate the derivatives market, when Ali appeared.

She'd changed into a flowing pale green pantsuit, and when she leaned down to kiss David, I noticed that she'd removed most of her makeup. I was studying her when she looked up. "Lionheart, let me tell you the story about some of the women before they get here. I told David about our plan and, although he is less than thrilled with the idea"—she looked at him and he grimaced as confirmation—"he can also give you his perspective." She slid down the arm of the sofa and snuggled in next to him. He kissed the side of her face.

"Good idea." My headache was finally fading, and I was beginning to get excited about our plan. "Tell me everything I need to know."

"I don't have time to tell you about everybody, and some of the more radical leaders I know only by name. Let's focus on the real power players, starting with the ones who are most likely to go for the idea of a sex strike." I nodded, and she pulled away from David, leaning her elbows on her knees, sheaves of paper extended toward me. "First, and probably most important, is Savannah Moran. She's black, about our age, smart and tough—been around about fifteen years and is the closest thing there is to a bridge between the old school and the young radicals."

David summed her up. "The Reverend Moran is an extraordinary woman. In my book, she's the soul of this crowd. She could be this generation's Martin Luther King, but she told me once that her calling is simple—to do God's work, one person at a time. "

"Wait a minute," I interrupted. "I remember you telling me about Savannah. About how she's an ordained Episcopal priest and how she's got this huge ministry in the worst part of Washington . . ."

"That's her." Ali nodded. "And she represents black women, period. If we're going to convince this crowd, it's going to be because we convince them that this is really doable. If Savannah says she can deliver African American women, we're halfway there. She's also responsible for bringing several of the younger feminists into the power crowd, and they idolize her. If she likes it, they'll like it."

"Sounds like Savannah Moran may be my new best friend."

"Don't count on it. She's a very tough cookie and may assume that you're just a dilettante. Let me take care of Savannah, OK?"

"Whatever," I said, annoyed.

Ali smiled and looked down at her notes. "Kimlee Ma. Asian, mid-twenties. The historic oppression of women is her field of expertise. Seems her grandmother was forced to be one of the comfort women for the Japanese soldiers during the Second World War. Kimlee would probably like the idea because of its great poetic justice. But its media value is what'll ultimately appeal to her."

"What's her story—she like to be on TV or something ?"

"No, no. She's totally behind the scenes, but she's a marketing genius."

David nodded. "She's got a dazzling sense of what will make the evening news. Remember the banners about deadbeat dads that hung over the balconies at all the major sports arenas?" The two of them were smiling like proud parents. "That was Kimlee's idea," he said.

"Yeah, she's a star," Ali agreed. " And she'll dig this."

So far so good. I nodded for her to continue as my eyes were drawn to the window where the peach-and-yellow roses swayed gently in the morning breeze.

"While we're on the subject of people who'll dig a sex strike—Lisa Pidgeon and Suzanne Millow—they're our public relations wizards." I turned back to look at her, and she nodded toward David.

He shook his head in distaste. "I know they're very good at what they do but I find them—what's a nice word?—grating."

I didn't care about personality traits, I wanted to make sure my old pal was coming. "Is Jinx on your list? It'd be under Howe."

"Yeah, here she is—M. L. Howe." And in an aside to David, "This is a friend of Lauren's from college."

If she wasn't going to get into it, I certainly wasn't. "Jinx is also going to like this idea."

"You think?"

"Trust me. I'm sure Jinx will be on our side." This seemed custom made for her. "So, Johnny. Who's our next contestant?"

"Lynette Valentine. Lynette is a feminist from the early days. I'm talking about the very early days—the days when feminism was about equity in the workplace and reproductive freedom, not separatism and victimization. She's really the last of the Mohicans to still be hands-on involved. The others will show up for the photo sessions, but Lynette is still in the trenches. Besides, she's one of my favorite people in the whole world, the original earth mother. You'll love her!"

David put his arm around his wife. "She adores Ali and she'll like you for the same reason. She's tough and she appreciates women who are tough, who don't play victims."

"Besides, Lynette is the one person who won't suffer from the celibacy part." Ali laughed.

"She doesn't like men?" I asked.

"It's not that. I mean, she's not one of these men-are-the-enemy types you started seeing in the last decade. She likes men a lot—after all, she was married twice. She says she's just not willing to give herself away again. She's a powerful woman, very complete in herself, and as far as Lynette's concerned, that's what it's all about.

"Besides just loving her, I have a huge amount of respect for Lynette. She's faced an uphill battle in the last fifteen years as her kind of feminism has disappeared and been replaced with this 'we're so pitiful and tragic' crap. I know Lynette would like to retire, but she won't until she feels like the movement is back on solid footing."

"If Lynette had her way, feminism would still be about powerful women, not women as victims . . ." David explained. Ali finished his sentence. ". . . and the feminist movement wouldn't be looked on as a malcontent fringe either."

"Anyone else I should know about?"

"Yeah, there's Carl Barnes. She'll be here although she's not the head of any group; she's our lawyer."

At that moment the doorbell rang and I jumped. I looked up at the clock on the carved mahogany mantel and was amazed to see that it was already 11:32. I knew Ali would be looking for signs, so I smiled.

"Are you OK?"

I nodded.

"Look, sweetie, I know how you get in groups of women, but please relax. Most of these gals are really nice, and we're all on the same side."

I nodded again, then excused myself and ducked into my room. I paced around for a few minutes, trying to clear my head. The more women's voices I heard, the more nervous I got. My instincts were screaming something about tanks massing at the border. I walked over to the mirror. "Get a grip, Blanche," I said to my reflection. "All you have to do is go out there and talk to these women, convince them that this Lysistrata idea is a good one. This is your chance to make a difference." A few more trips around the room and back to the mirror. "Maybe you can even make some new friends." I said a quick prayer, opened the door and made my way down the long hallway. My walk was confident, but I felt like Peter Rabbit entering Mr. McGregor's garden.

Ali turned, smiled at my arrival and introduced me to the four women standing with her. There were faces I recognized, but I was too nervous to listen to names. Mostly middle-aged women, they were soft spoken, articulate. If I hadn't known who they were, I would probably have guessed department heads from Vassar or Bryn Mawr. I don't know what I expected, but they didn't look like activists to me. They laughed easily with one another, like sisters, and they were dressed in loose, flowing clothes the colors of fading days—dark green and soft rose and honey and gray blue.

The bell rang several more times, and I turned to meet the new arrivals. Young, most of them were in their early- or mid-twenties, strong voiced, and dressed in the kind of outfits that are ugly on purpose. There were no soft colors here. Like the value judgments of the young, everything was either black or white. This was a very different crowd. This group I would have pegged as performance artists from Soho. As I listened to them, it was clear which way this crowd would vote.

There was curiosity and respect between the two groups, but little mingling. A tea party between the Crips and the Bloods. Ali made her way through the living room, chatting and making introductions and trying to put everyone at ease. She knew enough to knit connections between women who had never met. She knew who had mutual friends or similar backgrounds, who had studied at the same college, even who shared the same critics. I stood on the periphery and watched.

The doorbell rang again and Moore opened the door. Two women screeched and fluttered into the foyer, and Ali introduced me to Lisa Pidgeon and Suzanne Millow.

Lisa was thin and had hands that seemed too large for her body, hands that would be perfect for clawing one's way to the top or someone else's eyes out. She wore blood red press-on nails and had selected Fu Manchu length. She had bright little eyes, a sharp nose, thin lips that barely covered large yellow teeth, and a pointed chin. She wore bright yellow and shimmered with energy.

Suzanne was tall and deeply tanned, with round shoulders. Her green eyes were set in a permanent squint, in a face that looked like an old pocketbook, creased and mottled at the forehead with tiny brown splotches. She had streaked blond hair that she wore in a Nancy Reagan do that was too big for her head, which was too big for her thin, corded neck, which protruded from her purple suit. She looked like a scarecrow dressed up for Lent.

She was one of those women who appear to have been smoking five packs of cigarettes a day since birth—crow's-feet, nicotine yellowed fingers and a voice as deep and crackly as a fading radio station. In fact, she was exhaling a face-full of smoke and extinguishing a cigarette butt on Ali's limestone walk when Moore opened the door. She practically knocked Moore down to get to Ali. "This house is divine! The whole thing is just divine. I want you to know that we are *so* excited to be involved and *so* happy to be here."

I was backing away when Suzanne caught me, and between coughing fits, stared into my eyes. "Ooh and we are *so* thrilled that you're here. I just love your outfit. It's divine, really divine."

Suddenly, the door swung open and there stood a black and watchful woman. Five feet three or four, she was dressed in black and wore a white clerical collar and filled the doorway with her presence. Her face was heart shaped and her silver hair, cut close to the scalp, showed off her regal bone structure. She had large prominent brown eyes, a broad nose that spread across her face, high cheekbones and thick wine-colored lips that barely contained an enormous mouth full of blindingly white teeth. She might be a priest in this life, but she had to have been a high priestess in another.

I stuck out my hand. "You must be Savannah Moran."

She took it and looked at me appraisingly. "And you are?"

I started to say "Being sized up and I don't much like it," but before I could open my mouth, Ali hurried over and threw her arm around me. "Ms. Moran, you have just met my best friend in this life, Lauren Fontaine."

The beginnings of a smile appeared on Savannah's dark face. In an Alabama drawl, she challenged, "This scrawny white woman is the great Lauren Fontaine?"

"And this cantankerous black chick is the gracious Savannah Moran?"

"Right on both counts. Now you two be sweet to each other, because you're going to be allies." She lowered her voice. "Lauren's got an idea that you are going to like—a lot."

Savannah looked at me and nodded. "Lamb, I sure hope you do 'cause I've had as much of this shit as I intend to take."

"Yeah? Well, don't consider yourself a circle of one." I sighed.

The door cracked open and an earthy voice sang out, "Tell all the men to go hide. We broads are taking over!" Everyone laughed and a beautiful brunette in her early fifties sauntered in. She was voluptuous, dressed in red, with stacks of silver bracelets on both arms accompanying her movements like tambourines. Her hair was shiny brown, shoulder length and softly waved, she had wide-set eyes that twinkled and a small nose.

Savannah Moran was the first one to greet her. "Ms. Lynette! I am sure glad to see your glorious self." They hugged fiercely.

Ali was next in line. "I second that emotion," she said as Lynette embraced her. Other women were lining up, and Ali grabbed my hand and pulled me into the group. "Lynette, this is my oldest and closest friend, Lauren Fontaine." The next thing I knew, I was being enfolded by two strong arms into an ample bosom. She smelled like gardenias, and my heart slowed its thumping. "Lauren, this is Lynette Valentine."

"I'm glad you're here," she said, and braced herself for the onslaught.

"Me too," I said honestly, pulling away now that my turn was over.

The doorbell rang again and I opened the door.

Jinx.

We looked at each other and burst out laughing. Ali stepped into the doorway and held out her hands. "Jinx! Lauren told me about running into you on the train. Come in, come in. It's been such a long time." She put her arm around Jinx's shoulder and ushered her into the living room. I let out a sigh of relief.

We'd finished lunch and Moore had cleared the plates. I was on the sofa with Jinx on my left and Lynette on my right. Savannah was in the club chair opposite us, her disciples at her feet. Everyone was getting comfortable, when Ali stood up and cleared her throat. "This is without question one of the most critical moments in the history of feminism. We have just witnessed what can only be described as an assault against every woman in this country. Today, we have the responsibility of determining the response of American women. Never has it been so important that we unite in action. Tomorrow, the world will be watching, waiting to see if we're going to fight back or if we're simply going to take whatever they dish out."

Nice setup. I looked around the room and saw the eyes narrow and the mouths tighten. "There are those who think that we—"

One gal in her fifties stood up. She had pretty blue eyes, a little button nose and a pageboy flip. Gidget goes feminist. "I don't think we want to overreact until we know how the President is going to deal with this. Our sources tell us that he is absolutely livid—"

"Livid he may be; he can't do anything. It's not like he can veto this decision." This from a young woman with blond dreadlocks and Granny Clampett boots.

I looked at Lynette and she answered my unasked question. "Carl Barnes," she whispered.

Ali regained the floor. "It's up to us." She looked around the room. When no one challenged her, she looked directly at me, and I thought for a second that she wanted me to stand and give my little recital. I should have known that she was just warming up. "It's up to us to stand up with all the fury and passion that women feel about this abomination. Stand up and let them know that we will not suffer this outrage in silence, we will not sit back and let them protect this monster. We need to call women to battle and show those bastards that they better rethink their decision or they are going to have a fight on their hands the likes of which they have never seen."

Too militant. You could see it in the faces of some of the older contingent. They were whispering to each other with alarm. On the other hand, the younger women were squirming in their chairs in anticipation.

"Just exactly what do you have in mind?" asked the most famous woman in the room, a face synonymous with feminism—Florence Fienman.

Oh, God, we're dead now. Damn it, Ali! Sometimes you have absolutely no finesse. You're like a teamster in a tutu!

"Before I tell you what I think we ought to do, let me ask this question: who thinks we should react at all? And when I say react, I mean a deliberate and announced response, civil disobedience, whatever." Eight hands went up. Just as Ali predicted, they belonged to Ali herself, Savannah Moran, Carl Barnes, Lynette Valentine, Suzanne and Lisa. And just as I predicted, Jinx. A young Asian woman who was sitting at Savannah's feet also raised her hand. She had perfect skin and black lipstick and hair that appeared to have been cut by a weed-eater. I guessed her to be Kimlee Ma.

"Who thinks we should do nothing antagonistic and simply make a strong statement against this decision?" Eight hands.

Feeling like an ambassador from a third world dictatorship during an executive session of the UN, I did not raise my hand at all.

Florence Fienman spoke. "C'mon, Ali. This is all political. It's about the Speaker of the House making sure that the President doesn't get to name another judge to the Supreme Court. I think all we need to do tomorrow is have a big turnout. Those politicians aren't stupid. They'll get the message."

I kept watching her, even when she stopped speaking. Something told me that Florence Fienman and I had some kind of connection, but I couldn't imagine what it was.

Savannah responded: "I agree with you on at least one point, Flo. Those politicians aren't stupid. Tuesday's verdict wasn't an accident—it was carefully orchestrated. They think they can get away with this because it isn't an election year and because the American public has a very short memory. Besides, we've got to look at the big picture here: If we don't make these fools realize what a mistake they've made, we're going to be stuck with this monster. I don't know about the rest of you, but Mother Moran isn't about to let that happen."

The young woman with blond rattails harmonized. "The last thing on earth we need to do now is give up the battle. I think we need to do something shocking!"

"All you want is to start a fight!" shrilled one of the older women.

"All you want is to avoid one!" Jinx replied.

At that point the room erupted. Ali raised both hands and waited for silence. A minute passed. "That's enough! No fighting! Both sides have valid points, and if circumstances were less dire we could spend weeks debating them. That, unfortunately, is a luxury we can't afford." Her hands went to her hips.

"One side wants to articulate the anger that we feel about this terrible breach of trust by our elected officials . . . and the other side wants to focus on an appropriate counteraction." Everyone was nodding. "I think we can accomplish both goals. Those who believe that we should focus on what we say tomorrow will work on that front. Those who think we need some sort of ongoing action can focus on that. I mean, let's face it, there's more than enough to do, and there's no reason why we can't do both."

It was the obvious answer. Ali looked at me and smiled. This time I was the one to wink. *Great job, AliCat. And I didn't really mean that about the teamster in a tutu.*

She knew she had them. "The key to this is that, to the public, we show a united front. Flo, you-all can speak about why this is unacceptable to women, and we'll decide what we intend to do about it. All in favor of a joint response, raise your hands."

Seventeen hands. I took the liberty of including myself in the united and unanimous group.

"Good. Why doesn't each group spend an hour working? Then we can get back together and begin to organize." She thought for a second. "Flo's group stay here. The rest of you, in the dining room. It's 12:20. We'll meet back in this room at 1:30."

I had to hand it to her. It was a stroke of pure genius. The reaction crowd would be much more responsive to our idea than the moderates, and now we only had to convince them. Once this group was in agreement, the others would be much more likely to go along.

We moved on to my favorite room of the Wolvertons' house. With the Chinese red walls, the Louis XIV sideboard and dinner table, it's a little jewel box of a room. Moore was taking orders for coffee and soft drinks, when Ali turned to Kimlee. "What do you think?"

"I think that whatever we do should be very radical, and very showy, something that neither the media nor our enemies can ignore," Kimlee said, then looked to her idol. "I'd like to hear your ideas, Savannah."

"I'm going to tell you my concerns first. We cannot impose any financial burdens on our women. We cannot ask them to forgo wages or job security to make a point, even an important one." This, I knew, was a comment on the possibility of work stoppages and was so perfect for our case that I didn't even dare to look at Ali for fear we would give ourselves away. Savannah sat back in her chair and continued. "Whatever we decide to do, we better make damn sure that it puts our women in a position of power, not one of victimization. I am not abiding any more of that."

That was an intro if I'd ever heard one; I looked around the table and said in my most persuasive voice, "I'm Lauren Fontaine, and unlike each of you, I am not the leader of a women's organization. But I am every bit as appalled at the events of the last week. I agree that our response should be very radical and very showy. I also think that it should be both novel and appropriate. Something that's never been done before and something that's custom made for this situation. I think Savannah has an excellent point in that it should put women in a position of power and control."

Carl interrupted, "Well, it'd be great if you could figure out how to do all that—."

"As a matter of fact, I think I have. I've got a plan that I think accomplishes all of those things." I stopped for effect and looked around the table. Ali was nodding to Savannah, indicating that this was the idea that she'd referred to earlier.

Lynette laughed. "Well, don't keep us in suspense. If you've got a plan, let's hear it!"

I took a deep breath. "Distilled down to its essence, this is a fight about power." I looked at each woman and sat back in my chair. "True or false: men as a group, through the political process, control women as a group."

"True," they agreed, some with words, some with gestures.

"For almost thirty years, feminists have been trying to wrest control from men, and they have failed. We can't afford to fail this time and we won't—if we play our strengths against their weaknesses. Now, forgive me for stating the obvious, but every group of men is made up of individual men. Men in groups are powerful, men as individuals are not." I shifted to the front of my seat.

Ali was anticipating me. "Divide and conquer."

"Exactly!" I pointed at her as a teacher would at a particularly bright student. "How does an individual woman control an individual man?"

"With sex," she answered with all the confidence of an expert.

"Thank you. Sex is the one bargaining chip that women have used since the beginning of time. And there is a reason they've always used it. Because it always works. There was a play written about twenty-five hundred years ago called *Lysistrata*—about a group of women who stopped a war that had been going on for ages by refusing their husbands sex until the husbands were absolutely desperate. It worked then and it will work now." I tapped on the table to underscore my point. "We've got to turn up the heat, show the men in this country that if they don't support their women"—I dropped my voice almost to a whisper—"they can fuck themselves, as it were."

I could see them formulating opinions, but I wasn't finished. "You want something radical? Something showy? You want something that will grab the attention of the world media as well as every single red-blooded American male? You want to put the power in the hands of our women? This is how we do it. We just say no."

Jinx grinned. "A sex strike?"

"Yep. A sex strike."

"I think its an incredible idea!" Ali said, as if hearing it for the very first time.

Carl was whispering to Kimlee. They nodded to each other and Carl said, "This is a neat idea. But will it work?"

I spread my hands on the table and leaned forward. "It'll work 'cause it's based on a simple but absolutely certain premise: men will do anything for sex." I turned toward Jinx. "What's your take on this, Ms. Howe?"

"I love it. And Savannah's right. We've got to start operating from a position of power. This is a perfect time for the feminist movement to stop being about women as victims."

Kimlee nodded. "The good thing about this is that if it's handled right, it'll get enormous publicity." She glanced at Lisa and Suzanne, who were grabbing each other's hands in excitement. The sight seemed to drain her enthusiasm. "The bad thing is, if it's not successful, if we can't get the average woman to go along, then we're really going to look stupid." She thought a second. "But the other good thing is that it's sooo unexpected!" And a little girl's giggle escaped from her black lips.

"I like it. I think it has great possibilities," Carl agreed. "I think we can convince the average woman to participate, at least for a time—the only danger I see is that if this thing drags out very long, we'll lose support."

"Men would give in before women would," I said. Lynette had been sitting perfectly still, not even her bracelets had made a sound. I wanted her to like the idea. "Lynette?"

She came out of her reverie with this little Mona Lisa imitation and responded cryptically, "Yes, it's time we finally take the plunge." Jinx looked at me and I shrugged, then looked at Ali, but she was too busy studying the others' reactions to look back. I started to ask Lynette what she was talking about, but she wasn't finished. "Still, there are real dangers associated with such a plan, and they can't be ignored."

I groaned inwardly. "Like?" I asked.

"Like the fact that we have no idea what the repercussions will be for the women who do go along—and they could be quite serious."

I hadn't thought of that, and she saw my disappointment.

"That doesn't mean I'm against this idea—because I'm not. " She paused. "It just means we better think this through and we better be prepared for the worst-case reactions."

Boy, was she a fast thinker. I focused my energy into willing Savannah to love the idea. But I could tell that she didn't. She caught me staring at her and spoke. "She's got a point. Frankly, I think this idea is flat-out crazy . . ." Her voice drifted off, and I looked at Ali. Even if everyone else liked the idea, without Savannah, we couldn't convince the others that it was viable. Without Savannah, the game was over.

I'd been praying for her enthusiasm, but it was her despair that saved us. Her voice was tired and hollow as she finished. ". . . but crazy ideas and crazy actions might work in this crazy-ass world we're operating in. Besides, I haven't heard any other great ideas, and we are about out of time. So this seems like it needs to be our choice." She took a deep breath. "Here's what we're going to do: first, we're gonna sell this plan to our sisters in the other room, then we're gonna sell this plan to our sisters at the march." She shook her head. "Then we're gonna figure out what in the hell we're doing."

Everyone nodded, and Ali went in for the close as if no objections had been voiced. "It's the perfect response for the situation, it will get worldwide media attention, it's something that any woman can do to assert her power and it will put those creeps on notice that we will fight back. We've got to do it!"

My heart was pounding when she called for a show of hands. Eight hands rose. This was absolutely unbelievable. These women were serious. They had bought this wild idea. Excitement gave way to shock, and I sat there quietly, trying to make myself believe what had just happened.

"Certainly the speech calling for a sexual strike should be the focal point of tomorrow's march, but who," Jinx asked, looking around the table, "is going to give it?"

Silence. Lisa looked like she was on the verge of climax. Savannah and Ali looked at each other with alarm. Just as Suzanne was clearing her throat to speak, Kimlee said, "Savannah, you give the speech."

Savannah smiled and shook her head. "It's Lauren's idea. She needs to give the speech."

What if she didn't want to give the speech? The fact that it was my idea didn't have anything to do with anything. I was searching for the words to decline gracefully, but Lisa jumped in. "Lauren might not want to give the speech. I mean, she's not really even involved, except that she's Ali's friend. I would be willing to do it if she didn't want to . . ." I looked up and saw Lynette and Jinx silently begging. I turned to Kimlee and Carl; they had the same look.

"It's Lauren's idea. She talked us into it and she can talk the average American woman into it. Lauren needs to give the speech," Savannah repeated in a voice that dared challenge.

Ali jumped in. "I've known Lauren since we were in the ninth grade, and she is the single most persuasive person I have ever known. Those of you who know me know that I've been in this arena a long time, and I'm telling you—she's the person to do this."

Lisa wasn't finished. "Maybe Flo could give it . . ."

"It's my idea, I'll give the speech." I heard the words as they came out of my mouth and looked frantically for the ventriloquist who'd put them there.

They parceled out responsibilities for different things having to do with the march, then the group in the other room began to break up. Ali directed several people to various bathrooms, and Moore came around taking drink orders. There were pairs and clumps of women, some parked against walls, some drifting, all with heads close together. The whole scene made my stomach churn. Whispering women always make me feel like Julius Caesar in the Roman forum . . . on a lovely spring day . . . in the middle of March.

Jinx, Ali, Savannah and I stayed in the dining room. Moore appeared and received three Diet Coke orders. He turned to me. "And you, *Ms.* Fontaine?" Moore knows me pretty well, and I could see that he was tickled at my being at one of Ali's femfests.

"Nothing carbonated for me, dear. Just water and maybe a couple more aspirin." He nodded and disappeared into the kitchen.

Ali motioned for us to sit down at one end of the table. "Look, " she said in a muted voice, "I don't know how this is going to be received by the others, but I've got a sneaking suspicion that it won't be unanimous rave reviews. Here's how we pull this off. First, Savannah and I will be the ones who sell it." Jinx looked at me and I nodded. That suited me just fine.

Moore returned with three tall glasses of dark brown liquid and a short one of clear. I picked the aspirin off the tray and washed them down with a big slug of water.

"Here's to abstinence." Jinx laughed and held up her glass.

"To holding out," I responded, and we all took a sip of our drinks and a collective deep breath and it was then that it hit me.

The connection I had with Florence Fienman was Jake—they'd been lovers. I remembered the stories in all the magazines several years ago about their big breakup. As Jinx and I rejoined the crowd in the living room, I stared at Flo, sitting there like the grande dame, in Ali's chair. She saw me and gave me this dismissive little look.

The chairs and sofas were taken, and as we looked for places, I was sizzling with adrenaline. Jinx moved through the bodies to stand next to the fireplace, joining Lynette, Kimlee and Carl. I followed her.

Ali and Savannah made their entrance a few moments later. They waited until the room fell silent. They looked at each other, and it was Savannah who spoke. She might have a bad disposition, but her voice was wonderful, deep and rich. She started out low and slow. "Ladies, this is an historic occasion, so listen up. As of tomorrow, we American women are on strike." The room started humming, and she picked up speed and volume. "We are going to tell those gentlemen that from now on, the question won't be about what we women can and can't do, it'll be about what we will or won't do. And from now on, it's the sisters who'll be giving the answers. Any problems with that? " she challenged.

The looks on a number of faces showed, if not problems, then at least surprise and concern. "What kind of strike, Savannah?"

"A sex strike."

"Oh God," someone groaned, and the room exploded into chaos. From my vantage point, I could see every face. Some showed shock, a couple were laughing in disbelief, but the prevailing emotion was outrage. It was more than just not liking the idea, it was as if they thought we had somehow tricked them. My heart sank. There was no way those women were ever going to allow a sex strike.

There was so much discord, it was impossible to hear any one person. As I watched the fury on their faces, I wanted nothing more than to escape, until Savannah's strong alto voice resonated through the din. "I can't hear a damn thing with y'all squawking. Now, *shut the hell up* so I can finish."

Amazingly, they did just that. She puffed up like a blowfish and looked around the room, which was now completely silent. "I would be happy to hear your thoughts on this as long as you understand that it's me hearing your thoughts; it's *not* a debate."

Damn, I liked her style.

Out of the corner of my eye, I caught an exchange of looks between Lynette and Flo. It was that exchange that stole my attention from Savannah's magnificent performance. It spoke of a long, shared history, of mutual respect and affection—but something more. They had been down this road before.

"And before we get to the part about y'all talking, I'm going to talk. I understand that this idea is risky, that it may not work and that, even if it does work, it could cause a bunch of trouble. I also understand that we are on the ground, we are bloody and beat-up and we are down for the count. We've got one move left—we've got to kick 'em in the balls. And that's exactly what we're going to do. I have had it with all the whining and crying and being put upon. It's time we fought back."

A woman in her late fifties, whose face was fairly familiar and whose name was on the tip of my tongue, started to interrupt, but Savannah focused those big eyes of hers on her, and the sound died. "Y'all have had every chance to call the shots and you chose to take the path of least resistance. That was your choice. This is ours."

I looked at Lynette, and she read my mind. "Don't worry about a thing," she whispered. "The Reverend Moran is swingin' now and nobody's going to get in her way."

I looked again at the faces, and she was right. They weren't happy, but there wasn't a woman in that room who was steeling herself to do battle with Savannah. A few minutes passed, and she was allowing questions, one at a time. She might not be easy, but I certainly admired the way she handled herself. "Yes, we think that women can be convinced to go along." . . . "No, we don't think boycotts or work strikes would work." . . . "Because we don't want any woman to have to risk her job or her wages in order to show her support." And the one she kept repeating until the questions died down: "No, we haven't decided that yet."

Then it was time for the good cop to take over. Ali nodded to Savannah and began to speak. "I'm sure you can tell that what we have here is a skeleton idea and we are going to need a lot of suggestions to fill it in. If we put our heads together, we can flesh it out and emerge with a solid plan. We need your help, we need your ideas and we don't have much time."

Ali held her palms out. "Our group will hold a week's planning retreat immediately following the march, so make sure if you have ideas, you let one of us know. I guess the first thing we have to have is a stated goal. That seems to me to be the removal of Lawrence Underwood from the Supreme Court."

"And his being barred from practicing law," offered one of older women. There was a collective *hmmm*. I liked it. Everyone seemed to like it.

Ali grinned. "A stroke of genius! That's just the kind of great thinking we need." The idea's author beamed, and the tension in the room began to dissipate. "We've got a stated goal, now we—"

Kimlee jumped up. "Have petitions demanding his impeachment! The women would sign when they join and the men would have to sign before the woman would have sex with him."

Ali looked at Savannah, who cooed, "That is some smart thinking, girlfriend. It'll be a great way to bring things to a close. But I'm not sure we want to do it at the very beginning."

"Why not?" Kimlee asked, sinking back down to the floor.

"Because we don't know how much of a following we're going to have at the very beginning. We may need a little leeway when it comes to the numbers. If we have petitions at the beginning, we can only claim as many supporters as we have names."

No one seemed disturbed by Savannah's plan to inflate the number of participants. Damn, I thought, I certainly have a lot to learn.

I was watching Flo out of the corner of my eye. She raised her hand, and when Ali pointed to her, she stood. "I don't want to rain on anyone's parade, but this is not a new idea. It has, over the years, been suggested a number of times and rejected—for one reason: men are not going to take this lying down." Someone made a comment and there were a few snickers. She ignored the interruption. "This is not about sex, it's about power. We can expect retaliation and we can expect it to be brutal. Is that what we want to lead women into?"

I stepped forward. "Brutal? What Larry Underwood did to his wife was brutal. The travesty we all witnessed on Tuesday was brutal. I agree that this isn't about sex. It is about power. But if we aren't willing to fight for the power, we won't ever have it. I don't mean to be offensive, but if you had ever tried this idea, instead of rejecting it, the men in the House of Representatives wouldn't have dared pull this kind of shit, because they'd know better. "

They looked at each other, and I could see that a couple of the older women had once argued for such a response. Flo made a conceding gesture, but the look in her eyes told me that I'd made an enemy.

I changed the subject. "I have a friend in AA, and they do some things there I think would work for us. The women who participate in this movement are going to need to share their emotions and experiences with each other, and we should have groups or chapters, like they do in AA.

"That way, chapters could be part political organization and part support group. We can give every woman who joins the movement a chip. Each week that she holds out, we give her a different chip. When we're ready to call for the petition, she gets a gold chip for the every man she causes to sign."

"Every man?" Lynette asked, amused.

"Sure. We all have men who would join if we asked them—fathers, grandfathers, sons, gay friends. This doesn't all have to be about being deprived of sex." That seemed to make sense to them. "So, anyway, we could have each chapter support and encourage its members at daily meetings and new members could have sponsors who help them stay celibate—as opposed to sober. That's the way AA does it. They'd be given their sponsor's number to call if they have problems or feel themselves slipping."

Savannah laughed. "That may be fine for those Junior Leaguers who need a hug when things get rough, but my women are going to need a whole hell of a lot more than that. They're going to need a place to hide if they start saying no to their men. So you better put that in your plan. If this is a war, my ladies are going to be on the front lines—and I won't have *any* of them be casualties."

"Good point, Savannah. Not only are we going to have to provide encouragement, we're going to have to provide shelter. Safe havens— which just may turn out to be a good thing. The closer we stand together, the tougher we'll be to beat!" To hear me talk you'd have thought that I was intending to host a big slumber party, when in fact the only people who were going to be living at my house were already there. Despite my complete insincerity, I sounded good, and they ate it up like no-fat cookies.

And they couldn't have been more gracious when Ali announced that because the sex strike idea was mine, I would be giving the speech. They all seemed perfectly happy for me do it. Suzanne raised her finger. "One last thing. What about us?"

I cocked my head. "What do you mean, what about us?"

"I think we need to be very careful that these women know that we're making the same sacrifices they are. We all have to promise not to have sex until Underwood's been removed from both the bench and the bar."

She was right, and we all knew it. "No sex with our men until we win," Suzanne pledged, holding up her right hand.

"What about sex with someone else's man?" someone yelled.

Everyone laughed, then we all raised our right hands and swore: "No sex with our men until we win."

There were a lot of jokes about hurrying up and ending the meeting so everyone could go home and get enough to tide them over, but our group spent the next couple of hours hammering out our strategy. Then the other group talked about what they planned to say. By the time they got to logistical matters, my mind was elsewhere, trying to decide what the opening line of my own speech should be.

Finally they all left, Ali sang "Climb Every Mountain," and I went to my room, called Jake, told him that I was working on a speech for tomorrow and couldn't meet him for a drink at 5:00. No problem, he said, he was going to stay in and write. Room 906, he said. Just come over whenever I got finished.

There was a knock on the door. "You in there?"

"Yeah, come in," I yelled from the bathroom, where I was soaking in a bubble bath and putting finishing touches on my masterpiece.

I told Ali what I was going to say, which she liked. She said she would call the others to report that my speech was both solid and persuasive, and I told her I'd be going out later.

Ali guessed at once this was a romantic venture. "With who?" she asked.

"Jake Ward." I watched her face out of the corner of my eye. It took a second for her to react.

"Jake Ward. You're kidding? God, he's one of the sexiest men on the planet. How'd you meet him?" she demanded, her eyes glittering with interest.

"At Hank's."

"What's he like in real life?"

"Smart, delicious, *very* sexy." I reached for a towel and stepped out of the tub.

"Did he kiss you?" Ali and I are capable of mature conversation, except when it comes to men. Then our dialogue is strictly seventh grade.

"Yeah, he kissed me."

"I can't believe it! Is he a good kisser?"

"Great kisser. We're having drinks." I had finished drying my hair and was rolling it on big Velcro curlers.

"Can I go meet him?"

"Absolutely not."

"I'll trade you David for him."

I was laughing. "No you wouldn't. You would have an apoplectic fit if David so much as looked at another woman."

"True. OK, we'll leave David out of this. Just a simple ménage à trois."

"Fine. I'll call him and set it up."

She laughed. "God, this is so exciting. Where's he taking you?"

"I'm meeting him at the Four Seasons."

"He staying there?"

"Yeah."

"So, maybe a drink or two, then he whisks you upstairs for incredible sex." She was clearly savoring the thought.

"No chance."

"What do you mean no chance?"

"Well, first off, he's writing a piece for *Esquire* on the Underwood debacle, and when he invited me, he said it was because he wanted my opinion on it."

"Well, what's he going to say to you? 'Gee, Lauren, could you come for drinks at my hotel 'cause I'd like to slip you the big one?' C'mon, you're being obtuse. He wants to get you in the sack. Otherwise, there are lots of other places he could meet you for late cocktails."

"Well, it's more convenient for him there."

"Sure it's more convenient, more convenient to his bed."

"Nah, he probably just wants to pick my brain."

"Yeah, right, sugarplum. As if you have one to pick."

I threw a Velcro curler at her. "Well, anyway, I'm not going to do it. I've already decided."

"How come?"

"First off, because this guy is a famous womanizer and I have absolutely no intention of being just another of his conquests."

"Yeah, that's certainly something to think about." Her eyes searched the ceiling. "But you never know—maybe he's changed. All that stuff about him being the great cocksman was a pretty long time ago. I haven't read anything like that about him in years. Besides, Hank wouldn't introduce you to him if he thought all the guy wanted was to screw you and disappear."

"I know. And the thing about it is that I really like him. But I'm real balanced about it so far, and I know good and well that if I slept with him, I wouldn't be. I know myself; I'd be ricocheting off the walls, spending fifty hours a day attached to the damn phone, either waiting for him to call or talking to my friends, dissecting every word he says for hidden meaning. I'd be whining and obsessing about him every waking minute, and I just don't have the time or the inclination for it. I'm just too old."

"Too old. God, you're so full of shit. Finally you've found a guy who's fabulous and *single* and he's interested in you and you can't be bothered?" She arched her eyebrow up to her hairline.

"No, it's not that at all. It's just that I do like him and he is fabulous and I don't want to screw it up and if I sleep with him, I won't be able to keep my perspective."

"Let me ask you this—do you want to sleep with him?"

"Yes, I do want to sleep with him, and I probably will sleep with him —but I think it's too early."

"That's fair. What's your plan to stay out of his bed? Hairy legs or ratty underwear?"

"Ratty underwear." Of the two temptation avoidance techniques used by women since the beginning of recorded time, I prefer hairy legs.

Unfortunately, I had been caught off guard and would have to fall back on the pair of dingy underwear with loose elastic that every woman keeps for those occasions where her brain may be calmly saying no, but her libido is screaming *YES!!!* Over the years I have learned to never leave home without a dinner dress and a really nasty pair of undies.

"What about the bra?" The second critical decision: an ugly bra means that you intend to stay totally clothed and completely demure, and a sexy bra means something else entirely.

"Hundred dollar, black lace, demicup, killer diller, handmade exclusively for me by blind virgin nuns in the south of France."

" 'Nuff said."

Chapter 7

I knocked on his door. No answer. I strained to hear the sound of someone moving inside. Silence. I knocked again, louder this time. Then a deep voice, thick with sleep. "Who is it?"

It was past 11:00 and I wished that I had called first. Very bad form to have come so late without calling, but I had woken him and I couldn't exactly walk away now. "It's me, Lauren."

"Just a minute."

I heard him moving around heavily, an "Ouch!" low and guttural, followed by another minute of silence, and the door opened. The heavy hotel curtains had obviously been pulled closed, and it was pitch black in the room. I sensed him more than saw him.

"What's the matter?" I walked in, a study in nonchalance.

"I stubbed my toe."

"Poor baby. No wonder, stumbling around here in the dark."

I was turning around as he reached into the bathroom and turned on the light, which must have been on a dimmer, because the glow behind him was golden and very thin. His eyes were only half open, and he was wearing a faded pair of Levi's that were almost completely zipped and topped by a button not quite fastened. The hair on his chest was gray, and he was barefoot with the injured toe sticking in the air.

He rubbed his face with one hand, looked at me, smiled very slowly like a sleeping child lost in a good dream. "You're late."

"I warned you."

"Mmmm . . . so you did." He took my hand and walked wordlessly, as if sleepwalking, to the bed.

What are you doing? Stop. Don't go to the bed. Lauren, stop. Shake his hand off. Pull away! What are you doing? Lauren! The voice in my head was going like an Alabama auctioneer, but I followed behind him to the side of the king-size bed. As he dropped back into it, I kicked off my shoes and slipped in next to him, docile as a house pet.

His left arm held me tight against him, and my face was gently pressed in the sweet warm crook of his neck, the hair on his chest tickling my chin. My free arm lay across his stomach, and my palm rested half on his smooth skin and half on the dry, rough material of his denim waistband. Neither one of us made a sound, and he was rocking almost imperceptibly back and forth. It may not have been the smart thing to do, but it felt so natural, so right, so good. We lay like that for a long time.

I thought for a minute he had gone back to sleep, and I was dreamily contemplating the two urges I had: one, to pull up my arm and see what time it was, and the other, to stick my tongue out a millimeter and taste the delicate skin of his throat. That's when his right hand appeared and found the top button of my shirt, and I watched, mesmerized, as his fingers slid the pearl disk from the black material. They ran down the two inches of silk and were just about to liberate the next button when I sat up, supported on the arm that had been beneath me, and turned to look at him. "Hello, Lauren, so nice to see you again," I coached. "Nice to see you too, Jake." Then back in tutorial voice: "Gosh, Lauren, would you like a drink?"

"Gosh, Lauren, would you like a drink?" he repeated after me huskily.

"Why, yes, Jake, what a gracious host you are!" I said, and slid out of bed before he had a chance to pull me back.

He leaned over, clicked on the bedside lamp and sat up, blinking like a lion after a late afternoon nap. After a moment, he threw back the covers, got up and walked slowly to the mahogany minibar.

"What would you like, my dear?" he asked, his back to me.

"Scotch, unblended if you've got it."

"Glenlivet suit you?"

"Fine."

"Ice?"

"No, just a rumor of water."

"It'll have to be tap water," he said, walking to the bathroom.

"I'll live."

He brought me my drink, went back to bed and stretched out, this time on top of the covers. "I'm not sure I understand about this speech you're giving tomorrow," he said, putting his hands behind his head, exposing the hairless inside of his arms and the bulge of his biceps. "Do you mean you're one of the speakers at the march?"

I nodded. "Main speaker."

He was incredulous. "You're the main speaker? What are you going to say?"

"I'm going to call for a sex strike on American men until our political demands are met."

"A sex strike. Are you serious?"

I was rubbing my fingers over the rough material of the spread, tracing the fleur-de-lis of the stitching. I didn't look up. "Dead serious."

Then he laughed. I mean he really laughed. This really pissed me off, a fact he eventually noticed. "Oh." He was still chuckling. "I've hurt your feelings."

"No, you haven't hurt my feelings," I lied, the windchill of my voice minus twenty degrees. "This is a decision reached by some of the smartest, most powerful women in this country, and although I know this will come as a shock to you, they did it without enormous concern for what Jake Ward would think."

He made an exaggerated face of contrition, and although I was still furious, I started laughing. Then he looked at me suspiciously. "But why are *you* giving the speech?"

"Because it was my idea."

"By any chance, does this have its origins in our little lesson at the museum the other night?"

"Actually, it does," I admitted.

"Well, I guess it's a good thing that Ms. Mickel wasn't a visiting lecturer on Middle Eastern terrorists."

I wasn't going to give him the pleasure of a response; besides, I was having a hard time not staring at his biceps, which for a forty-eight year-old man were amazing. For some reason my silence turned him serious. "Do you really think it will work?"

"I have no idea, but I'll tell you one thing—every woman in the country has taken this personally. I can't even describe the fury and the feeling of helplessness this thing has touched off. It's as if each outrage against women was an unlit stick of dynamite. No one paid any attention to it and the pile just got larger and more dangerous. The Senate's decision to allow Lynn Underwood's murderer to continue to sit on the Supreme Court set the flame to the fuse.

"Women are not going to take up guns, or riot, or burn cities, or do the other violent things that men do when they're pushed too far. Will this work? I have no idea, but at a certain point winning means less than venting."

I shifted in my chair until I was leaning toward him, my weight over my extended leg. "So what are we going to do? It has to be personal, something to channel the fury that women feel. Something that each woman can do to make her outrage known. No," I corrected myself, "to make her outrage felt."

"I see. And how long do you anticipate this sex strike will last?"

I shrugged. "As long as it takes."

He was serious now, rubbing his jaw with short strokes, like a man in a shaving-cream commercial. "Lauren, do you know what you're doing?"

"Of course, I know what I'm doing." But as the question sank in, I realized I was lying. I sat very still for a moment, thinking. "No, come to think of it, I haven't the slightest idea."

"That's what I thought. C'mere." He waved me back to him, and I picked up my drink and walked to his side of the bed. He took the glass from me, set it on the nightstand and took my hand in both of his. "Sweetheart, you'd better be real clear about what you're doing before you give your speech, because frankly, the best thing that could happen to you is that you get branded a lunatic and laughed off that podium. If by some weird chance this thing succeeds, your life will never be the same. Whatever else you do, you will be remembered for the time that you spend on that platform tomorrow. It will define how you are looked at and how you are remembered. It'll be the description that sits next to your name for the rest of your life and the headline of your obituary when you die."

That's when it dawned on me that he was describing his own life, his own experience, and that he knew exactly what he was talking about.

That's when I first began to understand. They say that animals caught in car headlights are paralyzed by the brightness, but I've always thought that it wasn't the glare that froze them, it was the realization of what was about to happen. I sat on the edge of Jake Ward's bed, unable to move or to speak, disabled by the full understanding of what I had so easily promised that afternoon.

"Lauren, you talk about the rage and frustration that women feel, but let me tell you something, men feel frustration and anger too. The world has changed so much, and most of the things that we were taught simply aren't valid anymore. Not only have all the rules suddenly changed, but we're being vilified for having played by them all these years. Men who were raised to think and act one way now find themselves ridiculed and censured."

He rubbed his face hard and looked up. "The men who feel this the most are the men of my generation. And it's the men of my generation who are, at least for now, in positions of power. They will feel, and rightly so, that you are punishing them for something they didn't do. So, if they see you taking away one of the few and most important comforts left to them, they're going to focus all that anger straight at you. I understand why you feel so strongly about this, but there are much safer ways for you—"

I interrupted. "But they don't work. No one pays attention . . ."

He wasn't listening. "Before you decide that you want to be a revolutionary, think about what happens to people who take on the powerful. They *always* get hurt." Now I had my face in my hands so I couldn't see him, I could only hear those chilling words. "If you go through with your plan tomorrow, you will have accomplished one thing for sure: you, Lauren Fontaine, will stand alone as the target. Unless, of course, this is to be a joint effort."

"You mean the speech?"

He nodded.

"Nope. It's a solo appearance—but there are sixteen women's organizations standing behind me."

"OK. Let me ask you this question. How hard did you have to fight to be the one who did this, who gave the call to arms?"

"I didn't have to fight at all."

"Thought so," he said, and his expression said it all.

I'd been set up.

I sat there for a long moment, staring at the heavy curtains. I could go back and announce to Ali in the morning that if she thought the idea was so great, she could give my speech, or Lisa or Suzanne or anyone else they chose. I could tell them to do their own dirty work, that no matter what it accomplished, it wasn't worth the cost, and I wasn't interested in the job.

I got up as if in a trance, opened the curtains, put both hands on the cool glass and stood with my back to him, quiet for the longest time, looking at the stars. "I'm still going to do it," I said softly.

"Why?"

"Why?" I repeated the question to myself and explained to the night sky. "Because in every life there are moments when we define ourselves, when we stand alone with God and call out who we are and who we intend to become. This is certainly one of those moments . . . and there is nothing that could happen to me that would be worse than standing here now and breaking God's heart and my own by declaring myself a coward."

"Considering the cost, is that so important?"

"Jake," I whispered, "you of all people should know that it is." I turned around and he was looking at me, unsmiling, with an almost stricken expression on his face. I met his eyes and a look passed between us that snatched the breath out of my chest. It was not love, yet it was unmistakably tender; it was not lust, yet was undeniably erotic. It was a shock of recognition, a look of understanding so pure that neither one of us could speak—or needed to. I turned back to the glass, unable to sustain the gaze, and he came up behind me and wrapped his arms around me.

" 'But the bravest are surely those who have the clearest vision of what is before them, glory and danger alike, and yet notwithstanding go out to meet it,' " he whispered. I tried to turn and look at him, but he held me still. "Thucydides," he said. The password given and returned, we stood at the window, strong as soldiers.

No moment like that ever lasts very long, and he was the one to finally break the silence. "Now, tell me, brave woman, what time is your debut?"

"Three o'clock."

"Mmmm. I guess anyone who wants to make love has between now and three o'clock tomorrow, huh?"

"I think that's probably right," I murmured, tilting my head back slightly.

He kissed my hair and then my neck, murmuring, "I certainly feel sorry for all those people who don't have any advance notice of this sex strike."

"Really? And why is that?"

"Because there's just no way of knowing how long it will last . . . it could be years. And those poor souls who don't know to take advantage of the next few hours will surely regret it, maybe for the rest of their lives."

"Then again, maybe the men will just give in and give us Underwood's head on a platter."

"There are two chances of that happening: none and none. No, I think we may be in for a very long, very bitter siege."

It took a second for that to sink in. I sighed. "Well, I guess the good news is it will give people a chance to get to know each other so much better before they jump into bed together. You know, it's always better if you wait until you know the other person and—"

He was running the tip of his tongue up my neck and around my ear, and every nerve in my body was on red alert, sirens screaming from every erogenous zone. I couldn't speak another word, my mind was like regular programming on a television station during an emergency, automatically shut down and replaced by alarms.

He turned me around and kissed me, not the teasing kiss of the other night, a kiss of need and fury. He had his hands on either side of my face and I had my hands on the back of his neck, pulling him closer. We stood like that for no more than a minute, then we backed up and tumbled down onto the bed.

Delicious. Warm. Hard.

I drew back and took a sip of my drink, not so much because I was thirsty, but because I needed to collect what few coherent thoughts I might have left. The first thing that came to me was how turned on I was. This was a good one to start with, because it didn't take a lot to figure it out. The second thought I had was that I had promised myself I would not sleep with him, followed immediately by the thought that I had simply changed my mind. Then it hit me ... the dingy, big-girl underwear with the loose elastic. *But,* I thought to myself, *I'll just slip them off with my slacks, no problem.*

You see, this is always the danger of the ratty underpants method, and why hairy legs are so much more dependable.

I looked down at him and he was waiting and I remembered that what I really wanted was to be important to this man, not just one more name on the long list of bed partners. He took the drink from my hand and started to pull me back to him, and I put my hand on his chest to keep my distance. "Jake, honey, you are the sexiest thing in the history of the world, and I would adore making love with you, but I can't—"

I was about to tell him that I just wasn't ready, that I didn't know him well enough, when he interrupted, "Does this have anything to do with the guy you work for, the one you're having an affair with?"

I was so shocked that for a moment I couldn't speak. "What?" I stared at him. "What do you know about that?" It was clear from both the look on my face and the tone of my voice that I was furious. Furious and offended. Now it was his turn to be surprised.

"Now you're angry," he noted.

"You bet I'm angry," I repeated, so angry that I thought I might have an aneurysm. "Just what in the hell is going on here?!"

"Your friend Hank has talked about you for years, he adores you, he worries about you, and the fact that you were involved with a married man has been a source of real concern to him."

This was hardly news to me, we had only had fifty fights about it. "So what does that have to do with you?"

"You're turning purple, take a deep breath and I'll tell you. I'm forty-eight years old and I've had more than my fair share of women ..." He frowned as if displeased with the thought. "Hank and I used to have these conversations about women, and he always said the reason that I had never found a woman who didn't eventually bore me is that I'd never met you. He was convinced that you and I would make this legendary couple. So I told him that if you ever got over this married guy, I would come down and . . ." He held out his hands to signify that I knew the rest of the story.

I was floored. I had this visual flash of the famous baritone and the famous writer sitting around planning that dinner party. He could not have surprised me more if he'd sprouted another head. "And . . . ?"

"I didn't mean to offend you, but I don't want to waste my time. If you're in love with someone else, I need to know."

"OK. Then let me see if I can explain this. The guy in question, as you probably already know, is John Moriarty. I call him Slick. As you also know, he is married, which complicates things a bit."

"But why would you let yourself fall in love with someone who was married?" he asked rather indignantly.

"That's a really stupid question. The obvious answer is that love, real love, doesn't take into account religion or race or marital status. Love is seldom convenient, and we sure as hell don't get to pick who we fall in love with . . . and unless it happens to you early in life, there's a good chance that there will be other people involved."

"But you *do* love him?"

"Yes, I love him, but we are not going to have a life together and I no longer sleep with him and we are the very best of friends and that is that." I was looking at the corner of the nightstand, then I faced him. "And I'm not going to lie to you, it still hurts." I couldn't stand to say another word about it so I changed the subject. "But since we're on the subject of romantic pasts . . . maybe you could give me a little background on yours. Not that I haven't read about it since I was a teenager, of course. But perhaps you could sort of separate fact from fiction for me."

Maybe it was because I'd been unsuccessful in keeping the edge out of my voice or maybe he was just sick to death of the subject, but he stiffened and pulled away. I was immediately sorry that I'd brought it up, but after a very deep sigh, he said quietly, "OK, let's get it over with. What do you want to know?"

"Uh, let me see . . ." I was racking my brain to think of a question that would lighten things up. "Oh, yeah. Is it true that Carlo Caldilari-Finaldi drove his Porsche through the door of the Beverly Hills Hotel, where you were screwing his wife, what's her name, the movie star?"

"It wasn't a Porsche, it was a Lamborghini. It wasn't in Beverly Hills, it was in Malibu. And she wasn't his wife, she was his ex-wife."

"Well, I'm certainly glad you cleared that up. Seriously, Jake, I don't like the idea of being one of a cast of thousands."

"I think I just told you that you're not."

"Yeah, but—"

"Let me try to explain this. I've been divorced for a long time and, yes, I've had lots of romances. And because a lot of the women I've met have been public figures in their own right, people act like livestock judges with a five-legged calf.

"I'm a romantic and I believe that each one of us has a soul mate." He shook his head and laughed at himself. "It may be stupid, but I really believe that, always have. So, after my divorce, I counted on the law of averages. You know, the more women I dated, the better my chances of meeting the one I was looking for.

"Then I decided that if I couldn't find my soul mate, maybe I could distract myself until she found me." He said it in a way that was part teasing and part just stating a fact. "That's when I started settling for the interesting gals, the attractive ones, the fun ones. It's not hard to figure out why my romances didn't last too long. There'd come a point, usually sooner than later, when I'd feel this absolute panic to get away, to disappear." He pulled back to look at me, and I motioned for him to go on.

"Then I came to accept the fact that it probably wouldn't happen for me. I have this theory I call God's Law of Compensation. It works on the premise that each one of us gets a different set of goodies. Some people get looks, some people get money, some people get a perfect mate or fame or whatever. But no one gets everything. So it was like God had given me this spectacular life, and love was the one thing He'd decided I should do without. I completely dropped out of the social scene, spent lots of time alone. Then I was diagnosed with cancer, and fighting that took all my energy for about three years."

He held out his hand and, terrified, I took it. What was he going to say that was so awful he wanted me to hold his hand while he told me?

"Then about five years ago, I met someone. I thought it would last forever. It didn't. When it ended, it *did* make the tabloids and several weeks of stories for *Hard Copy* and *Inside Edition*, not to mention the front page of *People* magazine. We were even the subject of a ten-page article in *Vanity Fair*."

"Was that Flo?"

"Yeah, it was Flo. After that fiasco, I lost all interest in having a relationship. It was too risky and too humiliating. I swore I'd never do it again—take a chance on having my heart broken, then have the pleasure of seeing a commentary on it in the goddamned newspapers. You said yourself that you've been reading about my romantic exploits since you were a teenager." He took a deep breath and exhaled slowly. "Did you ever wonder what that's like? I'll give you a hint. You know that nightmare where you find yourself naked in the middle of town? Well, it feels like that. In real life, though, not only do you stand there helpless and vulnerable, but then everyone gets to comment on your shortcomings in a sort of spirited public debate.

"You look at me as one more person to hurt you. I have to be honest, I look at you as one more soon-to-be-public figure to make my personal feelings something for the writers of David Letterman to use."

"Maybe we ought to just forget the whole thing," I whispered as the air conditioner clicked on and the vent under the window began to hum.

"Maybe we should." He sighed.

I was suddenly afraid. "Do you want to?"

He was too. "Do you?"

"No. But you need to understand one thing. If you break my heart, I will hunt you down, kill you and eat you."

"Fine, as long as you understand that my feelings for you are just between us."

"What exactly are your feelings for me?" I whispered.

"I think I'm falling for you . . . and to tell you the truth, it scares the shit out of me." He let out a little laugh and shook his head. "Just my luck too. I find a woman who just might be worth coming out of retirement for and she suddenly decides to be the Lysistrata of the twentieth century."

"Well, just think about how wonderful it will be when the women win and we can celebrate. As a matter of fact, I think you should write that in your article . . . you should tell the men to hurry up and give in so that we can get this thing over with."

"And how do I know that you're not just using me to further your insurrectionist goals? And how do I know you're even going to be worth the wait?" His fingers were tracing my spine.

"The answer is you don't. Then again, how do I know that you are going to be worth the wait?" I challenged as I slid one leg over his and began kissing the tiny hollow under his earlobe.

"Well, let's see . . . why don't I tell you exactly what it is I intend to do to you when this is over, then you can make up your own mind whether I'm worth waiting for."

I called his bluff. "I think that's a splendid idea. Start talking."

He laughed and shifted his weight until I was lying flat and he was supporting himself on his elbow. "Hmm, where to begin? Well, I think you should know that you are the most exquisite woman I have ever seen. You should also know that from the second you walked into Hank's living room, I've been thinking about you, thinking about fucking you, so I'm very clear on what I plan to do.

"Of course, the first thing I'll do is take your clothes off, very, very slowly. The second thing I'll do is kiss every beautiful inch of you. I intend to memorize all of you; your taste and fragrance, every sound you make, every response, every curve of your body, until I could pick you out of a thousand naked women, blindfolded, using only my mouth. I'll start with your face, I'll kiss your forehead, your eyelids, the tip of your little nose, your mouth . . ." And he leaned down and brushed his lips across my forehead and eyelids and nose and mouth.

I smiled at the feel of it.

"I'll kiss your mouth gently at first, to taste you, to tease you, then I'll kiss you harder; I'll show you with my tongue what I'm going to do to you later with my cock . . ." And he leaned down and did and it was indeed a delicious promise. "When I think you've gotten the general idea, I'm going to lick and kiss your beautiful neck. I could tell at the window that you've got a neck as sensitive as it is elegant."

He took one finger and ran it from my jawbone to my shoulder so slowly and so gently that I shuddered. "It is sensitive, isn't it, Lauren?" As certain as a sheriff with eyewitnesses. Caught, I could only nod.

He smiled at the confession. "Then I think I'll kiss and lick your ears until your nipples are erect, until you think you can't stand it anymore. Then I'll kiss your shoulders and your hands, tickle your palms and suck your fingers, and when I'm finished with your hands, I'll raise them over your head and you'll have to promise to keep them there," he whispered as he took my hands and raised them over my head until I could feel the cool and the coarse fabric of the headboard.

His hands moved a few inches away to test me, to see what I would do, and when I did nothing, he slightly raised his eyebrow and smiled like a hypnotist whose subject has proved surprisingly susceptible.

"That's a good girl. Then I'll run just the tip of my tongue down the inside of those slender arms to your perfect breasts. I wanted to touch your breasts at Hank's. I wanted to unzip your dress and tongue and taste your sweet nipples until you moaned and begged me to fuck you there in that room, in front of all those people. I didn't do that then, but I certainly thought about it. I'm going to pinch and suck and bite them, gently at first, then harder, until I can tell just how you like it, until your back arches and your legs part . . ." He ran his hand over the black silk, tickling his palm on the little knots he'd made.

I was watching his hand as it slowly disconnected the two sides of fabric, revealing a bra so delicate it appears to be the handiwork of talented and exotic spiders. "Beautiful, so beautiful," he murmured and slipped his hand inside and I couldn't look anymore, I closed my eyes and concentrated on how good his fingers felt. "I'm not going to let up either. I am going to feast on your exquisite breasts until you'd just give anything if your arms weren't over your head so that you could push me away. Now, I don't want you to be thinking that this is going to be any quick thing; because it's going to last until you thrash and moan; not out of pain, of course, but out of pleasure. Then I'm going to kiss your lips again. At first you'll be relieved, but then you'll be dying to have my mouth back on you. I'm going to kiss your lips, then I'm going to run my tongue up your neck to your delicate little ear. I'm going to explore all the tiny little curves with the tip of my tongue until you arch your back . . ."

Oh, Jake, I thought, your voice alone is making me wet. Just right, just perfect, make me give in, do whatever you want . . . please, be that good.

". . . And press your hard little nipples into me, and once again you're going to wish you hadn't promised to keep your arms above your head, but now instead of wanting to push me away, you're going to want to pull me down to you, to feel my tongue and my teeth on you again, and I'm going to oblige you. Then do you know what I'm going to do, Lauren?"

His voice was so low that I was straining to hear. I was watching his mouth form the words, watching his lips and his pearly teeth and his pink tongue. I managed to shake my head no.

"I'm going to kiss my way down the shallow valley between your ribs down to your lovely navel, down the curve of your belly. I'll have my hands on your legs and I'll spread them ever so gently and, one by one, I'll kiss the inside of your thighs until you're thrusting your sweet pussy at my face. See, you're going to think you're ready, but I'm going to know that you're not. I'm going to know that you aren't near ready. Then I'll turn you over."

He touched my shoulder and I rolled onto my stomach, arms still above my head, face turned to the middle of the bed. I was unable to see him at all. My head was turned away from him, my cheek on the cool, smooth sheet, as I focused on the deep husky voice over my right shoulder.

"Once I have you like this, I'll explore the curve of your waist and your hips, the small of your back. I'm going to kiss you so gently all down the curve of your pretty little ass, down to the place where I could taste you, where I could stick out my tongue and touch your pink sugar candy. I'm not going to, not yet. You'll be waiting and wanting me to put my tongue there, and you might even spread your legs so I could smell your perfume. I'm still going to make you wait.

"You're not the type to beg, but you might ask nicely. A 'please,' something like that . . . and if you're real nice to me, I'll lick you, part your thighs and tease you with my tongue down the length of your creamy lips to your clit. You're going to have your ass in the air, and I'll tongue your little hot button until your legs shake. I'm going to wait until you're on the edge, then I'll move to the backs of your legs. I'll kiss my way to your ankles and the arch of your foot and put your toes in my mouth and rub them gently against my bottom teeth until it feels like little electrical shocks traveling straight up to your pussy. Then, I'll kiss my way back up your legs until I get close enough to tickle my face on your fur. Now I'm going to turn you over, " and he very gently took my shoulders and turned me until I could see him, until I was looking in his eyes. He smiled slightly and lowered his voice until it was a whisper, our secret. "You're really going to want me then, aren't you, sweetheart?"

And I nodded. He couldn't possible know how much.

"And I really want you too. See, through all this kissing and teasing, you need to remember that it's not just you that I'm holding back. All my instincts are to grab you, throw you on the bed, rip off your clothes and fuck you till you beg me to stop. It's going to take everything I've got to be gentle and slow and not to just ravish you." He let out a ragged little laugh. "God, woman, it's taking everything I've got not to ravish you this very minute. Now, where was I? Oh, yeah," and he took his finger and ran it up and down my zipper. "And I'll lick all the sweetness from the inside of your legs, then I'll take your clit in my mouth and rub it against my rough tongue until you're on fire. Then you'll finally be ready and I'll unzip my pants and take out my dick. I'll look in your eyes while I push it in. I don't think I'll have too much trouble and I want to watch your face when I enter you for the first time. I want to remember that forever. Then I'm gonna kiss you again and thrust myself into you, slowly and gently then faster . . . and harder. I'm gonna fuck you till you wail like a harmonica on a Louisiana night. You're gonna wrap your legs around my hips and—" My eyes were closed and he was tracing the seam of my pants, touching me through the wool, and it felt like chiffon.

"Please don't, please don't, please don't." Not out loud because it wasn't Jake I was talking to. I was four heartbeats away from slipping, from unconditional surrender, from holding his hand and grinding myself into his fingers.

Teeth clenched, heart pounding, legs spread, sweat trickling into my hair, the silk shirt stuck to my arched back, I said, "For God's sake, Jake, please stop, you are boring me to death."

He pulled back for an instant, then a laugh, rich as dark chocolate, and I pulled him to me and he pulled me even closer and tighter and his heart was just under mine and I could feel it thumping and he was laughing and so was I.

I was too smart to let him own me, too clever to let him know how close he'd come. My brain was congratulating itself on the victory, but my body wasn't impressed. It was humming like a tuning fork. I could feel his erection against my belly; I refused to allow him to control me. I could smell his cologne; I would not give him that power. I pushed him away, until he was on his back, until he stopped laughing, then I slid my leg over and straddled him. I didn't say a word and neither did he. I smiled, savoring the view and the sensation, and he smiled back, patient, waiting.

We were motionless, joined, smiling. Then almost imperceptibly, he increased the pressure. If I weren't as sensitive as a homemade bomb, I wouldn't have noticed it. But it was exactly what I was waiting for and I began to move on him, up and down the length of his erection. I tilted my hips until we weren't touching, then back until we were. We weren't and then we were and then we weren't. I never took my eyes from his as I shrugged off my shirt, not breaking the rhythm, and his smile expanded and I leaned down and kissed him and he was thrusting his hips to make contact, but the more he did, the higher I raised myself and the slower my movements became. He got the message and stopped trying to control the friction and the pace. As soon as he did, I went back to my rocking. I was watching his face carefully and I could tell the second his expression went from insolent to needy. The smug little smile disappeared, replaced by a grimace of pleasure, and his eyes closed and his head tilted back and I had him.

He had taken great pleasure in my response and I took no less delight in his. We had each proven our dominance. In our game of sexual power, we had come to a draw. I stopped and dismounted. "Gotta run, darlin'. I had a delicious time. See you tomorrow at the march." He stared at me, he opened his mouth but no sound came out. I put on my shirt and buttoned it, I found my shoes and slipped them on.

By the time I had everything I'd come with, he was shaking his head and grinning. "Touché, baby."

I smiled at the acknowledgment, leaned down and kissed him. "Jake, I'll really be looking forward to the end of this strike."

He kissed me back. "Hold on," he mumbled and got up, found his shoes and put them on.

"You don't have to see me out. I'm just going to grab a taxi," I protested. He didn't say anything, he just turned his back to me, undid his belt, then his pants and tucked his shirt in. I opened the door and walked into the hall, he was right behind me. "I can take care of myself," I said.

"I don't doubt that for a moment, but when you're with me, I'm going to take care of you."

We rode down in the elevator in silence. My brain was trying to formulate an appropriate response, but my heart was too busy smiling. He led me through the side door onto the street. There were no cabs, only a homeless man; Hispanic, mid-thirties, smelling like stale wine, whispering to himself and shifting his weight from one foot to the other in some private dance.

Jake put his arm around my waist, stopped and nodded to the man, who immediately went into a verbal jig, asking for a dollar: "Mister . . . a dollar . . . just one, one dollar . . . OK, mister? OK?"

Jake shook his head but he didn't walk on. "I'm not going to give you a dollar, but I can see you're having a hard time. You want to go to a shelter? There's one about five miles from here. I'll pay for the cab."

"No. no. I don't want no cab or no shelter, mister. I need a dollar for food, just one dollar."

"I know what you need a dollar for and I won't help you hurt yourself by giving you one," Jake said, and his tone left no room for debate and the man turned and two-stepped away.

"I couldn't give him any money 'cause he was just going to use it to buy another drink," he explained.

"Why the eye contact then? Seems to me like an invitation."

"Giving them money and acknowledging their existence are two different things. I almost never give them money, but I always try to let them know that I see them. There are probably few things worse than being a homeless alcoholic or addict—except maybe being treated as if you don't exist."

I nodded. "I know what you mean. I have this almost primal fear of being invisible."

He looked at me, obviously surprised. "What do you know about being invisible?"

"I was the third child of five."

He laughed. "You want to know invisible, try being the fourth child of eight."

"Oh yeah? You want to know invisible, try being the mistress of a married man."

He thought about that for a second and smiled. "Well, you're going to make up for all that tomorrow."

I whirled around. "What is that supposed to mean—that I'm giving the speech tomorrow to get attention?"

He started laughing. "I'm not saying that's the whole reason, but it's a part of the reason—and how do I know that? Because it was part of the reason I faced off with the National Guard that night so long ago."

I was flabbergasted. "So it's not courage or great lives, it's about a need to be noticed?" My voice was becoming shrill. "So it's not about being noble, it's about being neurotic, it's not about passion, it's about pathology?" He was trying to explain, but I wasn't having any part of it. "You let me talk about being brave and doing the right thing and you were probably laughing your ass off."

He reached out gently and took my wrists. "I most certainly was not. And I didn't say it was the reason, I said it was part—"

I was in no mood for explanations, "My God, you—"

"We're alone, dear. You can just call me Jake."

I ignored that. ". . . are such a cynic!! And I guess all that stuff I was saying about love, you probably thought that was pretty stupid too, huh?"

A cab pulled up, and he motioned the driver to stop, then he turned and took me by the shoulders. "I think what you said about love was the perfect description of what I feel right now for you." I got in and rolled down the window. He leaned down as if he were going to give me another kiss, but he didn't. Instead he whispered, "Rest up, darlin'. You're going to get lots of attention tomorrow and you don't want to miss a minute of it."

"Oh yeah? Well, your fly is open." I smirked.

He backed up a step and looked down, then he winked. "Thanks for noticing." He walked off, laughing. It wasn't until he thought that I couldn't see him anymore that he stopped laughing and zipped his pants.

Chapter 8

"Wake up, sleepyhead." I opened an eye and found Ali in a shrimp-colored silk robe, hot rollers in her hair, sitting on the side of my bed with a steaming porcelain mug in her hand. Ali is a morning person, a fault I excuse only because of her other good qualities. "It's your big day, rise and shine. Here, I brought you coffee in exchange for all the dirty details of your midnight rendezvous."

I sat up and took the coffee. "What time is it?"

"Seven o'clock."

"Seven o'clock? Ali, if you want to wake someone at this ungodly hour, why couldn't you pick on someone in your own family?"

"I did," she said, "and when I finished with him I let him go back to sleep. I want to hear about you and Jake Ward."

Jake Ward. Just the sound of his name made me tingle. I couldn't help smiling, which, of course, she took as an admission.

"You did it. I can tell. Was he incredible? Did you love it?"

"We didn't. I said no."

"You said no? He wanted to and you said no? You had a chance to do Jake Ward and you didn't take it? Girl, what are you thinking about?"

"Calm down or I'll call the orderlies to bring you your Thorazine."

"Scoot over, I'm about to fall off the bed. So, if you didn't have sex with him, how come you were gone so long?" she asked, patting her curlers to see if they were still warm.

"We were talking."

"About what?"

"About having sex."

"Lord have mercy, what is this world coming to? Well, what did you say about having sex?"

"He said he wanted to make love to me and I told him I wasn't ready and we talked about why and about Slick and about the plan for today. Then he told me in excruciating detail what he plans to do to me when we finally do make love."

She put her hand over her heart and fluttered it to signify palpitations. "Was it a turn-on?"

"I had to throw my panties away when I got home."

She laughed and shook her head. "Too bad, and they were so lovely."

I was sipping my coffee, savoring the memory. I could hear his voice, and I closed my eyes so I could see him.

"Should I leave you alone for a few minutes?"

It took me a second to figure out what she meant, then I laughed. "Not necessary. I took care of that last night. Besides, if things go well today, we'll all have plenty of time for self-abuse."

"Well, in that case, I want you to tell me every word he said so that I can use it too. But first, what did he say about the plan?"

"He said if I give this speech today, it will change my life forever; that I'll make myself a target for all the male anger in the country. He said he thinks that we're in for a long siege and that if anyone gets hurt in this, it'll be me."

I watched her eyes as I repeated what Jake had said. She didn't seem to want to look at me, she leaned against the headboard and looked up at the ceiling for a long time. "He's probably right."

"That thought has already occurred to me."

"Do you still want to do it?"

"Do I want to? That's not the pertinent question. The pertinent question is do I still intend to. And the answer to that is yes."

"You scared?"

"Yeah."

"Well, if it makes you feel better, everyone thought the speech sounds great. They were really impressed."

I shrugged.

"Look, I wouldn't have put you in this position if I didn't honestly think you were the only one who could pull it off."

"Don't worry about it. I figure it's just another test." My bladder was about to burst. I stood up and started toward the bathroom.

I made my way back to the bed and then I thought of something really frightening. I had to call Elizabeth and tell her that I was going to give the speech. I was trying to think of what I could say, when Ali derailed my train of thought.

"So what else did he say?"

"Who?"

"Who? Get with the program, Lauren. Jake Superstud Ward. What else did he say?'

"Let's see. Oh, he thinks he's falling in love with me."

"You're making that up."

"I am not."

"Swear to God?"

I nodded.

Her eyes widened. "I am so impressed! Can I be friends with you?"

"I'll think about it and let you know. Now I have to call Elizabeth and Razz and tell them about this afternoon. I don't know how Razz will feel, but Elizabeth is going to be furious. She was worried about my coming, and I told her that I'd be one anonymous marcher in two million anonymous marchers! She's going to kill me when I tell her about the speech."

"I don't envy you. I'd hate to get on Elizabeth's bad side."

"No kidding. I may have to ask Moore to come back to Atlanta and protect me. Now tell me the plan for the day. How is all of this supposed to work?" I slid back under the covers and propped a pillow under my head.

"We'll meet with the organization people at the Hay-Adams at 9:30 A.M."

That put me in a very bad mood. "Damn it, Ali! I'm exhausted. Why do we have to go so early?"

"Because we expect over two million people at this march and hundreds of thousands are already here. Because newspaper and television reporters from around the world will be there early, setting up. Because we want this to go off without a hitch."

"Well, I don't know what that has to do with me. I'm the featured performer. I mean you never saw Elvis Presley setting up chairs before a concert."

"So now you're Elvis Presley?"

"As a matter of fact, we share many similarities. We both have about the same energy level right now, and you have the same chance of raising us at this ridiculous hour."

"Lauren, I happen to know that you get up at 6:15 every morning. What is your problem?"

"I get up at 6:15 every morning during the week. I sleep until 10:00 on the weekends—as if you didn't know. I didn't sleep worth a damn on the train, nor did I get much sleep last night, and I'm tired. That is my problem."

My voice matched hers in irritation, but that was not my problem. My problem was that I would soon be breaking a promise to someone I cared very much about. I'm a good promise keeper, and it's something I happen to like about myself. This morning I had reason to like myself less. My problem was that if giving this speech would change my life, it would also change Razz's life and Elizabeth's life, and these were the people I was really responsible for, not some nameless, faceless group of women. My problem was I wanted so much to do the right thing and I was clueless about what the right thing was.

"Look, I know you're tired. I'd leave you here and arrange to get you later but the logistics of getting you to the right place at the right time in a crowd of a two-million-plus people would be just impossible. Besides, the women from yesterday are going to want to brief you, and it's really exciting to be at one of these things. You'll forget about being tired. I promise."

"All right, let me call home and I'll jump in the shower."

"Meet you downstairs in an hour." She walked to the door, then turned. "Lauren, you're about to make history. Aren't you at least a little excited?"

"I'm dreading this phone call. I hate the idea of making Elizabeth unhappy and afraid. I'll be excited once I get this out of the way." She closed the door, and I looked at the phone on the bedside table for five minutes before I picked it up and dialed.

"Fontaine residence."

"Hi."

"Hi yourself. What are you doing up so early?"

"We're getting ready to go to the march in about an hour. How's Razz?"

"Fine. Still asleep."

"How are you?"

"You called me at the crack o' dawn to find out how I am?"

"Actually, no. I need to talk to you about something."

Silence.

"You still there?"

"I'm here. What've you gone and done now?"

She certainly wasn't going to cut me any slack. "I haven't done anything yet."

No response.

"Elizabeth, I had lunch yesterday with the people who are putting this thing on . . ."

"Mmm."

I switched the phone to my other ear. "You remember the story I told you? The one you liked—about the Greek ladies who got what they wanted from the Greek men by refusing to have sex?"

"Mmm."

"Well, I told that story yesterday to those people, and they thought it was a terrific idea for these women up here. They think we should do it now, to show these men they can't push us around and get away with it. They think it really might help and they want to use the march today to ask the women to kind of, you know, band together and stop having sex —until they get rid of that bastard Underwood."

The line crackled with her suspicion. "What has this got to do with you?"

"Well, it was my idea. But you really liked it too, didn't you?" I had a pain in my stomach and wondered for a second if my ulcer was coming back.

"I know you haven't called me at daybreak to remind me about a story I liked. What has this got to do with you?"

"They want me to be the one to give the speech, because of it being my idea and everything."

She snorted. "They want you to give the speech 'cause you're the only one fool enough to do it."

Well, this was certainly a growing school of thought. "Look, Elizabeth, you may be right. It may be a really stupid thing to do, but you know what? It also may work. I may have a chance to really make a difference, and I can't walk away from that. I told them I'd do it."

"Uh-huh."

"I know I told you that I wouldn't do anything to bring attention or trouble to this family, and giving this speech today is probably going to do both. I've broken a promise to you and I'm really sorry about that, but you've got to know that we're going to be all right. Whatever happens, we're going to have each other and we're going to be all right."

Silence.

"Talk to me, please."

"You did break your promise and you're right about one thing, there's gonna be a heap of trouble for this family because you've set yourself in the middle of everything. You've got to be the one always trying to fix stuff when it's none of your concern. If you didn't think you could do everything better than everybody else, maybe you'd learn to let other folks do their own dirty business. I'd like to jerk a knot in your head. Now, what else you want me to say?"

"Nothing, thanks."

"You're welcome."

I tried to be mad, but every word she said was true. I did fancy that I could do everything better than anyone else. I swear to God, my ego is so big you could tether it and use it in the Macy's Thanksgiving Day Parade. Somebody certainly should jerk a knot in my head. I had absolutely no business doing this, except . . . "What if I don't do it and it would have helped? What if it would have worked, but I didn't bother to try?"

"Why does it have to be you?"

"I have no idea," I said and felt as tired as I have ever felt in my life.

"You're not just breaking a promise to me, you're breaking a promise to that boy too."

"What promise?"

"He asked you not to go up there and embarrass him, and you told him you wouldn't. Now, he's going to be embarrassed to death."

God, she could be brutal when she wanted to. Too bad there wasn't a loaded gun I could use. "Elizabeth, I'm sorry. Please tell Razz that too. I'm real sorry, but this is something I need to do. I'll call you when it's over. It might be on TV, in case you want to see it . . ."

I can't describe the noise she made, but it didn't leave me with the impression she wanted to watch me cause our family's downfall on television. I hung up the phone. I didn't make any sound, but there was a volcano of pain and terror erupting inside me and I lay there for a long time, breathless and unable to move.

Davidwas in the kitchen cooking when I came downstairs. The smell of bacon and eggs made my stomach growl, and he looked up and smiled. "Hello, troublemaker, how about some breakfast?"

"You talked me into it. David, you're not mad at me, are you?" I was prepared for the general male population of the country to hate my guts, but I didn't want to lose the men friends I already had.

"No, I'm not mad at you, although I wish you had come up with a different plan."

"Yeah, sorry about that. Let me ask you a question though . . ."

"Shoot."

"You were in the news business how long?"

"Twenty-four years."

"And you've seen lots of rebellions and protests and stuff . . ."

"I've seen a few . . ."

"What do you think our chances are?"

"Depends," he said as he slid two eggs and a piece of toast onto a blue-and-white plate and set it down in front of me. "If you can get enough women to go along—then I think you've got a good chance of getting what you want. I think I can speak for most men when I say that the idea of celibacy is extremely unappealing."

"So you think it'll work?" I asked between mouthfuls.

"I didn't say that. I said if you can get enough women to go along—then you've got a good chance. Your problem is going to be getting enough women to go along. The key to your success is momentum. If you can convince enough people with this speech, then you can expect to build on that in coming days. On the other hand if you can't get real momentum today, I think your Lysistrata Movement will be history in two weeks." He saw the look of despair on my face and patted my hand. "On the positive side, you have a very angry group of people, and rebellions have a better chance of succeeding if they're in response to a specific outrage—as opposed to a general feeling of mistreatment."

"So it all boils down to today?"

"Yeah, I think a lot of it probably does."

"And you think we've got a chance?"

He nodded and cracked another egg into the frying pan. "And for your sake, sweetheart, I hope it works."

I didn't want to know what he meant by that. "Well, I intend to make it work," I announced.

"What on earth are you wearing? Zsa Zsa, this is a march, not a party," boomed Ali as she walked in, took my hand and led me back upstairs. "You're supposed to wear white, it's what the suffragettes wore in the first marches and what the leaders and organizers all wear now!"

I changed into my white jeans that are tight but not obscene, and she lent me a beautiful off-the-shoulder white blouse that had little cap sleeves. I put on a black alligator belt with a gold buckle and gold earrings.

"You look fantastic. Just fantastic," she enthused. "You're going to make those men eat their hearts out. Lauren Fontaine . . ."

". . . poster child for sexual abstinence! Speaking of abstinence, don't you find it a little weird that this is a cause the two of *us* are espousing?"

"Very. Put it in the category of things we never thought we'd see."

I drank another cup of coffee while the Wolvertons ate. During breakfast, Ali gave me one of her famous pep talks. She made it sound as if the future of the world hung in the balance and I was the only one who could save it. I'm certain that she was trying to make me feel important, but she was only succeeding in making me queasy.

The feeling was familiar. I'd had it a million times as a trader. It was the mixture of fear and nausea that always comes right before you make a big bet. Once you've committed, the fear and nausea are replaced with calm and total focus. Which is not to say that they don't return with a vengeance if the bet turns out to be a poor one, but it's never as bad as the moments right before you jump.

"Shake a tail feather, Lauren, we don't want to be late," Ali announced, and we hugged David good-bye.

David squeezed me hard. "I know you'll be wonderful. Knock 'em dead."

"Thanks, love. Keep your fingers crossed for me," I said and squeezed him back.

The day was perfect. High, thin clouds and a nice breeze. I took that as a good omen. Ali had taped a white cardboard sign that said March Official on the inside of our windshield, which allowed us to pull into the driveway of the Hay-Adams. There were thousands of people swarming outside the building. Inside the lobby, everyone seemed to be attached to television cameras, bright lights or cables, walkie-talkies or badges.

At the top of the stairs, we had to show the IDs that had been brought by messenger to the Wolvertons' early that morning. An enormous woman with dark circles under her eyes took them and demanded driver's licenses. Then she studied us and them carefully to make sure that we were the people in the photos. Once we had passed inspection, we were escorted to the main ballroom, where there were hundreds of women in white racing around. I waved at several of the women from the day before, and they seemed delighted to see me. I wondered if they were just grateful that I hadn't come to my senses and disappeared.

Ali wandered off and I was standing by myself when the blonde with the dreadlocks saw me, rushed over and grabbed my hand. "How are you? Are you nervous?" I assured her that I was fine, a little nervous but I'd be OK. She grinned and rushed off.

Whispered rumors floated through the ballroom, and everywhere I looked there were women staring intently at me. As soon as our eyes met, they immediately became fascinated by something directly over my shoulder. Ali still hadn't come back, and I was looking for her when I literally bumped into Lynette. She gave me a hug. "How are you?"

"The only thing I'm sure of is that I'm here." I laughed.

"Don't worry, you'll be great."

"The word seems to be out about me."

"Yeah, you can't keep a secret in this crowd. They're all very curious about this mysterious, unknown woman who will lead us all into battle." We walked around the room as she explained what was happening and how all the pieces fit together. She was the perfect guide, weaving in history about the movement and funny stories about the people.

Every two or three minutes, someone would run up and hug her, and it was easy to see how beloved and integral a part of everything she was. Her power came from the acceptance and joy that radiated from her like the tinkle of those silver bracelets. I was impressed. "How long have you been involved in all this?"

Her eyes narrowed as if she were trying to see back to that time. "Gosh, let me think—late spring of '69."

"Wow. That's amazing. You've seen it all."

"That's the truth. I've seen it all and I've seen it all come full circle."

"What do you mean?"

"Yesterday, do you remember Flo saying that the sex strike was an old idea?"

I nodded.

"Well, it is. There was a march in New York thirty years ago—the first major Women's Rights March. Flo, Gloria, Betty Friedan, myself and a bunch of other troublemakers organized it. The march was a big, big success and was touted as a radical move, but it was actually the most timid of compromises. It was a downgrade from what had been planned as a work strike, which was a downgrade from—drumroll please—a sex strike."

"I wondered about that."

"It's still a sensitive subject for Flo. She was originally for the idea, actually she was one of its first proponents. But thirty years ago, she wasn't the world-famous Florence Fienman, she was an insecure twenty-five-year-old from Hackensack, New Jersey. There were some older women in the movement, women who had much more forceful person-alities, and they intimidated her. It was labeled a compromise, but I was there and it wasn't a compromise; it was a fight and Flo gave in. When it came to a vote, she folded. She still carries that."

I thought about what I'd said to her at the meeting: "If you had ever tried this idea, instead of rejecting it . . ." No wonder she'd looked at me that way. Well, to hell with her—after what Jake had told me, I'd just as soon run over her with my car as look at her twice.

"There you are. C'mon, it's time to go!" Ali's yell from two feet behind us startled me. I looked at my watch. It was quarter to eleven. I looked up, bewildered. "Where are we going?"

"What do you mean, where are we going? We're going to the march, Miss Alzheimer's."

Lynette leaned over and whispered, "The march starts at noon and you'll be leading it."

I looked to see if she was joking, but neither she nor Ali cracked a smile. It was like one of those nightmares where you're onstage and you don't know your lines or even what play it is. I looked at her and whispered, "Have you lost your mind? I don't even know where in the hell we're going. What if I lead everybody down the wrong street or get lost or something? I said I would give the speech; I didn't say anything about leading the march!"

They both burst out laughing. Ali patted my shoulder, "Cupcake, you won't be alone. We'll all be there with you. And you don't have to worry about getting lost, we know where we're going."

I felt so stupid that I started laughing too. "What a bimbo! I seem to have lost the last vestiges of both my intelligence and my sanity! Sorry, I guess I'm just a wee bit overwhelmed at this point."

"Of course you are," Lynette said. "That's to be expected. But don't think that we're going to leave you on your own or expect you to do something that you don't know how to do. Besides, this is the fun part!"

The three of us walked to the door and were joined by Jinx, who gave me a big hug and giggled "Don't you just hope Professor Daly's watching TV today?" and a jubilant Kimlee, who had locked arms with the blonde. The only one of us not dressed completely in white was Savannah, who wore the traditional uniform of the clergy. She stood out like a majestic black cat in the snow—a black cat who wouldn't cross your path but would dare you with insolent eyes to cross hers. Then came Lisa and Suzanne and, finally, Flo. I thought about apologizing, but there wasn't time and, besides, she didn't look like she had any interest in talking to me. Behind us, the other women who had been at Ali's began to gather. Everyone was laughing and talking excitedly as we walked down the stairs, but as soon as we hit the door to the lobby we stopped as if by silent command.

There was a giant antique mirror in a gilded frame on the wall next to the French doors that led to the lobby, and there was a sudden flurry while everyone smoothed her hair and checked her makeup and clothes.

"Lysistrata called together the Council of Women," I said, sotto voce. I looked at my reflection and flashed myself a smile of the powerful. The whole thing didn't take a minute, and when we were finished, we walked silently to the door. Ali whispered, "Show time!" opened the door and all hell broke loose. There was a rush of photographers, and I was blinded by the flashes. When the blue dots in front of my eyes faded, all I could see was a wall of television cameras with their hypnotic, blinking red lights. There were so many people, jumping and pushing for a view, and easily a hundred reporters competing at yelling questions. It was like the commodity pits in Chicago. "Is it true that you'll be calling for a work strike?" "Just how mad are you women at the Underwood decision?" "We hear you're planning to announce something big today, any hints?" "Why are you holding your press conference after the march instead of before?" All these questions and about a hundred more shouted at the same time. A very inquisitive bunch, and loud too.

Still, I'd be lying if I didn't say that it was a kick. I felt like I was in a movie and my heart was pounding and I was scared and excited and for some reason I started giggling. It was just that the whole idea of my leading a march of two million people was so patently absurd that the more I thought about it, the funnier it seemed. Flo shot me a dirty look and I tried to stop but I couldn't help it and I immediately started laughing again and the more I tried to suppress it, the worse it got, and then Ali got tickled and then Lynette and then Kimlee, and the next thing you know we were all laughing. It was a great moment and it was that picture of us all laughing that eventually appeared in every newspaper from New York to New Zealand. The captions were all different but the photo was the same. Laughing feminists.

As we got past the cameras, I couldn't believe how many people there were. Enough women to fill a city: college girls with ponytails and t-shirts; women in their seventies with corded necks and curved backs; black women with big African earrings; Jewish women with shiny black hair and sparkling metallic accents on their white outfits; short women in white tops and matching leggings; large women, perfectly made up and draped in flowing caftans. A great white swirl of women who had been horrified enough, outraged enough, frightened enough to travel here from all over the country.

It seemed the greater the distance traveled, the more prestige the travelers were awarded. "You came from San Francisco? All the way from Santa Fe? Wow! How did you get here?" They had come in cars and private planes and buses and trains, and they had come for one reason: because enough was enough and this was way too much.

I needn't have worried about leading everyone off course; there was a group of women talking into walkie-talkies who led us through the crowd. Thousands of pairs of eyes followed our steps, and adrenaline sang through my veins. Each cry of "There they are!" and "Look!" brought another surge of the sweet drug, and then there were uniformed police walking beside us, their dark blue shirts and black uniforms, the flash of silver badges and medals over their hearts and insignias over the brims of their caps, separated us from the other women in white like parentheses. Women's voices began to sing out to us. "We're from Jackson, Mississippi, and we love you!" and "Don't give up!" and "Give 'em hell!" "The women of Tacoma salute you!" Flo and Lynette waved and set off whistles and cheers, and Jinx picked it up, then Lisa and Suzanne. I didn't until Ali nudged me. "Wave back." Once I had permission, I was instantly transformed, grinning and waving like some demented pageant winner.

We passed tall, fluttering blue-and-white banners, each announcing the group below, who they were and were they'd come from—Milwaukee NOW, Reno Riot Grrls. Depending on the group, they'd scream "Savannah!!" or chant "Kimlee! Kimlee! Kimlee!" and I thought that soon they'd all be yelling my name and I shivered.

There were colored banners and homemade placards dancing in the breeze, borne by their owners with a mixture of homicidal fury and gaiety, signs saying WE WANT UNDERWOOD UNDERGROUND and LET'S KILL LARRY. There were lots of banners with Underwood's picture. One had him in his black robes and the statement CRUEL AND UNUSUAL PUNISHMENT FOR WOMEN. We pointed out the best ones to each other and shouted our approval to their creators.

The clouds had thinned and fanned out, covering the sun and leaving the sky pale white. The wind had picked up and we were holding our hair so that it didn't blow in our faces and I felt so light that I thought I might float away.

Ali was on my right, and we were trying to estimate the size of the crowd when one of the women with the walkie-talkies announced, "Almost there!" and pointed to the top of a hill a hundred yards in front of us.

The closer we got, the faster my heart beat. The sounds of the crowd grew louder and more excited, and the wind blew and when we came over the crest of the hill, I turned around and my breath caught deep in my throat. In the distance there were government buildings and monuments, enormous and still, but surrounding them was the flood of people as far as I could see. It looked as if the Capitol had sunk into an undulating marsh of white, all the way to the horizon, where it blended into the bleached sky.

Glorious heart and graceful movement, this is us, I thought. Us. It was probably the first time in my life that I felt a part of the body of womanhood. I looked down on that safe harbor and knew I was not alone, a refugee from my gender—I was a part of this, I belonged. It was a sweet seduction and I willingly surrendered. Added to the feeling of connection, was the indescribably delicious thought that Jake was somewhere in this crowd.

There were hundreds more photographers at the starting point of the march. Whirring and clicking; snap, snap, tick, whir, snap click, click. There were two movie stars, two women senators and several congress-women on a raised platform, and they were holding a fluttering white banner with blue lettering that said IMPEACH UNDERWOOD and having their photographs taken. There were introductions and more photographs, then Savannah leaned over and whispered something to Ali, who nodded and looked at me. "Are you ready?"

I grinned and nodded and she caught the eye of one of the women with the walkie-talkies and held up one finger and the march began.

Lynette's bracelets shimmered as she took my hand, and I winked at her as I took Ali's, who took Jinx's. Kimlee and Savannah and Flo and the others reached out until all of the women who had been at the Wolvertons' were connected, and we started to walk. Hundreds of people fell in behind us and thousands after them and the sound of all those feet on the pavement sent a thrill singing through me.

I had always wondered why people in parades looked so pleased with themselves, and now I knew. For a short time you lose the bitter taste of isolation and become a part of something much bigger. You fill the hollow of anonymous, unspoken emotion and declare in procession what you hate or what you celebrate. Caught up in the sweet euphoria of connection, I kept saying to Ali, "This is so great, I just love it!"

As we walked down the wide avenue, the group in back spread out, taking care to keep a few steps behind us. We could hear them; a procession of voices that resounded in the distance. We marched and we chanted, and the knowledge that all these other people cared so much was confirmation of what I felt, and the affirmation of two million women made me feel recklessly powerful. "Get out of our way or suffer the consequences!"

I was giddy, heading this female army, thinking of which famous leader I felt most like. I had narrowed it down to either Patton or MacArthur when we passed a group of about forty Underwood supporters. If I'd had a sword, I would have pointed it at them and yelled "Charge!" but I didn't, so I just tried to ignore them.

They started screaming insults and I caught Ali's eye and in a show of leadership and maturity, I gave them the finger as we passed.

It was 3:20 and we had reached our destination. The sun had broken through and the wind rested and everyone had taken their places on the podium, which was surrounded by the D.C. police, shoulder to shoulder, white-gloved hands clasped in front of dress uniforms. Flo was speaking to the two million people gathered around us and the millions more watching at home.

"This is a terrible time for women, a time of blatant disregard for our safety, our rights and our intelligence. As women, we have carried the burden of oppression for centuries. It is the mantle we assume at birth. In some societies, we are left to die for the sin of being female. In some societies, we are mutilated by custom. In some societies we are property to be traded or disposed of at will. Others can speak of persecution, but what race has had to endure what we have had to endure, what religion? Others have surely been mistreated, but only women have suffered *betrayal* at the hands of their own fathers, their own brothers, their husbands.

"We have comforted ourselves that it is society that plagues and controls us, but what is society if not the men who make it up, the men that we comfort and care for and welcome into our beds?"

Flo wound down to great applause, then she introduced Savannah to even greater applause. She took the podium like it was a pulpit. "The deceitful, duplicitous fraud perpetrated by the House of Representatives on the American people is the most offensive piece of work by any group in the history of this country. It is not only offensive, it is criminal—just like the man at the heart of this horror. I cannot imagine what the men who conspired to commit this outrage thought they would accomplish." She held out her hands. Then she leaned over the podium. "We are going to show them that they have vastly underestimated us. We are going to convince them that the days of men being perpetrators and women being victims is over. Today we have a powerful and audacious plan. It gives me enormous pleasure to introduce to you the woman who conceived it and will lead us to victory using it."

My heart was about to explode with fright—and excitement.

"Ladies and gentlemen, I'm honored to present Ms. Lauren Fontaine!"

There was a rumble of benefit-of-the-doubt applause, and I rose slowly on legs of Jell-O and wobbled to the lectern. My lungs were filling, expanding, as if for flight. I felt faint, shaky, and I looked down at the wood-grain Formica to steady myself, then looked out at the crowd.

"Earlier this week, American women were dealt a terrible blow. We each felt personally assaulted by the refusal of the Congress to impeach Larry Underwood. On that day each one of us knew what it felt like to be Lynn Underwood or any one of the millions of women in this country who are abused. But our days of being punching bags are over. We are angry, we feel betrayed, *we are going to fight back! And we are going to win!*"

The crowd began to cheer. The most amazing sound that I have ever heard, it sounded like thunder, a roar beginning below me and traveling back until it rang like an echo out to the horizon. But it wasn't the response that stunned me. It was the power of the word *we*. I felt as if I had never understood the word before, and I was certain that I'd never known its comfort. When I started again, even my voice was different. "Men have underestimated us. They have underestimated our resolve, they have underestimated our fury and, more than anything else, they have underestimated our power. We are about to show them that our resolve is strong, that our fury is awesome and that our power is mighty. And when we are finished, everything will be different. We will never again grovel for mercy or fairness. We will never again stand by as atrocities are committed against us by men. There will be no more requests for decent treatment!"

Another roar of applause, I turned to look at Ali and she saw that I had finally made it over the wall and adrenaline was pumping into my heart and lungs and I looked from Ali to Savannah and put aside what I'd written.

"As women, we have not been set upon by warring nations or invading tribes, we have never donned a scabbard or a gun and gone out to defend our homes." My hands gripped the podium for balance as I leaned out. "Yet I am here to tell you that the enemy is not at the gate. He is inside.

"There comes a day when, regardless of gender, each of us must stand up and say 'No. Not now. Not ever again!' There comes a day that the only noble response, the only honorable response, is to fight. Today is that day. It is the day that our great-granddaughters will point to when they tell *their* great-granddaughters how we began a battle that changed everything, that changed the way society looked at women, that changed the way men looked at women, that changed the way *we* look at women. Each other. And ourselves.

"It is a battle that will be as extraordinary as the circumstances that have called for it. It is not a battle that will be fought in the jungles. Or in the fields. Or on the beaches. It is a battle that will be fought in our homes." I looked down into their faces to make sure they understood that I was not calling them to fight a theoretical war. "It is a real battle and it will be fought in New York studio walk-ups. In Nebraska farmhouses. In Atlanta apartments and Beverly Hills mansions." I looked again into their faces, and their eyes did not slide away. "In Louisiana shacks and penthouses in Chicago. And it will be no less important than those battles that have bloodied the dirt and stained the grass and soaked the sand at Gettysburg and Normandy and Okinawa and Pork Chop Hill!"

I was cooking. This crowd belonged to me. I went in for the kill.

"We are through talking, now is the time for action. We will not allow a wife beater to sit on the Supreme Court. That is unacceptable to us and to decent people everywhere. We want Lawrence Underwood impeached. We want Lawrence Underwood punished. We want him ruined. We want him to stand as an example of what will happen any man who mistreats a woman.

"We're calling for American women to go on strike until the men in power understand that basic decency is a part of their jobs and the protection of their constituents is as important as the promotion of their personal agendas. We will not lie down with men until they learn to stand up for us.

"*We are here to announce to the world . . . that we will not have sex again until Lawrence Underwood is removed from the Supreme Court, disbarred and punished for the torture of his wife!*"

I boomed the last sentence in my most resonant voice. Winston Churchill in drag.

And there was absolute silence.

It's hard to describe my reaction, except to say that it was pure and visceral. I had felt this way once before. On a flight to Palm Beach when the captain had come on the intercom and announced that he was experiencing some difficulty lowering the landing gear. The same exact feeling and the same exact words formed in my mind: "oh, shit."

Chapter 9

Slow-motion silence hung in the air. I could not think what to do, I could not think what to say, I could not think how to escape. I stood at the podium like a statue, wishing that the earth would swallow me whole. Then the ground started shaking. I had never been in an earthquake, nor had I ever had a prayer answered so quickly, and my very first thought was, "Hey, thanks, God."

The ground continued to rumble, but the crowd hadn't dispersed. I looked at the faces of those in front of me and they were smiling. Smiling and crying, their fists thrust in the air, jubilant, ferocious and powerful. The noise may have been 6.4 on the Richter scale but it wasn't a geological tremor. It was two million women stomping their feet, vibrating the world with the force of their agreement. Then they started clapping. Then they started yelling. It went on and on and on. Minutes passed and still the reverberation was deafening. There is no way in the world I can describe the sound or explain the feeling except to say that it was like getting a standing ovation from heaven.

It's funny, but I have absolutely no recollection of what happened next or how we got from the podium to the press conference back at the hotel, and even that's a little bit of a blur. I do remember that Lisa practically body slammed Kimlee off the dais to stand next to me, and that I couldn't hear the questions until someone gave Suzanne a cough drop. I remember the way my heart jumped when I looked down and saw Jake in the throng of reporters who were asking questions. Who are you? Where did you come from? What do you do? What would you say to Judge Underwood? Are you married? Have you ever been? What have you got against sex?

I answered everything they asked and looked into Jake's smiling eyes when I responded. "Yes, I like men." ... "No, this is not a hoax." ... "Yes, I believe we can force the Congress to act." ... "It'll take as long as it takes."

I also remember how wonderful Savannah and Ali and Jinx and everyone made me feel afterwards and how I kept thinking, So this is what Jo was talking about.

Even Flo was gracious enough to tap me on the shoulder after it was all over. "I thought you did a wonderful job," she said, in a voice totally devoid of pleasure.

B y the time we got back to the Wolvertons', I was coming down from the high and so exhausted I could barely remain vertical. I promised Ali and David that if they let me take a nap, I would happily rehash every moment of the day when I woke up.

I must have slept for several hours, because it was dark outside when I rolled over and heard voices downstairs. I pulled my watch off the bedside table and turned on the light and it was 8:40 P.M. I had completely lost my place in time, and it took me a moment to get my bearings. Then I remembered and I wrapped the delicious memory of the day around me and snuggled into it. As good as that felt, I wanted to share it, wrap it around my friends and huddle with them in its luxurious pleasure. I got up, brushed my teeth, pulled on a t-shirt and a pair of cotton shorts and went downstairs.

I could hear voices coming from David's library. Ali was on the big leather sofa, and David sat in the dark club chair across from her, one leg thrown over the ottoman. They were polished and perfumed and dressed in uncreased linen as if they were on their way to a casual night out. I was trying to make sense out of that when I came around the corner, and standing at the tobacco-colored marble desk where a bar had been set up, in a white Lacoste shirt, an unbuttoned navy blazer and pleated khaki pants, stood Jake Ward. My heart jumped.

David looked up. "Well, here's our superstar! How was your nap?"

Still a little groggy, I looked at them. "Did I miss something?"

"No, no, Jake called while you were asleep and we invited him over for drinks," Ali said.

I shot her a look that said, "And thanks for not warning me so I could come down here looking like the Sea Hag." I turned to Jake. "Mr. Ward, how nice to see you again."

His craggy face broke into a grin. "Why, Ms. Fontaine, the pleasure is all mine," he said, bowing deeply. "I've come to congratulate you on your speech. It was mighty powerful."

I couldn't help grinning. "It was pretty grown-up, wasn't it?"

"Honey, it was very grown-up," Jake said and put his hand on my thigh, high enough to connote ownership. "I still don't like this idea but your execution of it was spectacular. You were masterful. I was proud for you." All in all, they made me feel like a combination of Socrates, Shakespeare and Spielberg. Then David described CNN's coverage. "They did an amazing job. With no advance notice, in less than two hours from the time Savannah introduced you by name, they had a complete dossier on you."

I crossed my arms and pulled back. "Define complete dossier."

"Marital status, age, hometown, education, employer. They had background information about you being on the debate team at UVA."

"You can't keep a secret in a small world," Ali teased.

I didn't say anything, but I felt like the wind had blown my skirt up in the middle of a crowded street. I looked at Jake. "Any advice on dealing with the media?"

"Yeah, don't tell them one damn thing."

David and Ali looked at each other, then David cocked his head. "Jake, do you think that's productive, considering what she's trying to do?"

Jake answered, indignation peppering his deep voice. "Opening up yourself to the media is never productive. It's a sucker game," he said, turning to me, "a game you cannot win. And it works like this: the media picks you out, plucks you out of thin air and holds you up to the world's attention and love. Then just when you start to depend on it, they come with the bill: 'Share yourself with us, we want to get to know you.' Seems reasonable, so you pay. Then, next time, they come wanting to know things that are intrusive, but by then it's not just a bill, it's a threat."

I got the sense that he wasn't just describing his own experience. Was this the way he rationalized what Flo had done? Did he still care about her? I watched his face for clues.

" 'Keep talking or we'll make up our own answers and they won't be as nice,' they tell you. So you can keep paying, telling things that are deeply personal, but it's never enough. First they want your clothes, then they want your flesh, then they want the marrow in your bones. Then one of two things happens: either you go along until they pick you clean, or at some point you tell them no. Either way you end up garbage. The result is the same. The only thing that varies is the amount of time it takes. I've seen what it does to people and it's not pretty."

Now it was David's turn. He brushed his silver hair back and squared his shoulders. "That's quite an indictment, Jake. And I can't say I think you're wrong, but it's not going to help Lauren. If she doesn't define herself for the public, the other side will."

I drained my drink and handed my glass to Jake. "Will you get me another, please?" He stood up and walked to the bar. "Make this one a scotch, if you don't mind," I said. "Now, can we talk about something besides me and this movement?"

The three of them looked at each other, and Ali shrugged. "Let's talk about dinner. You hungry?"

I wasn't, but I nodded.

"Good, I've got some cold chicken in the fridge and I can whip us up some salad." She looked up at Jake, who handed me the drink. "Jake, will you join us?"

"I'd like to, but I have to catch the last shuttle back to La Guardia. My brother is in Sloan-Kettering with pancreatic cancer. " He turned and looked at me with such a mix of concern and pride I almost cried. "Thank you for inviting me here to share this triumph."

"It's great to see you again, Jake. My prayers are with your brother and I hope we'll get to spend more time with you in the future," David said. Ali nodded agreement.

"Me too," he replied, looking straight at me.

The Wolvertons left the room, leaving Jake standing by the fireplace. "Do you know the difference between making love and a hug?"

"Is this a riddle?"

"No, I just want to make sure that you won't push me away if I try to hold you."

"I'm very clear on the difference between making love and a hug." I walked over to where he stood. He took my face in his thick hands and we looked at each other and I noticed the razor-fine hatches around his eyes and the almost invisible scar high on his tanned forehead. I put my arms around him and buried my face in his shoulder, and he brushed his lips across my cheek and whispered, "I finally found you." And he pulled back and again I felt his callused hands around my face. "I was afraid I'd look for the rest of my life and never find you."

We clung to each other for a very long time, until he groaned and disengaged. "You can't expect me to honor your vow of chastity from this proximity." He stepped back and smiled. "I'd give anything if you hadn't put yourself in this position, but that doesn't mean I'm not honored to know such a brave woman. As I stood in that crowd and watched you, I had the sense that this was simply your destiny and it was . . ."—he searched for the words—". . . a joy to watch."

I looked away before I started to cry. "Maybe it's like the thing you told me at Hank's—about lessons being kisses from God, and how He reserves the best ones for the brave."

"I think that's exactly what it is." His eyes smiled again and he took my face again in his hands. "But, *ma chère*, you have put me in such a terrible position."

I backed up a step. "What do you mean?"

"It's only natural that a man wants to protect the woman he loves, but I don't know how to shield you from this great kiss you're about to get from God."

At that moment, I didn't care about anything else but being in his arms and him talking about loving and protecting me, but he'd said something else. "I'm sorry, what'd you say?"

"I said I know some of the women you'll be working with, and my advice to you is 'Keep your guard up.' Now, I don't mean that's necessary with all of them, of course. Some of those ladies are extraordinary." He stopped for a second. "What do you think of Reverend Moran?"

"She's my hero," I said, hoping that he wasn't going to tell me that she was one of the ones I should watch.

He grinned. "Yeah, Savannah's one of my heroes too. And Lynette Valentine's a pretty terrific lady."

I nodded, happy that we agreed on those two, but I didn't want to jump to any conclusions either. "Jake, what are you saying? Are you warning me about Flo?"

"Yeah, I guess I am. Don't misunderstand, Florence Fienman is not a bad person but she is in tremendous pain and that's made her do some things that ordinarily she wouldn't. Just understand that by leading those women today you're a fresh wound to her, and when she finds out about us, it may get pretty uncomfortable."

"Well, she and I didn't exactly hit it off anyway." I ran my hand through my hair.

"I'm not surprised," he said. "Just be careful."

I thought about that, then he looked at me and I could tell I'd missed another question. "Could you repeat the question?"

He smiled and repeated his question loudly, slowly and deliberately, like he was talking to an idiot or a deaf person. "When are you going back to Atlanta?"

"Oh, I don't know. Probably Tuesday," I answered, slowly and deliberately. Then, "All the women are meeting at Ali and David's house on Chesapeake Bay tomorrow to do whatever it is that we have to do to organize the strike. I'll either take a late flight home Tuesday night or leave first thing Wednesday morning."

"I'll find you." He kissed me ever so gently and walked out the door.

"You better," I whispered.

We had just finished dinner in the kitchen when the phone rang on Ali's personal, private, unlisted, only-a-very-few-people-know-the-number line. She picked it up and I knew from the way she smiled when she heard the voice on the other end that it was her twin brother. Whatever he was saying made her laugh out loud, and she kept nodding her head like he could see her, then finally she said, "Yes, she's right here," and held out the phone to me.

I picked up my cup of coffee and walked to the phone. "Yes?"

He didn't even say hello, he just started raving. "I wouldn't have believed it if I hadn't seen it with my own eyes. I can't believe you did this—and without telling me! Just wait till those poor men find out who they're dealing with! Oh, heaven help this country. Now, of course, the gay men will put you up for sainthood. Although, if there's anyone I know who is woefully unqualified—"

He took a breath and I jumped in. "You hush; I think I'd make a wonderful saint. Saint Lauren—has a kind of a ring to it. Anyway, I didn't plan it—it just happened and everybody says I'm a fine leader and even Jake thinks it's my destiny and why don't you shut up and tell me what a good job I did."

He laughed, then he hesitated for a second. His voice was different when he spoke again. "I thought you did an exquisite job. I wept through the whole thing. I was so proud of you."

That made my eyes sting, and I blinked back tears. I turned toward the wall and wrapped the long cord around me. "Thanks. I guess you know how much that means to me."

"But I have to be honest, Lauren. I'm not completely thrilled about you doing this. Have you thought about the ramifications?"

"Not only have I thought about them, I intend to personally ramificate the next person who mentions them." I turned back around, and both Ali and David were watching. Suddenly I felt very tired. "Hank, I'm a big girl. I can handle this."

There was no mistaking the steel in his voice. "Listen to me. You've put yourself in a very difficult position, and this is certainly not the first time . . . but this time you can get in big trouble. I have no right to tell you what to do, that's something for your own heart to dictate, but for God's sake, be careful!"

"I will, I love you, I gotta go, bye," I said and hung up. I didn't have time to turn around before the phone rang again. "Wolvertons' residence."

"Mom?"

"Razz! Hi, sweetheart. How are you?"

"Fine. We saw you on TV."

"What'd you think?"

"Swear you won't get a big head?"

"Yeah." I was already grinning.

"I thought you were pretty cool."

"Thanks."

"I have to warn you. Elizabeth doesn't exactly share that opinion. She's real mad."

"I know. We talked about it this morning . . ."

"Yeah, I heard. She thinks you're doing this on purpose to ruin everything for our family."

"Razz, I would never do anything to hurt this family and you know it. So does Elizabeth. I'm doing it because it's the right thing, and Elizabeth is just going to have get used to it."

"Mom, don't be mad at her. She's just scared, that's all."

"I know, honey, and I'm not mad at her. Tell her not to worry, everything's going to be just fine."

He laughed. "You're crazy if you think I'm going to tell her I've even talked to you. Speaking of crazy, you wouldn't believe some of the Loony Tunes who've called here. The phone started ringing as soon as your speech was over; people you know and people who said they know you and people I never even heard of and people from newspapers and TV, and every time I'd hang up the phone, it'd ring again. I didn't want to be rude or anything but some of the stuff they were asking was pretty personal.

"Like I was talking to this guy from some big paper in Chicago and he started asking me who was your boyfriend and I said you didn't have one and then he started this crap about did you like men and I was really getting pissed off and Elizabeth whipped the phone out of my hand and started yelling at him to mind his own damn business and quit bedeviling us and did his mama know he was acting like that? Then she slammed the phone down and told me if I put it back on the hook, she'd tan my hide."

I had a vivid picture of that. "Good for her," I said.

"Well, if that makes you happy, this should make you delirious. About an hour after we took the phone off the hook, these idiots started knocking on the door and asking a barrage of questions, and Elizabeth about gave one of 'em a free nose job.

"Next thing you know, there are about fifty reporters camped outside the house like gypsies. So she turned the sprinklers on them until they left. But now they've all come back and it's pretty funny because they're all wearing raincoats and carrying umbrellas.

"She's says if they're still here in the morning, she's going to boil some Wesson Oil in vats like they did during King Arthur's time and get rid of them once and for all."

I couldn't help laughing. David and Ali were watching me, so I put my hand over the phone and explained. "Elizabeth is doing for journalism what Richard Speck did for nursing." Then back to Razz, "Should I come home?"

"Nah, I think in her own way, she's having a pretty good time," he said.

"Just don't let her do anything that I can be sued for. What about you —you OK?"

"Yeah, but I have to admit it's kind of bizarre, all these bouffants and toupees hanging around here asking questions about you."

"I know, babes and I'm afraid it's going to get a lot worse before it gets better. Do you want to go stay with Hank or Gigi?"

"They've both already offered, but we said no. Gigi came by here this afternoon. She was freaked about you giving the speech and everything, said she wished you'd told her you were going to do it. But I think she was pretty proud of you too. She said she'd come back tomorrow and check on us. Hank's coming tomorrow too. Speaking of which, when are you coming back?"

"Probably sometime Tuesday. I've got to go meet with the women who'll be running this thing, then I'm coming straight home. I tell you what—I'll call you tomorrow night after Elizabeth goes to sleep at . . . let's say midnight, on my private line. Take care of yourself and keep Elizabeth away from the Crisco. I'll get there as soon as I can."

"I'll try—but if the driveway's slippery when you get here, you'll know I failed."

"In that case, I'll get some coleslaw and chips and we'll have fried reporters for dinner."

Chapter 10

The dawn was sweet-talking the sky into pink and orange as Ali pulled into the Sheraton at 6:15 Monday morning. She was driving the Mercedes, I was sipping my third cup of coffee and Jinx was standing outside the hotel lobby, waiting for us with her bags and a stack of newspapers.

Five minutes later, we were back on the freeway and I was pouring Jinx a cup of coffee from our thermos, when Ali demanded, "Well, Jinx, don't keep us in suspense. What do the gentlemen of the press have to say about my friend's speech and our little plan?"

"I haven't had a chance to look. I just woke up about twenty minutes ago. Hold on . . ."

I turned to the backseat and watched her open the paper. Ali was watching in the rearview mirror. Jinx's face relaxed as she located the article. "We made the front page—but just barely. Bottom left, under the fold."

Ali and I traded looks of disappointment.

"The headline reads 'Anti-Underwood women call for sex strike.' "

I took another sip of coffee but it was cold and disgusting so I lowered my window and poured the rest out onto the freeway. "What does it say?" Ali demanded over the sound of the wind.

I rolled the window back up but Jinx didn't respond. I turned to see her searching for a page toward the back of the section. Then she grinned. "Ooooh, look—here's a picture of us all laughing."

"Let me see, let me see!" yelled Ali.

"Forget the picture," I said as I swiveled my head to see it. "What does it say?"

"It says, 'The impeach Underwood demonstration march on the na-

tion's capital took a bizarre turn yesterday when its keynote speaker
called for American women to launch a sex strike.' "

Ali and I looked at each other and I shook my head. Maybe Jake was
right, maybe I was going to be branded a lunatic. I stared out the
window as Jinx's voice got lower. "It says that few experts believe the
movement will catch on."

"Obviously, these experts weren't at the march yesterday," Ali said.

"It says that the surprise speaker and leader of the celibacy movement
is the stunning Lauren Fontaine . . ."

"Try stunned Lauren Fontaine." I sighed.

" ' . . . who is employed in the financial industry by the firm of Sterling
White. In a press conference following her speech, Ms. Fontaine announced that she and her followers will withhold their sexual favors
until Chief Justice Lawrence Caine Underwood is impeached, removed
from the Supreme Court and disbarred.' "

"Well, damn. They make it sound like my friends and I have been
personally servicing the nation," I fumed.

I looked back at Jinx who continued without an upward glance,
" 'When questioned about Fontaine's demands, a spokesman for the
congressional leadership replied, "This matter has been dealt with. We
looked at the evidence and found Chief Justice Underwood innocent of
all charges." ' "

"Innocent, my incontinent grandmother's ass!" Ali muttered.

"Wait," Jinx said. "It gets worse. Then it says, 'We have no comment
on such ridiculous threats as were made by this woman. We have,
however, increased security around Chief Justice Underwood as a pre-
cautionary measure.' "

"Christ, now I'm not only a lunatic, I'm a dangerous lunatic." I
slumped back against the seat. Everybody said they thought I'd done
such a great job. What in the bloody hell had happened? Maybe it was
nothing more than a good execution of a crummy idea. Suddenly, I felt
carsick. I glanced at Ali, who was shaking her head.

"Well, that's just one paper," Jinx said, tossing the *Times* into the front
seat so that Ali could see the photo. "Let's see what the *Post* says. We
made the front page and they've got the exact same picture . . . and
here's another picture of Lauren on the podium, giving the speech . . ."

"What does it say?" I asked, not at all sure that I wanted to know.

"The headline says: 'Underwood controversy turns personal,' " she said. " 'At a demonstration march yesterday in the Washington Mall, a group estimated by the Park Service at 700,000 watched as a radical new leader emerged from the militant feminist pack.' "

I was now holding my face in my left hand. I turned and glared at Ali through my fingers. "Pull over. I'm going to be sick."

She glanced at me, then into the rearview mirror at Jinx, who was still reading. " 'Lauren Fontaine made her debut with an unprecedented demand of American women. She called on them to forgo all sexual relations until Lawrence Underwood is impeached, removed from the Supreme Court and disbarred. The initial response of the crowd was stunned silence, but extremists responded to the call to revolution with screams of joy and soon the mob was in a frenzy.' "

"Make that a dangerous, extremist, radical lunatic," I said.

" 'There is speculation that yesterday's events may signify a fundamental change in the direction of the women's movement. But experts agree that such aggressive tactics could serve to topple the already precarious position that feminism holds in the lives of average women.

" 'There was no official response from Capitol Hill, but unnamed sources noted that lawmakers were unimpressed by Fontaine's threats. Said one, "It's way too weird to take seriously."

" 'The White House refused to comment on the sex ban except to say that "It is clear that the American people are not satisfied that justice has been done and the Speaker of the House should be ashamed of himself for forfeiting the public's trust in our nation's highest court for his party's political gain." ' "

Jinx lowered the paper. "You know you're in trouble when even your allies don't want to be associated with you."

I practically choked. "Jesus, it says *that?*"

"No. I say that," she replied, folding the paper.

I put my head back and stared at the ceiling. "It looks like the only thing they forgot is the requisite quote from my neighbors saying that I'd always kept to myself and never caused any trouble before this."

Ali reached over and patted my leg. "Don't get discouraged, cupcake.

We've just started, and what do you want to bet that both those articles were written by men?"

"You're right," Jinx said. "The byline for the *Post* says Benjamin Jenkins, and . . ." she reached over to get the *Times* from the front seat and turned back to the front page. "Yep, the byline for the *Times* is Chris Yeoman. Typical jackass male response."

That made me feel a little better. And Ali was right, it was silly to think that we'd be taken very seriously before we even organized the movement. Still, I'd have liked to give both Chris and Benjamin a karate chop to the mouth.

We rode in silence for a few miles, then Ali reminded me how much I'd enjoyed the march and teased, "Well, punkinhead, I remember yesterday you thought it was pretty much fun being a feminist leader."

"Now I'm older and wiser. Now I know that being a serial killer is the only thing that would be more of a laugh riot."

"Come on, nobody said it was . . ."

I faded away, no longer listening, thinking about the newspaper reporters and their male experts. The more I thought about how smug they were, the more furious I got. "I'm going to show those bastards how wrong they are," I interrupted. "I'm going to make them eat every single word of this!" I picked up the paper that was lying on the seat, crumpled it and held it up for effect. "By the time I'm finished with those guys, they're going to wish they never heard of me!" I threw the wad of paper on the floor.

"Like so many men before them," Ali said, and turned off the freeway onto the road that leads to the Wolvertons' fishing cabin.

We were sipping the rest of the coffee on the stone porch overlooking Chesapeake Bay when we heard the slamming of car doors. Ali went back into the house and reemerged a few minutes later with the blonde with the dreadlocks and Kimlee.

Then there were more car doors slamming, and everyone turned right around and went back to the front of the house except the blonde and me. She was wearing a shapeless dress and those same awful boots. As I set my mug down and stood up, it occurred to me that underneath the strange garb, she was both very exotic and quite pretty—like maybe she was the offspring of a fling between Grace Kelly and Bob Marley.

"I don't think we were introduced before," she said, and stuck out her hand. "I'm Carl." I was nodding politely when she added, "It's short for Carlton. Carlton Edith Barnes."

I was thinking that Edith wouldn't be my first choice for a name either, but I was pretty sure I'd pick it before Carl. Instead of sharing that observation, I smiled and shook her hand.

"You did a fantastic job yesterday."

"You're nice to say that, but I'm afraid that yesterday was the easy part. Have you seen the papers yet?"

She started to reply, when Ali returned with Savannah and Lynette. There was no doubt they had. "Do not be discouraged," was the first thing Savannah said.

A few minutes later, the door opened and Lisa and Suzanne burst in. Lisa was carrying enough suitcases for a trip around the galaxy and Suzanne was talking a mile a minute with a cigarette hanging out of her mouth. They hoped that Ali didn't mind that they had let themselves in, they just loved the house, thought it was sooo cozy and wasn't the view just divine. They were so busy ingratiating themselves that I thought I could slip past with a wave and an insincere smile.

I thought wrong. Suzanne caught me with her bony arm and almost strangled me, and it was all I could do to keep from visibly cringing. "Lauren, you must remember the first rule of PR—the only bad public-ity is no publicity. I know things don't look too good right now but we've come prepared," she said, holding up a large alligator briefcase in her other hand. I wondered for a second if she had flattered the alligator out of it.

"We can do wonders with you, dear. You've got so much to work with —you're beautiful, successful, you're a mother, you have a divine figure . . . by the time we get finished with you, you're going to be a major force, a cultural symbol of female empowerment."

I didn't know whether to laugh or cry. Was being a major force like being a tropical disturbance? or an army with advanced weapons systems? What did my figure have to do with empowerment? What on earth had I ever done to deserve this?

She turned to Ali to ask for an ashtray, and I took the opportunity to escape into the kitchen and make myself a Bloody Mary. I took a sip and decided I needed more vodka. I was in the process of pouring it when I heard a noise. I whirled around to see Savannah standing at the door, hands together, watching me.

"Want one?"

"No, thanks."

"I don't usually drink in the morning," I said, suddenly self-conscious.

She nodded toward the living room. "This is not as bad as it seems."

"I sure as hell hope not. I'd hate to have to see Larry Underwood's ugly face for the next twenty years." I took a big gulp, wiped my mouth with the back of my hand and looked into her deep eyes. She was a priest, she'd tell me the truth. "Do you think we have any chance of actually pulling this off?"

She smiled. "It depends. I think there's a lot of confusion about what we're trying to do. People can't get their arms around whether or not we're serious. If we can show 'em that this isn't a joke, it's about female solidarity and power, then we've got a decent chance. If the press or the other side can make this seem silly, it'll be all over, nothing more than a footnote in the history books."

That struck a chord of selfish horror. Suddenly, it wasn't about the bad guys winning, it was about how stupid I'd look if no one showed up at my revolution. Would I qualify as one of the Top Ten Losers of the Decade? Would the next edition of Trivial Pursuit ask, "Whose sex strike was a strikeout?" Could I tell people I was just kidding? Could I blame it on an evil twin? On a terrible childhood? a brain tumor? too many Twinkies?

"What do you think will make the difference?"

"You."

"Me?"

"Yeah. You. You gotta start talking. You did a damn good job yesterday, but the real work starts now. You've got to persuade the women in this country that if we stand together, we can move mountains. If you can do that, then not only will Larry Underwood be punished, but the women's movement might seem relevant again."

"Lauren! Come back!" It was Lisa, yelling. "We have not yet begun to fight! C'mon, dear, we're about to position yooou."

Savannah laughed at my Edvard Munch's *The Scream* impression. "The bad news is that this is an unfortunate but necessary evil these days. The good news is that Lisa and Suzanne are really good at it. If you're going to get 'positioned,' these are the people to do it." Her smile was apologetic. "Try to relax—it should be almost painless."

"Sounds suspiciously like a gynecological exam," I said, and returned to the living room with a commensurate lack of enthusiasm. Lisa and Suzanne were spreading files on the floor and the others were getting settled. I sat next to Jinx on the sofa.

"First of all," Suzanne announced, "we have a list of all the newspapers that have covered the story so far, and we've ranked them in order both of importance and sympathy with our cause. Here are the highlights—in the major-paper category, the West Coast papers like the idea better than the East Coast papers: The *L.A. Times* likes it a lot. They called the plan 'daring' and Lauren an 'exciting new presence.' San Francisco said they admired our chutzpah and said it was the first really interesting march since the sixties. Seattle called it hilarious. We're not sure that's a positive," she said and pulled a cigarette out of her expensive purse. "They may have missed the point, but we included them in the pro-movement category because they were so enthusiastic." She lit up with a cheap lighter and exhaled.

That was Lisa's cue. "On the East Coast, basically everybody hated it. *The New York Times* was dismissive and the *Washington Post* was downright hostile, called us 'extremist and radical.' Miami liked Lauren and hated the plan. Philadelphia hated Lauren *and* hated the plan. Atlanta played up the local angle and called Lauren an unlikely troublemaker."

Kimlee leaned over to Carl. "What's the local angle?"

"I'm the local angle. That's where I live," I said. A picture of Elizabeth reading this morning's paper flashed in front of me and I took another long swallow. I hadn't mixed the drink very well and now, mercifully, I was getting to the vodka.

Lisa was looking down her list. "We did a little better in the Midwest in that there were more 'let's wait and see what happens' articles, but we didn't have many friends in the South, especially the Bible Belt." She put down her list and opened another file. "The results are pretty much what we expected when broken down by the sex of the reporter."

At that, Ali looked over at me and nodded.

"Most of the positive articles were written by women. As a matter of fact, the only two editorials we got were penned by gals, one in Denver, one in San Diego. We've got copies of everything for your reading enjoyment, but I wouldn't take any of it to heart," she warned. "Television coverage has been disappointing too. We have a set in the car. Lots of giggles at our expense on the morning shows."

Lisa waved her hand. "Speaking of which, is there a television around here?"

Ali pointed over Lisa's shoulder at the big-screen TV against the living room wall. Lisa picked up the remote, turned on the set and found CNN. We sat silently through a piece on the Japanese economy and one on the President's visit to some VA hospital in Oregon and then there we were, followed by a group of women waving Impeach Underwood banners on the parade route. Bobbie Batista called it the latest skirmish in the battle of the sexes. Then they showed a reporter on the street in New York, stopping people for their reactions to the sex strike.

We had a brief moment of audience participation, we booed the creep who said if women wanted to fight dirty then so could men, and if his wife cut him off, he'd throw her out on the street. We booed the asshole who laughed and said he had two girlfriends and that he thought it would be great if one of them joined the movement so he could finally get some rest.

We cheered the young woman who said she was joining the movement and so were all her friends. When they cut to the head of the sociology department at Harvard and she explained why she thought the movement had a chance of success, we went crazy. We whooped and danced and hugged each other.

Then, as if to teach us a lesson about premature celebration, they showed a montage of responses, one after another saying basically the same thing. "Are they serious?" ... "I don't understand what they're trying to do." . . . "I'm not sure I know what they want." The effect was devastating. After about six of those, Ali grabbed the remote control and the picture went to black.

Suzanne started coughing. She was hacking and barking and Kimlee ran into the kitchen to get her a glass of water and Lisa pounded her on the back until she had the total attention of everyone in the room. Finally, she caught her breath. Then with her cigarette hanging out of her mouth, she wiped her eyes. "Like I say, we were disappointed with this morning's response. If we can generate enough heat with paper coverage, the television folks will follow. We have to get television to take us seriously. When that happens, eighty percent of the battle will be won."

"Why's that?" Jinx asked.

"A couple of reasons. It's much easier to write a biased story in the paper than it is to show an event on television and convince the viewer that he's seeing something other than what's on the screen. We also think that Lauren is very telegenic," she confided, winking in my direction.

"Lucky me," I mumbled and rolled my eyes at Jinx.

"So, we're now going to focus our energies on the paper media with an eye toward television, especially CNN. The more Lauren appears on TV, the better off we are."

Lisa clapped her hands and startled the hell out of me. Then she jumped up and pointed at me and started pacing around the room. "Lauren, you're our voice, our spokeswoman. We want you talking to the media as much as possible, but the key to this is that you say the right things. First thing we need to address is the radical label. You have to make clear that you're not an extremist, that you're just a woman in the mainstream who thinks things have gone too far."

"Well, that shouldn't be too hard," I said, recovering. "I can't recall having been swept up in any philosophical vortex lately."

Suzanne, who obviously didn't know me well enough to tell whether I was being smart-ass or evasive, stared intently at me and cleared her throat with one more little bark. "We just have to make sure we don't say anything that can come back and bite us in the butt."

I turned to face her. "Like?"

"Like have you ever belonged to any militant organizations? Signed petitions for or given money to any group that might be construed as seditious?"

I sighed. "I was raised to be an old-school Episcopalian, a group that looks upon activism as tacky, akin to masturbating in public." I looked over at Savannah, who was shaking her head and grinning. "It's not that I don't care about issues; it's just that I'm organizationally inhibited." Neither Suzanne nor Lisa seemed satisfied, so I went on.

"Specifically, I was briefly in a college sorority, that hotbed of social rest. I was in the Junior League for about a week and a member of the Book-of-the-Month Club for a couple of years in my twenties. I give money every year to Planned Parenthood, the Red Cross, the Metropolitan Opera and the Atlanta Zoo. I also give money to the Girl Scouts, but I get mint cookies in return. That's it—the full extent of my radical affiliations."

"What about criminal behavior?" Lisa challenged.

I leaned back. "What about it?"

"Have you ever been arrested or had a brush with the law?"

"Only that twenty-month stint in Brushy Mountain State Prison." Lisa's eyes darted to Ali to see her reaction, and I started laughing. "Shouldn't you have asked me all this before I gave the speech?"

Ali smiled. "Lionheart, I vouched for you before you gave the speech. What they're trying to find out now is whether you have anything in your past or present that can be used against us."

I took a deep breath. "OK, I don't have any criminal record nor am I engaged in any antisocial behavior. I have a sixteen-year-old son and I run the Atlanta trading office for Sterling White, and those two things keep me busy."

Lisa and Suzanne looked at each other. "That's what we wanted to hear," Lisa said. Suzanne was nodding, scribbling notes on her pad. Lisa pulled some printouts out of a green folder, then she looked up at me. "You've left no fingerprints at all except in your career. Everything we pulled about you is quite positive—you've been very successful but some of these articles are several years old. Are you still well thought of?"

"Jesus, what a weird question. Yeah, I'm still well thought of and I thought this was about Larry Underwood, not me."

She completely ignored that. "What we've got is good, but we need to get going, get some more positive articles about you. We want to pack Lexis/Nexis early."

"Nexis?"

She stubbed out her cigarette and explained. "The Lexis/Nexis system houses all the articles that have been written in newspapers or magazines. Any subject, any person, anything you can think of. Every reporter in the world has access to it, and reporters are notoriously lazy. Their idea of research is to pull up the subject on Lexis/Nexis and read what everybody else has written. We want to use that to our own advantage and pack all the positive articles we can, right here at the beginning."

The cigarette hadn't gone out and was sending smoke in my direction. "Our people are setting up a conference-call interview for Lauren with as many of the sympathetic reporters as we can get. That'll be this afternoon. What we need to do right now is decide on our audience and our focus."

I waved away the haze. "I thought that was pretty obvious. Our audience is women and our focus is getting that private terrorist off the Supreme Court."

"Only in the broadest sense," she said, oblivious to Ali, who reached over and tamped out the butt. "We've done some preliminary polling— a brief questionnaire answered by three hundred women across the nation—and here's what we've got: eighty-six percent believe that Lawrence Underwood is guilty of beating his wife. Of those who think he's guilty, seventy-one percent think he should be punished but only sixty-four percent think he should be removed from his position as chief justice."

Savannah groaned. "Lord, save us."

The others were shaking their heads but they didn't seem shocked. I waved my hands "Wait a second, wait a second. That doesn't make any sense. I don't understand what you're saying!"

Kimlee sighed. "The rest of them have either convinced themselves that Lynn Underwood brought it on herself or that it's not that big a deal."

I let my mouth hang open. "You're shittin' me."

"No she's not," Lynette said.

Suzanne picked a piece of tobacco off her tongue and continued. "Here're some more interesting figures. Of the women in our sample who think the bastard is guilty and should be punished, eighty percent feel strongly that, without intervention, Larry Underwood will be protected by conservatives as a political maneuver." She held up a finger for our attention. "Only twelve percent of our respondents think this issue should be settled in Washington."

"So our audience is the woman who believes he's guilty," Lisa broke in, ticking off points on her right hand. "Who believes that he deserves to be punished and that, unless we intervene, he won't be. That means we have to make this personal instead of political."

Ali looked up. "So instead of liberals vs. conservatives, it's got to be Lauren vs. Larry."

"Exactly," Suzanne said.

"Wait a minute," I said with some force. "Back up. Where do you get this Lauren vs. Larry business?"

I felt like I was being hustled, and Ali saw it. "Lionheart, we'll be trying to keep this about him, but at the same time the other side will be trying to make it about something else. It's possible that they'll make it about you.

"And to be honest—we want it about you. We wanted you to give the speech for a reason. If American women see you as a leader, someone who can stand up to the Washington political machine and speak not just for Lynn but for them too, they'll follow you. They'll join our sex strike, and Larry Underwood will be punished for what he did to his wife. You're charismatic, Lauren, and that's a plus . . . but that's not what matters at the end of the day. This is going to require more than appeal, it's gonna take finesse and a thick skin. And more than anything else, it's going to take guts. Not to mention your greatest talent—the ability to talk the white off rice. Ultimately, this is going to be about how well you make our case that the guy is slime."

I looked to Savannah to see if this was something the two of them had rehearsed. She didn't flinch. "She's telling you the truth. If you can make this about Larry, then Lynn Underwood, who was an incredible women and dear friend of mine, and who deserved a *helluva* lot better that she got, can rest in peace. And so can Nicole Brown Simpson and every other woman who died at the hands of a man who supposedly loved her. On the other hand, if Larry's pals can convince the media that you're some radical nutcase, then you're going to be hung out as an example to uppity women everywhere, left to twist in the wind, alone."

Ali, who knows me so well, stood up and held out her hands. "Lauren, it's simple. High stakes. Smartest player wins."

So this was a game and one where I didn't have to be the stationary target . . . a game of skill and wits. I've always been good at games, I thought, and rubbed my hands together like a villain in a silent film. This could actually be a lot of fun.

"I understand," I said. "And don't worry about me. I'm pure as driven snow—a single mother who works hard and wants to make the world safe for other women."

"That's a killer combination. Especially when compared to a slimy wife batterer. I'm feeling much better about our chances," Lisa warbled. "Now we just have to let the media get to know you, my dear."

A quick note before I forget: I can be found in the *Guinness Book of World Records*—under the category of Stupidest Person Who Ever Lived.

It was almost noon, and Suzanne and Lisa were in the living room where they'd been all morning, hustling up reporters for our cellular confab. The rest of us were gathered in the kitchen, making lunch and organizing the movement. Lynette was saying, "I think we should challenge each woman who signs up to recruit two new members."

I thought that sounded more like Amway than a radical political organization, but Savannah hooted, "Lynette, honey, that is a splendid idea! Now, how'd you get so smart?"

"That is a great idea," Kimlee said. "Just think how fast we can grow the movement that way." Then she started talking about mailing a letter outlining that idea to all the members of every major feminist organization, which led into a discussion of databases of members.

The longer I stood there, the less air the room seemed to have. It must have been pretty obvious, because Carl reached over and touched my hand. "Lauren, what do you think?"

I shrugged. "I have no idea. I don't know anything about databases or mailings or any of this stuff." I turned to Ali, "Where are your keys?"

"Where are you going?" she whispered.

"I don't know. Somewhere."

She went to her pocketbook and handed me the keys. "Want company?"

I shook my head. I got in the car and drove around the little neighboring town, looking at the old houses. I had so many thoughts circling around and stacked on top of each other, my head felt like O'Hare airport. Finally, I thought about the AA prayer that Hank was always reciting: "God grant me the serenity to accept the things I cannot change, the courage to change the things I can and the wisdom to know the difference." With wisdom doubtful and serenity clearly out of the question, I decided to focus on the one thing I could control—calling Sherry and making sure Vinnie had either hedged or closed his bond positions. That's when I found a phone booth outside a service station a couple of miles down the road and called the office.

Sherry was at the dentist so I had the switchboard connect me to the trading room. Between the noise of the traders and the eighteen-wheelers that seemed to pass every thirty seconds, I found myself yelling into the receiver.

"It's Lauren, let me speak to Vinnie."

A long second passed. "Kovacevich."

"What's the bond market doing?"

"Treasury intermediates are up 7/8ths. Long bonds up a point and a quarter."

That was the last thing I wanted to hear. My temples were pounding. I figured I had about one minute before a blood vessel burst in my brain and killed me, and I wanted to make use of every second. "You get your ass on the goddamned phone and close those stupid positions or I am going to personally rip off your—"

"I closed 'em."

"What?"

"I closed the cocksucking positions!!" He roared into the phone.

"When?" I roared back.

"At the fucking opening!" He'd made his trade at the opening bell.

"It's about damn time!" I yelled. I started to say something else, but by then I was talking to the dial tone.

I drove back to the cabin and waved to Lisa, who was pacing up and down the hall, talking to her secretary, checking on the details of the conference call with the reporters. I fixed myself a Coke and walked out to the porch, where the others were discussing different women and their organizational strengths, their standing in the feminist movement and their fields of expertise, and hacking slowly through a jungle of details and names and compromises.

Kimlee was talking about a list on her lap. "At the state level, each one of these women will be responsible for establishing chapters in her city. They'll also work with each of the organizations we represent to coordinate membership lists and arrange for meeting places for the chapters."

Ali motioned me over, but I shook my head and went back to my room. I was focusing on my interview, trying to anticipate questions and rehearse answers, arranging little sound bites on a verbal platter, ready to serve up as supposedly spontaneous insights and piping-hot witticisms.

At 2:40 there was a knock on my door. Suzanne stuck her head in. "You about ready?"

I nodded.

"Good." She came over to the bed and handed me a list of six names. Four of the names were followed by the names of newspapers. "This is the 3:00 interview. I didn't want so many people that they can't ask their questions and get a feel for who you are. If you'll look at the list, you'll notice that two of the names have blanks next them, Bob Fisher and Vicky Garrett—they're syndicated columnists. Bob by Gannett and Vicky by AP. Play to those two; between them they represent several hundred small papers." She turned away and lifted the window, sat on the windowsill and lit up. "I spoke to Bob a few minutes ago. His questions are going to focus on why you were the one that gave the speech. He seems a little suspicious—wanted to know if there was any connection between your financial support of Planned Parenthood and the fact that Lawrence Underwood has cast some important anti-Roe votes."

"How in the hell would he know about my giving money to Planned Parenthood?"

She shrugged and blew a smoke ring. "Beats me. I told him we knew you gave money, so do lots of us. No connection. Be sure to address this head-on; Vicky wants you on record with your personal reasons for doing this. You know, did your ex ever lay a hand on you? did your father beat your mother?—that kind of stuff." She flicked an ash out the window. "We're working on another set of reporters for an interview at 4:00 P.M. and maybe even a third one at 5:30."

"You set 'em up, I'll knock 'em down," I said with much more enthusiasm than I felt.

"Be careful of trick questions," was the last thing she said before the phone rang.

"No, I don't have an ax to grind, other that the fact that I believe the constitutional institutions of this country are what represent us and everything we stand for and believe to the rest of the world. Every day that Lawrence Underwood sits on the Supreme Court, that American symbol means less. This man is a monster and a hideous embarrassment to all of us, and under no circumstances should he be protected."

"Lauren, Thomas O'Dell at the *L.A. Times.* What's been your response to the mixed reception your idea has gotten?"

"Thomas, I'm glad you asked that. I'm not surprised that people are a little confused but I want to make this clear—this sex strike is no joke. Most of the people in this country believe that Larry Underwood is guilty and they also believe that he won't be punished if that decision is left up to the politicians. This is an act of power, something every woman can do to say 'Beating your wife is not acceptable, and if you do it then *you* are not acceptable, period.' I'm no radical, I'm just like every one of the other ninety million women who refuse to let Lynn Underwood's tormentor get away with murder.

"My only other reaction is disappointment with some of the people in the press—I don't understand how the same people who were so horrified with Congress's verdict could be so dismissive of our attempt to deal with it."

"Ms. Fontaine?—Betsy Bailey at the *Miami Herald*. Can you tell us what your significant other thinks about you leading this sex strike?"

Sure, Betsy, but let me answer that in two parts. One of my significant others thinks it's my destiny and he's all for it as long as his name is never mentioned. The other one is probably not too thrilled, because not only have I cut him off, now his wife will too.

"Betsy, I'm not romantically involved with anyone right now. But as you know, I'm a mom, so my significant other is my son. I've tried very hard to teach him about the importance of doing the right thing, so I think he understands why I'm involved in this fight."

It was almost midnight when I finished my fifth phone interview. My throat hurt like hell but I'd promised Razz I'd call. I picked up the receiver, dialed my number and heard Elizabeth's voice.

"What?" Cold as Eskimo boots.

"I wanted to see how you are."

"Well, we've got a bunch of fools hangin' around, asking every ridiculous question you can imagine. We've got the phone ringing off the hook with more fools asking more ridiculous questions. We can't even get out of this blessed house to go to the store. I told you not to do this and you wouldn't listen and now I'm stuck with all this foolishness while you're off junin' around up there. Now, how do you think I am? I am on my last nerve, that's how I am."

"For your information, I am not juning around. I am working on organizing this movement." She made a derogatory sound, which I ignored. "How's Razz?"

"He can't go outside. If he turns into one of those recluses, then you'll have your own self to blame."

"I hardly think a few days inside is going to turn him into Boo Radley." Now I was as testy as she was. "Look, I just wanted to check and see how you are."

"Well, now you know."

"Yeah, now I know. It's been a real pleasure talking to you."

"When are you coming home?"

"When I feel like it," I said and hung up.

Chapter 11

By sunset Tuesday, I had given at least seven phone interviews to reporters and I was exhausted. I'd wandered down to the bay in search of a little solitude and was standing in the olive green water, drinking wine and replaying the day's questions in my head, when I heard a noise and looked up to see Lynette. For a long moment we stood in silence as the sun snapped the surface of the water with golden sparks. I could tell she was deciding whether to leave me alone, and I wanted her to stay. I knocked back half the wine in one swallow. "How's the organization stuff going?"

She smiled. "I think we're right on track there. We've got a coherent plan and by tomorrow we'll have most of the details worked out." She put her hands through her hair and stretched. "The regional and local organizers are already at work, putting everything in place. The only thing left at that point will be coordinating all the organizations for maximum effect."

I nodded. "I never thought that running a revolution required so much organization. I kind of figured it was more like blowing up a bridge than building one."

"Blowing up a bridge takes planning too," she said. "Although we've never attempted anything on this scale, we've been through the drill a million times."

"Would you say you consider yourself a man's woman or a woman's woman?" I asked as I reached for my drink.

She considered the question. "I'd say I'm a woman's woman now, but I used to be a man's woman."

"What changed you?"

"Life," she said, and we both laughed.

"Could you be a tiny bit more specific?"

"Well," she smiled sadly and swatted at a horsefly, "about eight years ago, I went through a hideous second divorce, and it really made me think. That's when I realized that it was the women in my life who were always there for me—whether I was really up or really down; that none of my girlfriends had ever abandoned me because I was angry or I'd gained fifteen pounds or they had met someone whose thighs were firmer or whose self-esteem was smaller. It was at that point I stopped treating my relationships with women as secondary. I guess you could say that I'm a woman's woman because I've learned that men hurt you and let you down and for the most part, women don't. What about you?"

I leaned down and dipped my hand in the water. "Man's woman. Ever since I was little, I felt more comfortable with guys. At recess, the other girls wanted to play Barbie and jump rope, I wanted to play football and baseball and war. And it wasn't really any different when I got older— I'd listen to these conversations about prom dresses and fraternity pins and, later, redecorating and Junior League politics, and I always felt like I had dropped down from another planet. Guys are simple: they want to play the game and they want to win. I understand that. That makes sense to me."

I looked up and the translucent clouds were apricot, tinged by a golden sun. I looked back at Lynette and shrugged. "Anyway, my interests are more masculine than feminine, even though I think of myself as feminine. I'm probably not explaining this very well, but it seems that women care about things like beauty and security and romance, things that I think are nice—but basically unessential. Men care about things like honor and bravery and responsibility, and those are the things that really matter to me. Oh, I have women friends that I've had forever, like Ali, but I just don't feel like I have much in common with the average woman."

She grinned. "I think you're wrong. I think you have more in common with the average woman than you think. Besides, I think you're vastly overestimating men. Most of 'em only really care about getting laid and being taken care of.

"And you're underestimating women—they invented responsibility.

And as far as bravery goes, I know dozens of women who deserve a medal for the things they've survived. And honor . . . hell, how many people convicted of insider trading were women? And how many bigamists are women? And tax evaders and what about—"

"Do you know Jo Lewis?"

"No, why?"

"She's my therapist and I thought maybe she paid you to say this to me. It sounds like it came straight from her mouth."

She laughed and waded a little deeper. "I swear that Jo and I haven't conspired to brainwash you."

"Good, because my brain is so small and delicate, it has to be dry cleaned," I said and drained the last of the drink.

She looked at me with a puzzled expression. "I don't get it though. Why are you doing this if you don't feel like one of us?"

"Would you believe that one of my New Year's resolutions was to learn to speak in front of crowds and I thought the one yesterday would be a good place to start?" The way she looked at me made me nervous, so I changed the subject. "Ali says you've been celibate for a long time. Did you plan that? I mean, is it a political statement or something?"

She threw back her head and laughed. "No, it's not a political statement. After my divorce, I just couldn't bear the thought of being with a man. I didn't even think about it for seven or eight months. Then by the time I thought I might want to, there was no one even slightly interesting on the horizon. By the time a couple of years had passed, I figured it had been so long that I should wait until I met someone special, sort of a self-induced revirgination."

She put her hand behind her neck and stretched. "That was about the time three of my closest girlfriends were involved in relationships that were making them miserable, and I could see how the sex kept them connected to situations they should've walked away from. That's when I decided that sex was, excuse the pun, a sucker game for women. And I didn't want to play.

"Actually, I learned a lot from being celibate. We all have empty places inside of us, and we run around trying to fill ourselves up with shiny new things or work or booze or food or whatever. And as women, the most accepted way to fill our empty places is with other people—men, children, needy strangers." She brushed her hair from her face and smiled. "We all have a choice: we can fill our empty places . . . or we can close them. And closing them is work we do alone.

"It's really ironic, though, that after eight years I've been thinking about taking the plunge again—and you start this sex strike."

"Well, sorry. The timing of this thing seems to be universally off. If it makes you feel any better, I'm in the exact same boat, except for the eight years of celibacy, of course. "

"Really?"

"Yep. You even know him."

"Ooh, tell all."

"Jake Ward."

"Are you kidding? Does Flo know?"

"No."

"Good."

I was really disappointed. I wanted her to say what a great guy she thought Jake was.

"You know," she said, "the part of what I said about my girlfriends staying in relationships that had gone bad?"

I nodded.

"I was talking about Flo."

"Shit."

"Don't misunderstand. I'm not saying it was Jake's fault. It wasn't really anybody's fault, it was just a bad situation."

"What happened?"

"That's really not for me to say."

That frosted me. "Bullshit. I want to know what happened."

She sighed. "It was a great relationship until Flo started having problems."

This was not what I wanted to hear. I turned my face away from her voice. "What was Flo's problem?"

"Perspective."

I turned back. "What do you mean?"

"She lost her perspective. Flo, as you know, was one of the pioneers of the women's movement. She's been involved since she was twenty-four years old, it's been her life. She never married, never had kids, and when she met Jake, she believed that he was the payoff. Here was the guy she'd waited for and at just the right time."

"Just the right time?"

"Yeah, this was at the point that this generation of radical feminists came along, criticizing the old guard for letting the movement grow stagnant. They didn't understand or appreciate where we'd come from. They were too young." She shrugged. "But that's simply the nature of change and the impetus that's always driven young people to take the reins and continue the progress made by the previous generation. It's just that Flo couldn't see it as a natural progression and she took it personally.

"Flo was in a bad place, she felt completely negated and she started thinking that she'd given herself and her life to this cause and she'd made a terrible mistake. That's when she started holding on to Jake like a life raft in a storm. And nothing he could do or say was enough.

"The whole thing started getting to him and, eventually, he started pulling back, which she took as proof that her value as a person was diminishing. The less she loved and valued herself, the more she needed him to. Florence Fienman, who'd always been her own woman, got to the point where she hung her entire self-esteem on Jake Ward's opinion. She wasn't even Flo anymore, and she just couldn't leave it alone until she finally drove him away. It was sad, because otherwise he'd have never left. He's not that kind of guy. But what was really sad was that she couldn't see her part in the breakup, and she blamed him and that's when she started bad-mouthing him in the press. She was merciless. It was a real bad deal—it hurt her and it hurt him. I think he's one of the last great men around. I hope things work out for you two."

"Who two?"

We both turned around to see Savannah standing in the sand.

"Lauren and Mr. Jake Ward," Lynette replied, grinning.

"You and Uncle Jake?" Savannah was grinning too, hands on her hips. "Damn, some girls have all the luck. I'd give that old boy a run for his money if he ever got smart enough to ask." She laughed.

"Well, he thinks the world of both of you. He told me that."

"The old boy's got good taste too," Savannah said. "Does Flo know?"

Lynette grimaced. "Not yet."

Savannah looked at Lynette, then at me. "This will not make her happy."

Lynette arched an eyebrow. "That may be the understatement of the millennium. But I'm going to leave it to you two, because the human bladder is not meant to hold six gallons of wine. I have to find a bathroom before I explode."

We watched Lynette trudge up the hill, then I turned to Savannah. "Can I ask you a question?"

She nodded.

"How can you tell whose side God is on?"

She cut her eyes at me. "He's on my side."

"Ah, well that settles it." I laughed. "Seriously, I mean, you sure can't tell by the way things turn out. I don't know if I can explain what I mean but . . . part of me wonders if I should even be doing this."

"Why's that?"

"Because Larry Underwood is an evil man, *but* what makes me think that God wants me to the one responsible for punishing the guy. It's not like I've never done anything wrong . . ."

She looked tired. "Have you ever tortured anybody?"

"No."

"All right then. Quit worrying about whether you have the right to do the right thing. If God didn't want you to do it, He wouldn't have picked you out for this particular job. He had His choice of a lot of other people, you know."

That was an interesting concept. "I certainly never thought of it like that."

"Well, it's pretty obvious, don't you think?" She leaned toward me, her eyes shining. "Your background, your temperament, the things you've done and what you believe in all have prepared you to do His work."

It would never have occurred to me but it made complete sense. "That could be true," I said and thought back to the night it all started. Now I was whispering. "One of the first things Jake ever told me was that lessons are kisses from God."

She offered it back to me as proof. "He ought to know, don't you think?"

"Yeah, he should." This was simple. So simple that I couldn't imagine how it had eluded me for thirty-six entire years.

She said, "And knowing that has allowed our friend Jake the faith to do his work without fear."

But wait. Jake was just one person in a big world. "But if God gets everybody ready for the work he's picked out for 'em, then how come most people do such a crummy job?"

"Because they don't believe that their lessons are kisses from God, they think that those lessons are punishment. And they think all that punishment means that God doesn't love them—or that it means that there is no God."

Boy, she had sure hit my religious nail on the head. I wanted so much to have faith, and I felt like it was close enough to touch, that I could just reach out and snag it. "So if you think God loves you, then you have faith that he'll take care of you so you don't have to be scared all the time," I said.

"That's it," she said, pointing to me. "You get a gold star!"

"And if you're not scared, you don't need courage."

"You got it, lamb chop."

"*Wow*," I said and studied her face. "You are amazing."

"No question about it," she said, and we both laughed. We stood for several minutes admiring the sunset, then Savannah broke the silence. "You can trust these women not to hurt you," she said.

I was completely taken aback. "What makes you think I don't trust them?"

"Ali had told you about me, didn't you think she'd ever told me about you?"

"I guess. I just didn't know what she would have said about me." I drew the glass to my mouth. "What did she tell you?"

"Enough to have kept you in my prayers over the years."

I crossed my arms against my chest. "What exactly did she say?"

She shrugged. "That you've cut yourself off from women. That you focus only on the differences and not the things you have in common with the rest of us and that it's made you unhappy."

I started to deny that my separation from my gender had caused me a minute's discomfort, but that was Absolute Unbreakable Rule No. 2— Never lie: to a priest or a gynecologist. It was then that I flashed back to the meeting at Ali's house, and Savannah's words: "Lauren needs to give the speech." She knew. She knew before I did, and no blow to the solar plexus could have knocked the breath out of me more effectively. I stood there with my mouth open and she walked over and took the glass out of my hand and me into her arms and I squeezed my eyes shut and bit my lip to keep from weeping. She rocked me gently from side to side until finally I could breathe and I pulled back and whispered, "Thank you."

"Baby, everything that happens, happens for a reason. God's touch is everywhere, if you're paying attention, not only can you see it, you can be a part of it. Don't forget that."

"I won't," I lied.

We went through three more bottles of wine while we fixed steaks and salad, which we ate in the living room in front of the television. About halfway through the evening news, the screen dissolved into a clip of all of us as we came out into the lobby of the hotel before the march. Suzanne started screaming, "Turn it up! Turn it up!" Ali, who had the remote, did as she was told.

In the background there were the voices of reporters yelling, "Is it true that you'll be calling for a work strike?" and "Just how mad are you women at the Underwood verdict?" and "Why are you holding a press conference after the march instead of before?"

I was completely unprepared for what happened next; the film went into slow motion and zeroed in on my face as I shook my head, then grinned, then started to giggle. I can't describe what it felt like, except to say it was like watching yourself appear in the Zapruder film.

The background noise faded, replaced by the reporter's voice. "Americans were stunned Sunday when the women's movement introduced both a new leader and a surprising strategy at a protest march attended by an estimated two million people in the nation's capital. The march was organized in response to last week's congressional refusal to impeach Chief Justice Lawrence Underwood."

Then it switched to me at the podium at the end of the speech and the audio returned. "We will not have sex again until Lawrence Underwood is removed from the Supreme Court, disbarred and punished for the torture of his wife," then silence, then the whole incredible deafening response of two million screaming, stomping people.

Then an old photo of me from the cover of *Institutional Investor* appeared on the screen. "Lauren Montague Fontaine, well known in the financial world as a talented trader and the first woman ever to be named managing partner in the prestigious investment firm Sterling White, amazed her associates on Wall Street yesterday by becoming the spokeswoman for the women's revolutionary sex strike.

"The charismatic thirty-six-year-old currently heads Sterling White's Atlanta office. While Sunday marked her debut as a leader of the controversial sexual boycott, little else is known about her other political affiliations. Conservatives are questioning Ms. Fontaine's motives and why she was chosen as a spokesperson for this campaign."

As soon as the next story began, Ali switched channels. There was a blond reporter in a raincoat, standing in front of the stock exchange, "The one place where Lauren Fontaine is not a mystery is here . . . on Wall Street. Old-timers and Young Turks alike speak about her in tones of respect. Said one floor trader, who spoke only under condition of anonymity, 'I don't know why she's doing this, but if I were Larry Underwood, I'd be guarding my gonads. Lauren Fontaine is not somebody you want to tangle with.' "

After more wine and celebration, I went back to my room to rest and ended up falling asleep. It was after 10:00 P.M. when I woke up to voices in the living room.

Kimlee was talking. "At some point you grow weary of the game. It gets so that instead of hoping for what you want, all you hope is that you don't get your hopes up. But I'm finished with men. I am just over it in a big way."

Lisa sighed. "Believe me, I know what you mean. I am so tired of being disappointed by men. So sick of praying that this time it'll be different, that this one will really be there for me . . . that he won't just disappear, emotionally or literally. And yet in the end, it's always the same."

Then Carl's voice with an emotion I couldn't describe. "There comes a day that you just quit putting candles in shit and calling it chocolate cake, when you just aren't interested anymore."

I sat on the edge of the bed, on the edge of the conversation, thinking in the dark about what they'd said. Then I heard laughter outside, and it drew me like the Pied Piper onto the side patio. There were two wine bottles beside the Jacuzzi, and Ali, Jinx and Suzanne in it. They were deep in debate about what kind of women get beat up worst by men.

"It is strong women who get beat up! Men are too stupid to figure out that strong women have the exact same feelings and emotions and needs as pathetic, whiny women—" Ali said.

"Or maybe," Suzanne interrupted, "men can figure it out. Maybe they know tha' we need to be encouraged and supported and cared for every bit as much as some wimp who can't balance her own checkbook or even cross the street alone. But they jus' refuse to give us what we want or need."

Jinx gained the floor by waving her drink around and spilling half of it into the water. "So true, so true. If you're poor Pitiful Pearl, men will fall all over themselves to take care of you and boost you up; if you're strong they'll fall all over themselves to knock you down. They reward helpless women and beat up strong ones."

"Yeah, maybe," Lisa said, appearing on the deck, "but I think it's not strong women, it's sexual women that get beat up by men. The more comfortable you are with your sexuality, the worse it is. If they're single, they never call you back for a fifth date. If they're married, they revel in your appetites, then rush home with jewelry for wives who wouldn't know anal sex from Oral Roberts."

They went on with their debate, and I stepped back into my room. That's when it hit me that out of eight of us, Ali was the only one who was married. I thought of what Jinx had said on the train about writing off the opposite sex, and of Lynette's comments down at the water, and I wondered if the engine of the women's movement was fueled not by a hatred of men but by a profound disappointment in them. Was that the difference between ordinary women and those who considered them-selves feminists—one group was still hopeful while the other had given up? Those who still believed in Santa and those who knew better? Is that why feminists made other women so nervous?

The thought depressed me profoundly.

Chapter 12

"Please remain seated with your seat belt securely fastened until the captain has brought the aircraft to a complete stop at the terminal."

It was Thursday afternoon and I had barely noticed the landing. I'd called both Razz and the office to say that I'd be staying a couple of extra days, both of which were spent working feverishly on planning our strategy for the strike. But that wasn't what I was focused on—it was the scene that had taken place the night before; me, accidentally walking in on Carl and Kimlee. It wasn't their sexuality that bothered me. I couldn't care less that they were lesbeterians. But it made me wonder if it was why neither one of them was chosen to give the speech. Was I really the voice of the revolution or simply the hologram?

My car was still at the train station, so I grabbed a taxi at the airport. We rode in silence until we turned off the main road onto my street. There were cars and white vans sporting satellite dishes and network logos parked along the curb, on my neighbors' grass, blocking their driveways, narrowing the wide street down to one lane. The cab slowed to a crawl and the driver became animated. "Will ya look at all these news trucks! Must be something big. Yeah," he decided, "probably some rich guy murdered his wife."

"No, it's probably some housekeeper getting ready to murder her employer," I mumbled. From a hundred yards away their silhouettes were visible against the pale gray limestone—the reporters with black television camcorders perched on their shoulders looked from a distance like hunchbacked birds, their jutting lenses, the birds' heads. It was as if a gristle of enormous and grotesque vultures had landed on our lawn.

We topped the hill and came face to face with them and they swarmed around the cab, pushing microphones at the windows and yelling questions. I grabbed my bags and stepped out into the melee.

"Is it true that you've been in hiding?" challenged a man with a long face and huge teeth, thrusting a microphone at my chin. He reminded me of the big bad wolf, and I straightened.

"I most certainly have not been in hiding. I have been with the other organizers of the movement, planning our strategy."

"What's your personal opinion of Chief Justice Underwood?" called a man with a beak nose and the kind of handlebar mustache that's been out of style for about eighty years.

I stared Snidely Whiplash straight in his beady little eyes. "I think he's a repugnant, slimy, cowardly, disgusting piece of rat excrement who should be thrown off the Supreme Court, disbarred and punished. And American men will be sleeping alone until he is."

"What do you think of the USA Today poll showing that only twenty-three percent of sexually active women have joined the Lysistrata Movement?"

I had read that in the airport. "I'm delighted! That's almost one out of every four women. I think that's a pretty good start for the first four days. Don't you?"

A man in desperate need of a Kleenex sneered. "Do you understand that means that at least one out of every four men in this country hates your guts!?!"

I turned to face the boogeyman. "Do you understand that I'm not running for Miss Congeniality? I intend to see justice done for Lynn Underwood and every other woman in this country, and I don't care who hates me for it."

Another voice with a hostile question, and they all started jostling to get closer. I was about to lose my temper and knew that, once lost, it might only be found years from now, huddling in a cave in New Hampshire. I held up my hands, "Thanks so much for your interest. That's all I intend to say. Now, if you'll excuse me . . ." I stuck my bags out in front of me and used them to clear my way through the throng.

The door opened as soon as I hit the front step and slammed behind me before I was two feet inside the house. I turned around to face my beautiful son, hugged him hard and nodded toward the door. "You invite all those people over here?"

"Yeah, I thought I'd have a party while you were out of town," he said with the bravado of a man but holding on to me like a frightened little boy.

"Oh, Razz." I just held him and wiped my eyes with the back of my hand.

"You know you're always saying you want me to have lots of interesting experiences? Well, I gotta tell ya, this one's been an extravaganza." He pulled away and looked at me.

"Mom, don't cry. It's OK, I'm fine. I swear. The question is, are you OK?"

"Yeah, if you are, then I am. Where's Elizabeth?"

"Gigi's with her. She's been kind of freaked for the last couple of days. When all the reporters and stuff came, she kept thinking that if we didn't open the gate they'd go away. But they didn't, they stayed; and I swear, it was like they were spawning at night, every morning there'd be more of 'em.

"Finally, Elizabeth had enough, so she went tearing outside and started yelling. She called the reporters white trash and told them to get away from our property and never set foot on our land again."

I stood dumbfounded, but he continued. "The whole scene was like something straight out of the movies, and finally I had to go talk her back into the house, all because this smart-ass reporter started taunting her through the gate. Big mistake. I'd been in the kitchen, getting something to eat, and all of a sudden I hear this big commotion. Elizabeth had gone around to the shed, gotten about ten things of fertilizer—you know, that stuff that's basically just shit in a bag—and dumped them right at the front gate." He was grinning at the memory. "Mom, you've never seen people take off so fast. It was like dropping a stone into a school of minnows.

"Then, of course, a film of it ended up on *Inside Edition* and they made her look like some kind of psychotic or something. When she saw that, she got so mad I had to call Hank to come over and calm her down."

"Is she all right?"

"Yeah, Hank started saying that she's the bravest thing since John Wayne. Then he did this routine about trying to convince her to be his bodyguard. After that she calmed down. But every time she looks out the window and sees all the reporters, she goes off on another tirade."

"Sounds pretty grim."

"Yeah. We've managed, but it hasn't exactly been a frolic. Gigi and Hank have been taking turns staying here, but she's waiting for you."

"Why? So she can stab me with a butcher knife?"

"Nah, I think she wants to kill you with her bare hands."

I pulled him to me again, "Oh, Razz, I'm really sorry. But don't you worry, I'm back now and I promise you that everything's going to be OK. It's gonna be fine. We'll get through this together. That is, if we can talk Elizabeth out of murder or mayhem."

"If I were you, Mom, I'd settle for mayhem and consider myself fortunate." We left my bags on the floor in the entry hall and walked through the living room and the den with our arms entwined. I was just so happy to be home.

My pleasure was short lived. It lasted until the second we walked into my room and saw the two of them sitting on my bed. Gigi was talking in a soothing voice, and Elizabeth was rocking back and forth. I let go of Razz, knelt before them and took Elizabeth's hands. Her eyes were drained of light, and Gigi whispered, "Now look who's here. Didn't I tell you she was on her way?" Elizabeth nodded and looked at me and my heart broke into a million pieces.

My chest was aching from the impact, and I hardly noticed Gigi and Razz leaving. Minutes passed and neither one of us had moved or spoken. Elizabeth's head was bowed and her hands were lying in her lap. She didn't seem to have the words, and I was trying so hard not to fall apart that I couldn't open my mouth.

I got up and sat next to her and held her so tight that my arms hurt. Finally, I took a painful, deep breath and said, "Elizabeth, do you remember when Razz was so sick that the doctors thought he might die?"

She nodded, her eyes never leaving the floor.

"Remember how scared we were? And remember when that plane crashed taking off from La Guardia and you and Razz thought I was on it? That was really scary too, wasn't it?"

Another nod. "Now, you didn't know this, but when we didn't have any money, Razz came to me and wanted to know if you were going to leave us because we were poor. I had to tell him that I thought you might, and we were so scared of losing you." I had never shared that with her, and her eyes flickered at the thought.

"Those were all things to be afraid of. Because if we lost each other, nothing else in the world could make up for it—we belong together. But right now, we've got each other—so everything'll be OK. Right?" I bumped her shoulder with mine until she smiled. "Like Shadrach, Meshach and Abednego, or Winken, Blinken and Nod, or the Three Musketeers."

She nodded. "Bobby, Darlene and Annette?"

"Yeah, them too. Anyway, we've *got* each other and that's all we need. And don't worry about this other stuff, because I'm going to take care of it."

"Well, you better take care of it 'cause this is all your fault," she said quietly, still rocking.

"Yeah, I know." My arms were still around her, and I was getting rocked along for the ride.

"You make me so mad sometimes I'd like to smack you into September."

"I wouldn't blame you if you did."

"You're stubborn and pigheaded and you think you know everything in the world."

"You're absolutely right."

We went on like that for about five minutes as she enumerated every last one of my grievous and myriad faults, then she fell silent and I held her some more and told her that I loved her and that I'd always be grateful for the way she protected Razz. I also told her that I appreciated her newfound interest in gardening, with all the watering and fertilizing she'd done lately, and she laughed. Then she took a deep breath, squeezed me back and went into the kitchen to start dinner.

I found Razz and Gigi at the table in the sunroom, working on a 1,000-piece jigsaw puzzle. The front of the box had the famous photograph of the German students tearing down the Berlin Wall. I guess I'm old-fashioned, but I associate jigsaw puzzles with picturesque scenes of grazing horses or covered bridges. I picked up the box. "What is this, the Revolutionary Series? When you finish this one, what's next, Tiananmen Square?"

"No, we're doing the Soweto Riots next," Razz said without looking up.

"And after that, maybe you can work on the Women's Revolution, the one that has a close-up of me on the podium," I teased.

Elizabeth called from the kitchen, "Revolutionary Series, my tail. You're in the Criminally Insane Series."

Razz and I looked at each other and his eyes were blue and we smiled. Things were back to normal.

We were still in the sunroom, working on the puzzle, when we heard the front door open and Hank's voice. "Is she here yet?"

"Yeah, she's here!" we all yelled back.

"Well, thank God!" he said, coming around the corner.

"Hi, babe. Miss me?" I said, trying to figure out whether the piece I held was part of an arm or just graffiti.

"I would have liked to, my dear, but I wasn't afforded the opportunity. I saw you every time I picked up a newspaper or turned on the television. Now that you're here, tell me how on earth you ended up in this mess."

"It's a long story and one I'll tell you another time. Right now, though, we're re-creating a moment of ebullience for the German people. Want to help?"

"Absolutely. After all, I'm known in some circles as a master re-creator of ebullient moments." He pulled a Coke out of the refrigerator, then he turned to Razz. "So, sport, what do you think about your Mom calling for an end to sex on the planet?"

"It wouldn't be that big a deal but . . . um . . . uh . . . never mind." He turned tomato red, got up and excused himself.

"Well, I think it's a very good idea," Hank announced.

"Yeah, but that's because it doesn't really narrow down the field for you," Gigi said, reaching over for a piece of the sky. "I'm going along, but I have to say that I don't like it a bit and neither does Tom."

"That's not why I think it's a good idea," Hank said defensively, "I think the whole world might be a better place without sex."

"Easy for you to say, Hank," I teased. "You've already had about everybody in the whole world."

"OK, but I'm serious. I've really been thinking about how different things would be if we didn't have sex."

"So how different would things be?"

"Well, the first thing that would change is how people would choose their partners and what attributes they'd look for. If there were no such thing as sex, youth and beauty wouldn't be that big a deal; but wisdom would, and character would, and a sense of humor would too."

"Yeah, that'd be great," I said, suddenly loving the idea. "You show me a single woman in her thirties who's interesting and smart and fabulous and I'll show you a gal who hasn't been on a date in over a year. It'd change things, all right. I mean, can't you just hear it? Two guys at a bar . . . 'Wally, you wouldn't believe the woman I met last night. I'm not exaggerating when I say she had brains out to here! And the advanced degrees on this chick—like nothin' you ever saw!' "

"No kidding." He laughed. "I'll tell you what else would be different. The world would be a kinder place. Look at the way people who sleep together treat each other. They say horrible, hurtful things that they'd never say to a friend, and perform routine acts of cruelty that they wouldn't dream of inflicting on even the most casual acquaintance."

"There would be a lot fewer crimes of passion," Gigi agreed, refilling her glass and mine with chardonnay. "Men wouldn't have to take out their little sexual frustrations and insecurities on everyone else. There would be no more rapes, no more wars . . ."

"No more Corvettes," I offered. "And no more toupees."

"No more corporate takeovers."

"Yep, the world would be a much better-behaved place," Hank mused.

"And less stressful," Gigi chimed.

"And deadly dull," I said.

"And deadly dull," everyone concluded in unison and finally settled down to concentrate on the puzzle. We were actually making pretty good progress and might have finished it if everyone hadn't been so exhausted. Razz and Elizabeth went to bed about 11:00 P.M., and I walked Hank to the door a few minutes later. "You OK?" he asked, examining my face.

"Yeah, I'm fine. Just a little tired." I smiled to make him believe me. "Hank, this may sound crazy but I really think we're going to pull this off."

He hugged me tight. "It wouldn't surprise me a bit. Be careful though, the more it looks like you might, the more danger you'll be in. I think you ought to get a bodyguard."

"Excuse me?"

"I'm not kidding. You've pissed off a whole lot of guys—from the rednecks who are mad because none of the girls at Tiny Acres Trailer Park are putting out anymore, to the religious right, and honey, the radicals in that crowd make the Shiites look like paragons of reason."

I was trying to decide which crowd he was talking about when he leaned in close. Concern pulled his brows together. "Please promise me you'll look into it."

"Let's see how things go. If it looks like we might have a problem, I'll call Ali and get her to send Moore," I promised.

"I've got to be honest with you, little baby. Part of me loves you doing this. The high drama and all that. The other part of me is scared to death for you. The guy you've picked a fight with is one of the most powerful men in the country, and if he comes after you, not even Moore can keep you safe. I couldn't stand it if anything happened to you or Razz, and I need to tell you, I've got a real uneasy feeling about this," he said as he kissed my forehead and slipped through the door.

Gigi had poured another glass of wine and was waiting in the kitchen when I returned. "Something's the matter."

She took a slug. "Yeah, something's the matter."

"Is it Mom and Dad?"

She shook her head. "Daddy's concerned. You know he thinks whatever you do is great, but he's worried. Mom, on the other hand, thinks this is the greatest thing ever and reminds anyone who'll listen that she always predicted that you'd end up on the cover of *Time*. But that's not the problem."

"So what's the problem?"

"Tom." She looked up and her eyes were filled with tears.

I grabbed her hand. "Sweetie, what's the matter with Tom?"

Now the tears were falling. "He's so furious over this whole thing."

"Wait a second. He's furious over what whole thing?" I was genuinely stumped.

"This sex strike thing. It's like this personal insult to him that I'm a member of the movement."

"I don't get it. You've hardly been secretive about your support of the women's movement. He knows what happened to Sofia, doesn't he?"

"Yeah."

"Then I can't believe he would have the gall to take this as a personal insult, to think this has anything to do with him. Jesus, what an asshole!"

"Yeah, but he says nothing I do now can change what happened to Sofia or Lynn Underwood and that he should be the person I'm concerned about. You can't believe how bad it is. We had this huge fight two days ago. He says I'm sacrificing his needs to make a point and that makes him wonder about my commitment to him. 'I thought you married me, not the goddamned women's movement!' He's so mad I can't even reason with him." She was wringing her hands, and they were red and raw.

I reached out and put my hands on hers to still them. "Sweetie, I don't even know what to say. I have to tell you I'm real disappointed in Tom. I think he's being unbelievably selfish . . ."

She threw my hands off and narrowed her eyes. "Lauren, this is my second marriage. I don't give a shit how disappointed you are, I can't lose him! I don't make millions of dollars being a big Wall Street hotshot. I'm not like you. I'm not that strong. I need Tom."

I stopped myself from saying that needing someone was a luxury I'd never been able to afford. It wouldn't have helped her, and she was there for help. I reached out and again put my hands on hers to quiet them. "Do you want me to talk to him?"

She laughed, then she stood up and blew her nose on her paper napkin. "Not unless you want to hold my hand through another divorce."

"What does that mean?"

"Let me put it this way. Right now, you're not exactly on Tom's short list of favorite people," she said and popped me on the arm. "That's OK though, little sister. I still love you. In spite of the fact that your little idea is ruining my marriage." She laughed bitterly and walked to the door.

"Wait a minute." I was trying to think of some sort of compromise. "What if you made a way to keep track of how many times he wanted to do the deed and promised him that you'd make up for each and every time when the strike is over. You could tell him that you weren't sacrificing his needs, you were just postponing them."

She shrugged. "I'll try it, but I don't think it'll work. Listen, I've got to go. Staying here isn't exactly going to make things better."

I nodded with my back to her. I didn't turn around until after I heard the door open and close. Then I got up and locked it and watched out the window as her taillights slid down the hill. When they were gone, I just stood there and watched the darkness. It made me sick to think that this was causing such a rift between the two of them, and it made me sad that my wonderful new brother-in-law was acting like a jackass.

Then, as is my style, I started beating myself up—about my motives, about my judgment, about any personality defect that might have played a part in my decision to become a part of this circus. Whenever my neurons synapse, they usually do it wearing little hair shirts and screaming mea culpa! mea culpa!

It was almost midnight when I pulled back the covers and found the phone receiver buried under my pillows. I set it on the bedside table, but the incessant beep was driving me crazy. Reasoning that no one would dare call so late, I placed it back in the cradle. It rang about two seconds later.

"What do you want?" I growled.

An understated, unmistakably upper-class voice replied. "To tell you that I thought about you the whole time I was in Europe, to let you know that I miss you and to assure you that I'm fighting as hard as I can to save your sweet ass."

Chapter 13

"Oh, Slick, I'm so happy to hear your voice! And what in the hell do you mean you're trying to save my ass?"

"My dear, you have the chairman of this company very upset."

"He didn't appreciate my speech?"

"He called it inappropriate and distasteful."

"Well, the Marquis may not like it, but giving a speech is hardly a firing offense." Slick and I refer to Merrill Kennedy as the Marquis because Slick's wife, Annie, and Louella Kennedy are best friends, and Annie has shared some of the more charming aspects of the Kennedys' marriage. She says that the Marquis de Sade would cringe at the way our venerable chairman treats his wife.

"Not if the speech is to the Atlanta Rotary Club on 'Using the Yield Curve to Predict Short-Term Rates.' If the speech is to the entire world on 'Why Guys Who Knock Their Spouses Around Should Be Cut into Little Pieces,' then you're getting a little personal."

"Well, what's he going to do? Stand up for wife beaters everywhere and fire me?"

He sighed, then after a long silence said, "Were you aware that Merrill and Lawrence Underwood were roommates in prep school?"

"No, where'd they go? Lieutenant William Calley Jr. Academy? Hannibal Lecter High? I'm not afraid of Merrill; he can't do a thing to me because I gave a speech. I have a flawless record—"

"If that were your only problem, I'd agree. But not only is that not your only problem, it's not even your worst one," he said in an ominous tone.

"What're you talking about?"

"I'm talking about Kovacevich's $30 million loss."

"What?!" I choked. "He told me he closed out the positions Monday at the opening."

"I don't give a happy damn what he told you. I got a call from your back office this afternoon, notifying me that they'd hit a loss limit. I couldn't believe it, so I called Allen McDaniel at Salomon Brothers. His guy, George White, had the other side of the trade."

"What'd he say?"

"He confirmed it. Needless to say, I closed out the position."

Now there was no question about it. My ulcer was definitely back. "Who else knows?"

"You and I and your back office."

"This is just charming." The tendrils of panic began to travel from my gut to my chest, around my rib cage, into my heart and lungs. "Now I've got to figure out what to do."

"Well, figure fast. You know company policy as well as I do—all significant losses are reported to the chairman immediately."

"What constitutes immediately?"

"Uh, 9:00 A.M. tomorrow."

"Fine. Don't bother calling, I won't be here. You may, however, reach me at my new job, the cosmetics counter at Eckerds."

"Lauren, we've got a big problem and panicking is not going to help."

"I'm not panicking, dammit, but I need some time. What's the longest you could go without telling the Marquis?"

There was a long silence, punctuated by a long sigh. "I guess I could stall until the department meeting at 11:30."

"Oh, sweetie, you're always on my side. You're the very best friend anybody ever had."

His voice sounded very old when he answered. "I'm doing it for both of us, because if you can't figure out how to fix this by noon, then I'll be looking for a new job too," he said, and hung up the phone.

At least I now had the perfect counterirritant to leading the Lysistrata Movement. I pulled the covers over my head. I even tried to sleep. Hopeless. I got up about 2:30 A.M., went into the kitchen and started working on the puzzle. Stumped by a new section, I picked up the top of the box. What a glorious time, the reunification of Germany. If they could just deal with their inflation . . . I almost knocked over the table in my scramble to get to the den.

A wash of moonlight through the window gave everything in the room a dark blue cast. I went to my desk and entered the Internet. Bright green letters and numbers glowed from the dark screen, and I clicked into World News, scrolling down until I found it. "German Institute calls for tightening of monetary policy." Then again, a half a page down, "Inflation worries put pressure on Germany to raise rates."

I pulled up the screen for World Spot Currency Rates. This is where all exchange rates are posted. I looked past the franc and the yen to the deutsche mark. In tiny neon green letters: *Bank of Montreal: deutsche mark 1.6252 bid against the dollar.* This meant that a trader at the Bank of Montreal was willing to pay one U.S. dollar for 1.62 deutsche marks. I opened the drawer, pulled out the firm's phone directory and, using the dim light from the screen, found the U.K. section. If it was 3:15 A.M. in Atlanta, it was 9:15 A.M. in London. I picked up the phone and dialed.

"Sterling White."

"Ronnie Wells, please."

"Who may I say is calling?"

"Lauren Fontaine."

There was a five-second silence, then, "Barracuda, is it really you?"

Just hearing the voice of my old friend made me feel better. "It's really me, darling. How've you been?"

"Busy." Then he laughed. "I hear you've been busy too. I read in the *Herald-Tribune* that you've become quite a rabble-rouser in your spare time."

"Yeah, well, everyone needs a hobby . . ."

"Still full of surprises." His voice was warm with affection. "It must be quite late there. What is it? You can't sleep and want to chuckle over our old adventures?"

"I'd love to do that, but I think it should be face to face. Anyway, that's not why I rung you up in the middle of the night. I'm calling because I need your help."

"Oh, love, if you want to enlist me in this anti-sex thing, I'm afraid I'm going to have to pass."

"No, I know better than that." I laughed. "I want to make a trade, a big one."

"The champ's coming out of retirement?"

"For one last bout."

"My, my, this should be fun. At least we'll be on the same side this time, and I shan't worry about you tearing me to shreds." Before he'd headed back home to London, Ronnie was the head bond trader for Morgan Stanley and my favorite competitor.

"Do you think the deutsche mark's runnable against the dollar?"

"Absolutely. Inflation is the bloody plague of the German economy. As a matter of fact, our sources are looking for an announcement this morning from the Bundesbank."

That's the German equivalent of our Federal Reserve Bank. "How far do you expect them to go?"

"I expect we'll see the Lombard rate rise from eight percent to eight and a quarter."

"How far do you think that'd send the mark?"

"Well, let's see. The mark is trading at 1.62 to the dollar, if we get a quarter-point rise I think you could see it at 1.41."

I smiled to myself. All I needed was for it to go down to 1.47. "I want to go long the mark."

"Amount?"

"Two hundred million."

"Pardon me?"

"I want to go long the deutsche mark for $200 million. Did you think I'd go back in the ring for an odd lot?"

"Christ, $200 million?"

"Yeah, if you don't want the trade, I can wait for the Tokyo opening and do it there." This is what is known in the financial world as a bald-faced lie. I didn't have time to wait for the Tokyo market to open, but I also knew that my old friend would hate to miss a megatrade. I waited patiently for the answer.

"The market opens here in forty minutes. I'll call you back when it's done."

"Thanks," I whispered, and made my way to my bathroom to see if I could find some old Zantac. I located some that had expired almost eighteen months ago. I figured one would either kill me or make me feel better. Believing either to be an improvement, I took two. Then I went up to Razz's room and sat on his bed. I watched him sleep, stroked his hair and whispered over and over, "I love you so much."

Then I walked to Elizabeth's room, cracked the door and listened to the rhythm of her breathing. I had told her that it would be all right, that I would take care of everything. As I gently closed her door, I sent up a simple prayer, "God, please don't let me be lying to her again."

I was back at my desk in the dark when the phone rang. I jumped. It rang a second time and I picked up the receiver. "You're the buyer of 324 million marks and a seller of $200 million at a rate of 1.62."

"Good work. What kind of action are you seeing?"

"A little sell-side pressure that may be worth a pfennig," he said.

"Honey, I'll take all the help I can get." A pfennig is 1/100th of a mark. The rate had gone from 1.62 to 1.61. On a $200 million bet that would be worth a little over $1 million. One down, twenty-nine to go.

"No doubt. I think we'll see a very narrow trading range until closer to 9:00 A.M., your time." Any central bank announcement about rate changes must come at a prescribed time. An announcement from the Bundesbank about the Lombard rate could only come at from 3:00 to 3:30 P.M., Frankfurt time, just as an announcement from the New York Fed must come between 11:05 and 11:45 A.M., New York time. This spares traders from having to worry every minute about surprise announcements and in turn keeps the markets relatively calm. So if news is expected, most of the trading in that currency will occur right before or right after the thirty-minute announcement window.

"Call me if you see or hear anything."

"Will do." The phone went dead, leaving me alone in the dark.

The dark blue room turned gray, then golden as I watched the screen. I spoke with Ronnie every twenty or thirty minutes throughout the night, mostly about the things that might have an impact on the exchange rate: world news, who was on the buy side, who was selling, what their strategies might be.

At one point, I got really punchy and started pretending to be Merrill Kennedy, except that instead of trading $200 million worth of deutsche marks, I was trading two dollars' worth.

"Yes siree, I have seized this market by the testicles—traders all over the world will quake when they hear that I, Merrill the fearless, have placed my bet . . . not ten cents, not four bits, but two entire dollars. Let no one dare say that Merrill Kennedy is not a large undulating penis."

Ronnie was enjoying the joke. "Merrill, I must confess," he said, laughing, "I didn't think you had it in you. Who'd have ever guessed that you had the guts to come into the market like such a madman."

"Well, I try to keep my nerves of steel hidden lest I intimidate the firm's less-confident traders," I said, and we both fell out laughing.

I realize this doesn't sound all that hilarious in the telling, but the reason it was so funny to us was that Merrill really did consider himself a risk taker in spite of the fact that he'd never taken a chance in his life. Because in our world, your title wasn't what garnered respect, your chutzpah was . . . it wasn't how big your paycheck was but how big your balls were . . . not how blue blooded you could claim to be but how cold blooded. In order to feel equal to the real gamblers in the firm, Merrill had convinced himself that although he had never rolled the dice when the stakes were high, he would if the chance were offered him.

Ronnie and I chuckled some more about what a player Merrill thought he was, then we hung up and he went to grab some coffee and I sat quiet and still and watched the numbers tell my future.

At daybreak I called a cab, and by 7:00 A.M. I was in my glass office in the Sterling White trading room, talking to Ronnie and skimming the *Wall Street Journal.* "Shit!" he yelled in my ear. I looked at the screen. There was a bid from Morgan Stanley for a $100 million at 1.64.

"Goddammit! What in the hell is that?" I yelled back.

"Your ass on a platter!" If anyone took the trade, I'd be down $4 million. "Hold on, I'm calling Mike Eldred to see if this is a trade for their own account." Mike had taken over as the head of trading at Morgan Stanley when Ronnie left and they were as close as fat ladies in a broom closet. I held the phone and looked in my purse for the Zantac. I'd forgotten to bring it. I opened my bottom drawer and pulled out an economy size bottle of Pepto-Bismol. I was unscrewing the top when Ronnie came back. "It's not for their account," he said, pleased.

"Who in the hell is it for?"

"Your old pal John Hollister."

"Swear to God?"

"Cross my heart and hope to die." John Hollister was one of the most notorious arbitrageurs in the history of American finance. He'd made his name and almost a billion dollars shorting silver futures when Bunker Hunt tried to corner the market in '78. But Hollister was also famous on the street for another reason: manic depression. He'd be fine for months, then all of a sudden threaten to kill the chairman of American Express or charter the Concorde and take a hundred Central Park bums to Paris.

"How long has he been out of Menninger?"

"About eight months, I think." Hollister divided his time between Manhattan, Cap Ferrat and The Menninger Clinic in Topeka, Kansas.

"Hold on. I think I'll give the sex machine a call," I announced, flipping through my Rolodex for his number. John Hollister looked like Lurch on the old television show *The Addams Family* but fancied himself a great ladies' man. He had spent the better part of a decade alternately trying to seduce me and cheat me on trades, and I absolutely loathed him.

He picked up his phone on the first ring, and we chatted about the weather and my recent notoriety. A minute or two more of small talk and he blurted, "You are such a sexy little witch, I'm going to buy you a cello! That's it. I want you to stand naked on your equity trading desk and play for me! I tell you what, I'll hire the Philadelphia Orchestra to come play with you."

Bingo. "Gosh, John, that sounds like a lot of fun, but I'm afraid I'm not very musical. Anyway, thanks for the thought. Got to run now. Bye-bye." I hit the lighted button that was flashing. "Crazy as a possum on the freeway. I'll take the other side of that trade."

"The whole $100 million?"

"The whole thing. Call me back."

He was back to me in two minutes, "We got it, and fast enough that it didn't impact the market." I looked at the screen and sure enough the 1.64 had disappeared from the bid side, replaced by 1.62. That was another quick $2 million. I started laughing.

"Don't you feel a little guilty, taking advantage of the mentally disturbed?" He giggled.

"If I did, I wouldn't have been able to trade with half the guys on the street. Besides, I've waited a long time for this, so don't try to talk me out of enjoying it."

"What do you want to do now?"

"Close out the trade."

"Hold on." I waited. I could hear him talking on his other phone. He came back, "You're done."

We were back where we started: 1.62 marks to the dollar. But we had $3 million in profits and had only $27 million more to go. Several of my guys had begun to straggle in, and when I saw Arthur Munroe, I waved him into my office.

"Hey Lauren, glad you're back. Was that really you giving that speech? Everybody's been talking about it. You wouldn't believe how many calls we got Monday morning. The joke on the street is: Why does everybody want to trade with Lauren Fontaine? Because you can be sure you won't get screwed." He narrowed his eyes. "Was this something you planned?"

"No, I didn't plan it, it just kind of happened, kind of a spur-of-the-moment thing." And while he was trying to digest that, I told him about Vinnie lying to me about closing out his positions and about his $30 million loss. He sank into a chair and stared at me. I told him that I'd bet $200 million on the deutsche mark and about the trade with Hollister. He stared at me some more, then shook his head and stood up, "*Un*-fucking-believable."

"My sentiments, exactly. Keep an eye on the equity market and let me know if you see anything that might move the dollar. OK?"

"OK," he said and walked out.

I was so focused on the pale gray machine that I didn't see the man who had reduced my career to a bet on interest rates, standing in front of my desk. He cleared his sinuses and I looked up; he started to speak and I cut him off. "You're fired." I went back to studying the screen.

"Everybody has bad trades now and then. You can't fire me for a bad trade."

I raised neither my eyes nor my voice. "You know exactly why you've been fired, and if you think I am going to debate you on this, you are mistaken. Your assistant has gathered your belongings and they are in the closet in the reception area. You are no longer an employee at this firm."

"I'll sue your ass off. You can expect a fucking lawsuit before lunch."

"You do that and by the time you've finished your second dessert, everybody on the street will know that you lost this firm $30 million in unauthorized trading."

At that point he began to swell and turn purple. "You fucking cunt, you think you can ruin me? I'll show you who'll be ruined!" His voice continued to rise until the glass in the office shimmered from the vibration. "I'm gonna make you pay for this, bitch!"

He was trembling, and it occurred to me at that point that he might really try to hurt me. The image held little appeal, but I didn't budge. In my softest voice, I said, "You do not frighten me. I find your opinions tedious and your threats uninteresting. I have nothing further to discuss with you. You are dismissed."

I was congratulating myself on the "you are dismissed" part. I thought that was a nice touch and I looked up. He didn't seem to think so; his eyes were glassy and there were bubbles of spit at the corners of his mouth. For a moment I stared at him, thinking that if he broke the skin while hurting me, I'd almost certainly have to get a rabies shot.

We stared at each other, and I put my hand on the phone. "If you don't get your repulsive self out of my sight in sixty seconds, I'm going to call building security and have you arrested."

He started to leave, then he turned, walked to the edge of my desk and leaned over it. "You just wait," he hissed. "You just wait. Next time we see each other, I'll be the manager and you'll be on the street."

I stood up and our faces were six inches apart. "I don't doubt that for a second," I said, smiling. "I'll be in the mood for fried fish and hush puppies one night and I'll come through the drive-in window and there you'll be. Now get out."

As I watched him waddle down the hall, the phone rang. It was Slick. "Good morning, Lauren. How'd you sleep?"

"I didn't. I've been a very busy girl."

"Oh? What've you done?"

"Well, let's see. I worked on a 1,000-piece jigsaw puzzle, caught up with an old friend in London, had a chat with John Hollister about his favorite musical instrument, fired Kovacevich and made $3 million of the $30 million back."

"Run that by me again."

"I worked on a 1,000-piece—"

"Not that part, the part about making $3 million back."

"Oh that. Well, so far, I've got trading profits of $3 million." The bright green flashed 1.61. "No, sorry, make that $4 million."

"What's the trade?"

"Two hundred million—deutsche marks against dollars."

"Good God Almighty! $200 million!?!"

"Yeah, we think the Bundesbank's got to raise the Lombard today."

He exhaled. "Is this the editorial 'we' or the royal 'we'?"

"No, we is me and Ronnie Wells." He knew Ronnie, and I could hear the smile in his sigh. "You're not going to report the loss to the Marquis yet, are you?"

"No, I told you I wouldn't and I won't. I've called a closed-door meeting with some of my people until right before the Marquis' little get-together—and left word that I'm not to be disturbed by anyone. That's the only way I can avoid telling him."

"Yeah, but I won't be able to get in touch with you."

"Don't worry, I'll call you right before I go up." Then his voice dropped. "We were scheduled to start five minutes ago and they're all outside my door. I've got to go. I love you and I'm counting on you to do great things. Bye."

As I walked through the trading room it was obvious that everyone knew about my trade. There were thirty computer monitors blinking the World Spot Currency Rates. I stopped at Arthur's desk and we stood together and one by one my guys came over. Some came bashfully, asking a question and staying after the answer, and some came wordlessly and stood at one of the seven terminals on that side of the trading desk. And we watched together.

The rate was now 1.60 and we were up $5 million but there didn't seem to be many buyers. It was 8:40 and the thirty-minute window that the Bundesbank had to lower the Lombard was rapidly approaching. Arthur shook his head and grumbled, "The damn thing's too soft."

"I know," I replied, and to the screen I said, "C'mon, honey, you know what I need."

We watched in silence for a few minutes. 1.59 . . . "That's it, darling. That's so good. Give me more, give me more."

1.58 . . . Arthur was nodding his head, "It's firming up."

1.57 . . . A voice over Arthur's shoulder, "It ain't just firm, it's rock hard!"

The phone rang and it was Ronnie. "The Yanks are beginning to come into the market and it looks like they're all on the buy side." And he hung up.

I turned to Arthur with a grin. "The boys are lining up."

1.56 . . . "Yeeha!" came a whoop behind me. "Looks like a gang bang!"

I was whispering to the screen, "C'mon baby, c'mon baby, c'mon baby." At 1.56 I had $10 million in profits: $2 million from the Hollister trade and $8 million in the original.

1.56 . . . 1.55 . . . 1.56 . . . High-stakes trading is like riding a roller coaster blindfolded. At any second, the thing can move, leaving your stomach in your chest cavity. I'd make $4 million and lose it thirty seconds later, lose $2 million and recoup it in the thud of a heartbeat. My nerves were doing the Watusi . . . and I was having the time of my life.

1.56. I yelled to Lamar Jones, whose screen was two down from me, "Lamar, flip to World News and watch for an announcement from Frankfurt." We waited, as did traders all over the globe. 1.56 . . . and holding.

"Lamar?"

"Nothing!" 1.56 and holding.

"Oh, baby, a little more. C'mon, I need just a little more."

1.57

"Fuck," whispered Arthur.

"Lamar?" I yelled.

"Not a thing." 1.56 . . . 1.57.

The phone rang and I snatched it. "I don't like the trend."

"I don't think it's irrevocable. We've still got fifteen more minutes."

"Still think we'll get it today?"

"Monday, by the latest."

"Ron, darling, that will be of less than no use to me. It's gotta be today."

"Jesus-fucking-Christ, Lauren!! You didn't tell me this was a kamikaze trade!"

"I didn't? Well, it is." 1.57 . . . 1.58 . . .

1.57 . . . Ten more minutes. I held the phone and watched my profits disintegrate.

1.58 . . . 1.59 . . . 1.60 . . . 1.61.

I turned to Arthur, "Who besides Chase Manhattan has lowered their rates?"

"A couple of regionals."

"Not Nations?" He shook his head. "Not Citi? Not Bankers?"

"Hell, those guys love their margins too much. They aren't about to lower their rates until the prime's lowered."

1.62 . . . five more minutes. They weren't going to announce. 1.63.

"Ronnie? You still there?"

"Yeah. Sorry, Barracuda, nobody wins 'em all. Want me to close it out?"

"No, I want to go another $100 million."

"Have you lost your mind? They're not going to announce today!"

"I agree, but that doesn't mean that the Fed won't lower the prime today. That's what the bond market's been anticipating for almost two weeks." I was looking at Arthur and he was nodding his head.

The voice on the other end of the phone turned wary. "Why are you doing this?"

"It's a long story. Place the trade, please."

"I'll be back to you in a minute." Click. He had obviously lost his enthusiasm.

It was 9:30 A.M. and my traders went back to their places for the opening of the New York markets. The rumble of voices grew louder, and I felt as alone as I'd been when I placed the original trade.

There are three things shared by every trading room that I've ever been in: deafening noise, frantic activity and food. The noise of thirty-two traders carrying on a hundred and forty simultaneous conversations, seducing their clients, harassing their assistants and trading the newest jokes with other traders is as loud as a heavy-metal concert and as frenzied as a pit crew at the Indy 500.

"I need a buyer for forty million IBMs . . ."

"Who stole my Dunkin' Donuts?"

"Who'd buy this piece of crap at seventy-five and an eighth for God's sake?!"

Stupid, stupid, stupid. I should have sold at 1.56. If I lose so much as a nickel on this trade, my career's over. Maybe we'll get some run-up before the Fed conducts open market operations. This time, don't try to make back the entire loss. Surely the Fed knows the big banks aren't going to lower rates any more without a drop in the prime. What in the hell am I going to do if this trade turns any worse? $100 million more—what in the hell was I thinking about? Maybe I ought to call Ronnie, cancel the order and close the rest of the trade.

The phone rang. "You're done at 1.62. I hope to hell you know what you're doing!"

"Yeah, me too. Thanks."

"Short at 85 . . ."

"Put me down for a hundred AT&T's . . ."

1.63 . . . 1.64 . . . 1.65. My ulcer had obviously become gangrenous. I was holding my breath to make the pain stop.

"I'll bid you a half . . ."

"Are there any more Egg McMuffins?"

A week ago, my life was fine . . . 1.65 . . . now it's in shambles . . . 1.66. Everybody hates my guts, and I'm going to have to move my family into the Union Mission.

Arthur leaned over. "How're you doing?"

"Fine." *Either way it goes, this is the last trade of the old career.*

"Christ, what an asshole!"

"Five million Floridas at 76 off the bond . . ."

"Rock, what do you have on a ten year?"

I opened one eye and squinted at the screen. 1.64 . . . 1.63 . . .

Fifteen more minutes to go. The trend's back on our side. 1.62 . . . C'mon, little baby, come on back. 1.61.

I was looking at the large strip of screen that hangs above the trading desk. Huge neon dots traveling from left to right announced U.S. business news: MICROSOFT ANNOUNCES RECORD GAINS.

So what else is new? What about the Fed?

"Hey, Edwin! How 'bout the treasury strips?"

1.60 . . . 1.59 . . . please, please, please . . .

"Goldman's a buyer of the 08s at 97."

Across the black screen: CELLCALL COMPLETES STOCK BUYBACK.

Maybe I'll call the chairman of the damn Federal Reserve. 1.59 . . . Nah, he'd probably recognize my name and raise rates just to spite me. 1.60 . . . Maybe I'll call him and make up a name. God, I'm beginning to sound like John Hollister, probably should have gotten the number for Menninger while I was at it.

1.59 . . . The phone rang and Ronnie was back. "They've still got fifteen minutes to announce. How're you holding up?"

"I've become a manic-depressive instead of just a depressive." One of the trading assistants ran over to me. "Mr. Moriarty on line three." I nodded. "Ron, hold on. I'll be right back." I picked up a second phone. "Where are you?"

"Standing at Merrill's secretary's desk. The meeting's about to start. What's the deal?"

"We're up about twelve million."

He exhaled, "Good girl! Have you closed out the trade?"

"No. I'm hoping for a little more run. Twelve ought to be enough to save us though, don't you think?"

"Depends on how angry he is about the Lysistrata thing, but it sure helps. Gotta run. Good luck."

I hung up that phone and got back to Ronnie. "What are you seeing?"

"A little sell-side pressure, maybe two or three pfennigs worth. If we get it, you may want to bail out."

"Yeah, that might be a good idea. Let's see what happens." 1.59 . . .

"So how d'you like being back in the ring?"

"I'm out of shape, I'm winded and all I want to do now is get out of this alive . . ." Arthur popped me in the arm and pointed to the screen. Green neon dots: FEDERAL RESERVE—My heart stopped. LOWERS PRIME RATE 1/4 POINT.

A cheer went up in that room that was so loud I couldn't even hear myself yell. A minute passed, and like the crowd counting down after a TKO, the traders began to call out the numbers as they appeared on the Spot Currency screen. "1.58! 1.56! 1.54! 1.53!"

"Ron, are you there?" I yelled over the din.

"Yeah, I'm here," he bellowed back.

"Close it out!"

"Hold on." Seconds passed, "I got you out at 1.52. Counting the Hollister trade, that's $34 million profit, Winnah and still Champeen!!" He was laughing.

I was laughing. "Thanks, Ronnie, I always knew that together we'd be unbeatable!"

"It's been a pleasure. Take care, Barracuda." And he was gone.

I got up slowly and walked back to my office to a standing ovation. There was no question about it, my luck had definitely turned. The phone rang thirty minutes later. It was Slick. "How'd you come out?"

"Thirty-four million and change. The big question is how'd *you* come out?"

"I talked them out of firing you. But I'll have to tell you, it wasn't easy. I told them that Vinnie lied to you about closing his positions and I told them that you'd made back a chunk of his losses already."

"So everything's OK?"

"For now. I have to tell you these guys are furious about you and this Lysistrata thing. I think the real reason they didn't turn you loose is because they believe your 'little movement' will soon be history."

"Well, I don't give a damn what they think, because I've saved their $30 million so now they don't have any grounds to fire me. Besides, I intend to run this movement from 'behind the scenes' from now on. So, thanks to you, I feel pretty safe. Baby, you're the best."

He laughed, "I could say the same thing about you. But be careful; you've made some real powerful enemies. I've got to run. I love you. Bye."

This is excruciatingly embarrassing to admit, but I spent the next half hour drinking coffee and marveling at my invincibility. Occasionally, I get it in my head that I must have some kind of extraordinary powers that allow me to do things that mere mortals can't.

The phone rang. It was Ali. "Guess what? The greatest thing has happened! . . ."

Of course. What did you expect? "What?"

"I'm so excited I can hardly talk. All our prayers have been answered!!"

"The men have given in?"

"No, not yet. But they will. The movement is starting to be taken seriously, I mean really seriously, and after this, there won't be any stopping us!"

"So don't keep me in suspense. What is this greatest thing?"

"*Time* is doing a cover story on the movement! And guess what?"

"What?"

"You're on the cover! It's going to send our membership numbers to the moon!"

And probably send me to the unemployment line. "Gee, that's super."

"You don't sound very excited."

"Oh, I'm excited all right," I said and swigged the rest of the Pepto-Bismol. "I was just on my way out the door."

"Where you going?"

"To pick up my car at the train station before it either gets broken into or towed."

"Call me later."

"Later." I hung up and was almost to Sherry's desk when Arthur caught me. "Can we talk about who'll replace Kovacevich?"

"Not now. I've got to be out of here by the time the Philadelphia Orchestra shows up," I said and walked through the door.

Chapter 14

"The Most Powerful Person in America?" asked the banner underneath my chin. Razz had brought the copy of *Time* to the breakfast table the next morning, and Elizabeth ordered him to read from it aloud. The picture on the cover was flattering and, shock of shocks, so was the article. It said that Operation Lysistrata was the fastest growing movement in American history. There was even a graph comparing it to the civil rights and the antiwar movements, from origination to mass awareness. This they attributed to the speed of modern information dissemination, especially instant news coverage on TV. God bless CNN and God bless Ted Turner.

It said that local chapters were reporting hundreds of calls a day and that new members were signing up by the tens of thousands. It quoted several congressmen who'd voted not to impeach who said they were following events with great interest. It quoted Ali and Savannah and noted that I had been unavailable for comment.

"Cool," Razz said almost to himself. " Mom, here's a whole separate article about you."

"Yeah? What does it say?"

"Well, it's got two pictures of you," he said, and turned back the page so Elizabeth and I could see. One of the photos was of me standing at the podium and the other was from an old article about me in *Forbes,* where I'm standing at my trading desk in New York. He flipped the page back and cleared his throat. "It says, 'While the world may have been stunned at the women's demonstration march last Sunday, when Lauren Fontaine strapped on the big guns of female power and faced down both Washington politicians and 98 million American men, no one in the financial industry was surprised. For over a decade, the beautiful Ms. Fontaine has been famous on the streets of Lower Manhattan as a shoot-from-the-hip gunslinger.' "

He looked over the top of the magazine and mimed sticking his finger down his throat and we all laughed.

"Read on, read on," I said, still laughing.

He searched for his place. " 'Legend has it that Ms. Fontaine won her place on the trading desk of Goldman Sachs in a poker game with a Goldman partner. During the stock market crash of 1987, she coolly and single-handedly made that firm $58 million in one trading day.' " His expression changed and he looked at me with new eyes. "Is that true?"

"Yeah. You impressed?"

He considered the question. " Maybe. How much of it did you get to keep?"

"Half a million," I said and took a sip of cold coffee.

"You got gypped," he decided.

So much for impressing a sixteen-year-old. Or a forty-two-year-old. "What do you mean *she* got gypped?" Elizabeth said, then looked at me with a raised eyebrow. "Honey, I want a raise."

I grinned and motioned Razz to continue. He did. " 'The thirty-six-year-old Ms. Fontaine is currently a managing partner of Sterling White, one of the world's most prestigious investment firms. She is the only female ever to be named partner in Sterling White's 106-year history.

" 'But what would make even this gambler climb up on a podium and risk all to avenge a woman she never met? Is there something in her past that Lauren Fontaine's not talking about, or is she simply an old-style American hero?' "

Elizabeth stopped Razz to ask for my autograph, and I laughed. The article finished by saying that I was not a known activist, and a surprise to many experts.

Elizabeth announced, "Miss L., I think that's a real positive article."

"Yeah," Razz agreed, "I bet it'll help y'all get a lot more ladies to join the Listerine Movement."

"Lysistrata Movement," I corrected, knowing full well that he knew full well how to pronounce it.

"'Course it just means they still don't think you can make this thing happen," Elizabeth declared. "Once you really start scaring 'em, those folks are gonna turn ugly on you. You mark my words on that."

"So you think we're going to start scaring them?" I asked, pleased to have caught her in an almost-positive comment.

"Maybe. So don't be looking for those men to keep on saying nice things about you and putting pretty pictures of you on magazines."

"What about the part where it said the Senate is considering an inquiry into the way Congress handled the Underwood hearings? That's pretty spectacular, especially considering the fact that the strike has only been going for six days. Yes, indeed! Houston, we have liftoff!" I said and grinned.

"That may be true." She pointed at me. "But what goes up must come down."

"You know what I love most about you, Elizabeth? Your ability to always see the bright side of things."

"There is no bright side of this. That's what I keep trying to tell you."

"The bright side of this is that we're gonna win and that evil man is going to be punished. And the next time some man thinks about beating a woman, he can cogitate on the fate of Larry Underwood and tally up just how much it might cost him. The bright side of this is that we are going to make a difference. And that is the only thing that counts."

"To you, maybe," she said, and removed Razz's plate and started to walk away.

I turned to Razz. "Sweetheart, what's your take on all this?"

"I don't know. I guess I think you're both right. I understand what you're saying about making a difference and that being the only thing that counts, but I think Elizabeth has a good point too. It may just be that we won't know what the right thing was until we see the way it all ends up," he said, staring at the table.

"No!" I said and startled them both. "If you remember only one thing I've ever told you, remember this: There's a big difference between honor and fate, and doing the right thing can never be measured by the outcome of events. Judge yourself by what you do, not by what happens afterward." Then I softened and stood to kiss him on the forehead.

"Like King Arthur and the dudes of the Round Table?" he asked, referring to the book that, at his insistence, I'd read and reread to him every night of his third-grade year.

"Exactly. The greatest treasures are found behind the heaviest doors."

"Or stuck in the hardest rock."

"Spoken like a true knight." I took my knife, wiped it on my napkin and stood. "Kneel, dude!" I demanded imperiously, and he did. "By the power invested in me as"—and I held up the magazine—"the most powerful person in America, question mark, I declare you Sir Razz Do-right Fontaine."

At that point, Elizabeth, who had been watching from the door, yelled, "Boy, don't you have any better sense than to let that crazy woman near you with a knife!?"

"Pay no attention," I commanded. "The proletariat is notoriously distrustful of us noble types."

He leaned closer. "Mom, I don't know what a proletariat is, but I'm pretty sure I don't even want to be in the same house if Elizabeth hears you call her one."

Ali was on the phone the minute we cleared the dishes. "What did you think?"

"Other than the fact they made me sound like a cross between Annie Oakley and Cool Hand Luke, I thought it was a good article."

"Oh, I think so too, you old-style American hero." She laughed. "Anyway, you can't believe how fast things are happening. I keep getting calls from the state coordinators, who are unbelievably swamped with new members. Some of the larger cities already have twenty and thirty groups!" she reported.

"This is fantastic! I mean who could have guessed that this thing would take off like this? Have we heard from anybody on the political side?"

"Nothing direct. Mostly just rumors."

"Like what?"

"Like there have been several closed-door meetings at the Capitol about this. Like we're expecting an official response real soon. If impeachment hearings are reheld, you may be asked to come to Washington to testify."

I was giddy with the thought that the battle was almost over. "Wow. That's so grown-up. Are they really going to give in that quick?" I asked, took the coffee that Elizabeth set down in front of me and mouthed "Thanks" to her as she retreated.

"It's a real possibility. At least that's what we hear."

I took a sip of coffee, and the enormity of our momentum stunned me. I couldn't take it all in. "I'm not believing this, Ali. I keep thinking that I must be dreaming or something."

"Well, if you think that's something, listen to this. We've been contacted by all the major networks, they're begging for interviews with you," she bragged, laughing. "I must admit to being absolutely amazed at how much fun you can have with an unused pussy."

We talked about different reporters and how smart we were, about media strategy and how smart we were, about organizational issues and how smart we were.

"Have you heard from Jake?" she asked.

"No, and he's probably the only person writing about the Underwood story I haven't spoken to. Speaking of that, I better go. I've got six more interviews today and eight on Sunday and I'm rationing both my voice and my enthusiasm."

She laughed and hung up. She thought I was kidding.

It was around noon and I was on the phone with a woman from *Cosmopolitan* when I heard the door behind me close. I turned around. It was Gigi. It wasn't until she got within a few feet that I saw how awful she looked. There was no color at all in her face, just the charcoal circles under her eyes. "I have to talk to you," she mouthed.

I nodded and held up two fingers, signaling that I'd be off in a couple of minutes. As I wound up the interview, I watched Gigi gnaw her thumbnail to the quick. She had given up biting her nails at age eleven.

I hung up the phone and pulled her down on the sofa. "What in the world is going on?" I whispered.

"I'll tell you, but you have to promise you won't get all judgmental."

"I won't get all judgmental."

"Swear."

"OK, I swear. What?"

She sighed, "You know I told you the other night how mad Tom was about me being in the movement. Well, since then, things got worse— a lot worse—and last night he came home and told me if I wouldn't sleep with him, he knew someone who would."

"Oh. And who is that?"

"He wouldn't say. Anyway, I'm pretty sure it's this secretary at his firm. He swore that he hadn't done anything yet, but that he was beginning to think seriously about it."

I wasn't sure if this was the part I had promised to be nonjudgmental about, so I just murmured, "Uh-huh, uh-huh."

"This has just been a nightmare. Lauren, I love him so much and I can't lose him and yet I'd hate myself if I gave in. I have to do this for Sofia," she whispered and began to cry.

"Honey, I don't know what you want me to tell you."

"Tell me what to do!" she wailed.

"All right, but you're not going to like it. Tell him that this is something that you feel is extremely important and you expect his support. Tell him to grow up and suggest to him that if he so much as hints about cheating on you he'll be hearing from your divorce lawyer."

"You're right . . . I don't like it," she said, patting away the tears with the tips of her fingers.

"It's your call. Besides, if I weren't such a hard-ass, I might not have spent all these years alone." The phone rang. I looked down at the list Jinx had faxed me. Six reporters from Associated Press. It rang again.

She stood. "You're busy and I've got to go. I'll try to call you later. OK?"

I nodded and hugged her and picked up the phone on the seventh ring. I watched her walk out, while a man with a Texas twang asked me if I thought anyone was taking the strike seriously.

First thing Monday morning, all my traders were standing at the door, and as I walked through, they bowed deeply and chanted in unison, "Welcome to our humble place of commerce, O Powerful One!"

I looked around the room and raised my hands. "Thank you, thank you, O Meek and Wretched. I accept your lowly welcome and order you back to your menial tasks. And in celebration of my presence, I will allow the minion among you who makes the greatest profit today . . . to kiss my ring!" They all made wildly exaggerated faces and sounds of excitement and scuttled to their seats as I stood there laughing.

Sherry came in to report that the phones hadn't stopped ringing since last Monday morning and she'd taken 208 calls for me. Then she presented me with a stack of message slips about six inches high. I told her to hold all my calls except for Mr. Moriarty or Mr. Ward and started making separate stacks: return now, return later and who in the hell is this anyway?

I kept expecting Slick to call and I was getting worried. At 1:15, I was flipping through a new technical analysis report when Sherry knocked on my door. "I know you didn't want to take any more calls, but it's Mr. Kennedy's secretary. Line three."

I nodded and picked up the ten-thousand-pound receiver. "Lauren Fontaine."

"Ms. Fontaine, this is Mr. Kennedy's secretary. Mr. Kennedy would like you to meet with him and the executive committee in his office at 9:00 tomorrow morning. May I tell him that you'll be there?"

"Yeah, tell him I can hardly wait," I said and started to hang up.

"Ms. Fontaine?" Tentative.

"Yeah?"

"I just want you to know how much I'm rooting for you," she whispered and hung up before I could reply.

The fact that the call was hardly a surprise didn't make it one bit less sickening. I closed my eyes, put my face in my hands and rocked slowly in my seat. I stayed like that for a pretty long time, not really thinking, just feeling scared and sad. Scared and sad and very, very weary.

Finally, I took a deep breath and called Slick. His secretary informed me that he was at a Metropolitan Opera board meeting and wasn't expected in before 4:30. I left him a message to call me at the Park Lane Hotel, took a long look around the room and drove home to pack.

"What?" she asked when I walked in the door.

"I've got to go to New York."

She knew immediately and started in with her routine. "Now you've done it. How many times did I tell you what was gonna happen if you—"

I put up my hands. "Elizabeth, don't. I'm not up to it. You have made your objections to my leading this movement perfectly clear. But I have to do what I have to do so that I can live inside my own skin. I won't walk away from this just because it frightens you. I don't owe you that, and if you love me you wouldn't ask it. That's it. I don't want to hear another word about how bad I am for doing what I'm convinced is the right thing. Got it?"

She bowed back and glared at me. "Girl, you are so stupid you ought to be studied by scientists. I'm not afraid for me. I'm afraid for you 'cause you're the one who's spent the last twelve years trying to get all this money and power so that you and that boy are safe." She was so mad her head was bouncing left and right. "Well, it looks like you put that all up for grabs, and I hope you're pleased." She held up her hands. "That's it. I'm finished trying to talk sense to you. You just do what you're convinced is the right thing, and if it destroys you—"

"I'm only convinced that not doing it would destroy me."

She gave me one deadly look, turned around and walked out of the room. I was trying to decide whether to follow her when Razz walked in. "I thought you were at work," he said.

"I was and I got a call inviting me to a little powwow in New York tomorrow morning with the executive committee. I came home to pack."

"Are they going to fire you?"

"I don't know. They're not exactly thrilled about my involvement in the strike but I'm a partner in the firm. That means that I don't just work for Sterling White, I own part of it. That makes it pretty tough for them to get rid of me." I took a deep breath. "But if they really want to, they can probably find a way."

We walked down the hall and through the French doors in silence, with Razz just shaking his head. "Boy, this is turning out to be the suckiest summer vacation on record," he finally said.

"Anything I don't already know about?" I asked and motioned toward the patio.

He sprawled on a chaise lounge and looked at me. "To tell you the truth, Mom, I'm not even sure where to start. You know how I worked my ass off all spring quarter to get my grades up?" I nodded. "And how I was really looking forward to this summer to relax and spend time with my friends?" I nodded again.

"And, of course, last week was completely shot. So I go to the club this morning to see my friends and play some golf for the first time since all this stuff started. Big mistake! First off, I get followed by at least a dozen reporters. I decide to ignore them. Then they start yelling all this bullshit stuff about you to get a reaction." He was trying to decide whether to repeat what they'd said and decided against it. "Let's just say a couple of those creeps came real close to some free dental work." He held a clenched fist in the air for emphasis.

"Finally, I get inside the clubhouse. Mark has made a reservation for a 10:00 tee time and it's about quarter till. I go to the locker room to get some balls and a towel, and there are about six of these old geezers sitting around playing cards. One of 'em recognizes me and starts in on how stupid this sex strike is and why don't you mind your own business, and then they all jump on the bandwagon about what's the matter with you, ruining everybody's life anyway? On and on and on. The way these old codgers were talking it was like their world was coming to an end.

"I started to ask them why they cared since none of them had probably gotten any in the last century anyway. But I didn't, I just walked away."

"Excellent judgment on your part," I noted.

He shrugged. "So I get to the pro shop and everybody's there—Mark, Gary and Steve. When the guy at the desk sees it's me, our reservation mysteriously vanishes. Some misunderstanding. Mom, it was *so* obvious! At that point, I just said 'Forget it.' and came home."

"That's absolutely absurd!" I said, reaching for the phone. "I'll call the club manager."

He laughed derisively. "Oh, great idea. I'm sure they'll be sooo anxious to accommodate you."

"I get your drift," I said and sat back. "Well, why don't you invite your friends over here?"

"For what? To experience the thrill of being stared at like you were some kind of science project? Or to come place bets on how much longer it takes until Elizabeth snaps and unloads a few rounds into the crowd? Nifty plan, Mom. You call the caterers and I'll send out the invitations."

I couldn't think of a response so we just sat in silence. I could tell there was something else and waited to see if he would start. He didn't. I motioned him to move over and sat down next to him. "I get the sense that there's more to your tale of woe."

"I don't really want to talk about it," he said, studying his hands intently.

I stroked his cheek with the back of my hand, and there was stubble on my baby's face. "If you won't tell, then I won't know."

He turned away so that I could neither see nor touch his face. "I started to tell you the night you got home after the speech but I didn't want to say it in front of everybody."

"Yeah?"

"Well, there's this girl, her name is Lindy Barrett, and I'd almost convinced her to do it."

"Have sex?"

"Yeah, but now she's all fired up about this stupid movement . . ."

"A: This movement is not stupid, thank you, and B: I think you should admire her for standing up for her principles."

"I'm sixteen years old; admiration hasn't got anything to do with this! Principles haven't got anything to do with it! And I don't want her standing up, I want her lying down!" he fumed. "Just when I was finally going to do it, you found a way to ruin it for me!"

"Well, what do you expect. I'm your mother, ruining things for you gives me reason to live."

He exploded. "And why do you have to make a joke of everything? You always want me to talk to you about stuff, then you just try to be funny!"

"I'm sorry. I make jokes when I don't know what else to say. And I do want you to talk to me about stuff, but it sure doesn't mean I have the answers. I've got to be honest, it's hard for me to really put myself in your place 'cause it's been a while since I was your age."

"OK, maybe you're too old to understand, but trust me—this is making me crazy. I'm serious, Mom. I am practically a psychopath," he said and flopped back onto the cushions.

"Sweetheart, believe me, I understand. I'm actually in the same boat."

I don't know which surprised him more, that I was in the same situation or that I'd tell him.

"No shit?"

"I wouldn't exactly make it up. Look, the fact is that just about everybody is in the same boat right now, it's a boat with about a zillion people in it. I don't know what else to tell you except that, regardless of the way things seem now, this won't last forever. I'm sorry about the rest of it but I think you handled yourself beautifully. Now, I've got to go pack." I kissed the top of his head and left him staring at the sky.

B y 12:35 P.M., I was flying down the freeway, trying to make the 1:30 Delta flight, when the idea hit me. Turning around at the next exit, I headed back to the office. "Where's Jamie?" I demanded on my way to the operations room.

Jamie was the operations manager I'd inherited from my predecessor. Pudgy, pompous and pretentious, he had no more of a following than Kovacevich. Maybe even less, if that were possible. He saw me, stood up and adjusted himself, pulling his belt practically up to his armpits. "Can I help you?" he asked as if I were a homeless person who had wandered into Gracie Mansion.

"Yeah, you can help me. I want last week's tape from my phone in the trading room."

"Oh, I'm afraid I don't have it," he said, looking away for an instant.

I stepped forward until we were only inches apart. "May I suggest that you get it. And may I suggest that you do it now."

He backed up and cleared his throat, "I'm sorry, but that's going to be quite impossible as there are no tapes from last week."

"Why aren't there?"

"Storm knocked the power out. No one noticed it until today." I could tell how much he was enjoying this and it made me even angrier.

"Well, if the power went off, then why didn't the trading systems go off too?"

"Because the trading computers have backup power sources and the recorders don't. That's why." His voice had this singsong quality, and I stood very still, imagining how pleasant it would be to throw him out the window and listen to him scream for forty-seven floors.

I tore through Hartsfield and arrived at the gate just in time to see the plane being pushed back. I picked up my bag, cursing under my breath, and went into the bar for a drink and had two. I didn't think a third would help and I still had an hour to kill, so I walked over to the newsstand . . . and stood there in shock. Not only was my face staring from the cover of *Time,* it was plastered all over *Newsweek, People, New York* magazine and a half dozen others. I started humming the tune from the *Twilight Zone,* then walked in and, as quickly as I could, picked up one of each. I don't know if this makes any sense but I was embarrassed to be buying magazines with my face on them. It seemed egotistical or pathetic, like I wanted them for my scrapbook or something. I held out two twenties to the cashier, who never looked up, not even when I whispered, "I need a bag," in a tone more appropriate to a purchase of XXX-rated videos.

The next plane to New York was scheduled to leave at 3:10 but didn't actually taxi down the Atlanta runway until 5:05, which gave me plenty of time to read all about myself. *Newsweek* had a split photo—me on one side and Larry on the other with THE PROSECUTOR and THE JUDGE below.

The article began "Chief Justice Lawrence Underwood is a man comfortable with judging other people but he seems less content when those

roles are reversed. Now he is the defendant and it's his actions that are
under scrutiny. And his most unlikely prosecutor is a thirty-six-year-old
woman who may never have set foot in a courtroom.

"Lauren Fontaine may not know her way around a law library but
she's already swayed a lot of self-appointed jurors with a delightful
combination of Southern charm and Wall Street chutzpah. Neither strident nor whiny, she earned the nation's affection when she burst onto
the scene at the Impeach Underwood March, doing something no other
feminist has ever done in public: laughing. She's Scarlett O'Hara with a
social conscience, a sense of humor and a designer wardrobe. And she's
Lawrence Underwood's worst nightmare."

My armpits started sweating and I checked the byline, then closed the
magazine on the article and heaved a sigh of relief that my mother
hadn't written it. Then, after making sure my seatmates, a woman with
a shrieking four-month-old and a man I would have sworn was Abu
Nidal, weren't watching me, I reopened the magazine and found my
place. I skimmed through the parts about how I won my job in a poker
game and single-handedly saved Goldman Sachs in the market crash
of '87.

"It seems ironic that the famous jurist should find himself the subject
of an almost mythological pursuit of justice. In fact, his accuser went
back to the Greek classics for her playbook: Aristophanes' play *Lysistrata*,
written twenty-five hundred years ago. And Lauren Fontaine could easily be a modern-day Hellenic heroine. She's beautiful and strong and
fearless about mixing it up with the powerful Valhallans . . ."

The other articles were every bit as effusive. Actually, they were amazingly similar. An article in *The New Yorker* compared my deal with Larry
to Javert and Jean Valjean in *Les Misérables*, while *Rolling Stone* likened
it to Lieutenant Gerard and Dr. David Kimball from *The Fugitive*, and
Elle fell back on the old reliable Marcia Clark and O.J. Simpson.

People had on its cover a picture of me taken from behind during the
first applause for the speech. I was glancing over my shoulder and
grinning. I don't know what they did to it but I looked like a damn
movie star. The rest of the photos were pretty good too. I always wondered about how people in magazines always looked so great, how they
never had their eyes shut or their mouths full of food or anything like

that. Anyway, there wasn't a single picture that made me cringe (surely a once-in-a-lifetime event) and I, Lauren Fontaine, was the new media darling.

By the time we landed, my head was so big that I had to be removed from the plane by hydraulic lift.

It was almost 8:00 when I stepped out of the limo and into the hotel lobby.

"Oh, Ms. Fontaine, it's so good to have you back."

"Good to be back, Johnny. Hi, Abe. Hey, Victor."

"Saw you on the news, Ms. Fontaine. You were great!"

"What is this—the opening scene from *Hello, Dolly?*"

No mistaking it—that amused, aristocratic voice was Slick's. I turned around and he was smiling, and now that he was here and I was finally safe, I realized how scared I'd been. He looked smashing, as usual, with his jet black hair combed straight back, his custom-tailored suit hung perfectly on his six-foot-four-inch frame, a pink-and-white striped shirt with white collar and cuffs and an Hermès tie as bright as his smile.

"Yes, Mr. Moriarty, it is. And you should take me upstairs before I burst into song."

He laughed and shook my hand. "I hear that you've been invited to meet with the committee."

We got on the elevator and I pushed the button for the forty-fifth floor. "It wasn't an invitation. What's your read on this?"

"I don't know, I haven't talked to anyone. I was given the memo as I was walking out the door. It seems to me, though, if they were going to give you your walking papers, they wouldn't bring you all the way up here to do it."

"Yeah, I thought the same thing. Maybe there's still reason to hope." I comforted myself as he unlocked my door.

He closed the door, locked it again and turned around. I was right behind him and slipped into his loving arms. We stood like that for a long minute, then he picked me up and carried me over to the bed. Thirty seconds later, his jacket was on the chair and he was snuggled up next to me. "Now do you want to tell me how in the hell this happened?"

I hooked a finger under one of his alligator suspenders. "Well, I heard the story of Lysistrata at a dinner party at Hank's about two weeks ago. Then, as you know, I went to Washington for the march. The leaders of all the women's groups were coming to Ali's house to decide what to do. I told the Lysistrata story to Ali and said I thought it was appropriate for the circumstances. I was really just kidding, but she said they were desperate for a really radical response and she talked me into selling it as an idea to the women and I did. They said since it was my idea, I should give the speech, so I said OK."

"I must tell you I got quite a shock Monday evening when I found out. I was in the Admirals Club at Heathrow. I happened to look over at the television and . . . there you were, announcing a sex strike."

"What did you think?"

"The truth? My first thought was damn it to hell. My second thought was how much you seemed to be enjoying yourself."

"It *was* kind of fun," I admitted.

"Perhaps you could have a new career as a professional speaker," he said.

"I'm hoping I still have my old career."

He pulled me to him. "I know, sweetheart. Me too." Then he rolled onto his elbow. "Did you get any sense from Merrill's secretary about what was going on?"

I shook my head. "Only that she said she was rooting for me. What do you think this summons is about? The money or the movement?"

He scratched his head. "It's definitely the movement, but he's thinking he can make it look like it's the money. The last figure I had when I went into the meeting on Friday was that you'd recouped $12 million. As far as he knows, your office is still posting an $18 million loss. In his mind that's all the ammunition he needs. I bet you fifty bucks he's already promised his old pal Larry that he's going to take care of this. The Marquis is the kind of guy who doesn't want anyone to think he can't keep his women in line."

"Well, I sure hate to be the one to break it to the Marquis, but I'm not his woman." I shivered at the thought. "And as far as keeping me in line . . ."

"I could tell him his chances there are slim and none. I think we ought to be prepared for a fight, or should I say an ambush?"

"What do you mean?"

"I've seen Merrill in action and confrontation is not his usual MO. He doesn't, excuse the expression, have the balls."

"What about the rest of the executive committee? Any read on them?"

He shrugged. "Not really. The thing to remember about these guys is that whatever else you can say about them, and frankly that's not a lot, they are smart businessmen. They know you've made us a huge amount of money over the years and they know you did the same thing for Goldman Sachs. More importantly, they know you're dependable. You're not some flashy kid who'll make a fortune this week and lose ten fortunes next. Maybe they just want you to reassure them that you're still you—that you haven't gone off the deep end."

"I can do that. But can we talk about something else? I'm really kind of sick of this whole thing." I reached over and examined his cuff link. "So what do you want to talk about—opera?"

"I've spent all day long talking about opera," he said and freed the engraved gold disk from his shirt and handed it to me.

"Well, what's your position on the theory that Don Cornelius bobs his head like this because he isn't really a man, he's a marionette?" I challenged, doing my best Don Cornelius impersonation.

"That's ridiculous. I happen to think that Mr. Cornelius is the greatest thinker ever to come out of the London School of Economics. And anybody who says he's a puppet of the Keynesians is just plain wrong."

"I didn't say puppet, I said marionette. And besides, Don Cornelius isn't an economist, he was the host of *Soul Train* for about twenty years."

"I know that. I was just testing you. Actually, Don's a very good friend of mine. I was the best man at his wedding," he said and took my hand and brought it to his lips.

"Do tell?"

The phone rang and I was trying to stop giggling as I picked up the receiver. "Yes?"

"Lauren? It's Jake. You sound like you're in a good mood and I bet I know why. I just got finished with a stack of about twenty magazines, all with you on the covers. Nice articles, great pictures."

"Thanks. I hope it'll help," I said in my most neutral voice.

"Lauren?"

"Yes?"

"You're not alone, are you?"

"No."

"Your friend Slick?"

"Uh, yeah."

"Sorry to bother you." Click.

I dropped the receiver. It missed the cradle and bounced off the table and onto the floor. I leaned over, picked it up and slammed it down hard.

"Who was that?"

I wanted to make it his fault or to pick a fight. I glanced over my shoulder to say something hurtful and saw that there was nothing in his eyes but love and concern. "Jake Ward."

He sat up against the headboard and studied me. "I didn't know you even knew him."

"I met him a week or so ago."

"I don't like the guy, I don't trust him."

I rolled my eyes. "For God's sake, you don't even know him."

"I know everything I need to know about that guy. He's a damned opportunist! He didn't have the balls to go to war, but that didn't stop him from making a career cashing in on it."

"He didn't go to war because he thought it was immoral. And he didn't cash in on it, he wrote about it. He did what he thought was right, just like you did."

"Well, why was he calling you?" His back was ramrod straight, and he wasn't even looking at me.

"To tell me that he read all the stuff about me in this week's magazines and that he thought it would help the movement."

"And he thinks that it's a good idea for you to lead this movement?"

"Yes, he does and I take it from the question that you don't."

"That is correct. I don't. I wasn't going to say a word about it or do anything but be supportive of you, but since you asked—I think it's a terrible idea."

"I thought that you were a great advocate of women's rights."

"I am and you know it. I just don't want you to get hurt. I couldn't stand it if anything happened to—"

"I know," I whispered, putting my finger to his lips, "but I'm doing what I think is right. Besides, I think we're going to win."

"Not a chance," he said as if the decision rested with him and he'd already made up his mind.

I raised my eyebrow as far as it would go. "I am very curious to hear your reasoning for such an obviously flawed prediction. Not that I would put much store in the prophecies of a man who doesn't even know who Don Cornelius is."

"First of all, one doesn't have anything to do with the other. Do you think that we great prognosticators all sit around watching *Soul Trade*? We do not. We are much too busy foretelling the future, thank you. Now, to answer your question. You are not going to win because you underestimate men."

"I didn't think that was possible," I said, standing up and starting to pace.

"Well, it is. Seriously, sweetheart, I don't think you have any sense of how unfair this feels to men. In the last twenty years, everything has changed, and whether you and your pals believe it, most men have tried hard to be accommodating. We never seem to get any credit, though, just new charges and new demands. No women's group that I know of has ever stopped and said, 'Gentlemen, we've called for a lot of changes and we've still got a long way to go, but thanks for what you've done, what you've improved.' "

He reached out for me and I came around to his side of the bed. Then he motioned for me to sit. "No amount of change is ever enough or fast enough for the oppressed, but you might stop and think that there are a whole lot of men who are genuinely trying. And you are really pissing them off right now with this 'Let's work this out as enemies instead of allies' approach."

I started laughing. "Honey, I hate to break this to you, but you sound exactly like Jake Ward."

"I don't take that as a compliment and I thought you said that he was for you leading this thing."

"He thinks that it's what I was born to do, that it's my destiny. And I don't know what your problem is about Jake. I'm sure under different circumstances, you two would be great pals." I didn't know whether or not that was true, but I enjoyed taking his favorite little expression and serving it back to him.

He stiffened. "You are absolutely wrong. I have nothing in common with that son of a bitch."

Dread filled my lungs and forced the words out. "You have more in common than you think."

"Such as?"

"Me."

He looked at me, then closed his eyes. "What is that supposed to mean? Are you seeing this guy?" He opened one eye and I nodded. He put his hand to his face. "Are you sleeping with him?"

I put my hand on his exposed wrist. "I'm not sleeping with anyone right now, remember?"

He lowered his hand to break contact with mine. "Oh, yeah. Well, maybe this movement isn't such a bad idea, after all."

"Slick, he cares about me."

"Are you sure that it's you that Jake Ward cares about? And not the chance to relive his faded glory through your leading this movement? Maybe that's why he's so hot for you to be the militant of the year."

The accusation felt like a small-caliber bullet. "Yes, actually I am sure, because he cared about me before I even thought about leading the movement. I also know the last thing he wanted was for me to become a public figure. So thank you for your concern."

He pulled me back to him. "I should just keep my mouth shut, and I'm sorry. I just don't want that bastard to have you. I know that I made the choice that keeps me from having you and that I should hope things work out between you two, but I don't. I'm sorry I can't even pretend to be decent about it, much less noble."

"It's OK. Don't worry about it," I said.

"Well, I better go," he said and kissed me on the forehead. "See you tomorrow morning at the office." Then he picked up his jacket and opened the door. "Now you can call your friend Jake. And by the way, tell him I still love you." Then he was gone and I lay there alone and marveled at my ability to wound two men by simply answering the phone. I called Jake back but he didn't answer and his machine never picked up.

It was midnight when the phone rang. It was Gigi. "He's gone," she sobbed.

I turned on the bedside light and sat up. "What happened?"

"He came home and tried to make love. He was so romantic and sweet, but I stopped him and tried to explain why I couldn't. He turned beet red and started screaming. Then he just got in the car and took off."

"Don't let this freak you out," I said. "Just let him blow off some steam. He'll probably stop someplace for a beer, talk to other guys, see he's in the same situation as everybody else. They'll commiserate together, he'll realize he's being a jackass and come back asking your forgiveness."

"Do you really think so?" She didn't sound convinced.

"Sure. He'll be home before you know it." I didn't know what to tell her and that sounded reasonable. "Tell you what. If he's not home in an hour, call me back."

She did. All through the night, she called. More and more panicked, more and more hysterical. I was awake all night.

At 6:30 A.M., I flipped on the TV. It was clear the other side had chosen its strategy.

"When reached for comment, Justice Underwood said that he found Sunday's march offensive and cruel. 'I have not been charged with any crime and I am the subject of a carefully orchestrated plot to discredit me. I would like to be left alone to mourn the loss of my beloved wife.' "

I addressed the set. "You're just mourning the fact that you don't have anybody to beat up anymore, you sonuvabitch!" I said. "Now you'll have to make do with torturing small animals and pulling the wings off insects."

The phone rang and it was Ali, obviously watching the same channel. "Nothing like a little righteous indignation from a murderous sleazeball to start the day." She stopped so that we could hear what came next.

". . . the powerful Speaker of the House, Don Gertchen, who called the sex strike a militant response from the political left." The broadcast went to split screen, and there was my photo next to that of the Speaker of the House. I hit the volume button on the remote. There he was in person, with his Play-Doh face and his Kewpie doll lips, spitting into the camera. "This is a blatant attempt by the President and his partners to unconstitutionally remove the chief justice of the Supreme Court and replace him with another of his liberal cohorts."

I made a face of disgust for the benefit of the mirror behind the TV.

"What are you thinking?" Ali demanded.

"My first thought is how come nobody ever told me that I'm the President's partner. My second thought is if I am the President's partner, why haven't I ever been invited to the White House? My third thought is that if this is the tack they're taking, they're not planning to negotiate. They're getting ready for a fight."

"You're right," she said. "By accusing the President of being behind this, they're trying to reframe the issue, paint this as politics and take the heat off ol' Larry."

"Your basic accuse-them-of-what-you're-guilty-of trick," I noted.

"Yeah, and the worst thing the President can do is get caught up in their web. We need to get ahold of him and tell him to stay the hell out of this."

"Hold on a second," I said. "I, for one, wouldn't mind having the Prez on my side."

"No can do," she declared, as if the President of the United States reported to her personally.

"No can do?" I repeated with enough sarcasm to stop her before she sent another word screaming through the fiber optics.

"Lauren, we can't let them make this about the Speaker vs. the President or the conservatives vs. the liberals. It's got to stay about American women vs. Lawrence Underwood and the men who would let him get away with what he did."

I took a deep breath. "So what are you going to do—call up the leader of the Western world and tell him to keep his mouth shut?"

"Of course not," she said. "I'm going to get Savannah to call and tell him."

The elevator opened onto the eighty-sixth floor, and I stepped into the lobby of the chairman's office. Standing there was a trim, well-dressed woman in her late fifties who studied me for a long second.

"Excuse me, but aren't you Lauren Fontaine?"

Her face was very familiar and I was racking my brain trying to figure out who she was. "Yes." I smiled.

"We've met before, but you probably don't remember," she said. "I'm Louella Kennedy, Merrill Kennedy's wife." I thought about offering my condolences, but she smiled and pulled out a red chip. "I'm a member of your movement."

I grinned. "Fantastic! But it's not *my* movement, it's *our* movement. How's it going?"

"I'm saying *no*—and my husband is berserk," she confided.

I laughed. "How about you? How do you feel?"

She grinned and her eyes filled with tears. "For the very first time in my entire life I'm saying *no*. I spent the last fifty-seven years saying *yes*, regardless of how I felt or what I needed. Now that I'm saying *no*, I feel like the most powerful person on earth and I want to thank you for that." And she leaned forward and hugged me. I hugged her back, the elevator door opened and she stepped in and was gone.

I was thinking about her words as I stood at the enormous window and watched the sun reflect off the tiny Statue of Liberty below. If she was a member of the movement and it made her the most powerful person on earth, I'd just been made the least powerful person on earth. That thought so sickened me that the receptionist had to repeat it twice:

"Mr. Kennedy and the committee are ready for you now."

Chapter 15

Outside, it was a blistering, cloudless day, but the room was cool and dark and smelled of Dunhill cigars and big decisions. "Lauren, please come in. So nice to see you." Merrill Kennedy took me by the arm and led me to the table as if we had run into each other at the bar of the New York Yacht Club. "I believe you know all these gentlemen."

Merrill went to the head of the ebony table that had once been Napoleon's. I knew that because he'd told me the story at least twenty times. I took my place at the other end, declined the coffee offered and asked for a scotch instead. There was a moment of silence while they decided that I had made a joke, then an appreciative round of fake laughter.

"Lauren, we've asked you to come today to talk to us about this very troubling situation." Merrill looked at me for some reaction and I gave him none. "This firm prides itself on the many contributions that we make to the financial infrastructure of this country. A strong capital base is the foundation of all of those contributions. You have jeopardized our capital base and therefore our ability to honor our responsibilities to the American financial markets."

This really was too much; I was a full partner in this firm, not some errant peon. I smiled. "So what's the charge? Treason?" I looked straight in his eyes and caught in peripheral vision the looks that passed across the table.

"Lauren, I am only trying to explain to you the seriousness of your $30 million loss. Now, J.T. assured us on Friday that you had recouped a portion of it, and I sincerely hope that is still the case. I—"

"While we are explaining things to each other, I should say first of all that I am fully aware of the seriousness of such a loss. The second thing I feel I should point out to you is that the $30 million loss was not mine. It belonged to Vincent Kovacevich. The third, and surely the most important point, is that I recouped the entire thing."

For someone so concerned about the trading loss and what it might mean to his ability to be a good American, he seemed neither very surprised nor very happy at the news. All eyes turned to our leader, who took a long and leisurely sip of his coffee.

I then reminded myself that I couldn't afford the luxury of a fight with the chairman so I said in my most soothing and diplomatic voice, "Merrill, I'm sorry. I know that our capital is the lifeblood of our firm and that its protection is ultimately what we are all here for. Let me assure you that Thursday's $30 million loss was Friday's $4 million profit."

Marshall Cabot swung his bald head around and tilted his pointy little chin until he could look down the entire length of his long nose at me. "I, for one, am unclear on whether you cleared $4 million or $34 million."

"Thirty-four million."

I expected a round of applause or at least some kind of appreciation for what had been a spectacular piece of work, if I do say so myself. No such applause was forthcoming.

"I see. And just how much of the firm's capital did you have to risk to accomplish this?"

"What difference does it make?" Slick demanded and adjusted his shirt cuffs. "I, for one, am unclear on the point of this meeting. Kovacevich lost us a potful of money and Lauren made it back. And then some. Are we here to give her a bonus or beat her up about it?"

Merrill smiled patiently. "J.T., we're indeed pleased about Lauren's luck, but Marshall has a valid point." Then he turned to me and waited for me to speak. I stared at him long enough for him to figure out that I was offering nothing. "Lauren, how much of our money did you have at risk?"

I couldn't believe he was acting like I'd found $34 million in an old coat pocket. Anyone else at this firm who'd made that kind of money on a trade would be held up as a great hero and invited to take a chunk of it home. "Making $34 million in a day trade takes more than luck," I said.

"Of course. And I didn't mean to infer otherwise. But how much of our money did you have at risk?"

"Three hundred million."

Merrill leaned forward. "My goodness, Lauren, do you understand the enormity of the risk that you took with our money?"

The way he said our money made it sound like their money, which really pissed me off. It was like he'd suddenly forgotten that I was a partner. "Correct me if I'm wrong, but I thought that risking large amounts of capital in hopes of large profit was the function of this firm. I had assumed that's what we pay all these traders to do with *our money*."

"Yes, but $300 million! If you had lost that amount of money, you could have bankrupted this firm!" Marshall bellowed.

"If I had jumped from the top of this building, I could have landed on the shoe-shine man. If I had invented electricity, I could have been Thomas Edison. If I—"

Slick held up his hand for me to stop. "This is the stupidest conversation I've ever heard. Lauren has authorization to have $350 million in the bond market at any time. And since when do we call an executive committee meeting to rehash a trade, especially one that made us $34 million? If there is another point to this, then let's get to it. If not, then let's get back to work." He pushed back his chair and I held my breath.

"Sit down, J.T. There is another point, and if you're not too busy, I'll make it. My real concern about this situation is the lack of supervision that allowed us to teeter on the edge of disaster. Lack of supervision has destroyed and almost destroyed much larger firms than this one. Do I need to remind you about what happened to Salomon Brothers and their unauthorized purchases of treasuries, or E. F. Hutton and their check-kiting fiasco and of course, there was Kidder Peabody . . . not to mention Barings Bank."

I swallowed my anger, but its bitter gray taste lingered. "I understand your point and I agree. What you're saying about the dangers of lack of supervision is true. However, it was simply not the case here." I looked at Slick and he nodded.

"That's right," he said. "Lauren and I had discussed this matter and—"

I interrupted. "I had told Kovacevich twice to hedge or close the positions. On the Friday before last, I ordered him to pull out of the positions. On the following Monday, he told me that he was out. 'I closed the cocksucking positions,' were his exact words to me."

It made them flinch but it didn't save me. T. Arnold Howard, who was sitting on my left, leaned close enough to give me an ear exam and hissed, "Yes, but did you see him enter the order?"

I was at a loss to see what one had to do with the other and annoyed to have to answer such a stupid question. T. Arnold Howard was an idiot. He didn't know anything about even the simplest of procedures because he'd never set foot on a trading floor.

"No, I didn't see him enter the order. I'm the managing partner, not the order clerk. I told him to close the positions and he told me he had."

"So." Marshall smiled. "It's your word against his." He shimmied with excitement like a dog who's about to have a ball thrown.

I looked at Slick, who shook his head.

"What do you mean it's my word against his?"

"Vinnie and I have spoken," Merrill announced and rared back in his seat. "He has a very different memory of your conversations."

I raised an eyebrow and leaned back in my seat, "And I bet you're just dying to tell me about it."

"Sarcasm is so unappealing, Lauren, and so unnecessary. Vinnie says that you did have a conversation on Friday, a week ago, and during that conversation you did express some concern about the markets, but that you never ordered him to close out the positions. He assures me that he never told you that he'd closed the positions nor does he have any recollection of any conversation with you on the following Monday. Since you weren't even in the office that day, I have to say that I'm inclined to believe him. Maybe you were too busy posing for magazine covers to check on the position that almost destroyed this firm."

I wanted to say *Gosh, Merrill, you can beat up your wife and still have time to run this firm—why don't you think I can pose for a picture and still have time to check on a bond position?* but I didn't. Instead, I said,

"First of all, I didn't pose for any magazine cover, secondly, the photographs you're referring to were obviously taken on the previous day—a Sunday, a day the market is closed. Thirdly, the conversation that Mr. Kovacevich has so conveniently forgotten, took place over the telephone, a wonderful invention that allows two people to communicate from different locations. And hasn't it occurred to you that losing this firm $30 million in an unauthorized trade, a bit of a career killer, might give Kovacevich a reason to lie to you?"

"Just as it has occurred to me that failing to supervise a trader, also a bit of a career killer, might give you a similar motive."

I smiled, reached into my handbag, pulled out a tape and held it in my fist. "I guess we really need to hear the conversations in question. Thank goodness for those voice-activated recorders in the trading room."

Several jaws softened, and out of the corner of my eye, I saw Slick trying to suppress a smile. It was a flawless bluff and I loved every second of it. Which is precisely how long it lasted. I glanced at Merrill, whose face was as radiant as a high-stakes winner at Caesar's Palace. "I'm not certain what it is you have in your hand, Lauren, but I am quite certain what it is not."

My heart had dropped into my stomach, which was diligently trying to digest it. "Oh?"

He looked around the table, "Ms. Fontaine would like you to believe that she has the tape of her conversations with Vinnie. She doesn't. Due to a power outage, there were no recordings that week."

He had called my bluff, so I called his. "Why Merrill, how in the world would you know that?"

"I know because I asked for them Friday morning."

"Really? But you didn't even know about the trade until Friday noon."

"I misspoke. I mean Monday morning, yesterday morning," he said and took another sip of coffee.

Slick came out of his seat, thundering. "That's enough, goddammit! First you were concerned about the $30 million loss until there was no loss. Then you were horrified by the capital at risk, until you remembered that is the business we're in. Next, you were appalled by this alleged lack of supervision, and when you found that not to be the case, you had the tapes destroyed. I've had enough of this bullshit and I'll not sit here and watch you set her up!"

Jaws dropped. No one had ever seen John Moriarty lose his cool. There was a long silence while they looked at each other, then Merrill, who was more surprised than anyone, rose slowly. "J.T., you're absolutely right. This discussion has gotten out of hand and I take responsibility for that. I'm very sorry, Lauren. You probably feel like you've just lived through the Spanish Inquisition, but I promise you that's not why we asked you here."

Slick looked at me for a signal and I gave a little shrug and he sat down.

"Thank you," Merrill said, and he sat down too. "You know, when I first learned of this situation, the thing that hit me was how horrible I would feel if anything bad happened to this firm. I realized, maybe for the first time, just how proud I am to be associated with this company and how important it is to me to protect its great reputation." His performance was credible; not a lot of range, but pauses in all the right places and a nice little emotional vibrato. "We are unique in this industry in that there has never been even a whisper of a scandal associated with our name."

My right foot was falling asleep, so I slipped off my shoe and started rotating my ankle and flexing my toes while Merrill continued his soliloquy.

"The name Sterling White is known around the world for its history of integrity and discretion. When I was faced with the possibility of having that name and that reputation tarnished on my watch, I was sick." Another pause of heartfelt emotion. "And it made me realize what an enormous responsibility I have to the founders and the partners and the employees of this fine organization.

"That really got me thinking about how we've avoided the pitfalls that have damaged others, and I've come to the conclusion that it's because we've never let our egos get in the way." At this point, heads began to bob in agreement. "This is not a crowd that feels the need to call attention to itself—either as a group or as individuals. There is not one of us at this table who would ever allow our own agendas—social or political—to interfere with our responsibilities as stewards of this firm's reputation."

More head bobbing, and his expression changed to one of great sadness. "We value the job that you've done for us in Atlanta. I really mean that, Lauren. Frankly, if we didn't, you wouldn't be here now. We would sincerely like to work things out with you, but I must be candid. We will not allow you to use this firm to gain credibility for your ridiculous little movement."

"At what point in my speech or the press conference that followed did I ever mention this firm or make any reference to it? Not once. Not one time."

Merrill ignored the question. "I don't know how my colleagues feel about this, but frankly, I think that your whole involvement in this thing is a terrible embarrassment and your tour in the media is unconscionable."

"A horrible embarrassment to the firm," Marshall agreed.

"Unconscionable," Arnold hissed, amidst more head bobbing.

That did it. I smiled and in my most unemotional voice, I said. "Well, since we're sharing our thoughts on each other's behavior, let me tell you what I think is unconscionable." The smile left neither my face nor my voice. "I think your hypocrisy is unconscionable. You never let your egos get in the way? I think it's more accurate to say that your egos are never out of the way. And if they were laid end to end, they could stretch around the earth thirty-seven times and still reach halfway to the sun."

I shook my head sadly and looked around the room. "You're not a crowd that feels the need to call attention to yourselves? You have to be the only people alive who don't even know that the '80s are over."

I pointed down the table at Merrill. "You know, Merrill, I noticed that the new *Vanity Fair* issue also has an article about you. I read it on the plane. If you don't feel the need to call attention to yourself," I said, "explain why the readers of *W* and *Town and Country* are alerted every time you go to the bathroom, and the readers of *Architectural Digest* can describe in detail where you do it.

"Not one of you would ever allow your own social or political agenda to interfere with your responsibilities to this firm?" I turned to Arnold and smiled sweetly. "What about you? By acting as the finance chief to that miserable little racist in his pathetic mayoral bid, you cost this firm tens of millions in lost underwriting fees for New York bonds."

I turned around and flashed a grin at Marshall. "And you, who have used your position as vice chairman to put the squeeze on everyone who wants to do business with this firm—all to raise money for that ridiculous prep school so you can stay on the board and keep your sons from being expelled . . . again."

They stared, mouths agape. All except Slick, who was focusing intently on the gilt ceiling, alternately cringing and trying not to laugh out loud.

"I have had as much of this as I intend to take. I'm a full partner in this firm and I don't much care what you like. You've got ten seconds to tell me what you think you can do about it or I'm leaving."

Merrill exhaled slowly. "I'm sorry you find us so distasteful."

"Seven seconds . . ."

"Well, since your patience seems to have worn thin—I'll put it simply. If you want to stay a partner in this firm, you're going to have to resign as head troublemaker of this movement."

"That's it? That's the deal?"

"That's the deal."

"No can do."

"Then I'm afraid I have no choice but to call for a vote to terminate your partnership here. All in favor, raise your hands."

Every hand but mine and Slick's found the air.

"Done. You are neither a partner nor employee of this firm. Effective immediately. You will be replaced by Mr. Vinnie Kovacevich," he said matter-of-factly.

I felt like someone had cut out my heart with an X-Acto knife. I took great care not to look at Slick. I knew I couldn't survive it. Down the table, sad mouths in satisfied faces. They seemed to want to savor the moment, but I wasn't really in the mood to share it with them.

I located my shoe, slipped it back on and stood, in one movement, then I forced a smile and said, "Well, thanks for the memories. My attorney will be in touch with you in the morning to negotiate a severance package as well as the sale of my stock. So you might want to take the time to agree on an appropriate number while you're celebrating." I walked out and closed the door.

I stood for a long time outside the door, trying desperately to keep my composure. When I finally looked up, Mr. Kennedy's secretary was watching me and I shook my head. She shook hers too. "I'm so sorry," she croaked. And my tears fell from her eyes.

A few minutes later, I was wandering around the news shop in the lobby. A terrible tourniquet of numbness was wrapped so tightly around my chest I could catch only the shallowest of breaths.

"I'm glad I found you," he whispered, out of breath. "I was afraid that you'd just wander off."

I considered that. "I didn't know where to go. Meeting's over?"

"Yeah. It was certainly unpleasant, but I thought you handled it beautifully," he said, and hugged me for the very first time ever in public.

"What happened after I left?"

He cleared his throat. "A couple of things. First, we approved a severance package that I think you'll find very generous."

"Thanks, that'll help. Then what?"

"Then I resigned."

I pulled back to see if he was joking. "You what?"

"I resigned," he said and shrugged. "Did you think I'd sit through that debacle, go back to my office and have a cup of coffee and read the *Journal?*"

"Honey, you can't just walk away!"

"Not only can, did. Couldn't think much of myself if I stayed. Besides, there are lots of other jobs . . ."

"Maybe for you, 'the rich and restless heir to the Moriarty fortune, friend to Presidents, revered on Wall Street for his integrity,'" I said, quoting verbatim a recent *Barrons* article. "Not for me, order-clerking, magazine-posing, reputation-tarnishing, jeopardizer of the American way."

"OK, OK. So you're ruined forever." He laughed. "Don't make such a big deal over it." He put his arm around me and we walked through the lobby, to the entrance that said in tasteful brass letters: Please Use Revolving Door. We didn't.

"If worse comes to worst, you can always become a kept woman. I'll put you up in a fabulous apartment at the Carlyle . . ."

"Can Razz and Elizabeth come too?" I asked, stepping carefully on pavement so uneven it might be an ancient Byzantine mosaic.

"If it makes you happy, they can come. I'll shower you with exquisite jewels from Harry Winston . . ."

"Can I have a tiara?"

"If it makes you happy, you can. You can lie around all day eating bonbons and wearing silk robes . . ."

"Can I get a white silk robe with caribou feathers?"

"If it makes you happy. But caribou is a member of the moose family. You may prefer marabou feathers on your lingerie."

"Yeah, that too. But what will you expect of me in this arrangement?"

"For you to make me happy in return," he said.

"Oh yeah? How?" I asked, doing a little matador side step to avoid a courier on skates.

"Nonstop sex."

"Sorry, I belong to the Lysistrata Movement."

He sighed deeply. "Well, in that case, I'm afraid your pretty little ass is on the street."

"Unconditional love—how romantic!" I laughed and felt the tourniquet loosening.

"So," he said. "What do you want to do now? Talk to your lawyer? Call some headhunters?"

I shook my head. "I'll do that later. Right now I'd just like not to have to think about it. Let's just do something stupid, something to take my mind off the fact that those cretins have stolen my job."

"In that case," he said, "I have just the thing. Follow me."

He led me into the cool shade of the giant buildings, purchased a bottle of Taittinger, then we made our way onto the Staten Island ferry. I hadn't eaten breakfast and was drunk before I'd finished my third slug of champagne. I snuggled next to him and tilted my face to the sun. For someone who had just been ruined, I didn't feel too bad.

"I've got a question for you."

My eyes were closed. "Shoot."

"What was the deal with the tape?"

"A bluff. I knew that Merrill knew Vinnie was lying, so I figured he'd see the tape in my hand and assume it was the real one. I didn't know he'd already asked for the real one."

"Well, if the one you brought wasn't real, then . . ."

"Edith Piaf. I grabbed it out of my glove compartment at the airport."

"I see." He took a swig, kissed the top of my head and whispered, "Back in a minute." My eyes were still closed and the sun was warm on my face. The pressure around my chest was fading and I tested it by taking deep breaths. Then lilting music and the voice of the Little Sparrow. "May I have this dance?"

I blinked my eyes open as he set down a huge black boom box, playing music from *Paris Night*, and I stood and he took me in his arms. "Where'd you get the tape player?"

"Rented it from a couple of teenagers inside." He pulled me closer and we danced. The dark water of the harbor glimmered, and he picked up the bottle, tipping it up for me to drink as Edith Piaf sang *"Je ne regrette rien."*

Slick knows all the words and he sang them to me. Three tiny little girls giggled and gawked, an elderly tourist couple were alternately swaying to the music and shooting everything in sight with their camcorder and the Staten Island waitresses and bookkeepers watched with unabashed delight: a Harlequin Romance come to life. The spots of sun and water whirled around me and I kicked off my shoes, opened my mouth for more champagne and danced unrepentant into the light.

The ferry docked, the teenagers reclaimed their box, we bought return tickets and somewhere in the terminal of the New Jersey Port Authority, the magic disappeared. The diesel fumes and the oily water disgusted me, and the champagne was warm and made me sick but I drank it anyway. Slick was still trying. He put his arm around me and rocked gently but I didn't feel like moving and the sun on his wedding ring hurt my eyes, so I closed them and I wanted to be alone and he knew it.

"You're exhausted. Why don't you go back to the hotel and take a nap. I think I'll go get a *Journal* and check the want ads."

"Yeah, right."

"It's going to be fine, sweetheart. I promise. You just need some time to get your thoughts together, talk with your attorney, figure out how you want to handle this, and I need to go to Greenwich and break the news."

I nodded. Neither one of us knew what to say. I started to hail a cab and he caught my arm. "I love you," he whispered.

"I know. And thanks for today."

"I thought we had a chance there for a while . . ."

"Me too." I was blinking back tears and turned away. I wanted to be alone, but I didn't want to be alone while he was in Greenwich. He held out his handkerchief.

A friend of mine once told me that her lover's wife counted his handkerchiefs. I never forgot that. It summed up the entire exercise so exquisitely. Every woman who loves a married man has her collection of handkerchiefs; enough handkerchiefs to make a sail and take a tall ship across an ocean of tears, enough handkerchiefs to wrap around herself, like a mummy, carefully preserved in a state of perpetual hope.

I looked at the handkerchief and I looked at him and I shook my head. That was it. If he needed to go to Greenwich, he needed to stay in Greenwich. Why did I let this happen again and why did it never seem to hurt any less? A cab shot around the curve and I whistled.

I did not look back.

When I got to the hotel there were no messages from Jake, just an Urgent, Call Immediately!! message from Ali. I gritted my teeth, and prepared for the next load of excrement to strike the ventilator, but she came to the phone singing the chorus of "Oh, What a Beautiful Morning!"

"What are you so happy about?"

"Barbara Walters wants to interview you for a special segment on tonight's show! You're supposed to be there at 3:00 this afternoon, and I'm going to fax you all the new numbers so you can talk about how fast the movement's growing. God, I am so excited—this is exactly what we need! We're working with the phone people to get a central number that women can call. We're going to have a recording that tells them how to contact their local group. See, that way we can know the exact number of women who sign up because of tonight's interview. So, once again it's all up to you—but I know you'll be fabulous. I bet we'll see millions of women sign up tomorrow. But even if we don't get the kind of reaction we want, we can study the tapes and refine the message. So either way this is going to be incredibly valuable. Besides, this'll be great for our fund-raising . . ."

As Ali bubbled on, I sat on the side of my bed and looked out onto Central Park. I was picturing myself on television, hawking political celibacy like one of those long-fingernailed women on the Home Shopping Network. I was feeling more depressed by the minute and I wanted off the phone. "I gotta go."

"What's the matter with you?"

"Nothing is the matter with me. I gotta go."

"Well, I'd think you'd be excited," she huffed.

"Well, you'd think wrong. I'd prefer to stab myself a hundred times in the abdomen with a fork and become a human colander. And by the way, why didn't you bother to tell me about Carl and Kimlee?"

"What about 'em?"

"That they're Patsy Cline fans." That was our ancient code for gays.

"What?"

"Patsy Cline fans. I walked in on the two of them in bed. Why didn't you tell me?"

"Why didn't I tell you? I didn't tell you because I didn't think you'd care. Do you?"

"No," I admitted. "It's just that I'd rather talk about that than the fact that I'm unemployed."

"You got fired?"

"Yeah, I got fired."

"Oh, sweetheart. I'm so sorry! Did it have anything to do with—"

"Yeah. They wanted me to quit doing this and I said no and they canned me. Simple as that."

"Goddammit! Those stupid, little, asshole, scumbag, piece-of-shit, sleazoid, sons of bitches—"

"No argument here. So, anyway, I'm not feeling very jovial right now ..."

"In the interview, make sure and tell Barbara what they did to you!"

"No. I haven't told Razz and Elizabeth and I'll be damned if they're going to hear it on television."

"You could call them ..."

"I'm not going to tell them anything until I get home. So drop it."

"OK, I'm sorry. That was stunningly insensitive of me and I apologize. Is there anything I can do? Do you want me to come up there and cut their little peckers off?"

"That's actually not a bad idea. Bring a magnifying glass and some tweezers. Ali, no offense or anything, but I really don't feel very chatty. I'll call you as soon as I get back from the interview. OK?"

"Of course. Cupcake, I'm so—"

"Yeah, me too." I hung up the phone and slid into bed, fully clothed, pulled the covers over my head, curled into the fetal position and shivered until it was time to get dressed and go to the interview.

Chapter 16

The studio was set up to look like a living room. There was a couch and a coffee table, with cameras on either side. This thin woman with a forehead that looked like you could beam satellite pictures off it was holding a light meter around my face and calling out numbers, and an albino with a ponytail was hustling people around. There were cables all over everywhere. I looked up, and Barbara Walters was standing there. Perfectly coifed, flawlessly made up. She really was lovely. She shook my hand and looked in my eyes and told me that she was a fan. So I told her I was a fan, which I was. It was all very warm and girlie.

"Let me start by saying how much we appreciate your making yourself available for this interview," she said and led me to the couch. "I thought you did a wonderful job at the Impeach Underwood March."

I smiled.

"I'd like this to be a personal, intimate kind of interview. We'll talk briefly about the strike and your views on its progress and what you see in the future, but I want to spend most of the hour just getting to know you. Everyone is dying to know what you're really like, so just be yourself. Relax and remember that I'm on your side. I love what you're doing and I want to make you look good. If you feel emotional, just go with it. If you feel like crying, don't hold back."

I smiled and said, "Miss Walters, you have as much chance of making me cry on national television in front of sixty million people as I do of picking up this building . . . and throwing it—left-handed—from the prone position. I'm from the old school; we don't cry in public."

"Oh, but if you let your vulnerable side show, it'll make the audience see you as fragile and real and likable. You want people out there rooting for you."

"Ah yes. Tell 'em how pitiful you are and you might win a Frigidaire and be crowned Queen for a Day!"

Barbara laughed, although I suspected it was just to show that she was a good sport. "OK, OK," she said and smiled. "You don't have to cry if you don't want to, but remember, sixty million people will be tuning in. This is your chance to let them see the real Lauren Fontaine."

"Maybe the real Lauren Fontaine doesn't want to be seen." That stumped her for a minute, which gave me time to ask myself why I was picking on her when she was A: just doing her job, B: being perfectly nice and C: in a position to make me look like the Global Village Idiot if she chose.

I reached out and touched her hand. "Miss Walters, I'm sorry. So much has happened so fast, and I haven't even had time to gather my thoughts, much less my emotions. I appreciate your letting me be here, this is a huge honor and I apologize for being snotty. I'm just nervous."

She was perfectly gracious, and you could tell it was more that just professional, she was genuinely nice. "Please don't apologize. I understand the pressure you're under. Just relax. It's going to be fine. Maybe it would help if I go over some of things I'm going to ask."

"That would help a lot."

She flipped through her notes. "OK, here goes. I understand that you've just been fired by Sterling White because you refused to drop your role in the strike."

I made a mental note to strangle Ali and held up my hands. "Do not ask me that."

"Why not? Don't you want people to know what they did?"

"Absolutely. But not yet. Things are really precarious right now and I have a family to take care of. Sterling White holds about ninety-five percent of my net worth in the repurchase of my stock and severance pay, and I can't afford to give them a reason to keep it."

Her face fell.

"I tell you what—once I get my money from them, I'll give you an exclusive interview on the whole subject."

She smiled. "Is that a promise?"

I held out my hand. "That's a promise."

She shook it and laughed. "Remember, I've got witnesses."

I laughed too. "Fair enough. So much for the subject of Sterling White. What else do you want to talk about?"

She hesitated for a moment, then looked at her watch. "You really better get with Janine and Alex so they have plenty of time to make you gorgeous and you don't have to come out here in front of sixty million people with wet hair and no makeup."

I nodded. "No reason to cause a worldwide panic unless it would help the ratings." Then I smiled to let her know that there were no hard feelings. I mean I could hardly blame her. I'd already refused to cry and shot down one of her big scoops, and if she let me in on everything she planned, I might not leave her anything for the broadcast.

It wasn't until I was having my hair washed that I started wondering what else she had up her sleeve. I didn't get to worry about it. The next thing I knew, there was Janine with her makeup bag and Alex with his dryer. Then about two seconds later there was a man instructing me how to attach the tiny microphone to my blouse at the same time Barbara was attaching hers.

"Before the cameras start rolling, let me just remind you that we've got thirty minutes allotted for tonight. With time out for commercials, we'll have about twenty-two minutes of interview, so please, no yes or no answers. Try to be relaxed and just think of this as a chat between the two of us."

"And sixty million eavesdroppers?"

She smiled, but I could tell she wasn't listening, she was watching the producer count down the seconds by flashing first five fingers then four to three to two to one to a voice-over: "Ladies and gentlemen, welcome to this special edition of Barbara Walters Interviews. Tonight in this broadcast, carried by satellite around the globe, Barbara's special guest is Lauren Fontaine." Then there was this kind of swirly music.

She leaned over and touched my hand. Her voice was so soft that if it weren't for the lights and the cameras and the crew crouched around, you could almost forget that you were being broadcast to a zillion people.

"I'm Barbara Walters and tonight, in an extraordinary interview, I will get inside the head of perhaps the most provocative leader of our time, a woman who has turned the world on its ear in her quest for power for her gender.

"Now, Lauren, you appeared on scene for the first time as the main speaker at the Impeach Underwood March." She looked at me and I nodded. So far so good. "You gave an incredible speech about the need for today's women to fight for power." She looked at me and I smiled. "You were a real unknown when you stepped onto that stage little more than a week ago. As a matter of fact, the major news organizations were all having fits trying to figure out who you were," she confided.

I smiled. I was waiting for the question.

"How long have you been actively involved in the leadership of the women's movement?"

I grinned. "About ten days."

Her eyes got big and she let out a gasp. "Are you telling me that you have only been involved in the movement that you now run, for ten days."

This was fun. "Well, first off, I'm not running the movement. There are sixteen different women's organizations involved in this and their leaders are the ones who are really running the movement. I'm just the mouthpiece for that group. So what I'm trying to say is that I first got involved with that group of women the day before the march."

She was happy as a widow yelling bingo. "I had no idea!" she gushed. "Tell me how in the world this happened."

"I came to Washington to march and stay with my friends Ali and David Wolverton. The meeting where this strategy was decided on was being held at their house. I happened to be there and the rest is history."

"Was the sex strike your idea?"

"It's actually a very old idea, about twenty-five hundred years old. I just thought it might be appropriate for the circumstances."

"When you say the idea is twenty-five hundred years old . . ." She waited for me to take the cue.

"It was the subject of a Greek comedy by Aristophanes," I finished.

"Tell me," she said with a devilish look in her eye. "In the story, the women go on a sex strike to . . ."

"Convince their men to end the Peloponnesian War."

"And who wins?" She knew the answer.

"The women, of course." I grinned.

"Well, we'll see how this all plays out. But let's talk about you. You have a financial background." I nodded. "That is actually how the networks tracked you down, from all the articles about you in the financial press." I just sat there. "As a matter of fact, you've been in the news before—you shorted the stock market before the crash of '87 and made a great deal of money." I was waiting for the question. "You've proven that you have great instincts. How does the feeling you had then compare to the feeling you have now about your movement?"

"They're the same in that a lot of people thought I was crazy then and a lot of people think I'm crazy now."

The producer did her finger countdown again and then everybody relaxed. Time for the network to insert the commercials. Barbara leaned over and touched my arm. "This is wonderful. You're just doing great."

I thanked her and looked around the room. This was fun, my heart wasn't pounding quite so much. Another minute, then sharp whispers, then the finger countdown.

She smiled into the camera. "I'm Barbara Walters and I'm here this evening with Lauren Montague Fontaine, the leader of the country's nine-day-old sex strike.

"Lauren, let's go back to the fact that you've only been actively involved in the women's movement for less than two weeks. Do you consider yourself a woman's woman or a man's woman?'

I spoke each word, slowly, trying to figure out what I was going to say as I was saying it. "The older I get, the more I identify with and enjoy the company of women. To be honest, when I was younger, most of my friends were men. But I think that had a lot to do with the fact that I've spent my entire career in the financial industry, which has always been predominantly male. Like most people, I found my friends where I spent most of my time."

"But didn't you also spend four years at the exclusive all-girls school, Miss Porter's?"

"I did."

"But you didn't graduate there, did you?"

I laughed. "Barbara, you've done your homework. No, I didn't graduate, I was expelled at the end of my junior year."

She leaned over like I was going to tell her a secret. "'Fess up. What did you do to get kicked out of Miss Porter's?"

"Well, I didn't kill any diet doctors if that's what you're asking. I thought I could liven up our May Day program with a little Marvin Gaye, instead of the traditional processional, on the school's loudspeaker. Neither the headmaster nor the board of trustees was amused."

"So whether it's marching to a different drummer, going against the market or being the strategist and spokeswoman for the Women's Revolution, you've always been a rebel."

"I don't know if I'd call it that. I think it's more that I've always come to my own conclusions."

"How do you think history will remember you?"

"I think that's completely dependent on whether we're successful in removing this wife beater from the highest judicial position in our nation. If we win, I expect that I'll be remembered for my part in this movement. If we lose, I think I'll be lucky to get a headstone when I die that says something as charitable as 'It seemed like a good idea at the time.'"

"I think you underestimate yourself. I think that win or lose, you'll be remembered as a great fighter. Dr. Martin Luther King wasn't completely successful in achieving his goals, and yet he's remembered as a great man. As a matter of fact, I'm told that Dr. King is a personal hero of yours."

My face lit up at the mention of his name. "Absolutely. He was such an incredible man."

"Yet he died a violent death. You've also made some dangerous enemies. I hate to bring this up—but are you afraid for your life?"

"I wasn't until you asked," I deadpanned. "Just kidding. I knew going into this it would probably be both unpleasant and dangerous. Am I concerned? Yes. Am I afraid? No." Then I turned straight toward the camera and said as purposefully as I could, "And I'm not going to quit until we win."

She laughed. "Now, I don't mean to pry . . ."

"Yes you do," I teased.

She laughed. "All right. So I do. Is there someone special in your life, someone you're making suffer by being the leader of this sex strike?"

I blushed. "Yes. There's someone in my life who will be happy when this strike is over."

"Now, won't you tell us who the lucky man is?"

"No," I said, and smiled as sweetly as I could. "That's private."

"Oh, come on," she cajoled. "You know that public figures aren't allowed to have any kind of privacy these days."

"I think that's unfortunate," I said coolly. "But this is a person I care a great deal about and his privacy is important—to me anyway."

She tilted her head and smiled. "Fair enough. Earlier in this interview, you said that you've always come to your own conclusions. The verdict, if you can call it that, in the Underwood proceedings has touched off a firestorm of emotion. Why do you think that is?"

"As far as the response to the verdict," I said, and made quotation marks with my fingers, "I think the American people are damned tired of seeing people who are obviously guilty walk away, free as the vultures they are. Whether it's the Rodney King or the Reginald Denny cases, where it was right there in black-and-white moving pictures, or worse, like the Lorena Bobbitt or the first Menendez brothers trial, where the defendants sat down and took the time to confess, not to mention that there are those of us who believe O.J. Simpson was guilty as homemade sin . . .

"Irritation at that kind of injustice, I think, is the basis of the fury, in this case, and it's clearly magnified because the crime was so horrible, the victim was so loved and the perpetrator was so sure that his power would protect him. It's the same reason people were rooting for Richard Nixon to get his during Watergate."

"Fascinating," she said and nodded encouragement. "Realistically, what do you think are the chances of this matter being re-heard?"

"I think the chances are excellent. Out of the five cases I just mentioned, three were re-heard—all with different verdicts, I might add."

"You're referring to Rodney King, the Menendez brothers and O.J. Simpson."

I nodded.

"That's a pretty interesting twist." She looked into the camera and promised, "When we return with Lauren Fontaine, we'll find out under what circumstances she thinks citizen revolt is necessary."

I got back to the hotel about 4:30, put on my nightgown and robe and ordered a sandwich. I didn't want to miss Jake when he called me back. I even ordered a bottle of champagne, and at 7:30, I turned on the TV. Barbara (we're on a first-name basis, thank you) had said we'd air at 8:00.

It was every bit as good as it had seemed while we were doing it, maybe even better. I sipped my champagne and watched myself talk about the importance of women using their emotional as well as their sexual power to finally balance the political scales. I even impressed myself with my explanation of the unprecedented momentum of the movement so far, and my confident predictions of our ultimate success.

No question about it—I was good. I got so excited that I dismissed the morning's events as unimportant. I had a movement to run and powerful changes to effect and I didn't have time to be diddling around with some stupid little job, working for stupid little men like Merrill Kennedy. I was congratulating myself in the mirror when the phone rang.

I knew it would be Jake and it wasn't. It was Hank.

"Spectac-u-la-rama!"

"Do you really think so?" I asked with imitation modesty.

"Socks were flying in living rooms all over America!! Why haven't you ever told me that you could be so articulate?"

I laughed. "I guess it's just hard to explain in nods and grunts. Where are you?"

"I'm in your lovely home with my lovely godson Razz and my lovely bodyguard Elizabeth. And you have convinced us all to join the movement."

"I'm glad to hear that. So everyone's OK?"

"Everyone's just peachy. Hold on, Razz wants to talk to you."

A moment later. "Mom, you were really smooth." For my son, that was quite a compliment.

"Thanks. I'm so happy you liked it. You guys doing OK?"

"Yeah. We're still up to our asses in reporters, but now it's more like a game for us. They're just like a flock of crows. They stand outside, screeching and cawing at each other and watching the house with their beady little eyes. Every few hours, Elizabeth opens the front door and just stands there, staring at them. They get real quiet and you can see 'em trying to decide what she's going to do. Then when she goes back inside, they all start squawking again. If she opens the door again real quick, they immediately shut up. It's pretty hilarious. Anyway, terrorizing the reporters gives us something to do, so we're fine. By the way, we're waiting on you to finish the puzzle."

"Y'all go ahead. We can get another one when I get home."

"Which will be?"

"Probably tomorrow night. I'm thinking about taking the shuttle to Washington in the morning to check on things. So I'll see you around dinnertime."

"Sounds good. Just a sec, Elizabeth wants to talk to you."

God, please don't let her ask about the job. Just give us this one night of happiness.

"Oooh, honey, I'm so proud of you. Up there with Miss Barbara Walters, chatting away about power and putting men in their places."

"Thanks. That means so much to me, I can't even tell you." I brushed a tear away and poured another glass of champagne. "I swear I don't know what we'd do without you."

"I don't know either." She laughed. "Now don't you worry, we got everything under control here, so you just go on and concentrate on what you need to do."

"Thanks, Elizabeth, you're the all-time best. I'm going to stop by Washington in the morning, then I'll be home. Take good care of my boy. I love you all."

"We love you too."

The phone rang again. I knew it would be Jake.

It wasn't. It was Ali.

" 'You're the top! You're the Coliseum, You're the top! You're the Louvre Museum, You're a melody from a symphony by Strauss, You're a Bendel bonnet, a Shakespeare sonnet, you're Mickey Mouse.' "

I'm not sure if I've mentioned this before, but when Ali is happy, she sings, and when she's really happy, she sings Cole Porter. I let her finish the second verse. "So you liked it?"

"Loved it. Adored it. Am engaged to be married to it. Cupcake, you were flawless!" I laughed. "No, I'm dead serious. You cannot believe the reaction. The phone company keeps having to add circuits to our number. This phone guy told me they haven't had this many calls coming into Washington since Reagan was shot! And pledges? Enough pledges to give Jimmy Swaggart a hard-on. Hell, enough pledges to give me a hard-on. This is just what we needed and we—"

"I thought I'd drop by tomorrow."

"Here?"

"No, Kuala Lumpur. Of course, there."

"Oh fantastic. That'll be incredible. When?"

"I don't know. Sometime midmorning."

"I can't wait to tell everybody! They'll be so excited."

"Ali, don't tell everybody. I don't want to . . . just don't, OK?"

"Whatever you say," she chirped. "I can't wait to see you."

"Me neither. How're you and Jinx getting along?"

"Fantastic. I absolutely adore her and she's having the time of her life. Anyway, gotta run. See you tomorrow. And great work!"

I called Jake's number and this time was able to leave a message on his answering machine. I called Gigi and she sounded like she'd been crying. I couldn't tell for sure, because she mumbled into the phone that she couldn't talk and hung up in my face.

By 10:00 P.M., all the afternoon's happy feelings had worn off and I was back to the fact that I had lost my job, that it was probably all over with Jake and that Vinnie Kovacevich had won.

By 11:20 I was in bed with clumps of cold, wet toilet paper. Thick streaks of mascara started at my cheeks and bled to the middle of my neck. My head was pounding and I was too debilitated to get up and wash my face. There was a knock at the door. I lay there. Another knock.

I got up, caught a glimpse of a cranberry-eyed banshee in the mirror and opened the door. Slick walked right past me and sat down on the bed. His jacket and tie were gone and his face didn't look a bit better than mine and he sat there in silence.

I closed the door and sat next to him on the bed. "What?"

"Have you turned on the TV today?"

"Yeah, as a matter of fact I was on TV tonight with Barbara Walters. You didn't see it?"

He shook his head.

"Then what are you talking about?"

He didn't say anything, he walked over to the television and turned it on. Then he changed the channel. The weatherman was blabbering about a tropical storm. I looked at him and shrugged.

"Just wait," he said.

It didn't take two minutes. There we were, slow dancing on the deck of the Staten Island ferry and I was drinking champagne from the bottle and the voice-over: "Caught on tape: the antisex crusader turns up in the most surprising place with a very well known and very married Wall Street aristocrat. She makes celibacy look like so much fun. In a *Hard Copy* exclusive . . . Lauren Fontaine: Is she holding out on her man or on her followers?"

"Oh, no."

"Oh, yeah."

"Oh, shit. The tourists with the camcorder." We both sat there as if in a trance. Neither one of us said a word until the newscast resumed, then I turned to him. "Now, let me guess. Annie saw this . . ." He nodded. "And she demanded an explanation . . ." another nod "And you took the moment of truth and turned it into the hour of confession."

He nodded.

"What did you tell her?"

"That I had fallen in love with you a long time ago, that we were together while she was having her affair with that creep. I said that when she and I reconciled, I had stopped sleeping with you but that, even though I love her, I still have feelings for you and that I quit my job because I couldn't let them railroad you and stay."

"What did she say?"

"She threw me out."

"What about..." My mind was spinning with questions. Did Ali know this thing was going to be on? What would it do to the movement? What would Jake think? He waited for me to finish the question but I was so shell shocked by the day's events, I just shook my head.

We watched the "Lauren on the Love Boat" segment, and it wasn't as bad as I thought it would be. But I had no sense of perspective and neither did he. When it was over, we just looked at each other and shrugged.

"Could've been worse," he noted.

"Yeah, I guess. Let's talk about it in the morning. My head is killing me," I said. I found the aspirin in my bag and took four.

One thing I have learned over the years is that the more you fantasize about something happening, the less your fantasies will resemble the actual event when it occurs. Of all the times I'd envisioned Slick leaving Annie and coming to me, not once did I ever imagine that when it happened, neither one of us would be happy and that we'd both just take off our clothes, wrap our arms around each other and fall asleep.

Chapter 17

"Check this out!"

I was in the tub, shaving my legs. "I can't hear you. Come in here and tell me."

Slick stood in the doorway, wearing starched boxers and holding the *New York Times*. Even undressed, he looked regal. He arched an eyebrow at me. "Now, that's what I call a view."

I batted my lashes at him. "You can look, big boy, but you cannot touch."

"Not even a Fourth of July kiss?"

"Well, let's see. I guess kissing's exempt on national holidays."

"You're such a patriot," he said, and leaned down for his exemption. Then he slid his hand under the water.

I grabbed it and set it on the side of the tub. "Don't press your luck, cowboy. Now, what were you going to tell me?"

"This." He grinned and held up the front page. SEXUAL REVOLUTION SWEEPS COUNTRY was the headline. Not just *a* headline on the front page of the *New York Times, the* headline.

"Holy guacamole," I whispered as he walked away.

Before I could yell for him to come back, he reappeared with his glasses, polished them with the hem of his underwear, leaned against the sink and began to read. " 'Dateline: New York. An appearance on network television last night by the elusive Lauren Fontaine—' "

"Elusive?"

He shrugged " '. . . sent membership of her budding movement—' "

"Budding?"

He peered over the tortoiseshell frames. "Lauren, I did not write this, I'm only reading it."

"OK, sorry. Go ahead."

"Thank you. Now, where was I?"

"Budding movement . . ."

" '. . . Sent membership of her budding movement into the stratosphere. Preliminary figures from a call-in poll run by this newspaper show that an amazing 41 percent of previously sexually active women have joined what is now being called Operation Lysistrata.' "

"Forty-one percent? That is pretty amazing. Do you think that's accurate?"

"Beats me." He shrugged, then found his place again. " 'Critics claim that the numbers are overstated—' "

"That's ridiculous. They don't know what they're talking about. If the *New York Times* says it's forty-one percent, then it's forty-one percent. They know everything, they have all the news that's fit to print."

"Thank you, my dear, for that bulletin. Shall I read more, or would you like to rant a little while longer?"

I slid the soap onto its porcelain ledge. "I'm finished. You may continue."

" 'The movement, which began as a reaction to the refusal by Congress to impeach Chief Justice Lawrence Underwood, has been an unprecedented success, suggesting that there is more to this organized celibacy than a desire for removal of the tainted jurist—' "

"That's absurd," I hissed.

" 'Many strike-watchers think credit for a large part of the movement's momentum belongs to its charismatic leader, Lauren Fontaine.' " He lowered the paper and peered over his glasses.

"Well, yes, of course, there's that too," I said.

He laughed then pulled the paper back up. " 'The most appealing leader to appear since the '60s, Ms. Fontaine is mysterious, sexy, and tough, and her selection has proven to be a smart move on the part of the feminist coalition.' "

"Well, I certainly am fabulous, aren't I?" I said and threw back my head in a glamour-girl pose, cracking the back of my skull against the tiled wall. "Shit," I groaned, and we both burst out laughing.

He continued. " 'It is perhaps a sign of the times that Operation Lysistrata appears to have been based on the structure of Alcoholics

Anonymous and other twelve-step programs, down to the buddy system and the chips participants receive to signify membership. But unlike other recovery groups, membership in this is anything but secret. Millions of women have taken to gluing fasteners to the backs of their chips and wearing them as pins.

" 'In an interview with Barbara Walters last night, Ms. Fontaine credited the startling success of her revolution to the fact that its details were conceived and being implemented by every faction of the women's movement. She explained that the undertaking represented the first time that feminists—the conservative, the moderate, and the radical left—had joined together for the good of American women. "It is the unprecedented cooperation of all our sisters, from the national to the local level, that accounts for this breakthrough. Not only are we certain to change the power structure of this country, we are also able to offer a model of unity to change-minded groups around the world." ' "

He put down the paper. "I'm impressed."

I grinned. "Why? Did you think the only topics I can discuss are sex, love, my son and the capital markets?"

"No. I never thought I'd hear you talk about your sisters in any figurative sense."

"Well, maybe I'm changing my mind. Is that all of it?"

"No. Let's see. 'Male members of the Senate and the House of Representatives are reported to be meeting frequently to monitor the situation, but have given no signal that they are ready to negotiate the ouster of Underwood.' "

"Why do you think that is?" I leaned out and pulled down the paper so I could see his face.

"I guess they're waiting to see what happens. You can hardly expect them to give in after less than two weeks."

"That makes sense. Do you still think this isn't doable?"

He laughed. "I admit that I may have underestimated you." Then he shrugged. "If anybody can pull it off, my little radical, it's you. Now let me finish this article. OK?"

I nodded and he continued. " 'While there is no official response, there are already signs that the organized abstinence is being felt. An informal poll of prostitutes in several major urban areas shows an interesting state of affairs. A startling thirty-eight percent of prostitutes say they are supporting the sexual boycott, while their less political colleagues report a surge in business. A high-priced call girl from Manhattan, who asked not to be identified, said that prices for sex, both on the street and from escort services, have more than doubled.' "

"Never let it be said that women haven't done their part for capitalism," I noted and sank farther into the tub.

" 'Longtime political analyst Jim Law observes, "This movement is no different than previous ones in that along with victories come retaliation." Indeed, there are widespread reports of a strong and growing backlash, the reprisal taking two forms: the first being economic blackmail and the second, physical violence.' "

A shiver went down my spine and I turned on the hot water, partly because I was suddenly freezing and partly because I wanted to drown out the sound of his voice and this terrible news.

He simply talked louder and his patrician enunciation and resonant voice made what he was reading sound like a proclamation. " 'Homemakers and other financially dependent women are the primary targets for the economic coercion. As troubling as that is to organizers, physical retribution is a far greater concern. There has been a staggering increase in reports of domestic violence. Police spokesmen in several large urban areas agree that the escalation can be traced back to the beginning of Operation Lysistrata.' "

"I don't want to hear any more." I stood up, and shooed him back into the bedroom, dried off, put on my robe and lay next to him on the bed. I was high on the pillow, resting my face against his unshaven jaw and caressing his calf muscle with my foot while horns and firecrackers reverberated from forty-five floors below.

God, this was confusing. Slick was free. He was here with me in the middle of the day and I didn't have to steel myself for the moment he got up and announced he had to go . . . and yet I knew exactly how fast that could change. And what about Jake? I hadn't heard from him and . . . for all his talk about being there for me, he wasn't anywhere to be found. I decided it would be easier to react than act. "So how are you?" I whispered.

He shrugged. "I don't know yet." His stubble grazed my cheek as he turned ever so slightly away. "The word that comes to mind is ambivalent."

I felt cheated, partly because he had claimed my emotion for his own and partly because he wouldn't declare that this was what he'd prayed for, that this was what he wanted. He had to have known what I was trying to decide and he still wouldn't stand up and commit.

I managed a very small "OK."

"I'm sorry. I'm just trying to be honest. After all this time, I should be able to say that it's the happiest day of my life. I am happy but I'm also sad and scared and guilty and confused. But I want you to understand that none of those feelings has anything to do with how much I love you."

I didn't look at him. "I accept that. Or at least my brain does. My heart would like you to go fuck yourself."

"I don't blame your heart for feeling that way."

"My heart wants you to know that it doesn't need your permission."

"Tell your heart to give me a break."

"My heart says that you have given *it* a break and to eat shit." I got up.

His rich voice from the rumpled bed: "Where are you going?"

"I'm going to Washington. I have a revolution to run. And clearly, you need to spend some time alone, figuring out what you want."

"From my conversation with Annie last night, I don't think I have much choice."

At that, I spun around. "If you think for one damn minute that I want you by default, you are sadly mistaken."

"What's the matter, Lauren? Does it only count if you beat Annie? Is that the only way—you only win if she loses?" His eyes were narrowed, his tone accusing.

"Don't you dare try to twist my words, you son of a bitch in Prince Charming's clothing! I meant that if the only reason you're here is not because you love me like you always claim but because you haven't got any other choice, then you can forget it. I'll be elsewhere."

"Like where? With Jake Ward?"

"Yeah. With Jake Ward."

His eyes lost their steel, not angry now but stricken. "That's just fine, Lauren. You just go find Jake Ward. And I hope the two of you are very happy."

"Thank you. I'm sure we will be. And don't look at me naked."

"I can if I want."

"Oh no you can't!" I yelled, grabbing my clothes and slamming the bathroom door.

By the time I'd put on a black linen sheath, decided I couldn't survive panty hose and returned, he was dressed too. He looked impressive and impenetrable, but beautiful clothes were no defense against the sodden silence in the room. I couldn't walk through the weight of it, so I sat down next to him, took his beautiful face in my hands and shook my head. "When Annie left you the first time, I was waiting with open arms. But when she came back and you had to decide between us, you chose her. That's where your commitment lies. You have to go back and tell her that what we had was a long time ago, that you were the one who ended it and that yesterday was nothing more than one old friend trying to cheer up another. You can make her understand that."

He didn't look at me, he stood and his voice was thick with pain. "Lauren, I love you and if there's any way I can help, please promise you'll call me."

I thought about that for a second. "That's a deal—if you tell Annie that I think she's the luckiest person I know."

He smiled. Then he held me for a long time, for the last time. And he kissed me and walked out the door.

"Yeah, well that was before this thing took off. Tell them to call Flo and get over to Capitol Hill," Ali was saying into the phone as I walked in. "No, the Longworth Building . . . probably around 2:30 . . . yeah . . . OK."

As soon as she saw me, she came around the pink marble desk and gave me a huge hug, saying into the receiver, "I've got to go. Lauren

Fontaine just walked into my office." But it was strange the way she said it, kind of like I was a movie star or something.

"What's going on at the Capitol?" I asked, settling into a wing chair across from her.

"Flo Fienman and her crowd are working the place like crazy."

"Yeah?"

She handed me the front page of the *Washington Post*. There was the First Lady and Gloria Steinem and several women senators and congresswomen, all wearing chips, all standing with Florence Fienman and two of her followers.

I looked closely at the picture, then up at her. "Ali, weren't these three women absolutely livid when Savannah announced that we'd be calling for a sex strike?"

She laughed. "Yep, I seem to recall they were less than enthusiastic, but that was then . . . and this is now. Now everybody's claiming they loved the idea from the minute they heard it."

"I don't know if I trust Flo."

"No offense, babes, but it doesn't really matter. I know how you must feel about her being Jake's ex-lover and all that, but Flo was here a long time before you even knew what a feminist was. I don't want you looking for a fight. We can't afford it. We've all got to pull together if we're going to win."

She was right. "Fair enough. When are we going to get an official response from the men on Capitol Hill?"

"Soon. Oh, but on the subject of hearing from men, guess who called here looking for you?"

I shrugged.

"Jake Ward. He left a number for you to call. Oh, by the way, that was quite a show last night."

"So you saw it?"

"Me and about a zillion other people. It didn't exactly help our credibility, Miss Pure-as-driven-snow."

"No apologies here. I was minding my own business and I am big-time pissed about this. And please don't act like my friendship with Slick is a surprise to you—"

"You misunderstand. I don't blame you nor do I blame you for being mad. Actually, it's my fault for not warning you. That thing last night wasn't a coincidence and I'm certain that it wasn't a one-shot deal. The name of the game is character assassination and this is the way it's played. Anyway, now that you know you're a target, you have to be more careful."

I stared at her and my voice dropped to a growl. "Excuse me. I'd like you to repeat what you just said, because I know I didn't hear you right."

"What?" Her tone was defensive.

I made a face of exaggerated surprise. "Now that I know I'm a target for character assassination, I have to be more careful. I've already lost my job and my privacy and my family is suffering and scared and now I have to be more careful? And you set me up for this whole fucking deal and you forgot to warn me."

"Christ, Lauren. Don't put this on me, you're a big girl. Besides, we discussed the fact that you're going to be under a lot of media scrutiny. How in the hell did I know you'd be so stupid as to parade around in public with your married lover!"

"I wasn't parading and he hasn't been my lover for a long time."

"Parading, dancing, whatever, and nobody exactly announced your breakup in the press."

We sat in silence for a long time, then a sigh broke loose from my chest. "What about the stuff in the *New York Times* about the economic blackmail and domestic violence."

"They weren't lying. The stories we're hearing . . . I swear it's like somebody put a weed-eater in your guts. By the way, your idea to set up the local chapters as support groups has turned out to be a pretty good one."

"Yeah, how so?'

"I've heard it again and again. When one of our members is being hurt or threatened, the rest of her group will arrange for her to get money or a safe place or whatever she needs. It's really amazing. Sisterhood at its best."

"Good. Well, let's put a little pressure on our nation's legislators. Why don't we call a press conference for this afternoon. Let's say around 4:00."

Her eyes lit up. "A press conference?"

"A press conference?" Kimlee repeated as she and Carl appeared at the door.

"Yeah. A press conference. Ali and I were just talking about the terrible things that are being done to our members. It's logical to assume that the longer this goes on, the worse it's gonna get. We're going to have to speed things up. So I'm going to call on the gentlemen of Capitol Hill to respond."

"Fantastic!" Ali crowed. "It'll make 'em at least show their hand."

"I've got an idea," Carl said. "Why don't we call around and get some of the local chapters to stage a rally at the same time?"

"Extremely great idea!" Kimlee said and patted her on the back.

"OK, let's get cooking," I warbled in my best Julia Child voice.

When they left, I told Ali about the executive committee meeting and about Slick. She told me about how many calls had come in after the interview and how many women had picked up chips in the last eighteen hours. Then she showed me to an empty office and returned to hers to work on arrangements for the press conference.

The first thing I did was call Robby McCloud, my lawyer, and tell him everything that had happened about my getting fired from Sterling White. I told him to call Frank Davis, Sterling White's legal counsel, and arrange to sell my stock back to the firm and get my severance.

Then I called Jake at what turned out to be Sloan-Kettering, room 2302.

"Jake Ward," he growled.

"Lauren Fontaine," I purred back. I was about to ask about his brother, but he cut me off.

"I was returning your call."

"You mad at me?"

The way he laughed made me cringe. "Mad? Why should I be mad? You can't sleep with me, you have to save yourself for the cause. So what is it, Lauren? It doesn't count if you fuck old boyfriends? Certain dicks are grandfathered in? Is that it?"

"No, that's not it. And I think you're pretty damn presumptuous. First off, I didn't fuck my old boyfriend as you so delicately put it. Secondly, when I told you that I was going to be celibate until this was over, I meant it. Thirdly, my old boyfriend was there when you called because we were trying to figure out how to keep my career from going down the toilet."

"And your little Fred and Ginger number?"

"Christ, I can't believe you watch that junk!"

"Darlin', I wouldn't have missed it. It was really quite entertaining to watch you do the two-face, I mean the two-step, with your friend Mr. Moriarty."

"Jake, I can't take this. I told you it's over with me and Slick, and if you don't believe me, there's really nothing to discuss. You've caught me at a bad time—I just got fired and I've got to go home and tell my family. You trust me or you don't, you leave me or you don't. That's up to you, but the fact is—I just really don't want to hear about it right now. I gotta go." I hung up.

If he was going to break up with me, he could just wait until I had less on my mind. I walked out of the room and down a maze of corridors. I was looking for Jinx. I finally found her two offices down from Ali. She was wearing the most garish red-white-and-blue ensemble I'd ever seen. "Hey, girlfriend. You steal that dress from a car dealership?"

"Fuck you, it's July Fourth and I'm being patriotic," she said and hugged me.

"You having fun? Any of your bosses pressuring you for sex?"

"Not so far." She laughed. "I was—just this very minute—thinking of you and how much has happened since I ran into you on the train."

"Ah, yes. How time flies when you're having fun."

"Not that so much," she corrected. "More about how ironic it is that you've ended up the leader of the American women's revolt."

"Well, there have always been those who've found me fairly revolting. What can I tell you? It's past ironic. It's surrealistic. Did Ali tell you that I got fired?" She nodded. "I still can't believe it. I've never been fired from a job in my life. And men all over the country are sticking pins in voodoo dolls with my face on them. But you know what's just as weird?" She shook her head. "I was walking up and down the halls a minute ago looking for you . . ."

"Yeah?"

"And I'm peeking into people's offices . . . and they're glancing up . . . and from the looks on their faces you'd think they'd just seen Elizabeth Taylor or something."

She smiled knowingly. "Your fans."

"I guess." I shook my head.

"I don't understand why that bothers you. You have always elicited strong emotions from other people. I remember Lilly's comment the first time she met you. She said, 'The fire in that girl burns hot enough to set the rain forest ablaze.' "

"That's not it. I mean you're right about my always eliciting strong reactions from people. But now I'm eliciting even stronger reactions from people who don't know me. It's like I've stopped being a person and become an icon."

"The price of fame." She shrugged. "So from now on, I'll call you Carl Icon. And speaking of Carl, am I imagining things or are she and Kimlee an item."

"That's not your imagination, my dear. They are indeed."

"I thought so. Not that I care. I think they're both incredible. As a matter of fact, everybody here is."

"Oh my God, Lauren. I can't believe it's you in person," Lisa squealed.

"What? You were expecting me in theory?"

At that, Suzanne started laughing, then coughing, then choking.

"I've called a press conference at 4:00 to call for a response from our friends at the Capitol. See ya then." I slipped past them, back to the empty office.

I sat for a while drumming my fingers on the plastic receiver. I knew Tom would be at the office and was hoping I might get Gigi to talk. She picked up on the second ring.

"Hi. It's me."

"Hi, you. What's up?"

"I got fired and Annie threw Slick out. What's up with you?"

"You got what and Annie threw who out?"

I told her both stories in *Reader's Digest* form. "Back to my original question. What's up with you?"

"Nothing much. Sorry I couldn't talk last night."

"I noticed. You were so hysterical you couldn't even speak." I let the unasked question hang in the air.

"Well, Aunt Bea, if you must know, Tom and I had a fight. Now it's over and everything is perfect."

"You gave in." I went back to the desk and slumped into the chair.

"Yeah, I gave in. Don't hate me."

"Don't be ridiculous. I don't hate you."

"Well, I know you're horrified."

"I'm not horrified. You tried, you did the best you could. I'm not being judgmental, but if I'm disappointed in anybody, it's Tom."

"I don't want you to hold this against him! That's just the way men are."

I'd noticed that the desk drawer was unlocked so I pulled it out. It held a pencil and two lone paper clips. I sighed. "I guess. How much of this, do you think, was really about sex . . . and how much was about power?"

"I don't know and to tell you the truth I don't care. All I know is that I'm going to do whatever I have to do to make sure that red-headed bitch doesn't steal my husband. Whatever I have to do." She must have sensed how pathetic she sounded, because she added with great bravado. "You know what they say—all's fair in love and war."

"And war is hell." I looked up and Ali was standing in the door, pointing to her watch.

I told my sister I was glad that everything was OK, that I loved her and I had to go. Ali was still in the doorway. "Gigi," I said by way of explanation.

She nodded. "I'm sorry to interrupt you, but it's almost 4:00." As we walked down the long hall, she laughed. "Do you mind if I ask what that was all about?" I recounted that Gigi had given in and slept with Tom. We had just stepped into her office when she said, "Hell, tell her not to make herself sick about it. It's not that big a deal."

"What do you mean?" I said, as evenly and unemotionally as possible. I already knew what she meant.

She still had her back to me when she said it, "I mean it's not that big a deal. I'm still sleeping with David." She shrugged. "You know me, I can give up just about anything except the big banana, and besides, I'm not going to give David any reason to start looking around." She waited for me to speak, and when she realized that I wasn't going to, she turned around.

We stared at each other. "Well, say something," she demanded.

"I will. As soon as I can think of something besides 'You make me puke.' "

Her eyes narrowed and her voice rose. "You have no right to judge me. I'm making a contribution to this movement and I'm going to do it in the way that I choose."

My silence enraged her.

"I'm the one who's been here for twenty hours a day while you've given exactly one speech, one press conference and a few interviews. I am the one who has done the shit work while you have taken all the glory, cover girl."

"Is that so? You've done all the shit work while I've taken all the glory. Weren't you the one who asked me to sell this stupid idea to your pals at your stupid luncheon? Weren't you one of the ones who wanted me to give the speech? I never once heard you volunteer for the job, especially during our conversation about the fact that whoever gave the speech would become the dartboard for every straight man in the entire population. The fact is, you didn't have the vaginal fortitude to take the job and neither did anyone else. And I got stuck with it!" Blood was roaring in my ears, and my hands were clenched into tight fists. "And while we're on the subject of glory—how glorious do you think it is to have your family harassed by the goddamn media? How glorious do you think it is to be thrown out of a job that supports your family, a job that you've spent an entire lifetime to earn, a job that you know you haven't ever got a chance of replacing?

"And what about the millions of women who are holding out in the face of brutal beatings and financial strangulation, the ones who are doing the real shit work?"

"Oh, come off it, Lauren. You are so fucking self-righteous. This isn't about millions of women, this is about you."

"What are you talking abou—"

"I'm talking about the fact that I'm only doing what you're dying to do. That's why you're so furious. You want to fuck Jake Ward so bad you can taste it!"

"Well, I'm not tasting it, and in case you've forgotten, that's what this whole thing is about."

"I don't need you to tell what this is about! I've been working for the women's movement for over a decade. You waltz in here and in two weeks you're Miss Political Action Hero."

"So. Now we're down to the real problem. You were perfectly willing for me to make an ass of myself on that podium—because deep down you didn't really think any of this was doable. Well, I didn't make an ass of myself, I convinced those women and now you're pissed that you didn't do it. If you want to be mad at yourself, fine . . . but don't you dare try to dump it on me."

She glanced down at her watch. "You gave a good speech and that's great—but don't get confused, Lauren. If one speech was all it took to make a revolution, there would be a lot more revolutionaries. You don't have the first clue how to make this thing a success; the organization, the grueling—" There was a noise behind me and I whirled around. There in Ali's doorway stood Carl, Kimlee, Lisa, Suzanne and behind them, several others.

Their faces were rigid and ranged from stark white to pale gray. "Sorry to interrupt, but it's already 4:00," Kimlee whispered.

I flashed my most chilling smile. "Well, they can't start the party without us, so give me a minute and I'll be right down." They didn't move.

I took a deep breath, stared into Ali's face and let it out very slowly. "While it is possible that, at another time in my life, I've been more disgusted and disillusioned than I am right now, I'd be hard pressed to name it. You just decided that you were so damned important you could excuse yourself from the unpleasant parts of this and . . ." I couldn't finish, I just shook my head. It took me a minute to regain my voice. "This brings me to ask myself, 'Self, do you really want to put your family at risk and destroy your career for the privilege of being a patsy for this bunch?' And do you know what my answer is? 'No, Self, I don't believe that I do.' "

"So what are you saying?" Ali asked, and the panic in her voice pleased me.

"I'm saying that if you don't intend to practice what you preach, then you ought to pick my successor now and go announce it to the folks downstairs. I'm saying that I seem to be the only one of this crowd who's sacrificing anything, sexual or otherwise, and that if I'm going to be the point man for this little excursion into hell, then I'm going to damn well have some say in the way it's run."

At that point, Lynette and Jinx appeared, grinning like drunken Buddhas. "Look!" They thundered in unison, each holding up a magazine. Lynette had the new issue of *Vogue* with a picture of me laughing on the cover and GOTCHA! in hot-pink letters, and Jinx held the new *New York* with a picture of me smiling and the caption ANTISEX SYMBOL. Then a group on the street began to chant, "We want Lauren! We want Lauren!"

"There's the answer right there," Ali said, motioning toward the window. "They aren't going to accept any substitutes." She smiled as if presenting me with an offering.

I had no intention of letting her off so easy. I shrugged. "They don't have any say in the matter. That decision belongs to me." I looked at Ali and smiled. This was not a part of myself I'd ever shown her. I was a gambler by temperament and profession, and she was way out of her league.

She folded. "Look, Lauren. I'm really sorry about what I said, because the fact is, we wouldn't have this momentum if it weren't for you. Just tell me what you want. We'll do whatever you want. Right?" she said to the women. They nodded vigorously.

"All right, I'll tell you what I want. It's not a negotiation, it's a take-it-or-leave-it deal. I will not be associated with, much less be the figurehead for, a group of hypocrites. That's it. Take it or leave it."

"We want Lauren! We want Lauren!" The crowd had either grown larger or more impatient.

"Take it," Ali said.

"Take it," Lynette and Jinx and Carl said at the same time, and the rest of them a half second later.

"Fine. Here is the deal: Anyone who wants to help make the rules is damn sure going to live by them, Ms. Wolverton. That means keeping the vow we made to each other when we decided to do this. No sex with any man. The point of this exercise, if you'll remember, is to make men miserable. OK. Any questions?" I asked.

"I have one, " Carl said in a tiny voice. "If you aren't involved with a man . . ."

I thought for a second. "Then find one and refuse to sleep with him. Now let's go down and talk to the press."

Between the reporters from every news organization known to man and supporters of the movement, there were several thousand people standing on Wisconsin Avenue, outside the building, waving little flags. I came out, followed by Ali and the rest of the gang, and stood on the top step while an enormous, sweating man finished taping down the microphone wires on the cement.

I stepped to the podium and thanked them for coming. I spoke about the unstoppable momentum of the movement and our strong resolve. I said that I was fairly sure that the men in power had noticed the extraordinary events of the last two weeks and that it was time for them to act. I ventured that not only would we appreciate a quick resolution, but that perhaps their male constituents would too.

At that point someone yelled, "What about you and John Moriarty dancing on the Staten Island ferry?"

"What about it?" I challenged, holding out my hands like I didn't understand the point. It didn't work. Suddenly there were dozens of voices yelling questions. I held up my hands until they quieted. "Look, I really don't understand the hoopla," I began. They started up again and I shook my head. "Let me finish. John Moriarty is my friend. I am not sleeping with him or anyone else. I would also like to point out that everybody, except maybe the Amish, knows that sex and dancing are two separate things. The fact that Mr. Moriarty and I were dancing in a very public place might give you some sense of how racy we thought it was. This whole thing is simply a pathetic attempt to discredit me, and I have absolutely no intention of letting it become an issue. Let me repeat that. It's stupid and pointless and I'm not going to say anything else about it—but," I said, leaning all my weight onto the podium and dropping my voice, "I will tell you something important."

They all leaned in like I was really going to tell them a secret. Their faces were shining with anticipation—or maybe it was perspiration—but whatever it was, I had their attention.

"The men in this country have always fought for what they believed in, and their women have always honored them. When there was an important objective and men went into battle to secure it, from the Civil War to the civil rights movement, they counted on their women to support them. And their women did.

"I call on American men to return the favor, to think enough of the women they love—and themselves—to honor those women's decision to sacrifice their sexual pleasure and comfort in order to rid this country of a man who has horrified us all.

"I have heard stories of violence, of economic and emotional extortion inflicted by 'men' in response to this movement. This is the response of children, not men. If you don't like going without sex, then do something positive, something responsible and adult. Women don't like going without sex either; we all want to get this thing over as soon as possible. Call your congressmen and tell them to give Larry Underwood what he deserves.

"I'm afraid I can't answer further questions because I've got a plane to catch. Thank you very much for coming."

Ali and I didn't speak after the press conference, and I asked Jinx to drive me to the airport. When we pulled up to the curb at National, she popped the trunk. I pulled out my suitcase and she handed me a paper grocery sack with my name written on it. It was stapled at the top and must have weighed ten pounds.

"What is this?"

"Fan mail."

"You lie, Communist dog."

"Nyet, comrade. And this is just a fraction of it. I thought you might enjoy the ego massage on the flight home."

"Since that's the only thing I'm likely to get massaged in the near future, I'll take it. Thanks." I walked about ten steps and turned. She was getting back in the car and I yelled, "I sure am glad you were on that train."

"Me too. I've got a great feeling about your future," she hollered.

When I think back, and I have a million times, it was those words that prefaced all the horror yet to come, that innocent remark seemed to summon the cosmic furies that lay in wait for me, for all of us.

Chapter 18

It's got to be the biggest shake-up to the male psyche since Glenn Close made rabbit stew. Keep up the good work . . . Sincerely, Molly Donlon

I was happily ensconced in my seat, with my bag in the empty seat next to me, drinking scotch and reading my letters. They were from every kind of person you could imagine: Baptist deacons in Nashville to baby doctors in St. Louis to big deals in Hollywood.

I'd read about thirty or forty and they were running about ten to one in favor of the movement. Some of them were funny and several were so touching that I had to take a big gulp of my drink to burn back tears.

I opened the next letter. It had been typed on plain stationery and it said:

You think your so smart you meddeling bitch dyke. We're gonna show you smart is not as good as strong. We will kill you and your kid then youl be sorry. . . . Ps—We know where you live and this is not a threat but a promise.

My stomach constricted into an ice cube. I tried to reread the words, but I couldn't concentrate. My eyes kept skipping to the end, then back to the beginning, then to the middle, then back to the end. I picked up the envelope. The postmark was smeared. I could barely make out that it had come from Birmingham, but the date was a blur.

O-Heavenly-Father-please-help-me. I was praying like a soldier lost in enemy territory. Shivering and rocking and praying. *God-please-don't-let-'em-hurt-my-baby.*

I don't know how long I was in that blur of panic, maybe fifteen minutes. Eventually a flight attendant walked out with someone's drink order and noticed me. "Are you all right? Are you ill? Should I call for a doctor?"

That kind of snapped me out of it. "No, I'm all right. I need a phone, quick." I was by the bulkhead, which didn't have one of those airplane phones. She took my credit card and brought me one. I jabbed my home phone number into the handset. Busy. They probably still had the phone off the hook. I tried to call Hank and Gigi and the Atlanta Police, but as soon as anyone picked up, the static became deafening.

"Goddammit!" I slammed the phone down on the armrest. In my peripheral vision I could see heads appear above the tops of gray vinyl seats.

The flight attendant rushed back, and I think she was going to say something about please don't break the phone but the look on my face stopped her in her tracks. I had lost virtually all of my interpersonal skills. "If you can't hear the goddamn person you're calling on these fucking phones, then why do you put them here to rip people off?" I was practically yelling. More heads above the tops of seats.

"I'm sorry if there's too much interference between us and the place that you're trying to call. That's really a function of the weather. We're going to be landing in about fifty minutes and you'll be able to place your call from the terminal, if you like." Sweet but firm. They obviously teach them in flight attendant school how to deal with psychotic passengers. "Is there anything else I can do?"

I started to tell her that, yes, she could tell the pilot to hurry the hell up but then she would've cheerfully explained that airplanes have flight plans that must be followed and then I'd have had to beat her to death with the damn phone. It seemed like too much trouble, so I shook my head.

I knew I had to compose myself or I was never going to survive the next hour. Obviously I was the one they wanted, so surely they wouldn't do anything until they could find me. If they watched CNN, which had been broadcasting my comments live, they wouldn't be expecting me back in Atlanta so soon. I eventually calmed myself by focusing on the fact that whoever wrote this letter probably had no intention of going through with it, and even if they did, they sure as hell weren't going to do it in broad daylight with a hundred reporters hanging around. As soon as I got home, I'd call the FBI and they could put out an all-points bulletin for this creep with the language skills of a third grader and put him in jail and everything would be fine.

The first thing I noticed when I burst through the glass doors at the airport was the sky. Majestic and malignant clouds, steep and gray-black, the tops of which were flat. It was as if the devil had just taken them out of the box.

Less than twenty minutes after the plane had touched down I had my bags in the car and was racing down the freeway. Traffic was light and I drove up the hill to my house at exactly 7:10. I did not slow down, and reporters were diving for cover when I came tearing through the gate and up to the front door. I ignored their squawking, let myself in, came through the house like a twister and startled Elizabeth.

"Lord, you like to gave me a heart attack!"

"Sorry. Where's Razz?"

"In his room. Girl, what's the matter with you?"

"Razz!!" I yelled at the top of my lungs. My heart didn't start beating until I heard his footsteps on the stairs.

"Hey, Mom. What's wrong?" he asked.

I hugged him with all the strength I possessed and burst into tears. "I was worried about you."

"I was fine before you started with the death grip." I loosened my hold a little but I couldn't bring myself to let go.

"What's this all about?" Elizabeth said, hovering close.

"I got a . . ." I went to the control panel on our elaborate security system and punched in the code for maximum alert.

"Mom, what's going on? Somebody after you?"

"It's OK. It's fine," I said as the two of them just stared at each other.

"What is the matter with you?" Elizabeth demanded. "Carrying on like this—jumping around, scaring folks half to death and generally acting like a fool."

"I don't really know what it all means but I got this threatening letter and it said terrible things and it just scared me to death . . ."

"What'd it say?" Razz and Elizabeth asked in unison.

"It was a death threat . . . for me and Razz."

"Well, Mom, I can see how you might have pissed some people off, but I think you should remind your letter-writing friends, whoever they are, that I've just been minding my own business. I want it on the record that I have absolutely nothing to do with your politics."

I laughed. "Next time I hear from them I'll be sure to pass that along."

"So where's the letter?"

"In my pocketbook."

"I'll get it," Razz offered, and when he returned with my bag, I pulled the letter out and handed it to Elizabeth. She read it then studied the front of the envelope.

"It's from Birmingham, but I can't make out the date," I said, peering over her shoulder.

"We should call the FBI and turn the letter over to them. They'll be able to tell whether or not it's for real," Elizabeth said and handed it back to me.

"I'll do that right after dinner," I announced. "But I haven't eaten all day and I'm about to faint. Elizabeth, what's for dinner?"

"We're going to have us a Fourth of July feast; I was just fixing to fry up some chicken and whip up some coleslaw. I've got corn on the cob and a watermelon in the fridge."

"That sounds divine."

She nodded and led us back to the kitchen. We were trying to find the Cuisinart to shred the cabbage when there was a detonation of thunder. I thought I was going to explode right out of my skin. Instead, I screamed at the top of my lungs. They laughed, then I laughed, then more thunder shook the house. The sky had grown so dark it looked like night outside. A few minutes later, the rain came down in torrents and the thunder rolled again and again through the air, violently knocking down enormous and invisible things.

I don't know whether it was the sound of the rain or what, but I eventually relaxed enough to start shucking the corn. Elizabeth was standing by the stove, dropping the pieces of chicken into a skillet. Then she stopped. "I almost forgot. A package came for you yesterday." We all froze for a second, then looked at each other.

"Where is it?" I asked, in a voice that didn't sound anything like mine.

"On your bed," she whispered, looking at me.

"What did it look like? How heavy was it? Who delivered it?" I demanded as they followed me down the hall to my bedroom.

"Postman brought it. It was a big box but it wasn't heavy. As a matter of fact, the thing was light as a feather," she said as we stood at the door to my room. There it was, sitting at the foot of the bed. We surrounded it, and I leaned down, looking for a return address. There was none. "You recognize the handwriting?" Razz asked.

I shook my head. I looked closer. "It's postmarked Somethingville, South Carolina."

"Do you know anybody in—"

"Not that I know of. But at least it's not from Birmingham . . ."

"Is it ticking?" Elizabeth murmured.

It wasn't. I picked it up and gently shook it. Another crash and lightning and we all jumped a foot. Then we looked at each other and fell on the bed laughing. "I've had more than enough fear and paranoia for one day. I'm going to open this thing and find out what it is," I announced, ripped off the brown paper and pulled off the top. And there in the box, with a wide polka-dot band and a tiny spray of white paper flowers, was the purplest hat ever made.

"What in the world . . ." Elizabeth muttered as I slipped off the bed and onto the floor. "A present from a friend," I explained, lifting the hat gently and putting it on. It fit perfectly.

"Is it just me, or are things getting weirder by the minute around here?" Razz asked no one in particular.

I picked up a note at the bottom of the tissue paper and said, "Give me a second, OK?"

They left and I opened the envelope. It was stamped The Mt. Zion Church and the stationery was dove gray. I unfolded it and read. "*This was dictated to my friend and pastor Gerald for my friend Lauren.*" Then,

Dear Lauren,

The graduation was full of happiness and everybody was surprised about me and glad I came. I've been seeing you on TV and hearing about you on the radio. I guess you took my advice about things and I am terribly proud of you. You keep this hat to remind you that you got all my prayers and love going with you.

Love,

Queen Esther Lawrence.

I read it twice more, then returned to the kitchen. The two of them were rain racing at the kitchen window and talking about how long it had been since they'd played. Rain racing was a thing that Elizabeth had taught Razz when he was such a sick little boy. It's simple to play—each person picks a raindrop at the top of the window and whoever's raindrop reaches the bottom first, wins.

It's a long tradition in our house and the two of them claim never to have missed a match and I stood in the doorway and watched them joking and laughing. It might have just been the contrast with the storm outside, but that room had never seemed so warm and safe.

When I walked in, Razz started to comment, but I put up my hand, "This hat is a gift from a special friend of mine, and if anyone says one word about it, I am going to personally rip their face off."

At that, Elizabeth turned to Razz. "You know, it's that kind of talk that makes her such a role model for mothers." We all laughed, and about five times over the next hour, Razz repeated the line to himself and just cracked up.

When dinner was ready, we put our feast on red-white-and-blue platters that I'd bought years ago, specifically for such national events. Then we sat down in the dining room and dug in. I waited until Elizabeth was mid-cob, cleared my throat and began. "I got some bad news yesterday and I didn't want to tell you over the phone but . . ."

They looked at each other, then Razz picked up his chicken and beat me to it. "You got fired."

"How'd you know that?"

Unfortunately, Elizabeth wiped her mouth and blasted me before he could so much as swallow. "He knew it because I told him and I knew it when you decided you were going up there to that march and act like a big shot! Anybody with a brain the size of a pea could've seen it coming, anybody but you, that is."

I put down my fork. "Look, Elizabeth. You were right about all that and—"

"And save that crap about how it's gonna be OK, 'cause I'm not buying that anymore. I've got fall quarter tuition due in a few weeks and I don't think the financial director of the nursing school gives a toot whether we've got each other."

I looked at Razz's stricken face, then back at hers. "Damn, Elizabeth! I said I got fired, I didn't say we were poor. You're being ridiculous! Now quit acting like we're all going to be out on the street. We've got more money than the three of us could possibly spend."

"How much?" Razz asked, his eyes big, his mouth full of coleslaw.

"Don't speak with your mouth full and millions if you must know."

"Where is it?" he demanded.

I stuck out my tongue. "None of your beeswax," I said, then turned to Elizabeth. "Are you satisfied?"

She looked suspicious but she was starting to eat again, which I took to be a good sign. "Mmm. Where is it?"

I laughed. "It's in stock. Boy, you two missed your calling as KGB interrogators. Now leave me alone so I can eat my dinner." When I'd finished, I wiped my mouth. "Speaking of the police, I'm going to call the FBI and find out what they think we should do about my fan mail."

I called the number in the phone book and told the man who answered who I was and about the letter. He put me on hold, then connected me to Agent Bob Brown.

"I'm glad you called, Ms. Fontaine. As a matter of fact, we've been trying to contact you. Were you aware that your phone has been off the hook for over a week?" he asked and didn't wait for an answer. "Let me be brutally honest, Ms. Fontaine—I've been with the bureau for twenty-seven years and I've never seen as much activity focused on an individual."

"Activity?"

"People with plans to harm you or members of your family."

A sick and icy feeling enveloped me and I lost the ability to speak.

"Are you there?" he demanded.

I made a noise.

"Although we've been unable to contact you, I've had a number of my best agents close by. I'll radio the field agent in charge, a gentleman named Jim Brooks, and let him know that we've spoken. He and Agent Marty Wilson will be there in a few minutes to talk to you and take a look at the letter you received.

"When they arrive at your house, they'll show you identification. Only then should you let them in. And from now on, you should be extremely careful about who comes in and out of your home. I know this is frightening, and I don't mean to scare you, but I'd be doing you a disservice if I were less candid."

All I could manage was "I understand." I sounded like I was being strangled.

"Off the record, I will tell you that we've been given a great deal of both latitude and resources to protect you and the members of your family. That's compliments of the White House. When Agent Brooks arrives, he will give you the number of my private line. You can reach me at any time, day or night. Do not, I repeat, do not hesitate to call me—questions, concerns, or if you just want to talk—I'm here. OK?"

"Thank you, " I whispered.

"What did he say?" Razz demanded.

Elizabeth was out of her chair. "What do they know?"

It took me a second to respond. I was overcome with the thought that the box I'd so cavalierly torn open an hour before could have just as easily contained a bomb as a purple hat. I took a deep breath. "He said I've got a lot more enemies than I thought and some of them are hard at work preparing to—"

"Kill you?" Elizabeth demanded.

I looked at her as the words sank in. "Yeah, kill me."

Chapter 19

"You're up early," Elizabeth said.

"Never went to sleep. Got any coffee?" I had three extra-strength Excedrin in my hand. I pulled a juice glass from the cabinet, filled it and swallowed them before turning toward her. I felt like someone was trying to open my skull by tapping a wedge into a crack behind my right eye.

The only light in the room came from the fluorescent strips under the cabinets and the little TV on the counter by the kitchen. "Yeah, we got coffee. You want toast?"

I looked outside. The charcoal outlines of sodden trees against a gunmetal gray sky matched my mood. It was too dark to see the rain, but you could hear it waterfalling from the slick leaves to the grass. "No thanks. God, listen to this rain."

"We sure need it—"

"Yeah, hopefully this bad weather'll keep the assassins at home, cleaning their weapons and listening to Rush Limbaugh and G. Gordon Liddy."

I could only see the crescent of her face that wasn't in shadow. The lambent light was perfectly adequate to make out her wince before she turned back to the counter. She started to say something, when my picture flashed across the TV screen. I hit the volume button on the remote control.

"In a related story, a spokesman for the Wall Street firm of Sterling White announced that Lauren Fontaine has been asked to step down from her position as managing partner. The firm denies that the release is related to Fontaine's activities as leader of the sex strike that has swept the nation. While refusing to publicly discuss the dismissal, insiders tell us that Ms. Fontaine was implicated in an incident of unauthorized trading that may have involved some $300 million. Our reporters will continue to investigate and bring you more on this story as it unfolds."

We looked at each other. Then she sighed. "And it's only gonna get worse." She handed me a steaming mug. "By the time those jackasses are finished telling lies to those trashy reporters, you're going to have stolen that money . . . and it was going to be money set aside for a charity that buys wheelchairs for orphans."

"Wheelchairs for orphans born addicted to crack," I corrected. "No, wait . . . wheelchairs for orphans born addicted to crack who are blind and play the harmonica." I tried to laugh, but everything inside me felt bruised, and the sound came out more like a squawk. I slumped against the refrigerator. "And you tried to tell me and I wouldn't listen."

"Way too late for *I told you so* now, " she said softly. "But whatever else they can say about you, anybody who knows you in the least knows that you are completely honest."

I looked into her face, sepia in the shadows. "Yeah, great. What about the rest of the world?"

"You done nothing wrong, you got nothing to be ashamed of. What you've got to be thinking at this point is that this is going to be very tough on our boy and you're gonna have to be real strong for him." Her voice was almost a whisper.

"I know," I said and studied my bony feet against the pale floorboards.

"Then don't let him see you busted up."

"I'm not busted up, I'm furious." And saying the words gave me the energy to march to the phone. "I'm not going to let those bastards get away with this. I'm calling Ali. Now." I punched in the number.

"Hello." She was wide awake.

"It's me."

"I'm glad you called. We've got a problem."

"Yeah, tell me about it."

"What are you talking about?" She sounded wary.

"What are *you* talking about?"

"One of the tabloids has a full cover story on you and Slick. The picture's from the Staten Island ferry tape but the interview is with a guy, a room-service waiter from the St. Regis, who says that you and Slick are regular customers."

"Oh, Christ! We haven't been to the damn St. Regis in years. And we only went there a couple of times after Annie ran off with that Newton Wheeler guy." I was cradling the phone and looking in the drawer for a sugar spoon.

"That ain't the version this guy's telling. Of course, if he told the whole truth, his story probably wouldn't be worth the fifty grand they're probably paying him. You should also remember that the truth is not exactly the standard here, these are the folks who brought you the exclusive interview with Bigfoot."

I found the spoon and was poking at a grape-sized clump of sugar, lying in the bowl like a frosted gold nugget. "What's his name? I'll sue his ass off and the publisher's asses too. That'll be the most expensive story they ever printed. I can't believe this. Jesus, this is really charming. Anyway, I was calling to tell you—"

"Oh, wait. Is it the thing about you getting fired?"

"Yeah." I reached into the bowl, picked up the sugar nugget from its glittering bed and dropped it into the sink. It made a tiny clink against the stainless steel, and I dug into the now pristine mound of sparkling granules.

"I'm watching it right now. Hold on." There was just the sound of her breathing and a TV in the background for a minute, then, "I can't believe they're lying about why you were fired. You ought to sue them too."

"I'd be glad to if you'd give me a name. No chance of that. If you listen carefully, you'll note that there were no names mentioned, only the ubiquitous unnamed sources. None of those bastards is going to talk on the record. No, it's all insinuation and innuendo." I stirred the sugar into my coffee and took a long sip. "Talk to the others and see what they suggest. Maybe I should hold another news conference tomorrow."

"Don't worry. I'll take care of whatever needs to be done."

"Thanks." I sighed and looked across the room into Elizabeth's eyes. "I guess it's too much to assume that you have any good news . . ."

"Nothing but the fact that this movement is growing like bacteria."

"Well, I'm glad it's working. Listen, I need you to send Moore down here for a while. The FBI was here until 3:00 in the morning, and I'm not supposed to talk about this on the phone, but suffice to say they've got their hands full—seems the wackos are fighting over who gets to splatter my brains all over the front page of tomorrow's paper."

Her voice broke and she started wailing. "My God, Lauren, what have I done to you?" Then she spent the next I don't know how many minutes carrying on; weeping and asking my forgiveness for getting me involved and swearing that she never believed it would come to this.

I listened politely, but I wasn't at all impressed. I got off the phone and turned to Elizabeth. "Why in the hell did I get involved in this? Why didn't I just mind my own damn business?"

" 'Cause you did what you thought was the right thing, and you got those folks scared now."

"You really think so?" She nodded, and I smiled for the first time that day. "Well, I wish you'd never talked me into leading this stupid movement."

"I know you didn't want to, honey, but I knew all along it was the right thing for you to do," she deadpanned.

I laughed.

There were two stone-faced agents in the house and several others on the grounds and in the crowd of reporters at the gate. This made us feel pretty safe, so Elizabeth, Razz and I spent the rainy afternoon working on a new puzzle, this one featuring a scene from the Civil War. The two of them were about as subtle as a Molotov cocktail, which is precisely what I felt like I'd swallowed when Hank showed up.

He was let in by an unsmiling FBI guy after I identified him.

"Good Lord! For a minute there, I thought I was going to be strip-searched," he said as I led him to the breakfast room.

"Maybe next time," I promised.

He laughed. "What in the hell is all this?"

"FBI," Razz said out of the side of his mouth like a cartoon criminal. He jabbed his thumb in my direction. "Feds everywhere and she's the cause of it all."

"Well, I've got just the thing to get your mind off the proverbial murderous mob at the gate," he announced, batting the rain from his hair with the latest issue of *Esquire*. "Jake's article, hot off the press. You might want to sit down before you read it." He saw the look on my face. "No, come to think of it—you might want a drink first." He looked at the magazine then back at me. "I have a better idea—drink a bottle of scotch and lie down, then I'll read it to you."

"Is it that bad?"

"No, it's not that bad, but you're going to be pissed all the same."

I sighed. "Let's get it over with."

He sat down and opened the magazine and found the page. Then he looked up at the ceiling and took a deep breath through his nose like a person about to do a swan dive off the cliffs of Acapulco. "It's called 'I'm Not The Enemy Just Because I'm Wearing Pants.' "

"It's a stupid title."

He ignored me and began to read. " 'It's not that Lauren Fontaine and her friends don't have a valid argument, they do. It's not that Lawrence Underwood isn't a disgusting human being with no legitimate right to sit anywhere but in a prison cell. He is.

" 'It's just that the leaders of the Lysistrata Movement appear to believe that it is the male power structure that's kept Lynn Underwood and women like her from being safe in their own homes. That's why they've targeted the male population of the country. And in the short run, they've been successful in keeping the focus on their agenda. I think I can say, without fear of argument, they've certainly gotten our attention.

" 'In the long run, such a (excuse the pun) naked power play will not carry the day, especially since the average man is every bit as horrified by Larry Left-hook Underwood as the average woman. The leaders of the movement have confused friend and enemy and in doing so have severely limited their chances of success.

" 'This is not about women vs. men, and the withholding of sex to force the movement's agenda is going to do nothing but polarize this nation once again. Don't we have enough divisions with blacks against whites, gays against straights, liberals against conservatives, pro-choicers against pro-lifers? Can't we disagree about anything without getting into each other's faces?

" 'The leaders of the sex strike have said that it's a showcase for female power, but the strategy of making men so upset that they will step in and make Congress do the right thing is more an admission of power-lessness. If these bright and talented women want to really show off their clout, they should call off the strike and use their formidable political skills to replace every congressman who cast a no vote in Lawrence Underwood's impeachment hearings.

" 'Holding all men responsible for the actions of one man is not only unfair it's ineffective. You cannot force someone to become your ally by first making them your enemy. And that is why I hope Lauren Fontaine realizes that manipulation will do her cause more harm than good. I wish her and her friends good judgment and good luck.' "

"I hate him. He's a sunuvabitch, turncoat, sanctimonious shithead. 'I want to wish her and her friends good judgment and good luck,' " I mimicked. "I hate him."

"You already said that," Razz pointed out.

"It bears repeating. I hate him." I was spitting mad, which made them sit back in their chairs out of range. "Plus, I can't believe that he would just spring this on me. What a creep! What a cretin! What a——"

"He tried to tell you," Hank said.

I made a really ferocious face. "What are you talking about and why are you on his side?"

"It's what he called you at your hotel in New York to tell you about. And it's what he tried to tell you when he called you in Washington. In case you are unaware—sometimes it is extremely difficult to tell you anything, because you never listen."

Then there was a chorus of confirmation in surround-sound, and I glared at them too.

"Well, I don't care. I thought he was on our side and it turns out——"

"See, there you go!" Elizabeth chimed in. "You never let anybody else talk, because you think you've already got all the answers."

"And I do," I said in my own defense.

"And they're usually wrong," she shot back.

"Why are you all ganging up on me?" I demanded.

" 'Cause, no offense, Mom, but sometimes you're a real pain in the ass."

I went to the kitchen and retrieved the list of enemies the FBI had given me the night before. I brought it to the table and wrote in big letters at the bottom *Jake. Razz. Elizabeth. Hank.* That got a big laugh, then I sat without uttering so much as a syllable as Hank explained why he thought Jake was right.

"You're not doing anything but making straight men dig in their heels and see women as the enemy. And that is not going to get rid of Larry Underwood," he said, tapping on the page with Jake's article. "Why don't you try being more conciliatory?"

"Don't you see? We're in this situation because we've been so damn conciliatory. That's what men have always counted on—that when push came to shove, we'd do anything to avoid a scene. That's the problem with the fact that the women's movement was run by well-bred, highly educated women from paternalistic backgrounds. They burned bras instead of buildings. That's why when the gays wanted political clout, they did it with ACT UP, that in-your-face, militant, like-it-or-lump-it model for social change.

"That's what I bring to the table. I'm the debutante with the sawed-off shotgun, the librarian who'll knee you in the crotch if you put your hand on my ass on a crowded subway, the country-club matron with a switchblade in my Judith Leiber bag. I am the symbol for the fact that women are not going to be conciliatory anymore. I'm the Stokely Carmichael of the female sex."

"You're a lunatic," Elizabeth noted.

"Wait a minute," I said, looking around the table. "I can't believe I'm having this conversation. I would think that a black woman and a gay man could understand the feeling of fury that comes with impotence."

"Hey now," Hank shot back, "don't be casting any aspersions on my manhood. Gay—yes; impotent—no."

I laughed. "You know what I mean. Politically impotent. Sometimes, it takes somebody to stand up and scream 'Deal with me!' and for some reason I got picked to be the one. It's not my function to be nice. I'm the bad cop, the designated demon, the ultimate uppity woman."

"The nation's sex strike enters its twelfth day and not since the Iranian hostage crisis have Americans marked off every inexorable twenty-four-hour period with such grim resignation," said the TV newsperson. Authorities attribute a sharp rise in assault and rape cases as well as four domestic violence deaths to the strike.

"The weather hasn't helped tensions. The heat wave that has swept the Midwest and Southern states, bringing temperatures into the one hundreds in some places, has contributed to what many are calling the most miserable summer since the Depression."

"Five minutes, Christians," Hank said and disappeared into the dining room, which was set up as command central. We had four television sets around the room, each connected to its own VCR and each one set to a different network. Razz was keeping track of faxes from headquarters in Washington, and Gigi was manning one phone line while Hank was on the other.

"Bring on the lions," I said, reapplied my lipstick and, flanked by Agent Brooks on one side and Agent Wilson on the other, walked outside and up to the lectern, set exactly one body length from the door, looked at the mob of sweating reporters, cleared my throat and began.

"I'm Lauren Fontaine and I want to speak to the American people about the campaign mounted by those who seek to ruin my reputation. I'm talking about the accusation that I was fired from my position at Sterling White for an incident of unauthorized trading. That is false. I was fired because I refused to resign as a leader of this movement."

I looked into the cameras instead of the faces of the reporters. It was a tip I'd picked up from Hank, who'd given his share of interviews and knew all the tricks.

"I would ask the American people to consider the fact that if Sterling White really had a legitimate reason to fire me, they would have said so on the record. They would have said in a press release, 'Lauren Fontaine was fired because she engaged in unauthorized trading.' They knew it wasn't true and they knew if they announced it that way, I could and would have sued them for libel. It is neither an accident nor a coincidence that the firm of Sterling White has refused to make that clear, and in doing so, has left room for unnamed sources to make the accusation that my dismissal was the result of some wrongdoing on my part. I call on the chairman of Sterling White to state on the record why I was fired, so we can settle this matter once and for all."

Then I shook my head at the absurdity of the subject I was about to address. "There have also been reports that I am currently involved in a sexual relationship with John Moriarty. I am not. John Moriarty was my boss and is my friend. Period. Let me be crystal clear on this subject. I am not having sex with anyone. I have been and will continue to be celibate along with the other seventy-five or eighty million women in this country who are and will continue to be celibate until our demands are met."

The humidity was unbearable and I was starting to sweat. My shirt was stuck to my back, and for the first time, I started feeling sorry for the reporters. They were clearly miserable, with their frizzing hair and spreading stains under their arms.

"I'm here to ask the journalists of this country to stop allowing themselves to be used as pawns of character destruction. They must somehow return to the discipline of not printing that which they do not know to be true. What I'm suggesting is not complicated, nor is it difficult. I'm simply calling on the media to go back to that simple practice they used to call investigation.

"If an accusation is made, don't print it until it has been thoroughly investigated and proven to be true. If an accuser refuses to be named, then find someone who will go on the record with the accusation or find proof that the accusation is grounded in truth *before* it's printed. That used to be the foundation of journalism and must be again. It is up to you to stop the poison fog that has been used so frequently and so successfully, in recent years, to destroy people in public life."

I paused for effect and looked slowly through the throng as hundreds of pairs of eyes studied hundreds of pairs of cruddy shoes. There was no air and each word took effort. "Let me make this understood. American women are *finished* with being victims. From now on, feminism is not about victimization—it's about power. Forty-six percent of the women in this country are already participants in this movement. That's eighty million women and that's a number that's growing every hour. In case our so-called leaders haven't noticed, this country is in the middle of a revolution. Could we trouble them for a response?

"I also have a message for Larry Underwood's political cronies. You cannot simply duck this egregious example of immorality with politics-as-usual maneuvering. I would urge you to understand that the people of this country are disgusted and repulsed by this pathetic partisan performance, and that trying to make *me* the villain isn't going to work.

"The American people aren't stupid. They want Larry Underwood punished for what he did to Lynn Underwood, and I'm not going anywhere until he is. I'm not going to be intimidated by this carefully orchestrated character assassination. When this is over, I'll be the one still standing."

I stood for another short minute to accommodate the still photographers, but I took no questions and was hustled back inside.

"Ooooh, honey . . . What a tough talker you are," Elizabeth called as Agent Wilson secured the door. Moore had just arrived from the airport and she was giving him a tour of the house.

"You know it, baby," I replied, sounding a lot more jovial than I felt. I had tough-talked myself into this incredible debacle and I needed a scotch and water. I started to hug Moore but I was soaking wet so I grabbed his hand instead and thanked him for coming.

He kissed the top of my head. "Don't you be afraid of a thing, dear one. I'm going to make anyone who even *thinks* about hurting you very sorry indeed."

"Thanks, sweetie. I feel a million times safer just having you around. Moore, have you ever met my sister? Gigi, this is one of my favorite people . . ." We chatted a minute, then Moore and Elizabeth left and Gigi came and stood next to me under the air-conditioning vent.

"Want to talk?"

My jovial façade crumbled like my shoulders. "What's there to say?"

"It's not your fault."

"Yeah, it is. This is all my fault because I should have seen this coming."

"How in the world could you have seen this coming?"

"The better question is how could I have not seen this coming." I was practically yelling. "It's the standard response. It's not like it hasn't happened before; Lani Guinier, Zoe Baird, Kimba Wood! What do all those people have in common?"

"They all have weird names?"

"No, they were all people destroyed in the press by their political enemies. It used to be done using snipers on rooftops or in book depositories. Now it's also done in newsrooms and on television. It's worse now, of course, because you can't put a bulletproof vest on your reputation and all the bodyguards in the world can't protect you. Everybody tried to warn me but I didn't listen and now it's too late."

"It makes me sick," she said. "It's so unbelievably cowardly. Why take the time to debate the ideas when they can just destroy the person?"

"I feel like I have a piano wire wrapped around my neck and the tabloids hold one end and the regular press holds the other and it doesn't really matter which one pulls hardest; I'm going to be dead either way."

Hank and Razz walked in. I held out my arms and Razz came over and sat next to me. I patted his back.

"What are you two talking about?" he asked.

"We were just talking about the people who are trying so hard to make me look like a bad person and I was feeling sorry for myself. Poor me, pour me a drink."

After four drinks and a three-hour nap, I'd finally woken up. My brain was full and throbbing, the neural equivalent of what Slick called a piss hard-on. My mouth tasted like the bottom of a mushroom cap and I was sad to be conscious. A mere late-afternoon hangover tipped, then teetered, then tobogganed into despair, following the realization that Sterling White had issued their carefully worded statement to do more than discredit me and the movement. They did it to keep from paying what they owed me.

I figured the money they owed me for severance plus the current value of my Sterling White stock totaled about $2.88 million. Other than the equity in my house and about $30,000 dollars in the bank, that money represented all the work and the risk and the sacrifices and the hard-fought and harder-won success of my entire adult life. But that money represented much more than my success. It was the hard currency of my love for my family—our security, Elizabeth's nursing school, Razz's college.

I had told them last night that we had more money than we could spend. "Don't worry," I'd assured them. "We've got millions in stock." It might as well be in a herd of cattle with Mad Cow disease for what it would be worth once Sterling White's lawyers got started.

They were going to make me sue them for it and then the only thing for sure was that lawyers would get what the tax man didn't. At that point, it also occurred to me that with Slick gone, there was no one left at the firm to fight for my interests.

Fine. I decided, I'll just fight for my own. I pulled the phone onto my bed and dialed my lawyer. "Robby? It's Lauren. What'd they say?"

"I just got off the phone with their lawyer. I think you're right. There's no question in my mind that they're stalling. To top it off, Frank Davis says that Merrill Kennedy thought you behaved rudely at the meeting and he wants a personal apology from you before there will be any further discussions."

I was too stunned to respond.

"Lauren, don't let this rattle you," he said. "I've looked at your partnership agreements. You don't have anything to worry about. The only way they can keep your stock and avoid paying you for it, or your severance for that matter, is to prove that you committed fraud. They may not like your politics but that's not going to stand up in court and they know it. So don't worry. OK?"

"OK." I hung up the phone and cried ice-cold tears of rage. I pulled myself out of bed, and as if under dark water, numb and throbbing, tear-swollen blind, to the bathroom for toilet paper. Every time I bent down for more, my head swam until I sank onto the seat and could blow my nose without vertigo. Then the hot poison of fear twisted my intestines and I pulled down my underwear and held my head and had diarrhea and blew my nose and rested my forehead on my knees, then vomited twice for good measure. When I was totally dehydrated, I slowly got up and drank a glass of water and then even more slowly took a few aspirin and went back to bed. To make myself feel better, I picked up my Queen Esther hat from my bedside table and put it on. Then I pulled the covers over my head—purple polka-dotted hat and all.

Yeah, this was a kiss from God, all right. First the kiss, then the Vaseline, then the big one right up the ass. I got up and went into my bathroom for some more water, then I went back to bed and lay there watching the little antique clock on my bedside table, wondering what in the hell I was going to do.

That's how I know it was exactly 4:58 P.M. when I found out that the Congress had announced that it would rehold hearings on the possible impeachment of Lawrence Underwood.

This is how I found out. My private line rang. I picked it up. A choir of female voices, screaming in unison on a speakerphone. Not saying anything, just screaming. And laughing. I could finally make out Ali's voice. "Lionheart, we did it!" More screaming, then she hushed whoever else was there and repeated, "Lionheart, did you hear? We did it!"

"Did what?" Now I was yelling.

"We just got word that Congress is going to revisit the Underwood question!" She was drowned out by about six other voices. Then I heard a "Y'all shut up so I can talk," and I knew the gentle priest was there.

Savannah boomed, "Lauren, we did it. We are on our way now!" Then I could make out Jinx's voice yelling congratulations, then Lynette's, then Kimlee led a rousing rendition of "For She's a Jolly Good Fellow" and when they got to the part "that nobody can deny," I could hear Suzanne coughing in the background.

I spent the next fifteen minutes listening to them glow and crow and make plans, then I washed my face, pulled on my clothes and went downstairs to share the news with the home team.

The phone rang in the middle of our celebration, and Elizabeth talked for so long that I thought the call was for her, even though it had come in on my line. Finally, she called me to the phone.

"Who is it?" I whispered, holding my hand over the receiver.

She said, "It's Ali—she wants to talk to you."

"Hello?"

"Hail, conquering heroine," she said.

"Hail, yourself!" I laughed.

"I wanted to call and talk to you without a cast of thousands."

"Good idea," I said. "What do you think all this means? Are these guys going to give Larry up, or is this a trick?"

"That's hard to say. I'm a little suspicious of how fast this has happened. Underwood's been on the court for over a decade and that means he and his pals can pull in a whole lot of favors. I can't believe that they're going down without more of a fight.

"On the other hand, we've got almost a hundred million voters, and those congressmen have got to be scared shitless. If they're going to sacrifice Larry for their own political skins, this is the way they'd have to do it."

"I'm not sure I understand—"

"What I mean is that they can't just say 'OK, you win—you get off our backs and we'll give you Larry on a stick.' They reopen hearings, they hear some testimony that suddenly convinces them that he's guilty, they impeach him, the Senate votes him out, we call off the strike. Everybody's happy but Larry.

"Lauren, do you have any idea what an absolute, hands-down miracle it is that we've gotten this far? If I had to calculate the odds of actually convincing sixty-two percent of the female population to go on a sex strike and then keeping it going long enough to get to the point where the Congress may change its mind, I'd say they were about two hundred million to one. If I had to calculate the chances of it happening in less than three weeks, I'd say they were closer to about two zillion to one. But it was your press conference this morning that did it. Those little farts are scared to death of you."

"Not all the little farts," I said.

"What's going on?" she demanded.

I waited until Elizabeth was out of earshot. "I just got off the phone with my lawyer. He thinks Sterling White's stalling. Now they say they won't even negotiate until I apologize to Merrill Kennedy."

"For what?"

"I hurt his delicate feelings."

"How terrible. Has Moore gotten there yet?"

"He has and I feel much better just having him around. Thank you."

"It's the least I could do."

I didn't say a word. I poured myself a drink and stepped outside our back door. There were news helicopters circling the house, casting long shadows on the grass. I watched them until the last swallow of liquid anesthesia was gone, then I walked back inside.

"I also wanted to thank you," she said.

"For what?"

"For being our fearless leader." She laughed to cover the emotion in her voice.

"Think nothing of it," I said as I bolted the door and checked the security panel next to it.

Having Moore come down turned out to be a very smart decision. Every day brought hate mail and death threats, all of which were examined in detail by the FBI. The post office was told to send all packages, unopened, to the Bureau. Sometimes they asked me to look at the letters they received, but I avoided it when at all possible. Mostly the letters were stupid but some of them were brilliantly evil, and any reference to Razz could snatch my breath away and send me into a spin of dread and guilt. I told the FBI that Moore was in charge of my security and to deal with him, because I didn't want to know any of the gory details.

Which is not to say that I wasn't scared, I was. Moore suggested that we have these security lights installed on the back of the house. He felt like we were the most vulnerable from the backyard because it could be accessed from the river by anyone, but Agent Brooks argued that we'd just be making things easier for a shooter, so that idea got nixed. He said that they had agents patrolling either side of the Chattahoochee and that they could take care of anybody who tried to get at us from the water.

Moore didn't buy it though, and lots of nights I'd walk out of my room and he'd be standing there at the window, watching the gardens and the orchard and the vast lawn for anyone who'd come to keep a promise made in one of those letters.

Razz started sleeping on the couch in my room, which suited me fine. He thought he was there for my protection but it simply saved me from having to sit at the foot of his bed all through the night to assure myself that he was safe.

It was hard to tell which were scarier, the nights that came with silence and shadow or the dawns that brought the furious attacks of the media. The mainstream press took the "unauthorized trade" angle while the tabloids worked the Lauren and Slick story. They each had their own style; the *Hard Copy*s and the *National Enquirer*s simply went around until they found "insiders" who, for a price, would share their insider's knowledge; translated, that meant make stuff up. People came out of the woodwork claiming to have seen us in places we never went to, doing things we'd never done.

Slick's driver was offered big money to divulge titillating details of our romance on a television newsmagazine. I can only assume that the executive producers of said newsmagazine thought we rode around having sex in the backseat of his limo. I thought that was pretty funny in light of the fact that Slick put public displays of affection right up there in the same category as flossing at the table. After all, the hug he gave me after I got fired and our dance on the ferry were the only two times in five years he'd ever touched me in public.

The big newspapers told a version closer to the truth, although everything was twisted to suggest the most sinister or suspicious motives. Merrill Kennedy had declined to make any additional statement about why I was fired, saying that the firm had no further comment on the matter.

This opened the door to the half-truths and innuendos about the Kovacevich trade. Much was made of the fact that, had I lost all $300 million, I could have bankrupted the firm and caused a meltdown of the capital markets. The fact that I hadn't lost $300 million, I'd earned $34 million for the firm, was all but ignored.

On the few occasions where it was noted that the original trade was Kovacevich's, the blame was never his for lying about having closed the positions; it was always mine for not having known that he was lying. When all else failed, they would bring up the fact that my trade was done at night; the insinuation being that it was something I was trying to hide.

Kovacevich even had the nerve to go on TV and imply that the fact that he had ended up in my job as managing partner was due not to the dishonesty of his trade but the dishonesty of mine. I got so mad that I threw a bowl of Rice Krispies at the screen. I missed, but Razz and Elizabeth called me Elvis all morning.

That was the day I called a press conference to say that if the firm of Sterling White really believed that the transaction in question was so illegal or immoral or whatever, they should give back the $34 million in profits that I'd made.

What really made it nightmarish is that nothing we did seemed to help. Instead of trying to defend myself, I asked the people who'd been involved in the trade to speak to the press. I was more touched than I can describe when each one said he'd be glad to, in spite of the obvious fact that doing so might put his job in jeopardy.

Arthur appeared on *Nightline* and *Newshour with Jim Lehrer* but it didn't do any good. Ronnie even held a press conference about the trade, but he was no more successful than Arthur in diminishing suspicions that I had done something improper.

In one television interview, the host asked Ronnie about five times if I had told him why I wanted to do the trade. When he said no, the guy acted like that was proof of big-time shady dealings. Ronnie was great though; he laughed in the guy's face and said he hadn't asked me why I was doing the trade because it was none of his business why I was doing the trade and that if he spent all his time asking traders what their motives were, he wouldn't have time to execute orders and earn his salary, much less his seven-figure annual bonus.

Slick tried to tell our side of the story to Deborah Norville, but

Deborah seemed much more interested in our relationship than what happened in the executive committee meeting.

Larry Underwood was also in the news every day. He'd hired a big New York PR firm, and the spin doctors were working overtime. Every time you turned on the television, there he was, weeping about the tragic death of his beloved wife, while performing good deeds for the community. He spoke about the warning signs of depression at a mental health symposium in Vermont and dabbed at his eyes for all the network cameras. He established a foundation in his wife's name to continue her work with battered women and broke down at the press conference announcement. Every time you opened the newspaper, there was poor Larry looking stricken, blinking back tears. You would have thought someone in the media might pick up on the fact that Mr. Underwood's overwhelming sadness had occurred only after his wife had been dead for four months—in my view, a fairly long-delayed reaction. But no one did.

Larry was throwing himself on the funeral pyre and no one seemed to notice that he'd waited until the fire had gone out. What was really amazing to me was that people were actually starting to feel sorry for the bastard. I was being made into a cross between Hester Prynne and Ivan Boesky, while Larry played the grieving spouse with such flair that I kept expecting him to don a black veil and a pillbox hat.

Finally, I resigned myself to the fact that I had to make peace with Merrill since he was the one at the controls of this runaway train. I went to my room thinking about what I'd said to Jinx on the train about doing whatever it took to take care of your kid. I looked at my watch and it was ten till three. I called Merrill Kennedy's office. "This is Lauren Fontaine. Is Merrill there?"

"Yes he is, Ms. Fontaine. Will you hold?"

"Sure."

She came back on the line after a long second. "He says he can't talk to you right this minute but he'll call you back as soon as he can. He says it won't be long."

"OK. Tell him I'll be right here waiting." I gave her the number of my private line and hung up.

I waited. I sat on my bed with my hand on the phone and thought what I would say. I checked my watch and practiced what I would say. I waited and I perfected what I would say. At 6:15, I called his office again.

"Oh, Ms. Fontaine. Didn't he call you back?"

"No. Unfortunately, he didn't. May I speak to him now?"

"I'm sorry, he left about an hour ago."

I was so mad I could've chewed the skin off the back of my hand. "No problem. I'll just call him at home. Thanks so much."

I walked down to the den and rummaged through the box containing the contents of my stuff from Sterling White until I found the Partners Directory. Then I fixed myself a drink and took it upstairs. I dialed Merrill's home number, and the other end picked up so fast I still had a mouthful of scotch.

"Hello?"

I swallowed fast. "Louella?"

The voice on the other end was tentative. "Yes?"

I thought about our chance meeting in Merrill's office and smiled to myself; at least I had one friend in the Kennedy family. "This is Lauren Fontaine."

A gust from the polar icecap. "What do you want?"

"Um, well, I called to speak to Merrill. Is he there?"

"No."

"Do you have any idea when you expect him?"

"No."

"Well, I'm really hopeful about our chances of getting Larry Underwood impeached."

"That's nice." The way she said it, you'd have thought I'd said I liked sex with German shepherds or something.

I was searching for some connection. "Are you still involved? . . . with the movement, I mean."

"I'm not," she sniffed. "After I discovered what a hypocrite you are, I had no interest . . ."

"Whoa, hold on."

"No," she barked, "you hold on. I believed in you and what you said about women sticking together. That's before I knew that you were trying to steal Annie Moriarty's husband. Annie Moriarty is my best friend and you're a fake and a fraud and a liar and I'm glad my husband fired you!" Then she hung up with enough force to make my ears ring.

"Nice chatting with you too," I said and tossed back the rest of my drink. I called Hank.

"Do you hate me?" I asked when he picked up the phone.

"No, I adore you, I respect you, I admire you, I worship the very ground you walk on."

"Thanks. I needed that."

"You're welcome. Who is this?"

I laughed. "It's me, the most hated woman in Christendom. Lauren Fontaine."

"Oh, yuk. How'd you get my number?"

"Very funny. I'm in deep shit."

"What's up?"

"I'm afraid I'm not going to get my money from Sterling White." Just hearing myself say the words made me nauseous. "Hank, I've got to get that money!"

"Calm down, calm down. We'll figure this out. Why don't you come over for a drink and we'll discuss it."

"Good idea. Let me grab a bodyguard and I'll be right over."

Hank met us at the door. He shook hands with Moore and gave me a long hug. Moore asked if someone could show him around the house. We all knew the unspoken motive for that request was not architectural curiosity but a need for knowledge of the ways out in case we needed to make a quick exit. Hank called Walter to show him around. When the two of them left for a tour, Hank looked at me. "Little baby, you have *really* done it now."

I leveled a look at him. "Thank you for that news flash, Harry Reasoner. What we've got to do is figure out is how to get those rat bastards to give me my money."

"Have you talked to what's-his-name?"

"Merrill?"

"Yeah, Merrill."

"I can't even get the guy on the phone." I said. Then I told him about the calls I'd made to his office as well as my conversation with Louella.

"Does he like opera?"

"Yeah, he's always bragging about how he has season tickets to both the Met and Kennedy Center."

He winked and walked to the phone. "What's his number?"

I told him and he dialed it. When he spoke, it was with his most-famous-opera-baritone voice. "Hello. I'd like to speak with Mr. Kennedy, please. . . . Mr. Kennedy, this is Edward Williams. I believe we met at a gala after one of my performances. I can't remember if it was in Washington or New York. Yes, that's it—of course, it was at Jimmy Levine's house." He looked at me and winked. "Yes, yes. That was fun . . . Do you ever get down to Atlanta? Oh, really?"

I was staring at Hank, trying to hear the conversation through his eyes.

"Sure. Well, you must let me know next time you plan to visit and I'll throw together some fun people for cocktails and dinner . . . Splendid. Oh, it would be my pleasure.

"Merrill, let me tell you why I'm calling . . . No, no, nothing about fund-raising . . . I don't really get involved in that sort of thing at all . . . no, it's really a personal matter. Merrill, I don't make it a habit to interfere in other people's business, but you seem to have had a misunderstanding with a friend of mine. I hope you'll forgive my intrusion, but I was wanting to see if . . ." he pointed to the bar and then at me and himself.

I nodded and fixed us both a drink, careful not to make any sound that would keep me from hearing at least one side of the conversation.

He laughed a big baritone laugh at whatever stupid, self-serving, pretentious thing Merrill had said. "I know what you mean and . . ." He took the drink and rolled his eyes. "Sure. Sure. Lauren Fontaine . . . No, Lauren and I go way back, practically to childhood . . . I'm her son's godfather." Now he was nodding. "Yeah, she is a pistol. No, volatile *is* a good word.

"Oh, I know. I've been on the other side of that famous temper too." He laughed, "No, it's not any fun. Well, there's no question about it, Merrill, we're definitely talking about the same lady. No, I know she's very upset at some of the things she said." He turned his back to me. "No, I'm just trying to pave the way for that apology . . . Mmhmm . . . Mmhmm . . . I sure would consider that a personal favor."

He turned back so I could see how painful the conversation was. "No, we Puccini fans have to stick together, ha, ha, ha. You too. I meant it about calling me. Good. See you in September, if not before."

He hung up and looked at me. "What a colossal asshole."

"What'd he say? What'd he say?"

A smile. "He said he was sorry that you two had parted badly and that if you'll call him tomorrow, he's sure that the two of you can work out your differences and have an amiable parting."

I was so happy I burst out laughing, "Thank You! Thank you! Thank you!" I even started to do a little jig. I didn't even stop when I heard footsteps—Moore had seen me do tons of stranger things.

I looked up. It wasn't Moore. It was Jake Ward.

Chapter 20

Ever hear the term "mixed emotions"? I was thrilled, horrified, grateful, furious. I had missed him, detested him, needed him, cursed him. At that moment, I simply stared at him.

"Well." He smiled. "If it's not the dancing guerrilla."

I turned to Hank and huffed. "What's he doing here?"

"I came down to visit my old friend," Jake said, pointing at Hank as if he were evidence.

"Ha!" I said and struck a pose of jaded disbelief. "You came down to try to weasel your way back into my good graces," I said and tossed my head. "Which was clearly a lack of good judgment since I refuse to accept your apologies."

"Good. Because I'm not offering any."

"Good. Because your article was stupid and I know why you did it."

At that point, Hank set his drink on the table and shook his head. "I'm going to find Walter," he said, looking at me then at Jake. "Now I want you two to play nicely or there'll be no juice and cookies before nap time."

Jake folded his arms across his chest and challenged. "So, you think you know why I wrote the article."

"Yes. I do. You just did to hurt me because you were jealous of me and Slick."

"Is that so? Then again maybe I just feel sorry for him."

"Well, don't. He doesn't need your pity, 'cause he knows I hate you."

"You do not. You find me irresistible, but back to the subject. I wrote that article to try to help you. I think you're dead wrong in the way you're going about this, and it's not going to work. You are not going to get rid of Larry Underwood this way!"

"Oh yes I am! Congress is reconvening hearings next week and I'm going to testify. And when they're over, Larry Underwood is going to be gone and you can kiss my feet and say you were wrong."

"Well, we'll see who'll be kissing whose feet, Ms. Fontaine." He laughed and took a step toward me.

I took a step back. "And that last line 'I wish her and her friends good judgment and good luck.' That is so condescending and officious. I can't believe you wrote that! If you wanted to help me you could have told me that stuff yourself instead of writing an article to make me look bad!"

"I tried to tell you before not to make this about men and women, but you refused to listen." He still had his king of kindergarten stance, but the look on his face made me realize that making me look bad was the last thing he'd meant to do. "My writing that article may seem like a betrayal to you, but I did it because I want you to be successful. I want this guy punished too." He tilted his head and grinned. "Besides, none of those things have anything to do with how crazy I am about you."

"Yeah, sure. But then again, maybe you wrote that mean article so that nobody would know about us, so that nobody would suspect that you were, you know, with me."

His face fell. "Oh, Lauren. You don't really believe that. Do you?"

"The thought crossed my mind," I said and blinked back the tears that came with that admission.

"Honey, I'm not ashamed of loving you. I'm just a really private guy and I don't think it's anybody's business but . . ." His voice was now a whisper. "Oh, Lauren."

He took me in his arms and made these tsk and sigh noises that mean *How on earth could you possibly think something so stupid?* I was doing everything I could to keep from simply unraveling. "I'm still mad," I said into his chest.

"Oh, I know you must be." He laughed. "Especially when you're having such trouble."

Had Hank told him about my money problems? "What do you mean, having trouble?"

"Well, I happen to know you're dying to sleep with me and denying yourself and—"

I pushed him back with one finger. "Mr. Ward, you have the two of us confused. I am not denying myself, I am denying you."

"Well, denial is the right word, but it's not what you're doing, it's what you're in."

I laughed and tried to think of a clever retort, but I didn't get the chance. He cupped the back of my head with his hands and kissed me —hard. Then he pulled my chin up with his finger. "Why did you hang up on me when I called you in Washington?"

I couldn't move my face but I dropped my eyes. "I was afraid you were getting ready to dump me and I couldn't bear it."

"Listen to me, Lauren. Listen with all your heart. I've spent my whole life looking for you. It's taken me all these years to find you and I am not going anywhere. I wish I could be with you all the time but my brother is dying and right now I need to spend as much time with him as I can. But just because I'm not physically here doesn't mean I'm not committed to you. I may get mad, but I'm not going anywhere. Understand?"

"Yeah," I said and kissed him.

"Ms. Fontaine, this is Anita Wood. I'm the booker for *The Late Show with David Letterman.* We would love to have you on the show. Would you please call me at 212—"

I looked up at Moore, who shook his head. We were in the living room, drinking coffee and listening to the zillions of messages on my answering machine.

"C'mon, Moore," I pleaded. "Even Salman Rushdie did the Letterman show."

He shook his head again. "No. We're not taking any chances—"

"Lauren, Barry Ferral. I'm calling for the *Sally Jesse Raphael* show."

I hit the FAST-FORWARD button.

"Lauren, Lester Simmons here at the William Morris Agency. Have you given any thought to representation? We believe that we can help you turn your newfound notoriety into a very lucrative career as a professional personality. The William Morris Agency acts as—"

Fast-forward.

"Lauren, this is Pilar Green. You probably don't remember me but we were friends in grammar school." I almost reached for the receiver before it hit me that we were listening to a tape. "I just wanted to call and say how proud of you I am. You always were a feisty little devil. Remember the time Tony Tyler made you mad, so you knocked him down on the ground and gave him a nosebleed? Anyway, I just wanted to call and say hi and keep up the good work. Bye."

"Why is it the ones you actually want to talk to never leave their numbers?" I sighed and picked up my coffee. "And how come people figure that fame makes you an amnesiac?"

Moore laughed. "How come you never told me about the unfortunate Tony Tyler?"

"I didn't want to scare you," I teased, and took a sip of my coffee. "Besides, it wasn't as random as it sounds. He made fun of my hat."

"Oh, well in that case . . ." he said and rolled his eyes and we both laughed.

I punched the PLAY button and the next voice was barely audible. "Lauren Fontaine, you're dead." Click.

I put down my mug and pinched the bridge of my nose. "You and your pals at the FBI have any idea who that is?"

He shook his head. "But that's before we knew about 'The Tyler Incident.' Maybe it's your old archenemy looking for a rematch."

I smiled and the doorbell rang.

"I'll get it," he said and moved toward the door.

"If it's Tony, don't let him in!" I yelled.

It wasn't Tony. It was Jake. He walked in the room and looked at me, and I felt a million blistering needles pierce the skin in my groin and under my arms. He strode toward me, and after a few seconds, the stinging flush began to fade. He offered no greeting, simply pulled me into his arms, and that's where I was when the others appeared in the doorway, Razz and Elizabeth and, behind them, Moore.

I made the introductions and we settled back in the living room. Jake sat next to me on the sofa. "What are you guys up to?" he asked.

"Moore and I were just talking about my latest death threat," I said.

He turned to Moore. "Describe it."

"Unemotional, whispered but not disguised, left on tape."

Jake nodded. "Probably not dangerous."

Razz blurted, "How would you know?"

Before I could make a face at him for being rude, Jake answered. "Because I got enough of them in my day to usually be able to tell the dangerous from the merely deranged."

"You've gotten death threats too?" Razz asked with a mix of curiosity and admiration.

"Yep, hundreds as a matter of fact." He was enjoying the idea that Razz had no clue about his infamous past.

Razz looked at me for confirmation and I nodded. "Oh yeah? Well, is that where you guys met—in a home for the criminally unpopular?"

Jake roared and Razz blushed at this stranger's appreciation. "No, actually it was your godfather who introduced us—"

Razz turned to me, "Oh, is this the guy that you were whining to Elizabeth about, how he hadn't called you?" He ignored my glare and turned back to Jake, having made the connection. "I've heard all about you. Weren't you like a big revolutionary or something when you were young?"

I rolled my eyes. "Speaking of homes, I may commit you to a home for the criminally tactless."

"Aw, leave him alone. I think he's great." Jake laughed and Razz's face lit up like a candle.

"Seriously," Razz began. "Why does everybody seem to hate my mom? I know she can be annoying as hell, but I think people have gone a little overboard."

"Razz, most of the people who are threatening her are more scared than anything. They're afraid if your mom is successful then pretty soon someone else will stand up to them, then someone else and someone else, until no one is afraid of them anymore. That's the last thing they want to happen."

"Well, why did everybody say she was so great at the beginning then?" he demanded, "When the same people are trying to make her seem like a big crook now?"

"That's something different. It's the media who're responsible for that, and I think there are a couple of reasons for it." I was watching Elizabeth, and she was completely focused on Jake, listening intently.

"The guys who write for newspapers and magazines don't make much money. What they get instead is power—the power to make someone a hero or to completely destroy them. They like using that power, especially on people who are passionate and proud and unapologetic. It's people like your mom who really piss 'em off. In the old Greek myths, any mortal who exhibited what they used to call hubris and we now call pride was automatically on the shit list of the gods. Except now it's the writers for *Time* and *Newsweek* instead of Zeus and Ares."

"Yeah, but what god does that make you? I mean, didn't you write that article in *Esquire* that flipped her out?"

Jake nodded. "I did. And while I criticized the way your mother and her associates are going about this, I never questioned her motives or said that she wasn't trying to do the right thing."

That seemed to satisfy Razz, but Elizabeth was squirming in her seat. "You said there were other reasons why the media is trying to make Miss L. look bad."

"Culture casting. They say there are only thirty-four plots in all of literature and the millions of books out there are some variation of those basic thirty-four plots. In the news business, it's the same thing but with fewer stories. Anytime someone fresh appears they have to be put into one of these slots." He started to tick off examples on his fingers. "You've got your age-old warring-forces story with—fill in the blank: Arabs and Jews, Tutsis and Hutus, Serbs and Croats, whatever. You have your scary story about something you assumed was harmless that turns out to be hazardous to your health: asbestos, caffeine, drinking water, etc., etc."

I looked around the room and they were all mesmerized. It made me happy and I turned back to Jake, who was still talking.

"No newscast or magazine is complete without the story of neighbor helping neighbor in need, and then there's always the innocent in jeopardy—missing women, children trapped in wells, you know the drill. And one of everybody's favorites is the good guy against the bad guy. That one's a classic and that's what the story about your mom and Larry

Underwood started out to be. But there's a story that reporters like even more, and that's the one where the person who appears to be a good guy turns out to be a bad one. Reporters love that one because it can not only destroy the person involved, it can also make the reporter look really smart. That's what's going on now."

"So this is a game for these creeps?" Razz demanded.

"I'm afraid it is. But don't forget that the truth is a powerful force, and history has a way of showing very clearly who were the good guys and who were the bad guys." Jake leaned over and kissed me on the cheek. "And we know where your mom will rank. Now, as much as I hate to, I have to catch a plane."

He rose and said his good-byes and I walked him to the door. He kissed me until my knees went shaky, then he opened the door and stood for a moment. His foot hadn't hit the gravel before a reporter yelled, "Hey, Jake! Are you here to convince Lauren to call off the strike?"

"No, I'm here because I love her and I wanted to make sure she's OK."

There was a second of silence, then the reporters went absolutely nuts. Strobe lights exploded and we stood there together for a long moment, holding hands, posing.

"Thanks," I said without moving my lips.

"My pleasure," he replied without moving his.

I walked past Razz's room about an hour later and he was lying on his bed staring at the wall. I knew the second I saw him that something was wrong. I walked to the foot of the bed and he looked up. His eyes were almost coal black. "Razz, what's the matter? What's happened?"

He didn't move, but his face was ghostly white. "I got a phone call."

"When?"

"Little while ago. While you and Jake were outside."

I eased down on the mattress, never taking my eyes off him. "From whom?"

He looked back at the wall. "I'll give you a hint. He hasn't been heard from in this century."

"Oh, no." A canister of dread exploded in my gut.

"Oh, yeah. That paragon of mental health, that poster child for pharmaceuticals, my dear father."

My hand was at my mouth. "What did he want?"

"He said he wanted me to come live with him because you were too busy making trouble to take care of me. He can't make me do that, can he?"

"No. Hell, no." I picked up a book and slammed it down on the arm of his reading chair. I couldn't let on how stunned I was. I took a very deep breath and I held up my hand. "You do not have to worry, sweetheart. I'll take care of this." Another deep breath. "Don't give it another thought. Under no circumstances will you have to live with your father."

"You sure?" He wanted me to convince him.

"Positive." I grinned. "I'd give you to the gypsies first. Shoot, I'd even cut you up and sell you as bait down by the river before I'd send you to him."

A smile spread across his face. "That a promise?"

"That's a promise."

"Oh, yeah, he also said to tell you that an old friend of yours had passed away."

"Who?"

"Some guy named Irwin Hatfield."

I did not flinch. "He say anything else?"

"Not really. I didn't exactly try to keep him on the line. Mom, who is Irwin Hatfield?"

"He was a good friend of mine, of ours."

"He couldn't have been too good a friend of mine since I never heard of him."

I laughed and turned away before he could see from the panic in my eyes just how wrong he was.

I came through the door into the kitchen. The aroma of beef stew wafted up from the stove. Elizabeth was seething. "Why is that no-good white trash calling here and what did he want?" she demanded.

"He wants Razz to come live with him and he wanted me to know that Irwin Hatfield is dead."

The name Irwin Hatfield meant nothing to Razz because I had taken great care to shield him from the bitter machinations of his father's attempts to get custody. Elizabeth, on the other hand, knew that Irwin Hatfield was the only judge in Augusta who would give me a fair hearing against Teddy's family. Her eyes demanded comfort.

I paced around the butcher-block island in the middle of the kitchen, then I picked up the phone and called information in Augusta. Then I called the paper. A young woman answered, popping gum into receiver. "Obituary."

"I understand that Judge Irwin Hatfield has died."

"Yeah."

"Could you tell me the cause of death?"

"Hold on."

Elizabeth and I stared at each other.

The juicy smacking preceded the voice. "Heart attack."

"Heart attack," I said to Elizabeth, whose jaw was set. "But remember, Judge Hatfield isn't the only player who's dead now."

She shrugged, then the phone rang. It was Hank. He wanted to know if everything had gone well with Jake and I reported that it had.

He heard it in my voice. "What's going on?"

"Teddy called Razz a little while ago."

"What did that sonuvabitch want?"

"He wants Razz to come live with him and he also wanted me to know that Irwin Hatfield is dead. He died of a heart attack."

There was a very long silence. "What does this mean?"

"It means that the only judge in Augusta who wasn't owned by the Fontaines is gone." I sighed. "That's what it means."

He let loose a string of expletives so venomous that I don't remember anything specific, only that they were inventive enough to have come from his sister.

"Now I really need my money since I'm going to have to go back to court and this time I've got to have a major lawyer. I need to make a call. I'll let you know as soon as I know something."

I hung up and walked into the den, out of Elizabeth's earshot, thinking about who would be appointed to take Irwin Hatfield's place and the power he would have to ruin both Razz's life and mine. Would he take Razz away, even though he was sixteen and wanted to stay with me? Was his wife a member of the movement? For mine and Razz's sake, I hoped she wasn't. Could I screw up anything else? No, I decided, I'd about covered all the possibilities, there was nothing else left to go wrong.

I took about six of those deep breaths they teach you in Lamaze class and called Merrill Kennedy's office. He came immediately to the phone. "Good afternoon, Lauren."

"Good afternoon, Merrill," I replied, as jovial as a fat man at a Santa audition. "How are things in the world of high finance?"

"Why, they're just fine, thank you. I spoke to your charming friend Edward Williams last night. He's certainly a talented fellow, isn't he?" His voice was warm and kind of creepily intimate.

"Yes, he is and I'll tell him you said so. The opinions of real opera connoisseurs mean a lot to him." God, I was glad there were no witnesses to this conversation.

His oily voice poured out of the receiver. "Your friend said there were some things you'd like to say to me?"

"Merrill, I asked him to call you because I really do want to apologize for my behavior at the meeting." I thought of the way he'd railroaded me and dug my nails into my palm to continue talking. "I was completely out of line and I hope you'll forgive me."

"Lauren, you are awfully kind to call and admit that you were wrong and that you behaved badly, and I do forgive you."

I could feel my throat constrict. I closed my eyes. "That means a lot to me, Merrill. It really does. Now, if you've got a second, I'd like to go ahead and get our financial arrangements settled."

"Oh my goodness, Lauren I can't discuss that sort of thing with you. You should talk to Frank Davis about that."

I was now breathing so deeply that I thought I might burst a lung. "Merrill," I said as calmly as I could, "Frank has said that he is waiting to hear from you before sending my money. Merrill, let me be candid with you. My ex may be suing me for custody of our son and I've got to have the money to pay a lawyer." I couldn't believe I'd told him that, but I was so desperate and the guy was, after all, a human being.

There was a long silence before he spoke. "Well, you should have thought of that before you started throwing your weight around, shouldn't you?"

"Merrill, the money is mine. There's no dispute about that."

"The money is not yours until I choose to give it to you, *if* I choose to give it to you. You're a smart aleck who has never been grateful for what she's been given."

The question of what I'd been given raced across a synapse of my brain, but he was saying something else. "You're never satisfied— gimme, gimme, gimme. All of you are like that!"

"All of us?" Was he talking about the hapless Louella?

"Yes," he hissed, and the veneer of polish was gone from his voice. "All of you, you women and niggers and faggots. Push, push, push. That's all you do. Maybe you should be held up as a lesson on the dangers of—"

That's all I heard. I hung the phone up and got in the shower. I stayed there for over an hour. I could not get clean.

Chapter 21

It was early Friday morning and we were all in D.C. The original plan was for me to go by myself with Agent Brooks, but then there was a big fight over what to do with Moore. Moore said he had to come with me because I needed at least two bodyguards, but I wanted him to stay with Razz and Elizabeth and keep them safe. Finally, I decided we'd all go.

Brooks had called ahead and four airport security guys met us in an underground spot at Hartsfield, hustled us through parts of the airport I'd never seen and into a car on the tarmac. It was pretty impressive, they were talking to the Delta people the whole time and had the entire operation planned down to the minute so that we were the last ones on just before the doors closed and the plane took off.

David was waiting for us at Washington National with another set of airport security people, and we went straight from the plane to their car. There were as many reporters at the Wolvertons' as were camped around our house, but we were happy with the change of scenery. Teddy's threat to sue me for custody had hit the gossip columns Thursday and the questions focused on that. I answered a couple, then slipped inside where there was almost as much activity.

Ali was introducing Elizabeth and Razz to Lynette and Savannah and everybody was hugging everybody else. I didn't say anything; I just stood and took it all in. To me there are few greater joys than to be in a room when people you love meet each other, and this was a cool compress on a bruised heart.

Savannah saw me and hugged me for a long time. Long enough that I completely melted into her strong arms. Finally, she pulled back and studied me. "Lauren, honey, forgive me for saying so, but you look like shit."

She was right. I'd lost about six pounds, my jeans were hanging off me and my face had that gaunt, haunted look that you see in photographs of women in refugee camps. Under about a pound of makeup, my skin was completely broken out, and there wasn't a concealer made that could hide the dark circles under my eyes.

"Mother Moran, you ain't telling me anything I don't already know." I sighed and turned back to the others.

"Let's get you all settled," Ali was saying to Razz and Elizabeth, then she pointed to me. "The rest of the crowd's in the library, looking at how many votes we've got. Go on in. I'll be back in a bit."

Savannah and Lynette and I made our way down the hall to David's library, where there were more hugs from Jinx and Kimlee. Lisa and Suzanne both grabbed me with all the usual hoopla. That's when I noticed Ms. Fienman and two of her pals were there.

I turned around to speak to Flo, but she had her back to me and was talking to Carl. I stood there for a long moment. I knew she could see me from the corner of her eye but she made no move to speak or to include me so I shrugged and walked away. This little interchange was missed by no one.

Ali came back and handed me about fifty pages, stapled together. "Let's get started. We've got a helluva lot of work to do." She sat in David's chair and the rest of us took our seats—Savannah, Jinx and I on the big sofa, Lynette, Lisa and Kimlee in the leather chairs that flanked the sofa. Carl and Suzanne were on chairs from the dining room and Flo sat by the doors to the garden with her cronies.

"The sheets I've just given out list every congressman and how we think he'll vote. The first thing I need to tell you is that, as of now, we do not have enough votes to win."

I raised my hand. "How far off are we?"

"Further than we'd like. The way it stands now, we only have half the votes we need."

"Maybe that's why they're willing to come to the table so soon," I mumbled. The whole thing had seemed way too good to be true—this explained it.

She held up the paper. "We've broken this down into two sections. On the first two pages we have the legislators we know will vote to impeach, followed by the ones we think will probably vote to impeach; then we have the undecideds, then the little shitheads who will probably vote for Larry again and, finally, the big shitheads that we know will vote for him."

I put my paper in my lap and rubbed my face. "Before I say anything else, let me start by saying thank you to Flo. I think what you did in getting this through the leadership is nothing short of spectacular."

She acknowledged my compliment with the slightest nod.

"Here's my question: Is the timing of this good for us, or are we getting pushed into this before we're ready? I know I was surprised that hearings were called so fast."

"The reason they were called so fast is because I worked like hell to get them called so fast. The sooner we get a vote, the better off we are," Flo explained as if to a slow-witted child.

"How do you figure that?" I asked, careful to keep my voice level.

She sighed at my stupidity. "Because the longer we draw this out, the better the chances of our losing our momentum."

"I've seen no evidence that we're in any danger of losing our momentum," I said, but then I thought about Gigi giving in to Tom and the domestic violence and the financial pressure so many women were facing. I hated to grant Flo the point, but maybe she was right. I shrugged and looked around. "You all have been closer to that part of it than I have. What are you seeing in the ranks? Are we in danger of running out of steam?"

Savannah said, "I don't know about running out of steam, but Flo is right about one thing. The longer this thing goes on, the better the chances that we're going to suffer casualties. I don't want my women at risk for one more day than it takes to win."

"Well, back to my original question. Can we win now? Ali just told us we can't."

Ali set her papers on David's desk. "No, I said we don't have the votes right now. Once you and Savannah testify, we'll pick up support. Then we'll put Jerry Dixon on and he'll testify about what Lynn Underwood told him and that'll be that. Larry goes down in a ball of flames."

"Yeah," Kimlee said. "Jerry Dixon is the key to all of this. He's the closest thing we've got to an eyewitness. He treated Lynn in the emergency room that night. When he asked her how she got the concussion and the dislocated shoulder and she told him she'd fallen down the stairs. He fixed her shoulder, then she made a call to her husband's beeper for him to pick her up but the sonuvabitch never came so Jerry sat with her until she was well enough to take a cab, some hour and a half later. That's when she broke down and told him it was Larry that did it. This guy is convincing. He talks, we win. The rest of it is packaging."

I held out my hands. "Well, why don't we just put him on the stand and forget the rest of it?"

"Not that simple," Jinx said and leered. "The American people want a fight. They want you in the arena and they want Larry and they want Savannah and the rest of it. They want to be ring-side at the biggest bout since Muhammad Ali and Sonny Liston. They want fifty-yard-line seats at the Super Bowl of the genders, they want to be right behind home plate at the World Series of the sexes."

"This is sick," I said.

"This is showbiz," Suzanne corrected.

"Suzanne's right. That was one of my arguments," Flo said to the room in general. "I told the leadership that all the public wanted was for them to provide a legitimate forum. This strike happened because people feel cheated. They want to see Lawrence Underwood stand trial. That's much more important than the verdict."

"That's a good point," I said. "But what if we go through this and the verdict is not guilty? Then what do we do? At that point, we may need to rethink our strategy. There's an article you all might want to read that explains why the strike may be a mistake. It's in the most recent issue of *Esquire*, on the guest editor's page; Jake Ward wrote it." Then I couldn't resist a little plug. "I think it's a pretty good piece."

At that Flo hissed, "Yes, and I'm sure he says the same thing about you."

I smiled and thought, *Yeah, eat your heart out.* "Will we be the only people testifying?" I asked.

Kimlee started to answer and Flo rolled her eyes. I held up my hand to stop Kimlee and leaned into the room. "We appear to have a problem that I think needs addressing. I make no pretense now, nor have I in the past, that I know much about this process at all. That is not my function. I'm here because this movement needs what I bring to it— and that is the willingness to be unpopular. It's why I was the one chosen to take the podium, and do not for one second think I don't understand that.

"You said it yourself, Flo—this sex strike was an old idea. It was *your* idea, but you didn't have the guts to fight for it when you were twenty-five and you didn't have the guts to fight for it when it came up at the meeting before the march. Events have proven one thing: I am willing to stand and do battle and you are not. So spare me the superior fucking attitude, 'cause I'm not impressed."

"Oh, you're not impressed," Flo hissed. "Well, let me tell you something, Miss Fontaine, I'm not impressed with you either. We took you on face value when you sashayed in here a few weeks ago, and we let you participate."

"You let me participate?" I roared. "You didn't *let* me do anything! And face value—what is that supposed to mean?"

"It means we didn't think that you were going to be under suspicion for whatever it is you got fired for. Or that you were screwing someone else's husband and flaunting it. Or that you were going to be a huge embarrassment to this movement." The whole time she was saying this, several of the women she'd brought with her were looking at each other with glee. "It means that you forgot to mention that you might be sued for custody of your son because you're an unfit mother!"

The blood had left my face and was pooled in my pounding heart and hands. It took me a moment to find my voice, and when I did, it was lower than a whisper and not even recognizable to me. "You listen to me and you listen good. I will take you apart if you ever so much as breathe a word about my son again. I don't mean I will say ugly things about you to other people behind your back or that I will bad-mouth you in the press, things that you're so good at. I mean, I will personally, with my own hands, kill you! I will wipe your presence off the face of the earth."

Her jaw dropped in horror and that room was so quiet you could've heard a dancing angel fall on the head of a pin. "Well," Ali said, after a very long silence, "so much for sisterhood." Then the room exploded, each group squawking in outrage.

Savannah moved into the middle of the room between the two of us. "That is enough!" she boomed. "We have not got the time for this petty personal shit. Our women have waited decades for what we may be able to do in the next few weeks—*if we support each other.* I will smack you both bald before I let you ruin this chance, because this is not about either one of you." She turned to Flo. "God didn't let us get to this point to soothe your wounded ego." Then she whirled around to me. "Just because you've got the gloves on doesn't mean you get to use them on anybody you want.

"He has allowed you both a place in His plan and I expect you are both pissing Him off, acting like this. Let it go, girls. Let Him, in His infinite grace, use you in service to other women."

Well, what can you say to that? Nothing.

"All right then," Savannah said and sat down. Then she leaned over to me. "The answer to your question is no, we won't be the only people testifying. Larry's side will have their witnesses too. We'll go first and they won't testify until we finish. They'll have the last word. We think the best plan is for you to start, me to go next and Jerry Dixon to finish."

Ali leaned forward, resting her elbows on the marble desk in front of her. "Lauren, you represent the political stick. You're there to warn them that you've harnessed the fury of half the electorate and that they should not be so stupid as to incur your wrath. The message between the lines should be that you are taking names and are prepared to politically kick the asses of whoever tries to pull any funny business.

"Then Savannah will talk about Lynn Underwood. The other side may well use the blame-the-defendant trick. They may throw out all kinds of outlandish claims about what kind of person she was. You know, make up shit because she's not here to defend herself. It'll be Savannah's job to paint a clear picture of an extraordinary woman."

Over steepled fingers, Savannah said, "I'll be there in my little clerical collar telling the world what a fine, loving—" She stopped for a second and brushed tears away. Then she regained her composure. "I will tell them who Lynn Underwood was."

Ali nodded. "Then Jerry Dixon tells what he knows and we rest our case, so to speak. There'll be questions after each person testifies and my best guess is that each one of us will get an entire day and we'll be finished with our part by Tuesday or Wednesday of next week."

Lisa picked up a silver letter opener. "We've got our public-relations types preparing interviews," she said, pointing it at me. "Lauren, when you're not testifying, we need you talking to the media. Savannah and Flo and the rest of us will be working the halls. The hearings will be carried live by all the major networks, and if we pull together, by this time ten days from now Larry Underwood will be toast."

I was in my room unpacking when I looked up and saw Razz. "Can I talk to you?" he asked, leaning against the doorjamb.

"Sure," I said and closed the door behind him. He hopped up on the bed and held out a hand for me. I grabbed it and he pulled me up. Once we were situated, I patted his leg. "Tell me what's on your mind, sweetpea."

"How much longer do think all this fun and games will last?" he asked, studying his hands.

"I don't know. A lot of it depends on what happens next week. I hope it's over soon but I can't make any promises."

"Do you think it'll last all summer?"

"It could. Why do you ask?"

"Well, since you started with this quaint little idea, we've been knee-deep in trouble, every dork and dweeb in the universe has camped out at our house, we've got homicidal maniacs as pen pals and I haven't gotten to have any fun or see any of my friends." He looked up. "I'm ready for this stupid thing to be over. I especially don't want it going on by the time school starts."

I'd been too wrapped up in my own stuff to see how isolated he must feel. "I'm sorry about you not getting to see your pals. You blew me off when I mentioned it before, but you could invite all your friends over for a big party when we get back."

He shook his head. "One of the reasons I haven't seen any of my friends is that they're all pissed."

"About what?"

"God, Mom, you are so retarded you could be in the *Guinness Book of World Records!*" He shook his head in disgust. "Because of you, nobody's doing the bone-dance."

"Oh. I see. And you've been taking the heat for my politics."

He nodded. "I'm the biggest social piranha in Atlanta."

"Pariah," I corrected.

"Piranha, pariah. It's all the same," he said and flopped back onto the covers.

"What else?"

"If it weren't for this stupid idea of yours, my father wouldn't have reared his ugly head again. I hate to say this, but it seems like you're so busy trying to fix the world and being famous that you don't even care that you've completely fucked up everything for everybody else in this family."

I was speechless.

He shook his head and huffed. "It's not exactly like Aunt Ali and her friends asked you to come up here and start this whole damn war." He looked around for words to express his frustration. "Why'd you have to butt in, anyway?"

"Because I thought it was the right thing to do."

"It was none of your business, Mom! You didn't even know that Underwood lady. Why didn't you let one of those other women do this, one of 'em who was actually her friend?"

"They asked me," I said, simply.

"Hell, yeah, they asked you! None of them would put their families through the stuff we've been through on account of your nifty little plan. Do you think for one minute Aunt Ali would put Corinne and Uncle David through this kind of crap? Corinne, if you'll notice, is at camp, having fun during her summer vacation, not stuck inside a house, like some freak, because her mother's turned into a rabid, barking, political dog."

"Sweetheart, I understand. But what exactly is it that you want me to do about it?"

"Nothing," he said through gritted teeth. "I guess I just wanted you to know how much I hate this stupid idea of yours."

"Well, get at the end of the line . . . if you can find it," I said and slid off the bed. I went to the window and separated the blinds enough to peek through. There was still a big crowd of reporters. I dropped the blinds and turned around. "Razz, I'm sorry about messing up your summer and I'm sorry that I've screwed up a lot of things for us. Like I said, I only did this because I thought it was the right thing to do. In a perfect world, I'd be the only one who had to pay a price for that decision, but the world isn't perfect and I know that it's not just me, it's everybody around me who's having to ante up.

"I don't blame you for being mad, but what's done is done and I still think that something good is going to come out of this. Besides, this won't last forever. And if it makes you feel better, I'm having a pretty shitty time myself."

"Tell me about it. You ought to enter the Miss Morbid USA contest —I think you could win," he said, rolling over on his stomach.

"What else do you want me to say?"

"Nothing. But maybe I *should* go live with my dad for a while."

I closed my eyes. "No," was the only word I had the power to even whisper.

"Why not?"

"Why not?" I snapped. "I'll tell you why not! Because I didn't raise you to cut and run when things get tough, and because the only thing your father can teach you is how to abdicate instead of fight."

His eyes narrowed. "Are you deaf? I'm not cutting and running and I'm not abdicating anything, because *this is not my fight!* I don't give a shit about Lynn Underwood. I'm sorry she got beat up and I'm sorry she was stupid enough to stick around and let it happen again and again, and I'm sorry that her jerk-off husband got away with it, but you're the one that's always talking about taking responsibility for your own actions."

I ran my hands through my dirty hair and looked at him. "Can't it be your fight because it's important to me?"

"Couldn't you have asked me before you started it?" he countered.

"Yeah. I should've and I am very sorry that I didn't. Please forgive me."

He cut his eyes at me. "Yeah, OK, but you need to tell Elizabeth the same stuff you just said to me, because this hasn't exactly been a picnic in Paris for her either."

"More like a barbecue with the Branch Davidians," I offered.

"Or dinner with Dahmer." He walked to the door and stood silent, his back to me. Then he turned and said, "The thing I said about going to stay with my dad. I didn't mean that like running away, it's just that you seem like you're too busy with all this hoopla to have me around right now."

I jumped off the bed and grabbed him. "I need you around," I said. "It's the only thing that makes me feel like I can stand this shit for one more minute. I need to be able to look at you and hold your hand and whisper your name in the dark while I watch you sleep. You are my gift, my reward, my heart. You are . . ." I was about to cry so I rolled my eyes instead. "Too busy, my ass. That's the dumbest thing I ever heard."

"Mom, let's just get this over with. OK?"

"As fast as I possibly can."

Chapter 22

"... at the foot of the Capitol for our gavel-to-gavel coverage of this historic event. Here with me today are Democratic Senators Ashby Graham from Tennessee and Garth Dawson from New York, who have promised to check in with us throughout this special session. Senator Graham, what are your thoughts on ..."

Razz was searching for a country music station and I was staring out the window, mesmerized by the cheering crowds that lined the left side of the street. Savannah was in the front seat with Razz and Moore. Elizabeth and I were in the back, and the rest of our gang was behind us, following in our little five-car parade down Constitution Avenue. I'd thought Ali was kidding when she said we'd have to leave her house at 7:30 in the morning, but it had taken us an hour and twenty minutes, with flashing lights and full police escort, to get from her house to Capitol Hill, a trip that usually takes thirty minutes, max.

Elizabeth turned from the window and the screaming demonstrators on the right side of the street and nudged me, her eyes wide. "Oooh, girl, we're in deep now."

She turned back toward the window before I could read her face. "Yeah. You all right?" I whispered.

She waved her hand dismissively. "Honey, I'm fine. We gotta do what we gotta do." She turned just enough to give me a wink, then back to the window and the amazing crowds.

"Estimates by District officials put the number at close to 1.8 million people," said the voice on the radio. "Many of these people arrived over the weekend and have been camping in the parks in and around Washington. They tell us that they have no plans to leave until this emergency session has completed its hearings and voted on whether or not to impeach Chief Justice Underwood."

"Moore, don't you guys have any decent radio stations?" Razz asked and punched another button.

"Veteran newsmen agree that neither the civil rights marches nor the antiwar demonstrations compare to the success of the Lysistrata Movement. . . ."

I put my hand on the back of Moore's seat and leaned forward. "Do they still think this is a demonstration?" I was incredulous. "Do they just not get it?"

Savannah turned three-quarters around in her seat. "That's what you're here for, lamb. To make sure if they haven't gotten it yet, they get it now."

Moore followed the flashing blue lights and stopped and we got out of the cars and were surrounded by Capitol Police. There were white news trucks sporting satellites on towers of gleaming metal; sweating, kinky-haired, fat men in t-shirts emblazoned with my face, selling t-shirts emblazoned with my face; a crowd of reporters and, directly behind them, a crowd of Underwood supporters.

I can't remember what it was I said, but Razz started laughing. I was watching his face when there was an ear-piercing screech behind us. I whirled around as a thin woman came charging out of the Underwood crowd. Her eyes were narrowed in a hatchetlike countenance and she was close enough to point her finger up in Razz's face, screaming, "You think this is funny, you moron? It's too bad you weren't the one who committed suicide so your mother could know what it feels like to be falsely accused!"

Bad move.

The look on my son's face at that moment and the stress of the last weeks exploded into the rocket fuel of fury and sent my hands for her neck. But Moore, who stood a breath away, beat me to it and grabbed and held her until the police handcuffed her and pushed her into a police cruiser. She was shrieking and cursing and spitting as they closed the door and drove her off. The entire scene lasted less than two minutes and shook me to my core.

My hands went up again, this time to my son's face. "Are you all right?"

He nodded, still dazed; then Ali came running up and the reporters charged and we were immediately surrounded by Capitol Police and rushed through a door and down into what looked like an empty subway.

By the time we caught our breath, Savannah was calming me, Razz was embarrassed and Elizabeth was tending him, Ali was trying to find out what had happened. Moore was gesturing furiously to two policemen to show his displeasure for the security breach, Carl was looking for Kimlee, who was still outside.

Three Secret Service guys hustled me into this large golf cart and drove through a long cement tunnel that hummed with fluorescent panels on the ceiling. From there I was escorted through the hallways of the Capitol building and into the enormous chambers from the back. They introduced me to the doorman or the sergeant at arms or whatever he was called, who yelled out, "Ladies and gentleman, Ms. Lauren Fontaine," and they all stood up and clapped their courtesy applause.

I walked down the long steps, smiling. Up the steps to the lectern, then I stopped, turned and flashed my best smile, and enough camera flashes went off to create a sunspot.

My introduction came from the oily Speaker of the House himself, Don Gertchen. "Ms. Fontaine, I want to thank you for appearing here today. We do appreciate your interest in these proceedings, but you must understand that we are faced with the difficult job of determining the truth in this situation.

"While we understand that you and your followers feel certain of Chief Justice Underwood's guilt, the rest of us are less so. You have indeed made yourselves and your position clear with your well-organized and inventive demonstration. We have to balance the anger on the part of the electorate that agrees with you with Justice Underwood's right to a fair and unbiased hearing.

"We hope that your participation in this process proves to you and your associates that we are sensitive to the needs and concerns of all of our constituents. In return we would ask you to call off your boycott."

"Mr. Speaker, I thank you for the chance to appear before the Congress, but it's imperative that I make my position clear. The Lysistrata Movement is not a demonstration. It's not to be confused with a march, a boycott, a rally or anything else whose purpose is simply to make a point. We're not interested in making a point. We are at war."

There is no other way to tell what happened except to say all hell broke loose. It was described by news commentators as the closest thing to a riot that the chambers had seen since the first Congress. The whole left side of the aisle came up, en masse, like the horn section of a high school band, twenty or so guys on the right side of the aisle thundered out of their seats and started yelling "Point of order!" at the sergeant at arms. Meanwhile, in the gallery, the photographers were practically knocking each other down for the best view, while a bunch of people in one spectator section started chanting "Underwood's innocent, Underwood's innocent." Ali and Savannah and the council sat stunned in the front row, but above the din I could hear two separate and distinct voices: Elizabeth's, yelling "Go, girl!" and Razz's "Give 'em hell, Mom!"

I didn't move a muscle. The next day, a couple of reporters said I froze but it wasn't that at all. I was thinking about Samson and the Philistines and trying hard not to smile.

Twenty minutes later, when order had been restored, I started again. "I'm here today to address you and to answer any questions you may have about our position on the impeachment of Lawrence Underwood, why it is imperative and the enormity of the consequences if such action is not taken.

"There are very few people in the history of this country who have come before a session of the Congress to issue ultimatums. And yet that is my purpose as I appear before you today. Let me first say that it is not my wish to offend this august body or to show, in any way, a lack of respect. After I'm finished, I'm certain that you will hear adoration, praise and prayer from those who speak for Mr. Underwood. But that is not what I am here for.

"I represent"—I looked down at my notes even though I knew the figure by heart—"about a hundred million of your female constituents."

A huge cheer went up from the balcony. I looked up and could see Razz and Elizabeth and Ali and Savannah and the others in the front row. When the noise finally died down, I leaned into the microphones.

"I am here to speak for those women, and I'm here to speak for a woman I never met but admired for her kindness and generosity of spirit. And I'm here to speak for every person who ever felt powerless to fight back, who ever gave up because they were convinced that they had no other options. I speak for every person who wants to believe that bad guys, no matter how powerful they are, can be made to pay for evil acts.

"I have come here to make you understand that this is a campaign for justice. The people want justice, they want accountability, they want action. The man at the center of these hearings is not above justice and you must make him accountable for what he did just as you must be accountable to the people you represent.

"The hundred million citizens who are on strike know this isn't about politics, it's about the power wielded by one evil man. One evil man who counts on a system that cares only how many victories it can chalk up for the ideological team and how much damage it can inflict on those whose views are different. A system that has taken all of us prisoners.

"If you have the courage, you can help us face down those who would make this about political wins and losses instead of justice. If you don't, you'll be responsible for plunging this nation into a siege the likes of which it has not seen since the Civil War. You represent the American people and I know that two hundred million of those people are hoping that you understand that this is not rhetoric, it is not a demonstration —it is a revolution.

"We will wait as long as it takes but we will make the waiting as painful for you as it is for us. We will hold out because our right to justice is more important to us than you can imagine. We are not going away, we're going to hold on and fight until Lawrence Underwood is punished. Hopefully, you will see fit to do that now. If you do not, we will replace you with representatives who will. He *will* be punished, either by you or by your successors."

Playing to the cameras, the congressman from Louisiana pulled off his bifocals and wiped them with his handkerchief, then he slowly replaced them and pointed at me with a fat finger. "Miz Fontaine, my district in Louisiana is full of devout men, simple, hardworking Christian men who know right from wrong and who think that you are the evil one."

About fifteen people in the gallery jumped up, cheering and clapping, then surprised, they sat down and pretended not to notice that the huge chamber was silent. He was waiting for me to say something. I just watched him.

"Now, I don't believe that, Miz Fontaine, I think you're just real misguided. I'm sure you're a smart lady, and me—I'm just a country boy. A country boy, faced with a big ol' dilemma, so why don't you help me out here with a few questions. Justice Underwood is a man who has not been convicted of any crime. Justice Underwood is a man who has not even been charged with a crime."

He took a big breath and I jumped in. "Haven't you heard, sir? Larry Underwood has been charged by the American public with longtime, yellow-bellied, systematic, sadistic torture of his devout, hardworking, Christian wife. And how do you expect him to be convicted when the only body with jurisdiction to hear his case refused to spend so much as an entire day on it, much less ask one hard question or bother to speak to the witness who gave you a sworn affidavit that said the victim named Larry Underwood as her batterer?

"If that were the effort expended on other criminal cases, we wouldn't have one single soul in jail in the entire country. So you'll have to forgive me for thinking that your lack of a guilty verdict is hardly proof of his innocence."

Well, that seemed to really piss the old boy off. "Miz Fontaine, you interrupted me. I was not finished with my question. Now if you'll be so kind as to allow me to finish speaking."

My only response was silence.

"Thank you. Now, my question is this. Nobody elected you to anything, so how do you figure to have the right to come waltzing in here, telling us elected officials what we have to do?"

His studied country-boy accent was setting my nerves on edge, so I smiled and responded in my sweetest Georgia drawl. "I received a letter in the mail requesting that I appear here today. So, to answer your question—I came waltzing in here at the invitation of the Speaker of the House. And I'm not telling you what you have to do, I'm simply pointing out what you can expect should you elected officials choose to protect this monster."

B y 11:00 A.M., my blood pressure was about 300/190. The other side's hearing tactics turned out to be identical to its media strategy: provoke, intimidate and attack. Still, I felt like I was holding my own. This frustrated the other side and made them progressively more contentious, which in turn did nothing to improve my mood either.

"Ms. Fontaine, you're in a bit of trouble yourself, aren't you?" I was asked by the representative from Utah, a man with a narrow face, steel-rimmed glasses and teeth long enough to suggest possible beaver ancestry.

I cocked my head and he smiled, prompting me to wonder just how much wood could a woodchuck chuck.

"I mean you've been charged with unauthorized trading, have you not?" he thundered.

"Do you mean have I been charged by the Securities and Exchange Commission, whose jurisdiction that is? The answer is—no, I have not."

"Well, haven't you been charged by your previous employer?"

"My previous employer, who just happens to have been Lawrence Underwood's close friend and former prep school roommate, has not charged me with unauthorized trading. He has, in fact, refused to go on record with formal charges, preferring to allow insinuation and innuendo to do his dirty work. I should also point out that the supposedly unauthorized trade made my previous employer $34 million. I've said it once, I'll say it again: If Merrill Kennedy really believes that the trade in question was, in any way, illegal or unethical, then he ought to give that money back. I am not aware of any effort on his part to do so."

"But you're being sued for custody of your son, are you not?" He'd been saving that like a savory stump.

I leaned out from the podium. "I find that question offensive and presumptuous. I did not come here to answer to you about my private life."

"That's funny, since you seem to think that Chief Justice Underwood should answer to you about *his* private life."

I forced a calm that I didn't feel into my voice. "I don't find it funny at all and Chief Justice Underwood isn't answering to me, he is answering to the American people, and as far as I know, repeated criminal assault isn't covered under the right to privacy statutes."

"Will the lady yield to the gentleman from Rhode Island?" boomed the Speaker.

"I yield to the gentleman from Rhode Island," I said. It was almost 2:00 P.M., I'd been tied to the whipping post for hours, enduring personal insults and antagonism, pompous and condescending lectures as well as sarcastic and snotty comments. I was getting really testy.

Senator Scott Burkowski leaned forward into his microphone. "Is it really your intent to declare war on this body? "

"Senator Burkowski, I believe my words are on record."

"Ms. Fontaine, are you aware of the penalties for sedition?"

"I am fully aware of the penalties for sedition," I said with the certainty of a liar. I was not even sure what sedition was—I thought it had something to do with dirt conservation, but I wasn't about to say so. Instead, I changed the subject. "Senator Burkowski, you are the representative of the people of the state of Rhode Island."

He nodded.

"And you take your job seriously."

He nodded.

"I am the representative of a hundred million angry women and I take my job seriously too."

He cocked his head as if he were unsure of my point, then a grin spread across his face. "Are you saying that you'd like to go to prison to show how seriously you take your job?"

I stood up. "Mr. Burkowski, if you think your state and this country are better served by throwing your senatorial weight around, if you think that throwing me into prison is going to force a hundred million women back into bed, you shouldn't threaten me—you should *just try it.*"

Eleven hundred people hesitated for a second to make sure they'd heard right; then the place exploded again. The Speaker of the House leaned over to the sergeant at arms and growled, "Get the goddamned mace."

Blinding me with chemicals was the about the only thing they hadn't thought of yet. But the mace he was talking about appeared to be the proverbial big stick, black with silver wrapping, topped with an eagle perched on a ball. The sergeant at arms picked it up from the bottom rung of this big pedestal. I was relieved to know that they were only going to beat me to a pulp. But to my amazement, it wasn't used on me at all. Brandishing it is supposed to enforce order in the room. It didn't work. A second recess was called.

I glanced at my watch. Twenty more minutes and it would be over. I was exhausted, everyone was exhausted. I'd been warned by the Speaker to conduct myself in a courteous way when addressing the members and I had said that I would respond with courtesy if spoken to with courtesy.

Representative Dick Seibert had the floor and, mercifully, he was on our side. "Ms. Fontaine, one question. I'd like to clear up a discrepancy in your testimony. Earlier you said that you represented one hundred million women, then you said you knew that two hundred million people hoped we understood the seriousness of your position. Is it one hundred million people or two hundred million?"

I couldn't have asked for a better setup. "I said I represent one hundred million women. The other hundred million includes the corresponding number of *very* desperate men."

At that point, as if rehearsed, one male page raised his hand to substantiate my claim, then another, then another until every male page, photographer, legislative assistant and cameraman held their hands high and brought the house down. I laughed, they laughed, the nation as a whole laughed, and it was probably that single gesture that saved us as a country.

There is nothing quite so perverse as the media. While I was trying to be nice, they were intent on destroying me. Then when I turned into the flaming bitch on wheels, they loved me. The morning after my appearance, I was everybody's favorite girl.

The *New York Times* said, "Lauren Fontaine took on both an unnamed assailant and the U.S. Congress yesterday and never broke a sweat. It was the most impressive performance given in that body in decades. Democrats are already whispering about the possibility of high office . . ."

The *Washington Post* said, "Since the days of Senator Joseph McCarthy, Congress has reveled in its power. It has used subpoenas and inquiries and confirmation hearings to force the powerful to grovel at its collective feet. They call it eating the carpet, and they wanted Lauren Fontaine to do it. Who of them would have guessed that the cool blonde in the Chanel suit would decline so much as a taste of the old rug, and in doing so, show them for the bullies that they are."

The *Wall Street Journal* even credited me with a 121-point rise in the Dow Jones. They said, "Politicians found out yesterday what Wall Streeters have known for years: Lauren Fontaine is one cool customer. Traders honored her yesterday by bidding up stocks . . ."

But it was the *Atlanta Constitution* article that caused the greatest display of euphoria when Razz read aloud, " 'So strong was Lauren Fontaine's presence in front of the joint session of Congress yesterday that the chances of impeachment went from nonexistent to even odds as Ms. Fontaine won the most spectacular game of brinkmanship since John Kennedy made the Russians blink one hot October over three decades ago.' "

Chapter 23

"You were killer," I said and hugged her again.

She was. She had done an exquisite job. The Reverend Moran had been eloquent in her testimony about Lynn Underwood and who she was.

She beamed. "Thank you, my dear. I was pretty good if I do say so myself."

Elizabeth appeared in the doorway. "Savannah, darling, you did Lynn proud. You did us all proud," she said, shaking her head with emotion. Savannah bowed at the compliment.

I glanced at my watch and it was past midnight. "Where's everybody else?"

She stifled a yawn. "They're all still working the halls, and they'll be there as long as there's anybody left who'll listen. I am too talked out to be useful but I wanted to come by and see how y'all are doing."

"We're doing great, thanks to you."

She looked around the room. "Is Uncle Jake here yet?"

"So that's why you came by," I teased and shook my finger at her. "I'm on to you, Savannah; you better leave my man alone. Besides, he's at the hotel. He called about twenty minutes ago, said he'd just gotten in and he'd see us in the morning."

She winked. "I guess I'll just have to wait till tomorrow then. I gotta run, lamb. I'm beat."

I hugged her. "Get some sleep, you deserve it."

"You too. Sweet dreams." She slipped out the door.

I turned around in time to see Elizabeth heading to the kitchen so I followed her. David had retired early and Razz had rumbled off to his room after the eleven o'clock news and the house was quiet. Elizabeth and I had had so little time together since we'd come to the chaos of Washington, and I thought we might grab a snack and compare notes on the players before Ali came home.

She was several steps ahead of me and through the door to the kitchen when I heard Moore's voice. "There's the beautiful woman of my dreams." The door swung back and I took a quick step backwards to avoid it.

"And there," Elizabeth cooed, "is my fantasy man."

The door settled and I stood in Ali's Chinese red dining room. So much for a midnight snack, I thought. I guess I'll go back to my room.

I did. I took my clothes off, put on my nightgown, hung up my things, walked over to the television, picked up the remote control, tossed it onto the bed and went to the bathroom. As I was walking back, I caught my reflection in the mirror and I was still grinning my ass off.

I flipped on the TV to CNN, where there was a clip of Savannah. I turned up the sound. "To sum up the day's events, the impeachment of Chief Justice Lawrence Underwood came closer to becoming a reality when the well-known Reverend Savannah Moran, Rector of Saint Timothy's Church in Washington, D.C., testified in front of an emergency session of Congress today. The Reverend spoke eloquently about her twenty-five-year friendship with Lynn Underwood and her belief that Lawrence Underwood was responsible for his wife's suicide. She conceded under the sometimes strident questioning of the congressional leadership that Lynn Underwood had never told her that she was being abused by her husband. Still, insiders report that the Reverend Moran may have picked up several key votes for the Lysistratans.

"Jerry Dixon, an emergency room doctor who treated Lynn Underwood, will take the floor Monday morning and his testimony will be covered live beginning at 9:00 A.M., eastern daylight time. The nation is expected to be glued to their sets as the Lysistrata leaders, the doctors, and the politicians continue to play out their moves in a game where there are lots of surprises and anything can happen."

I flipped off the TV and wriggled into the pillows. "Yes indeed," I repeated to myself. "There are lots of surprises and anything can happen." I closed my eyes and drifted off.

I couldn't have been asleep more than an hour or two when I felt myself being shaken. I opened my eyes and Moore was standing over me, the dim light of the hallway behind him.

"Sweetie, I'm really happy for you, but can we talk about this later?" I groaned and turned over.

His tone was as dark as the room. "Lauren, you need to get up. The FBI's here and they want to talk to you."

I sat up and pushed the hair out of my face. "What's the matter?"

"Savannah's missing—"

"Oh my God." I was out of bed and almost to the stairs.

"—And they got a letter saying she was going to be murdered," he said quietly to my back.

I went cold.

I could see two men in dark suits at the foot of the stairs but I was frozen, my hand on the banister. One of them looked up. "Ms. Fontaine, we need your help." When I didn't move, he added, "Reverend Moran needs your help."

It's the only thing that got me down those stairs. Horror had filled me tight, swollen my feet and hands. Every step was bruising and I clutched the rail and it felt as if I were descending into the depths of a nightmare that I would never leave.

I was halfway down when I noticed David, standing in shadow. He was in his bathrobe and a tuft of his hair was sticking straight up on one side and it was the first time he had ever looked old to me. His face was haggard and he looked thin and helpless. He didn't move toward me, I moved toward him. "Where's Ali?"

"On her way home. She's safe," he said more to himself than me.

The man who spoke to me was in his early fifties; he had a silver flattop and soft brown eyes. He shook my hand. "I'm Agent John Lynch and this is my partner, Agent Johnson." I looked at Agent Johnson. He was powerfully built, with big shoulders and a baby face.

I reached for David's hand and turned back to Agent Lynch. "Tell me about the letter. What did it say?"

"Said she was a liar and a troublemaker. Said that by the time we received the letter she'd have been put to death for her crimes. Called it justifiable homicide, said that God would be pleased."

The room began to tilt. I closed my eyes and reached out for the wall.

"Come on, Ms. Fontaine, let's all sit down," he said and motioned toward the sofa. Moore took my other arm and we walked into the living room. Elizabeth was standing in the doorway to the kitchen. Her face was gray. We looked at each other and she shook her head.

"Elizabeth," I whispered and she looked up. I motioned to her to come and she did and we sank into the sofa, holding each other's hands.

"Could she still be alive?" I croaked, wedged tightly between David and Elizabeth.

"We don't know. We haven't found a body, so we're proceeding as if she is. She couldn't be reached at her home and we have reason to believe that she has not been home since early this morning." He looked up at Moore, who was standing beside the couch, like a sentry. "I understand that she came by here around midnight."

I answered. "It was 12:13 when she got here. I know 'cause I looked at my watch."

"How long did she stay?"

"Less than ten minutes."

"What did she say?"

"She said that she came by to check on us, that she was pleased with the way things went, that she was tired and she'd be by tomorrow."

Agent Johnson spoke. "Did she seem nervous, say anything about being followed, anything like that?" The lamp on the end table cast a deep shadow on his face, making him look like a character in an Edward Hopper painting, forlorn and morose.

"She didn't say anything like that, she just seemed tired." Then Ali and Lynette and Jinx came in with another FBI guy. They didn't even shut the door before Kimlee and Carl appeared, and more FBI men whose names I didn't catch, then Lisa and Suzanne and Flo. And then, there on the steps, eyes wide with fear, was Razz.

I watched it in slow motion, numb, not registering sounds or voices. I know I spoke but I don't recall what I was asked or what I said in return. People touched me, I watched them do it but could feel nothing outside myself. I could only feel the hot black tar of despair bubbling up inside me, drowning me from the inside, and I could hear only one voice—my own, crying silently, "Please don't leave me, Savannah, I'm afraid and I need you. Please don't leave me."

Ali and Lynette started calling people to see if anyone had seen her and no one had. The night dragged by, one airless hour after another, and in my high-pitched loneliness, even the sight of the people I loved gave me unbearable claustrophobia.

I walked into the kitchen and through it to the hallway and from there into David's library. I stood in the doorway of that umbral chamber, dark as a sarcophagus, then walked to the French doors and looked through them at the rose garden, lit by a repoussé moon. The air-conditioning was on high and the room was chilly and I didn't have the energy to open the door and step out into the heat. The roses that had been fresh and arrogant the night of the march were now faded, their petals dropped on the ground like shed ball gowns.

I put my forehead against the glass and wondered: Had this ever been a good idea? Was I responsible for this? Was it a punishment for my hubris?

Should I kneel like a beggar and plead with God to spare Savannah because I loved her? Would my audacity just piss him off? He must love her; had he taken her home to watch over us? Could I convince Him how much we needed her here?

I turned my face toward heaven. "So what's your point? This wasn't even her idea. And what's the deal about protecting Larry? Sometimes I don't get You at all. Wouldn't it be more honest if You just said, 'Hey, I'm God, I make the rules and I change 'em when I want and screw you'?"

"I came as soon as I could." It was Jake. He turned me around and pulled me to him, squeezing an enormous sigh out of my chest in the process.

"I was just talking to God," I said into his shirt.

He nodded. "I was praying all the way over in the cab."

"I wouldn't exactly call what I was doing praying, more like taunting."

"Do you think that's going to help?"

I shrugged. "No. But He doesn't help when I ask nicely either." I pulled away and opened the French doors to the garden. "Besides, I think you're wrong. I don't think His lessons are kisses, I just think He hates my guts." It was still in the low nineties and I stepped out and felt like I'd walked into a blanket fresh from the dryer, hot but not yet dry.

"He doesn't hate your guts."

I whirled around. "Well, why is all this happening to the good guys? Why would He take Savannah? And don't give me any bullshit about lessons. I need her—we all need her. Jake, I'm the mouth of this thing but Savannah is its soul."

He winced. "*Chère,* we don't know that God has taken Savannah. Have a little faith."

"Don't you understand?" I sighed. "I don't have any faith. I don't really believe that God gives a damn about me. And I don't I think He gives us lessons, only tests. That's why I said that at Hank's about courage. And you know what's so ironic? She'd almost convinced me with her faith. You could see how Savannah believed it. In spite of everything, she saw God as loving and good. if He let anything bad happen to her, I'll know I was right all along—that God is just plain mean."

He took my hand, kissed my palm and held it to his face. "If God is teaching you who He is through Savannah, then I'm sure she'll turn up."

This seemed preposterous, the most outlandish of claims. "You think that because God knows I need Savannah to learn about Him that He'll make her still be alive."

He nodded with absolute faith. "I don't think it, I know it."

This was a smart guy, but he was clearly off his rocker. I laughed. "Are you kidding me? Do you really believe that?" I was almost giddy with amazement at his wild assertions.

"I'm so sure of it that I'll make you a deal on behalf of God."

"Which is?"

"If Savannah turns out to still be alive, you'll take it as proof that God is loving and that He loves you."

This must be a trick or a joke or something. "Are you authorized to act as God's agent?"

"Actually, in this case I think I am. After all, I'm not making you any promises on His behalf. All I'm saying is that if Savannah is still alive, you'll know that God loves you and always will. If Savannah's dead, then you can keep believing anything you want."

"And you think she might be still alive for no other reason than just because I need her to teach me about faith."

"Yeah."

I put my hand on his cheek. "I am so lucky to have found you. Whatever happens, I'm sure of that. You're a sweet, dear, wonderful man," I whispered, and when he smiled, I added, "Even if you are crazy."

He grabbed me and pulled me to him as if he thought he could merge our flesh with the pressure of his arms and his love. "I can promise you one thing—I love you and I'm not going anywhere, ever. Understand?"

I nodded and we walked back through the house, through the gloom of the hall and the kitchen, white and silent like a morgue, into the melancholy that hovered in the living room. Before we came through the kitchen door, I slid away from Jake. I knew seeing us arm in arm would kill Flo and she was in enough pain. I didn't like her and she didn't like me, but we both loved Savannah.

That's the funny thing about times like that—you feel so sorry for everyone else, it keeps you from dying of your own emotions. "Do we know anything?" I asked the FBI men, who were all standing together. Agent Johnson was the closest to me; he shook his head. "We haven't located her car or anyone else who's seen her."

I nodded and sat on the floor in front of the fireplace for the vigil. Lynette and Elizabeth were making coffee and Moore was setting out food and it was almost 3:00 when the call came in to Agent Lynch. They had found Savannah about five blocks west of St. Timothy's. She'd been beaten almost to death. That was all the information they had. Could someone come to County Hospital? I didn't move. I couldn't do it. Finally Flo stood and she looked at Lynette and the two of them left with an FBI man whose name I didn't know. Jake looked at me and I just shook my head. I had known all along that the outcome was going to be violence, known in the instinctive dread that runs through the core of me like mercury through a thermometer.

I looked at my son, sitting silently at my feet, whom I'd brought here with me on this campaign so that he could see this up close, my own little drummer boy to keep time on the battlefield while the world exploded into loss and hatred and destruction and death.

I looked at Elizabeth, but when she looked back at me, I had to look away. She had known before I did and she had warned me and I had been so convinced of my power. *My name is Ozymandias, king of kings: / Look on my works, ye Mighty, and despair!*

There was not a soul in that room I could look at, much less comfort or be comforted by, and the night caught us all and encompassed us and refused to move forward. Instead, it came back on itself and encircled us again and again, thickening and entombing us in its aubergine cruelty.

At 4:20 A.M., Flo called. Savannah was in surgery. Her face was so badly beaten, they had only identified her by her clerical collar and she was in a coma.

We burst through the electric doors into the long hallway, and the only sound was our footsteps on linoleum and the hum of the fluorescent lights. Inside the glass door marked Trauma Intensive Care Unit Waiting Room you could see Flo, rocking back and forth in her plastic chair, and Lynette with her face in her hands.

Next to them was a big man with wispy red hair, his eyes closed, mumbling to himself. It wasn't until he looked up when we came in that I recognized him from newspaper photos—Bishop Paul Keeler.

He embraced Jake, then he spoke to the rest of us. "Savannah is still in surgery. That's all we know . . . except that the doctors are not encouraging." Then he bowed his head. "Please join me in a prayer. Holy Father, in your infinite mercy, please hear our prayers and supplications for your servant Savannah, who has been so valiant . . ."

When he finished and led into the Lord's Prayer, I couldn't speak. I felt dizzy and the room grew darker until I couldn't see at all and I was shaking furiously and clenching my teeth, trying to keep them from chattering, and it was as if I'd fallen into a river of ice water and been caught in the black undertow. I was too embarrassed to say anything.

Razz was standing next to me and nudged me with his elbow. "Mom, are you OK?"

"I'm fine."

I woke up with a horrible taste in my mouth in a hospital room packed with flowers and Mylar balloons. Razz and Jake were sitting next to the bed, Moore and Elizabeth were standing in the corner.

I didn't want to breathe on them, so I turned my head toward the wall. "Did I faint or something?" I croaked.

"You went into shock," Razz offered.

I remembered his comment the day I left for Washington about shock therapy being my only hope. I looked down at my hands. "Pretty pathetic." I took a deep breath and held it as a shield. Then, "How's Savannah?"

"She's in ICU in critical condition . . . in a coma *but* still alive," Jake assured me.

"What do the doctors say?"

"They won't make any predictions. The only thing they'll say is that she surprised them by surviving the first twenty-four hours. She's in pretty bad shape though . . . five broken ribs, collapsed lung, severely bruised kidneys, fractured pelvis. They operated again this afternoon to relieve swelling in her brain. That's the greatest danger right now. It's real touch and go . . ." His voice drifted off.

I rolled over on my side, facing away from them, and felt the pull of the IV line attached to my arm. In my peripheral vision I could see Jake sit back and fold his arms across his chest.

"I hope to hell you're not going to lie there wallowing in self-pity 'cause you feel guilty about Savannah."

I whirled back around. "Well, now that you mention it, Mr. Ward, I do feel guilty. I feel extremely guilty."

"Well, get over it," he whispered. "I hate to be the one who breaks the news to you, but you are not responsible for every event in the universe. We have a God, and you ain't it."

"Oh, yeah," I hissed. "Your God was going to take care of Savannah, remember?"

"The deal, as I recall, was that Savannah would still be alive. And Savannah *is* still alive. And that is a miracle for which the rest of us are pretty damned grateful!"

I sighed and spoke to the ceiling. "To tell you the truth, I'm so confused I don't know what I feel. Maybe it's not even guilt, maybe it's just a combination of fear and sadness. All I know is that I started this whole stupid thing—"

He put his fingers to my lips. "First off, Larry Underwood started this whole stupid thing. You, my little egomaniac, are only one player in this entire drama. You got involved because of your anger and your conscience and so did a lot of other people. This has been the kind of battle that Savannah's fought for decades, long before she ever heard of Lauren Fontaine. It doesn't have anything to do with you. OK?"

That did make me feel a little better. "OK," I said and looked around. There was a heavy plastic water pitcher on the table behind Jake and behind that a clock. The room didn't have a window. "What time is it?"

"It's 9:50 . . . Sunday night."

"When can I go home?"

"In the morning. Now get some sleep," Jake said and squeezed my hand. Then he slipped through the door.

Razz came to the side of the bed and kissed me on the forehead. "Don't worry, Mom. There's about a battalion of cops and FBI guys out here protecting you."

I looked over at Moore, who hadn't moved. "Please go with them and keep my baby safe," I whispered.

And my beloved friend didn't argue or make me explain. He followed my son out the door.

It took less than ten minutes to convince John Lynch to wheel me down through the empty hospital kitchen to the doctors' entrance of the ICU. The entire area had been cordoned off from the press, and there were several FBI guys that I recognized from Ali's house. I looked in the waiting room and it was packed with worried women comforting each other and somber clergymen whispering among themselves. Huddled in between were bewildered family members of other ICU patients, who'd pitched makeshift camps around the glass tables and cheap sofas.

Just inside the door, Lynette looked up from what had obviously been a long vigil. She hadn't changed clothes, her face was gray and her voice, muted. "Hi, baby, you feeling better?"

"Yeah, I'm fine. What about Savannah?"

"Hanging in there."

"She regained consciousness?"

She looked away and shook her head.

"What do the doctors say?"

She made a face of disgust. "Those jackasses are worthless. Absolutely worthless. They can barely be bothered to tell us anything and when they do, it's all clichés."

I nodded. There was no air in the room.

"Have you seen her?"

She nodded. "They let three people at a time in for about ten minutes at 8:00 A.M., 2:00 P.M. and 10:00 P.M. I just saw her. The priests are in there now."

I got up out of the wheelchair and pushed through the doors. There was a well-lit nurses' station in the middle, with about eight beds, each occupied and each with at least one visitor, lit like tableaus of tragedy in a large, otherwise dark, room. Shadow and light, plastic and stainless steel, machines and tubes, hope and death.

Three men in black stood at the foot of Savannah's bed and I moved past them to the rail. No one had warned me and I was horrified by the swollen pulp and fresh bandages. There was nothing that would have given solace that she was even still alive except the clear liquids still moving through tubes in her nose and her arms and the bright-red bloody gauze that protected the tracheotomy tube at the bottom of her throat.

The three priests backed away as I took her hand, careful not to disturb the needles taped into it. "Savannah, it's Lauren. I love you and I want so much for you to get better. We're all praying like crazy for you and begging God to let you stay here and keep working in His service."

I was trying to find the right combination of words, some magical challenge that whatever was left of her would respond to. Tears were streaming down my face now and I was struggling to keep my enunciation clear. "Don't let them make you a victim, Savannah. Don't let them think they can stop you with pain and fear. If you die, then they win. They will have proven us powerless to fight against their strength and violence and hatred. But if you get well, you'll prove that we can't be intimidated or beaten down. Don't you be like Lynn Underwood and give up. Get mad, Savannah, and get well. Focus your wrath on the men who are responsible for this and for what happened to Lynn and to Nicole Brown Simpson and every other woman who ever lay, broken and bleeding, in an emergency room in the middle of the night." My sobs were interrupted by an attack of hiccups and it took forever to get out the last sentence: "Do you hear me, Savannah?"

I could have sworn I felt her squeeze my hand.

I was released from the hospital at 7:30 Monday morning. Razz and Moore had come to get me, but we hadn't gone far—just downstairs to the ICU for the 8:00 A.M. visitation. Jake was waiting with Ali and the three of us were the first ones allowed in to see Savannah.

Never in my life have I been as happy to see anyone open their eyes. I promptly burst into tears.

Ali leaned over and kissed Savannah's hand. "Sweetie, the doctors are calling it a miracle." At the word *miracle,* Jake looked at me and smiled. "You wouldn't believe how many people have been praying for you. Now, you just concentrate on getting better 'cause we're on our way to victory. Jerry Dixon testifies this morning and I want you well enough to dance at Larry Underwood's impeachment party. OK?"

Savannah nodded and smiled ever so slightly.

"I gotta dash. Love you like crazy. Be back after the hearings." And she was gone.

"Savannah, darlin'," Jake cooed, "you are as strong as you are beautiful. And Ali's right—the world has been praying for you. You will, however, find interesting the obituary that was printed in the early

Sunday edition of the *New York Times*. Very complimentary, if a bit premature. As a matter of fact, I think I'm going to start calling you Lazarus."

She looked at him with the one eye that wasn't bandaged and let out the tiniest laugh.

I knew that there were so many people waiting to see her and I didn't want to be selfish but my heart was about to explode. I took the hand without the IVs. "I love you, Mother Moran," I said. "I'm so grateful that you're not dead." I leaned in close and whispered. "I was scared you were, but Jake said he knew you'd turn up because I need you so much. And he said if you did, that I had to take it as a sign that God loves me."

She was silent so I pulled away to see her reaction, but she wasn't looking at me. She and Jake exchanged a look of such shared grace that I knew I was witnessing a sacrament.

I came out of Savannah's room and the FBI guys took me straight to the Wolvertons'. I was too weak to show up at the Capitol for Jerry Dixon's testimony. It was just as well. Jerry Dixon never showed up either.

I was sure there was another person in the world who might be as pissed as I was by the recent turn of events but I had no idea who it might be. I should have guessed.

It was late morning, I had turned off the television and had my suitcase sitting on the princess-and-the-pea bed. I was packing. The door was locked and there was a loud knock.

"Lauren, open this damn door!" Ali yelled.

"I'm recuperating," I yelled back. "Leave me alone."

"If you don't let me in, I'm going to have Moore bust the door down. Then I'm going to have him throw your sorry ass out into that swarm of reporters downstairs," she threatened.

"Ha! Moore likes me much better than you and he'll do what I say. *I'll* tell him to throw *your* sorry ass out there," I noted as I opened the door and let her in.

She ignored the suitcase and we both climbed up on the bed. She sat there for a long time with a strange look on her face, then she turned to me. "When we started this, I just knew it would work. It seemed like the right thing, and the more women who signed up, the more right it seemed . . . now I'm not so sure." She exhaled, slumping like a week-old helium balloon. "Now, to tell you the truth, I'm not so sure about anything."

"I know what you mean," I said, gnawing on the little plastic button that held on my hospital bracelet. "The only thing I'm certain of is that when I get my hands on Jerry Dixon, he's a dead man."

She raised an eyebrow. "What makes you think he's not already a dead man?"

Immediate and major goose bumps. "You think they killed him?"

"I'd be willing to bet you a million bucks they did. Honey, I knew Jerry Dixon and he was a tortured soul. He held himself responsible for not reporting what Lynn told him to the police. She had made him swear he wouldn't tell anybody, but when she committed suicide, he felt like it was his fault for not helping her. I talked to him two days ago. The poor thing was overjoyed about having the chance to tell his story. He told me there was nothing on earth that could keep him from testifying this morning." She sighed. "If he were still alive, he'd have been there."

"Is it just me or is this is beginning to seem like a Scorsese movie?"

"Unbelievable," she said. "Absolutely nightmarish. The only good news is that the doctors are predicting a full recovery for Savannah. I guess we ought to call a press conference—"

"You can call a séance for all I care but I'm not talking to the press today. I'm going to round up my troops and go home. As soon as I can —hopefully this afternoon, but tonight at the latest. No offense but I've got to get the hell out of here."

She pursed her lips like she was going to say something but then she just nodded and walked out.

"Have you seen *USA TODAY* yet?" Ali asked.

"Ouch! Not yet. What does it say?" We'd flown home late the night before. Now I was talking to her on the phone and plucking my eye-brows, pathetically happy to be back in my own heavily guarded house.

"It says that House Speaker Don Gertchen has decided to postpone the impeachment hearings until Jerry Dixon can be located."

"Yeah?"

"He says that he has reason to believe that Jerry Dixon is in hiding and wants to recant his testimony in the sworn affidavit."

"You are making this up to annoy me," I said.

"I am not," she said. "That is a quote from the big butt-cheese himself. But wait, I haven't told you the best part . . ."

I pinched the bridge of my nose and groaned. "Don't keep me in suspense."

"He says that because they have shown their good faith in holding the hearings, you should show yours by calling off the sex strike."

"I'll show 'em mine all right," I said, leaning toward the mirror to see if I'd missed anything on my right eye. "Are we in agreement that such a statement is beyond absurd and should be treated as such?"

"I believe we are."

I took a swallow of coffee and started on my left eye. "A press conference, Amos?"

"By all means, Andy. Say noon?"

"Sounds simply divine. You set it up and I'll let old Don have it. On a more important note—tell me about Savannah."

"She's healing. Still asleep most of the time, though. Doctors say they'll take out the trach tube in a couple of days and maybe have her in a regular hospital room within a week."

"Tell her she's an inspiration."

They were all there. The same on-air reporters and their accompanying camera crews. The same maneuvering for a few feet of empty space to stand in and broadcast from. The same drill, but with a twist. This press conference came complete with metal detectors at the gates and four extra security guards checking credentials.

I picked up the antique hand mirror that my grandmother had left me, then Moore and I walked outside and up to the podium. He was so close behind me, I could have sworn I felt his breath on the top of my head.

As if on cue, Monica Kaufman called out, "Lauren, what's the mirror for?"

"I've been carrying it around all morning," I said and posed with my prop. "Ever since I read Mr. Gertchen's remarks in the paper. I keep checking it to see just how stupid I look."

That got a big laugh.

I put the mirror down and leaned over the podium. "Listen up, 'cause I'm going to tell you exactly what I think. I think Jerry Dixon is dead. I think anything about him recanting his testimony is bullshit. I think that I'm not going to believe anything so patently ridiculous unless Jerry Dixon says so to my face, in my house, sitting on my living room sofa.

"I think that Larry Underwood's cronies are completely responsible for this and I also think the American people aren't any stupider than I am. As far as Don Gertchen is concerned, I think I made myself clear earlier this week." I dragged each word out with as much sarcasm as I could. "But apparently Don and I have what used to be known as a failure to communicate. Let me say it again, Don. This sex strike will be over when Larry Underwood has been impeached and punished for the abuse of his wife."

I picked up my mirror and had started for the door when one of the reporters yelled, "Why do you think Jerry Dixon is dead?"

The sarcasm left me and sadness flooded my voice box. "Because if he were still alive, he'd have been there yesterday. And you'd have heard the story he tried so hard and waited so patiently to tell you."

"You're accusing the chief justice of the Supreme Court of having a witness bumped off. Isn't that just a little over the top?" asked a smirking man with teeth that looked like they were made of Roquefort cheese.

"Over the top? You mean like the cowardly cretins who tried to beat a woman priest to death or like the justice in question who tortured his wife until she killed herself or—" For a second, I was so mad I lost a sense of where I was; then another question from another reporter.

"What about you, Lauren? Are you still receiving death threats?"

"By the truckload," I said and walked back into my house.

Chapter 24

Hank was throwing one of his famous parties to boost my morale, which had reached an all-time low the week after Jerry Dixon disappeared. "Mr. Ward" had promised to fly down for the occasion and we were all looking forward to the big shindig.

I'd been giving interviews from the house by remote feed all day to various networks, and I had to do one for MTV before we could leave, so Razz, Elizabeth, Moore and I were about forty minutes late.

The door opened. "Well, look who's here," Hank announced and pulled us inside. He introduced us to his surprisingly young date, who was wedged between him and the delicious Mr. Ward. She never acknowledged my existence; she was too busy ogling Jake.

"Jake, I believe you know Lauren and Razz Fontaine." Jake shook Razz's hand, then he turned to me. "I'm very happy to see you again." He kissed my cheek.

"The pleasure is all mine," I said and mouthed a kiss right where Miss Invader of Personal Territory could see it. At that point, she turned to Hank and asked him to give her a tour of the house. Then Razz wandered off and we were alone.

"You look great." His voice was deep and warm.

"Thanks." I nodded toward Hank and his date as they disappeared. "I think Hank's date is curious about which is mightier, your pen or your sword."

"Well, she didn't put it in those exact words." He laughed, watching my reaction. "But she did happen to mention that I was her hero when she was younger."

I laughed. "What? She followed the Solidarity movement as a preschooler? Anyway, I don't care about her." Big lie. First of all, Voncile (my inner voice) had been checking her out and was not happy. And second of all, I was acutely aware that Jake was a hero to two generations —ours and hers.

Jake took my hand and whispered into my hair. "I don't care about her either. I missed you. I thought about you every endless empty hour and all I want right now is to hold you." He took me in his arms and squeezed me tight.

"You don't need to be her hero. You're my hero," I whispered and he blushed, which I thought was really cute. Then Gigi waved to get my attention. "Lauren, come over and introduce us." I did and Razz wandered over. We all chatted for a while, then Jake went to get us a drink. As soon as he was out of earshot, Gigi grabbed my arm. "Honeeey, he is a dream!"

I grinned. "Thanks, I think so too."

"And did you check out Hank's date?"

"Are you kidding? How could you miss her?" Razz grinned.

"She wasn't talking to you, she was talking to me." I said, punching him. "Are you kidding? How could you miss her?"

"Major man thief. She was all over Tom until Jake got here. She's been all over him ever since. And that dress she's wearing—It's so tight, it could be a Band-Aid."

"I know," interrupted Razz, "and I want to say right now that I'd gi—" Gigi and I looked at him and he stopped midword, smiled and walked off. Then she pointed at me. "You better keep an eye on her. She's done everything but put her hand down your friend's pants."

"I already noticed. I swear, I hate it when Hank gets in these heterosexual moods."

There were probably fifty people, not counting the waiters who were taking drink orders and passing hors d'oeuvres. Every single one of them had both an opinion on the movement and the mistaken assumption that I had an interest in hearing it.

Hank was moving through the crowd, making sure everyone was being taken care of, allowing his date to position herself so that she was practically making a human Jake burrito.

I stood there and watched. She pulled back and looked at him and kinda squeezed her shoulders together so her tits would jump out at him. Then—and this is the killer—she parted her lips and kept 'em like that. If there's anything I hate it's that Marilyn Monroe open pout that says, "I'm not quite bright enough to keep my mouth closed. As a matter of fact, you could probably stick the big one in here and I'd be too stupid to know it."

Jake was smirking that damn smirk and Hank appeared beside me. "Is something wrong?"

I flashed a big smile and said under my breath, "Yes, your date is a little friendly for my taste." He turned to look and she was whispering something to Jake and massaging his left shoulder with both hands.

Although, you couldn't hear what she said, you could guess by the way he pulled back, chuckled and said, "Honey, that's a real sweet thing to say and I'm flattered . . . and I don't believe I've ever heard it put quite that way."

I waited for Jake to see me, and when he finally did, I shot him a look of complete disgust. There was no way he could extricate himself without yanking his arm away from her clutches. He shot me back the most helpless look in the world and I turned around and walked out.

I knocked on the door of the guest bathroom and found Gigi and Elizabeth. Elizabeth was checking herself in front of the mirror, something I had never seen her do before, and Gigi was drinking wine and smoking. Gigi only smokes in other people's bathrooms during parties.

"I knew that bitch was trouble from the second I walked into this house," Gigi said, dropping her cigarette into the toilet.

I didn't have to ask who they were talking about. "Yeah," I agreed, flipped my dress up and my panties down and sat on the seat. "Times like this make me wish there was such a thing as the predator police." Blank looks. "You know, for women who go after a man they know is taken. Like I should be able to swear out a complaint tonight against Miss Twitch and the predator police would come and take her away for appropriate punishment."

"Like what?" Elizabeth asked into the mirror.

"Like sentencing her to a lifetime of Laura Ashley dresses and Talbot's turtlenecks," I said, standing up and flushing the toilet.

"And flannel nightgowns . . ." Gigi announced. "And big-girl under-pants."

"That isn't near bad enough. That heifer ought to be sentenced to two years of an unfaithful husband," Elizabeth offered.

"You know, I just thought of something," I said. "She's probably just young and insecure and it's easier for her to interact with men because they validate her in a way that we don't. It's not her fault that we're threatened by her youth and beauty and we shouldn't let it bother us."

Then I opened the door.

"Where are you going ?" Gigi asked, finishing off her wine.

I grinned. "To go out there and tell her if she doesn't leave Jake alone, she'll be leaving in a body bag."

She was standing in the corner with Tom. She'd positioned herself in front of him so that when he leaned down to talk to her, he was staring down her cleavage. And I don't believe that I'd ever seen my brother-in-law so talkative.

I'd just given the bartender my order when I felt a hand on my arm and turned around. It was Jake. "I've been trying to find you."

"Oh, really? Is that why you and Miss Kudzu have been intertwined all night?"

"Oh, come on, Lauren. That wasn't my fault and you know it. I've spent half the night looking for you."

"Yeah, right. And the other half—"

He put his finger on my lips to stop me. "That's enough, woman. I flew all the way down here to be with you for one night. Not her, you. Now come with me."

I didn't say anything. He was holding my hand and I was trying to figure out where we were going. Past the dining room and the kitchen, through the foyer and into the hall that leads to the master suite. I hardly ever went into this part of the house; nobody did. He knocked on the door to Hank's bedroom, and when there was no response, he opened it. Then he pulled me into the dark green room.

I still didn't say anything. I wanted to see what he was going to do. That actually is a lie, I knew exactly what he was going to do and I didn't want to distract him by talking. He picked me up and carried me over to the bed, threw me down and moved slowly onto the bed and on top of me. He had one hand under my head, holding it. He kissed me, gently at first, then harder and harder, then still holding my head, he started running his tongue down the side of my neck. His other hand was white hot and it was burning me wherever he put it and he wouldn't stop. I was guiding his hands and saying no and there was a knock on the door and I came off the bed and onto my feet in one heartbeat.

He sat up and snarled, "What do you want?"

"Oh, sorry," came a tiny little voice in reply. "I was just looking for an unoccupied bathroom. I'm sorry." Then footsteps disappearing and the moment with it.

We stared at each other. I was standing, the front of my dress wrinkled, and he was on the bed with a dark stain the size of a quarter on the front of his pants. I was stiff with shame. "Shit."

"Pardon?" he said.

"I feel like shit. I'm ashamed and frustrated and turned on and I feel like shit," I said, smoothing down the front of my dress.

He laughed. "And you think I feel—what? thrilled? proud? turned off? C'mon, honey, cut me a little slack here."

"Why won't you help me be good?"

"The obvious reasons: It's not my job and it's not my style." He laughed.

I couldn't help it, I laughed too. Then I got serious. "In that case, I can't see you again until this is over. Jake, I can't afford one more reason to doubt what I'm doing, I've got too much at stake already and God knows I'm having a hard enough time as it is." I wanted him to say that he'd be good, that I was going to be safe with him, that he was going to save me from the two of us.

He looked at me for a long time. "You're right. You're right and I'm sorry. Here you are, risking everything to be the person you hope to be and here I am, thinking about myself and how much I want you." He had his elbows on his knees and his face in his hands and he looked down at the floor then up at me. "I am so sorry, Lauren. I love you— for who you are and who you are trying to become—and I am going to support you, even if that means staying away until this is over." Then he stood up, kissed me on the forehead and walked out the door. I sat on that bed for fifteen minutes before I smoothed it and my hair, pulled on my party face and went out. By the time I did, he was long gone.

I was wrecked and the last thing I wanted was to go back to the party. I went upstairs. The door to Hank's library was closed, but I could hear a far-away voice so I knocked. The door opened a crack and Hank was standing there. "What's goin' on?" He didn't say a word, just opened the door and let me in. Elizabeth and Moore were sitting on the couch, Gigi was on the floor next to Razz. The television was on.

I took one look at their faces and braced myself. "What?" Hank took my hand. "It's not good news?"

"It's not good news." Gigi said. "They're charging you with securities fraud."

I looked at her blankly. "What?"

"Securities fraud," Gigi repeated.

Hank squeezed my hand but I still couldn't make sense of any of it. "What in the—"

"It means that you have to be on trial and it means that if they find you guilty, you've got to go to prison," Razz blurted.

"That's ridiculous. I'm not going to prison. I—" I couldn't finish, I had a flashback of my conversation with Elizabeth the day I left for the march: *There's no way anyone can do anything to hurt us just because I go to this thing. This is the land of the free, remember?* I couldn't bear to look at her, I couldn't bear to look at any of them. I stared at the Oriental rug and croaked, "I'm so stupid."

"Oh, honey." Hank pulled me into his arms. "Don't say that. You're not stupid."

My mind was ricocheting around my skull. "How'd you know this was on?"

"Ali called," Gigi explained.

Over Hank's shoulder, I could see the screen with the Special Bulletin banner at the bottom. John Pruitt was saying how the attorney general for the state of Georgia had agreed to present the case and had just announced the indictment by a secret grand jury.

I felt like I was in a dream, it seemed so unreal. I knew John Pruitt, and there he was on TV, saying it was widely believed that I would give myself up to authorities. Then he added that if I didn't turn myself in within seventy-two hours, I would be considered a fugitive and the FBI would become involved.

Hank put his arms around me. "From now on, you all are staying here. At least until we figure out what to do."

"They're not kidding around, are they?" I asked.

"No, they're not kidding around."

"Well," I said and pulled back. "Fuck 'em if they can't take a joke. I'm sick of all this and they can say what they want, but they're not putting me in jail. They think they're so powerful but they don't know who they're messing with. I've no more committed securities fraud than I've flown to the moon on gossamer wings. I'll get the best lawyers in the country and I'll get off, then I'll sue 'em for about a billion dollars. This is just a setup and it doesn't scare me a bit. Nobody here needs to worry, I promise you that. OK?" I challenged. They all smiled and nodded.

I was so whacked-out that it never occurred to me that I was being humored. I honestly thought I'd convinced them everything would be just dandy. Hank got up and turned off the set. "OK, we'll deal with this later. Now let's all go downstairs and mingle."

"Yeah, let's mingle," Gigi repeated in a fakely enthusiastic voice. So we went downstairs but I wouldn't go so far as to say that we actually mingled. It was more like we positioned ourselves in the same room as a group of people whose lives hadn't just been ripped apart.

Like Mennonites at an orgy, our presence did little for the mood of the party and it began to break up not long after we reappeared. It was certainly the first shindig at Hank's that I can ever remember being over at 10:30.

I was in the den with Gigi and Elizabeth, telling them what had happened with Jake and eating leftover caviar on little toast points, when Hank walked in with his date. I don't know if I can articulate this very well, but after everything that had happened in the last few hours, the very fact that She continued to live was an affront to me. That She would compound the felony by presenting herself in the same room was her big mistake.

Gigi broke the silence. "Everybody out of the pool."

She didn't get it. Holding on to Hank's belt loop, she flashed a big smile at me. "I am so glad I got a chance to meet you. I—"

"Save it," I said. "You don't give a happy damn about meeting me."

If she had said, "Yeah, you're right," or if she'd even kept her mouth shut, it wouldn't have happened, but no, she just had to say, "Why, that's not true."

"Yeah, it is. I'm a woman and as far as you're concerned, that immediately makes me your enemy."

"I don't think of you as my enemy!" she protested. Hank was shaking his head in an unsuccessful attempt to let her know that the less she said, the less bloodshed there'd be.

"If you didn't think I was your enemy, you wouldn't have walked in here tonight and made it clear to Jake Ward that you're an available fuck. If you didn't think of me as the enemy, you wouldn't come to my friend's house, stand right in front of me and try to steal my date. What's obvious to me is that it has nothing to do with Jake, it's about me. And your flirtation with Tom isn't about Tom, it's about his wife. If it was about men, you'd have been perfectly happy with the one who brought you."

She stood there with her mouth hanging open. Then, and I'm not making this up, she said, "You just don't like me, do you?"

"No, ma'am. I don't like you a bit. I think you're a flawless example of everything that makes women distrust each other. But my primary emotion here is not dislike as much as it is fear. You're the most dangerous kind of female—'cause you do one of two things to every woman you meet: Either you force them to reduce themselves to cunts to compete with you, or you humiliate them by proving to them how powerless they are if they don't. You hate women and this is the way you punish them."

It was suddenly as if a strong wind had blown across the mesa of awareness, dusted away all the righteous indignation and unearthed the skeletal outline of the truth. "You know how I know?" I said.

She didn't respond; she just stood there, frozen, chalk white.

"I know because I've been right where you are. I've done the same thing my whole life. It's not about sex, it's about power. It's not about attraction, it's about anger. I know how women make you feel, how they don't even give you a chance—how you're automatically the enemy the minute you walk into the room. I know what it feels like to be locked in a battle with your own gender, going around and around, taking turns wounding each other. I know that, on the other hand, men make you feel good. They don't snipe and gossip about you, they don't gang up and try to make you cry.

"But I also know that all women aren't mean and petty and at the end of the day, it's women who'll save your ass. Find some real women friends and stop playing pain boomerangs."

She stood motionless and silent. Finally, she whispered, "I don't know how."

"Well, first don't attach yourself to someone else's man. That tends to really put women off," Gigi said. "Second, look for the women who are laughing—"

"Not *mean* laughing—like at someone else's expense—*happy* laughing, fun, silly, joyous laughing. Women who laugh loud are safer than women who have tight little snickery laughs," I explained, holding out a toast point with caviar to her.

She came closer like a bird expecting a trap. She reached out and took it. "Thanks." Her voice was so low it was almost inaudible.

Gigi pulled out a chair for her and she hesitated, then sat down.

"Another thing to look for is strength," Elizabeth said and helped herself to more caviar. "The stronger the woman, the better the friend."

"That is absolutely true." I said, "You're not a member of our movement, are you?"

She shook her head.

"Religious or dietary reasons?"

She shook her head.

"Well then, you ought to join," Elizabeth said. "You'll meet a bunch of very cool ladies and they'll teach you a lot." Then she turned to me. "I think she ought to meet Lynette and Savannah . . ."

Hank eventually wandered off, and for the next hour it was just the girls, eating, giving advice, laughing and carrying on. Then the phone rang and Gigi answered it. "Purgatory Hilton. Oh hi, sweetie. It has been a long time. Me too. Yeah, we saw it. Mmhm, mmhm. That's a good idea. Mmhmm. Yeah, she's right here, hold on." She handed me the phone.

"Hello?"

"Hi, love." Slick.

"How'd you find me?"

"Called your friend Ali. Gigi says you've heard the announcement."

"Oh, we heard it all right. Charming, huh?"

"Well, that's one word for it. Scary's another."

"I'm not scared," I shot back. "I'm not scared a bit. Those creeps can't do anything to me."

"Sweetheart, I don't want to upset you, but they can do something to you. They can put you in prison."

"Well, dammit! I didn't do anything wrong."

"I know you didn't."

"What kind of securities fraud am I supposed to have committed?"

"I have no idea. I can't figure that out either."

"Well, what in the hell am I supposed to do now?"

"That's what I was calling about. I've just gotten off the phone with Townes Duncan. He's agreed to represent you."

"Wow, I didn't even know you knew Townes Duncan, much less that you could just ring him up and tell him to represent me," I said, and looked at Gigi and Elizabeth to make sure they heard.

He laughed. "Anyway, he said that in spite of what you've done, he really admires you and would like to be your lawyer. As a matter of fact, he's planning to fly to Atlanta tomorrow to meet with you. He's, um— hold on a second—he's coming in on the 3:10."

What could I say? "OK. Tell him to come to Hank's." I gave him the address.

"Are you all right?"

"Yeah, I'm fine. Thanks for doing that." There was a silence on the other end. "What about you? You and Annie OK?"

"Yeah, we're going to a marriage counselor and, though I think we've probably got a long way to go, we're both pretty hopeful."

I won't lie. I felt the sting of his words. "I'm rootin' for you," I said.

"And I, you," he said and hung up.

I was still holding the receiver when Hank appeared to take his date home. I took the last toast point, dipped it in the caviar and called out. "Nice to have met you, Jennifer."

"Bye-bye! Come see us anytime," Gigi said as she and Elizabeth escorted Hank and his happy date to the door.

"You don't even have to bring Hank!" Elizabeth hollered after them.

Chapter 25

The door to Hank's opened and there was the famous Townes Duncan. I think I was a tiny bit disappointed that he was merely life-sized. But there was something about him, besides the stocky frame, the square jaw and the Hershey-bar brown eyes. I can't explain it, but I understood immediately what *Vanity Fair* meant when they wondered if juries sometimes acquitted his clients simply because he was so likable.

"Come in, come in. I'm glad to meet you," Hank said and introduced us.

"This is a double honor. Mr. Williams, I'm a big fan, I've seen you several times at the Met and I've got all your CDs." Hank nodded graciously and said to call him Hank.

He sat across from us in a wing chair. He wore a blue-and-white striped shirt with white collar and cuffs, red tie, an exquisite suit and penny loafers. I smiled at the shoes.

"How about some coffee?" Hank gestured toward the silver service.

"Sure." While I poured, he looked around.

Hank turned to the figures standing in the doorway. "Oh, and these are our friends Moore and Elizabeth, and Lauren's son, Razz." They filed in to shake hands and I motioned for them to have a seat.

Townes pulled out a legal pad and set it on his lap. Then he put his hands together and brought them to his chin. "Although I've followed this story closely in the press, I think it'd be helpful if you started at the beginning and told me everything since Vincent Kovacevich opened the original bond positions."

I started at the beginning and talked for two hours while he took notes on the legal pad. He only interrupted to ask me to repeat dates or numbers. I told him everything I could remember. I recounted my conversations with Vinnie, with Ronnie, with Slick and Jamie and Merrill. "I'm a registered principal," I said at the end of my recitation. "And I know all the securities laws and I also know that I haven't broken a single one."

"John Hollister," he said.

"What about him?"

"Mr. Hollister has told the authorities that the trade between the two of you wasn't a legitimate transaction."

"What are you saying?"

"John Hollister is claiming that you didn't actually sell him $100 million in deutsche marks. He says you were parking his position for him."

My mouth dropped. Elizabeth stared at me, then she turned to Townes. "What is parking a position, and what's so bad about it?"

Townes leaned forward. "The parking of securities or currencies is basically a phony transaction that's done to hide the nature of someone's holdings. It's done to fake out either the SEC or the IRS and it's illegal. As a matter of fact, it's the charge that sent Michael Milken to prison."

"This is so stupid! I've never parked a position in my entire career, and if I was going to park for somebody, it sure as hell wouldn't be for that creep."

"I believe you. But he's signed an affidavit to that effect."

"I don't get it . . ." But as soon as I said that, I thought about my comment at the press conference that if Sterling White thought the transaction was so terrible, they should give the money back.

Before I could answer my own question, he did. "It's pretty simple. The guy loses two million to you, then he sees that your old firm is trying to make it look like you were trying to hide the trade for some reason and he thinks he can get his money back and send you to prison for good measure."

"Yeah? Well, I got news for John Hollister and anybody else who's wondering—I have absolutely no intention of going to prison."

"I'm going to be honest with you, Lauren. I think the fact that the attorney general is bringing this charge instead of the SEC means that this doesn't really have anything to do with securities violations. This guy is politically ambitious and I think he's trying to accomplish two things: one, to punish you, and two, to make you disappear long enough for them to break up the strike."

I looked at my son. "And long enough for Teddy to get custody of Razz." I turned back to Townes. "Well, they have to convict me first," I pointed out.

Townes was resting his face in his right hand. "Not necessarily," he said and looked up. "They can accomplish both things by setting your bail so high you can't pay."

Hank interrupted. "No such thing. Whatever number they set, I'll pay it."

"Or not setting bail at all."

I couldn't speak. I could barely breathe. "How could they possibly do that?"

"They can do it by getting the right judge, and by making a case that you're being sued for the custody of your son, that you're no longer employed and as such have no ties to the community. In short, by making a good case that you are a flight risk."

I was speaking slowly, mostly just thinking out loud. "So . . . what if I were to accommodate them by disappearing."

"If you were to accommodate them on the disappearing part, my guess is that the search for you would be weak. But when it's over, especially if the movement wins, they've got you just where they want you. You're a fugitive, so when they do catch you, they've got you for good."

"What do you mean 'for good'?" I was whispering at the top of my lungs. "I didn't park John Hollister's goddamn position. I haven't done anything wrong!"

"At that point, it won't be your business practices that are on trial in that courtroom, it'll be you and your movement. I guess you know you've made a whole lot of enemies in a very short time."

"Yeah, it's a talent," I said.

He ignored the remark. "I also need to tell you that attorneys are no longer allowed to strike potential jurors solely on grounds of gender, so your chances of getting an all-female jury are quite slim." He looked down at his hands. "Without an all-female jury, I think the outcome could be affected by things other than the evidence."

Hank put his arm around me and said in a strained voice, "What about options?"

"What sort of options?" Townes and I asked in unison.

"Like just disappearing for good. Going someplace that doesn't have an extradition treaty with the U.S."

Townes spoke slowly. "I'm an officer of the court and as such could be disbarred for even discussing that with you." We just sat there and looked at him. "I can't discuss *any* alternative to giving yourself up and standing trial. A decision on your part to not appear for arraignment is an option that I could not advise you on. I couldn't even be present during such a discussion."

I nodded and thought for a minute. "If I did decide to run, what would you have to do? Hypothetically, of course."

"Of course. I'd have to report to the authorities that I met with you and that I have no knowledge of your whereabouts. Lauren, listen to me. Don't do it. This isn't a John Grisham novel—this is real life. The claim against you is outrageous and we will beat it. Stand your ground. Now let me go back to the hotel, go through what you've told me and see what I can't figure out."

He rose so we all stood up. "Why don't you call me in a couple of hours and I'll have some more questions for you. Don't lose hope," he said, walking to the door.

Hank and I stared at each other. Then in a hoarse whisper, he said, "Heavens to Mergatroid."

"You took the words right out of my mouth," I whispered back, and sat down hard on the arm of the sofa.

"Oh, by the way . . ." We looked up and it was Townes again. "I charge $550 an hour and I usually require a $100,000 retainer, but because of the situation, I'll settle for $50,000 up front. Let me know." And he was gone.

Gigi and Tom showed up at noon the next day, and Ali and the gang arrived at Hank's around 2:30. I had Savannah on the speakerphone when I told them about the conversation with Townes.

"So what are you gonna do?" Ali asked.

"I don't know. Before that conversation, I never considered running. Of course, before that conversation, I never considered the possibility of actually having to go to prison. I watched this movie one time, about these women in prison, and it didn't look like much fun."

"Yeah, I hate those outfits they all wear," Jinx offered.

"No kidding," Gigi agreed. "Maybe they'll let you wear your own stuff."

Hank started laughing. "Yeah, I can see the society columns now: Ms. Lauren Fontaine was spotted at Rikers Island recently, looking smashing in a pink Chanel outfit complete with the signature gold and pearl necklaces. Always the fashion plate, Ms. Fontaine gives new meaning to the phrase 'women in chains.' "

"If you ran, where would you go?" Moore asked.

"I haven't exactly thought about it," I said.

"What about London?" Gigi asked.

"Yuk. I hate London. It's expensive and depressing and they only eat boiled food. Besides, it'd be too easy for them to find us in England. "

"What about Switzerland?"

I looked at Razz and Elizabeth and was suddenly very sad. "Where would you guys like to go?"

Razz shrugged and Elizabeth glanced at Moore. "How long would we be gone?" they asked in unison.

"If we go, we'll be gone a real long time," I said, and the air seemed to get sucked out of the room.

Razz crossed his arms. "How much money have we got?"

I was paralyzed. I could not bear to tell them another lie.

"Plenty," Hank said. "All the money you need."

"I always wanted to go to Monte Carlo," Elizabeth said, trying to sound happy.

I focused on Razz. "How does Monte Carlo suit you, babe?"

"I don't know."

"You would love Monte Carlo," Hank assured him. "Think flocks of supermodels in thong bikinis."

"Monte Carlo it is," he decided. "Come to think of it, Mom, things have been pretty grim in this neck of the woods ever since you started with this little social experiment of yours. I think it'd be good for us to have a change of scenery."

"Well," Elizabeth said, "who's gonna protect us from the lunatics?" Moore looked at me with such eagerness I almost laughed.

"Well, what about Moore?" I asked, straight-faced. "Moore, if we decide to go, would you go with us and keep us safe from the assorted fiends and nutcases we're likely to encounter?"

He nodded with such force that I thought he'd pull a muscle in his neck.

"Of course, you don't all have to disappear together," Ali said. "First off, it's not very realistic for you to think that you're just going to saunter through airport security. Lauren's face is plastered all over every newspaper and magazine and television in America and, no offense, but the rest of you are not exactly inconspicuous."

"Elizabeth and Moore can take Razz so that Teddy can't find him. And they don't have to leave the country, they could just stay at our camp on the bay."

Jinx turned from the bar, where she was mixing a martini. "Maybe this guy's not being straight with you, maybe you ought to talk to a woman lawyer."

I shook my head. "I trust him."

"Me too," Hank said. "Besides, the Townes Duncans of the world don't get to be famous by lying to their prospective clients. He thinks she's being set up. A woman lawyer isn't going to change that."

"Wait a minute," Savannah's voice commanded from the speakerphone. "We've got this whole country about to explode and these guys are trying to throw you in jail. Maybe you ought to let 'em take you—and see what happens."

"What are you thinking?" I asked, not all that pleased with the direction this conversation was taking.

"Maybe you just go. Hold your head up and let them put you in jail. It could be the last bit of rope those fools need to hang themselves with."

If that suggestion had come from anyone else in the world I'd have been horrified. But it had come from Savannah and I trusted her. That didn't mean I was convinced.

"What if instead of feeling bad about my being thrown in jail, people think I actually did something wrong—then I'd be the one hanging."

"Didn't you say the claim is really ludicrous?" Savannah challenged.

"Yes, but that didn't keep a grand jury from indicting me."

"Yeah, a secret grand jury who never heard your side of the story. Any decent lawyer can convince a grand jury to indict. Besides which, we know absolutely nothing about the gender makeup of this secret grand jury. Savannah's right—if this Townes Duncan is that good, he'll be able to convince the American public that you were set up." This from Carl.

"Yeah. All that's fine and good, but if I'm in jail, I can't take care of my kid. Razz's father is trying to get custody of him and I'm not going to let that happen."

"Trust me, dear. We will do whatever we have to do to make sure that your son is safe right here," Savannah said in that voice that means *take this as gospel.*

"Let me think about this. It's a lot to digest." What I couldn't articulate was the rising panic in the back of my throat. The only way to keep from screaming was to focus on something else. "While you're all here, let's talk about whether the strike is helping or hurting us now. Have we given any thought to abandoning it? That way we could probably pick up a fair percentage of support from men who want Larry punished but are mad at us because they feel manipulated."

Lynette scratched the back of her neck and said to the music of her bracelets, "This is an important point and one we need to wrestle with. We may be making enemies of friends, and besides, if we want all the American people on our side, this may be the time to make peace."

I could tell Lisa was going to say something by the way she was squirming in her chair. "But let's not forget why we did this," she blurted. "It's not to get the man on the street on our side, it's to force the legislators to remember that we represent the majority of the population. Those are the guys who will make this decision—the congressmen and senators who'll decide whether or not to impeach."

"No," Ali said. "Now is not the time to take the heat off. If Jerry Dixon doesn't show up, and we're all pretty sure he won't, *and* we call off the strike, they'll just postpone the hearings until such time as there is more evidence . . . which of course will be never."

"That's a good point," I noted. "For now, at least, the strike continues."

Townes called around dinnertime to say he was pleased with his progress and we'd talk again in the morning. I was exhausted and climbed Hank's stairs for bed at 10:30. I might as well not have bothered. Once I was alone, fear came to keep me company. There was no way I'd be safe in prison, nothing could protect me in there. My mind raced, trying to decide what to do, then simply trying to entice the peace that now came only with unconsciousness. But sleep, like a frightened animal, wouldn't be lured.

It was past 3:00 when I finally dozed off and not quite 5:00 when I woke up more dazed than refreshed. I couldn't stand the thought of one more minute in that bed so I got up and stood in the shower, and at one point it even occurred to me to turn it on.

I dressed, wrapped my still-wet hair in one of Hank's white silk tuxedo scarves, found his keys, wrote a note that I'd return soon, unarmed the alarm and drove his Rolls-Royce down the driveway. A few minutes later, I passed our house and heard two helicopters hovering, but it was too dark to tell if they were police or just vulture media. I didn't slow down to look.

I pulled onto the Perimeter, the freeway that circles Atlanta, and just drove. I had no idea where I was going, but exhilaration pumped through my veins as if I'd made it over the wall at San Quentin. I headed for the sunrise, put on Hank's shades and found a country music station.

The music was just what I needed. There I was, like a demented Dina Merrill, my head wrapped in white silk and gigantic sunglasses, tooling around in a navy blue Corniche, singing a Tammy Wynette song at the top of my lungs.

I came around the freeway in time to see a fiery sun hover over the stadium and to realize that I was famished. I swung the car off at the exit and spent the next few minutes looking for a coffee shop or diner.

I pulled into the parking lot of one of those waffle franchises, put the top back up and walked in.

There were only four other people in the place and I took the back booth. The waitress kept winking at me. I figured she recognized me, so I winked back a couple of times before it occurred to me that it was not a conspirator's signal but a facial tic.

I ate a huge breakfast and read the paper. The meal cost $3.56 and I threw a five on the table and walked out into the parking lot. That's when I heard it. A choir of angels. I looked into the sky and I couldn't see anything, but their voices were as pure and sweet as a child's love and I was as certain as I was surprised that this wasn't a dream, it was actually happening.

Those voices spun around me and I put my hand on the car to steady myself. Then the song faded and began again and the longer I listened, the more it sounded like the voices were around me instead of above me and by the hymn's third verse I could accurately place the direction they came from and I did the only possible thing. I followed them.

Around the corner was a dark red brick building. The sun wasn't high enough to light the street yet, and I walked down the shadow darkness until I came to a side door. It was heavy but I opened it and slipped into the darkened nave. Only the part of the church where the practicing choir stood was lit, and I was unnoticed in the side pew, listening.

Then they were dismissed and the church was first quiet, then still, and the sun began to shimmer through the stained glass. Tiny motes of dust floated through the golden iridescence and I looked down to the garnet Bibles with the morning's program tucked into them. I pulled one out: Welcome to Ebenezer Baptist Church.

I am such a sucker for stuff like that. I looked up and whispered, "Nice touch." I couldn't help it, I had to walk to the pulpit and stand where Martin Luther King Jr. had stood and I had to put my hands on his lectern. I closed my eyes and I could see him: courageous and serene at the Birmingham bus boycotts and the Memphis sanitation workers' strike. My eyes were still closed, and I could see him, radiant and calm at the Washington Mall and the Oslo ceremonies.

A voice from the back of the church startled me. "May I help you?"

I jumped. "I'm sorry. I was drawn in by your choir and I just realized where I was. It's pretty powerful standing here."

The voice was deep and melodious and its owner hidden by the darkness. It was sort of like talking to the Wizard of Oz. "What can you see from his pulpit?"

I didn't stop to consider what a strange question it was. "I can see the past. I can see him."

There was now a smile in the voice. "I do the same thing, sometimes. I stand right there where you are and remember him."

"You knew him?"

"I knew him," the voice said, and a man about my age emerged. "And loved him. Not because I really understood what he was trying to do. I loved him because he loved me, me and all the other kids; I loved him because he was our preacher. It broke my heart when he was killed."

"Mine too."

He nodded and came closer. He was short and thick with broad shoulders and close-cropped hair. His suit was black and his white shirt glowed against his skin.

"What do you remember about him?" I asked.

He looked at the ceiling and took a breath. "I remember his smile; mysterious like the Mona Lisa. I remember his voice. When he preached or spoke to crowds, it was that majestic instrument of his power, but when he spoke to you one-on-one, especially when he spoke to us kids, it was different; it was warm as a blanket, it was the music of love. And I remember a poem he taught us: 'Life is mostly froth and bubble, two things stand as stone / Kindness in another's trouble—

We finished together: " '—courage in your own.' "

He smiled that I knew it. I smiled back and surprised myself by saying, "I'm Lauren Fontaine, and I don't know if you know, but I'm in a lot of trouble."

His wide face registered no reaction. "This is a safe place. You could hide here," was all he said as he turned around.

"He didn't hide here," I challenged.

"It would never have occurred to him," he said and walked back into the darkness.

When I got back to Hank's, I could hear everyone in the dining room—eating, talking, waiting. I walked in and motioned Razz to follow me and he did. We walked into the living room and I shut the door.

"What are you gonna do?" he whispered.

"Only one thing I can do."

"Stay and fight?" His voice cracked.

"Yeah."

He studied the light switch on the wall. "I knew you were gonna say that."

He couldn't look at me and maintain his composure. I couldn't touch him and maintain mine.

I didn't say anything to anyone else. I couldn't. I just turned and made my way to the guest room and sat at the foot of the bed. Finally, I picked up the phone.

"Ramada Renaissance. How may I assist you?"

"Townes Duncan's room, please."

"Duncan."

"I'm ready."

"All right. Give me your number and I'll call you back in a little while," he said and hung up.

I must have fallen asleep, because the phone startled me when it rang an hour later. "Lauren?"

"Townes?"

"Yeah, It's all taken care of. I'll come over around 2:00 P.M. I've called a news conference for 3:00 at Hank's, then I'll go with you to give yourself up. I've told the federal marshals to expect us around 4:30. Pack a toothbrush. The arraignment will be tomorrow morning at 10:00. Your friends can go by your place later and get your stuff. I'll bring you something to wear to court tomorrow."

Once I hung up, I went downstairs. I met Hank in the hall. "I'm going in. I've talked to Townes and we're supposed to meet the feds at 4:30. He's coming over around 2:00 and holding a news conference at 3:00."

We walked out onto the terrace, our faces announcing my decision.

Gigi shook her head, muttering, "I just can't believe this is happening. I just can't believe it . . ."

Lynette touched my arm. "You OK, lamb?"

"I'm fine," I said. "I'll be back in a little bit. Right now, I've got to go upstairs, take a shower and pick out a cute outfit to wear to the slammer." I winked and left them all staring at each other.

By the time Townes arrived at 2:10, we were all in the dining room, where we'd just finished lunch. Hank introduced him to everyone and he sat down in the chair to my left. Hank was at the head of the table, on my right, and as I ran my finger around the Flora Danica plate, I thought back to the night it all started, the night I met Jake, and his words came back to me: *He has lessons for the timid and the fearful, but the really good ones, He reserves for the brave.* And then Queen Esther's, *Girl, every important journey is scary, and the big ones, you usually take alone, but if you got faith in the Lord, you gonna find that He'll pack your bags with enough courage to get you where you need to go.*

For the first time in my life I was unafraid. Was that possible? Could I remember a time when I didn't have to pack my own bag with courage? I was awed by the realization. I didn't have to be brave—because I wasn't afraid. And I wasn't afraid because I had faith.

"You ready?"

I looked up and Townes was standing. I motioned to Razz and we walked into the kitchen and I held my son for a long time. " I love you more than you know," I whispered.

He pulled away and looked at me. "Same here." The tears rolling down his face matched mine. "I never did tell ya, but I'm real proud that you're my mom."

"Me too," I said as we walked back out to the dining room.

I wiped the tears away with the back of my hand. I nodded to Townes. "I'm ready." I turned to my friends. "Do not tell me good-bye or anything resembling good-bye. That would just finish me off. We've got a ton of stuff to do and I'll be in touch from the joint. Let's all go out there grinning."

I didn't wait for an answer. Townes and I walked outside to the biggest crowd of reporters yet. When Ali and Lynette and Gigi and everyone were all standing behind us on the top steps, he began.

"Lauren Fontaine is being set up," he said, "by people who want to keep an evil man on the Supreme Court. As you know, she's been accused of securities fraud. I think it is important that everyone completely understand the charge. That way I think I can show you how ludicrous it is.

"She has been indicted on one felony count of securities parking. Let me explain exactly what securities parking is. It's a rare and illegal thing that some brokerage firms do for favored clients, and its purpose is to hide the client's holdings from either the IRS or the SEC.

"It's always hard to tell if you're explaining technical terms so that a layman can understand, and it is absolutely critical that you understand why this charge is so absurd, so I take the risk of being redundant.

"Securities parking has one purpose and that is to help the client avoid reporting his holdings. It is done in two kinds of circumstances. The first circumstance usually occurs while the client is amassing a large stock position in preparation for a takeover.

"The SEC requires anyone holding more than five percent of a stock's outstanding shares to file a thing called a Schedule 13D. The purpose of that rule is to allow the management of the company in question to know that someone is out there in the market buying up their stock.

"If the person who's buying up the stock doesn't want to file a 13D because he doesn't want management to know what he's doing, he might ask the broker he works with to park the shares in the brokerage firm's account. This is what Mike Milken did for Ivan Boesky and it's what he was sent to prison for. This is not the kind of securities parking that Ms. Fontaine is being charged with. There was no stock involved in the transaction in question.

"The other kind of securities parking occurs with currencies and its purpose is simple—to allow the client to underreport his profits so he doesn't have to pay taxes on them that year. This kind of parking occurs at only one time—on the last trading day of the year—December 31st. *This* is what Lauren Fontaine supposedly did for John Hollister on the morning of Friday, June 29th."

He let that sink in. Then he played another card. "As I said, securities parking is something a broker does for a favored client. The broker

doesn't get anything out of it but the chance to go to jail. If you ask
around, talk to your sources on Wall Street, you'll find that my client's
dislike of John Hollister is well known. He had tried to cheat her on a
number of occasions and she thought he was a crook. She'd always
thought he was a crook, she'd said so in public many times. He was
hardly the person she would risk her career for, much less a prison
sentence."

I could look at the crowd and tell that he was making his point. He
turned over another face card. "Much has already been made in the
press of the"—he made quotation marks with his fingers—"mysterious
$200 million trade she was in the process of making that morning.

"An employee of Sterling White, Vincent Kovacevich had incurred a
significant loss for the firm while she was away in Washington and lied
to her about it. She received a telephone call about midnight advising
her of the loss when she returned home on the evening of June 28th.
You have already heard this from Ron Wells and J.T. Moriarty and a
number of other people who were involved in or aware of that transaction. Those men have all given newspaper and television interviews
backing up my client's version of those events.

"Whether you believe that the fault for the loss belonged to Vincent
Kovacevich or to Lauren Fontaine, there is one thing everyone agrees
on—her career was on the line. So put yourself in her place. It's 7:30 in
the morning. You've been up all night because you have to make $30
million dollars in the currency markets before noon. Everything you've
ever worked for, even the survival of the 106-year-old firm of which you
own a piece, is riding on the success of this trade.

"Would you stop in the middle of everything you were doing to hide
a hundred million dollars for someone you detested? If you wouldn't,
then you understand our amazement at the charge here."

He was really enjoying himself at this point and flipped his last ace.
"The thing I think most interesting is that the attorney general of the
state of Georgia took it upon himself to indict my client when the
Securities and Exchange Commission, whose jurisdiction this is, has not
found grounds on which to bring charges."

Then he stepped back and motioned me to the microphone.

I stepped up and put my hand on Townes' arm. "Everything Mr. Duncan just told you is true except maybe his assertion that what the attorney general has done is merely interesting—it is more than interesting—it is horrifying," I said. "Maybe I'm just being paranoid—but I think this has more to do with my fight to have Lawrence Underwood punished than it does with any sinister securities trade." I raised an eyebrow. "What do you think?

"And that," I said with great emphasis, "is why I declare myself a political prisoner." I had absolutely no idea what I was talking about, but it seemed dramatic and I was on a roll. "And why I expect to be treated with all of the privileges afforded by the Geneva convention." I caught the look on Townes' face and decided to change the subject.

"I expect that the women of this country will continue to hold out for justice and continue the work that we've begun. We are so close! Don't let these little people get in our way."

The reporters started yelling questions, but Moore hustled me back into the house, through the garage and into Townes' limo. Townes was asking me what in the hell did I know about the Geneva convention and I said I didn't know anything and he said it just meant that my captors couldn't torture me and I said I thought that was good and he didn't say anything, he just shook his head. He didn't talk for a while, then he started filling me in on stuff like the fact that I'd be handcuffed and that I'd be strip-searched at the prison, but not to worry, it'd be done by a female guard, and a bunch of other charming little tidbits about life in the Big House. Finally I said that if he was going to tell me one more bad thing I was going to jump out of the car into the path of a semi and to please shut up and turn on some decent music.

It wasn't hard for the driver to find the building where I would surrender. It was the building swarming with helicopters and news trucks and reporters. That self-righteous prick, the attorney general, was standing on the front steps, pontificating for the press. He'd had plenty of time to change his clothes but he was wearing this ridiculous Hawaiian shirt and khakis like he'd come running in from this big manhunt à la Tommy Lee Jones in *The Fugitive.*

We got out of the car and had made it to the top step when he motioned for two men in uniforms to handcuff me. They did and were just about to lead me off when one of the reporters yelled, "Did you ever think this would happen when you started the Lysistrata Movement?"

I turned around. "Which part? Showing that women are incredibly powerful when they stick together or being thrown into jail by Don Ho?" Then I laughed and they took me away.

Chapter 26

It took four hideous hours to be processed into the Hardwick Women's Correctional Facility. Part of the deal that Townes had cut was the promise that I would not be housed in general population, meaning that I would have a separate area. The problem was that my separate area was a double-wide trailer that would not be available for eighteen hours.

I was lower than the sun when, with Townes and the warden and two prison guards on either side of me, I walked into a building with a sign that said POD 2. I knew the instant they stopped in front of cell 206 that there'd been a terrible mistake. There was an enormous man sitting on one of two narrow beds.

I turned around with my back to the cell, and Townes saw my face. "It's a woman," he whispered.

"And I am Marie of Rumania," I whispered back and moved my head just enough to see this thing with a dirty-blond crewcut out of the corner of my eye.

The guard on my right unlocked the door and the thing just sat there staring at me. Townes didn't linger, he said he would see me in the morning, then gave me a little hug and walked outside. The others followed and I heard what will go down in my memory as the most nightmarish sound I'd ever heard, the clunk of metal that left me locked inside with that thing.

I cleared my throat and held out my hand. "Lauren Fontaine."

It stared at me.

I looked around the cell and said, "Well, I just love what you've done to the place. Who's your decorator?"

It stared at my breasts straight through my neon orange jumpsuit and my crossed arms.

I shrugged and turned away. I sat on that bed and silently recited the names of the people I love, middle names included. John Ransom Fontaine, James Cannon Ward, Elizabeth Francis Martin, Charlotte Allison Williams Wolverton, John Tarleton Moriarty . . .

The lights went out and I slid under the thin blanket and lay on my back so that I could keep an eye on the hulking figure, and through the cavernous emptiness of cement and metal, a mellifluous voice sang a lullaby and then a dozen voices rose up screaming *"Shut Up"* and then quiet and again the same lullaby and again the screaming and it went on all night and then the lights went on at 6:30 in the morning.

I was so exhausted I was nauseous. I went to the sink and started to brush my teeth and it was then that hulking creature came to squat on the toilet and move its bowels and leave me sweating and dry heaving into the sink.

The doors opened and the prisoners walked out and one of the guards called the roll. This was notable for two reasons. When I answered to "Fontaine, Lauren," there was a hum of whispered comment, then a shrill voice called out, "Hey, Laureeeni, you big fuckin' deal, welcome to the slaaammer!" This was met with hyena laughter.

I yelled back, "That's Miss big fuckin' deal to you, and thanks so much, I'm just thrilled to be here." This was met with total silence.

The second thing was that I learned my cellmate's name. It was, and I'm not making this up, Rusty Nail.

Everything had been planned for my maximum humiliation. I was allowed to wear my own clothes but not to come to my arraignment with my lawyer, and so I was transported in a prison bus and unloaded at the back door of the courthouse, wearing handcuffs and shackles, and I felt like something that had been pressed between the pages of a Kafka novel.

There were reporters and supporters, all of them screaming, and police and bailiffs and something caught my eye and it was an effigy of me hung from a tree next to the building and I turned my head and there was Townes and he had this huge, fake smile on his face. "You ready?" he said and took my hand.

I smiled and sank my nails into his palm. "You get me the fuck out of there."

"I'm doing the best I can," was all he said, then he studied my clammy face. "Are you sick?"

I shook my head. He started to say something but I waved his concern away. "Merely a combo platter of stress and exhaustion and revulsion to my roommate, the lovely and elegant Rusty Nail. Any chance I could get some Gatorade?"

He sent an assistant to find some and the bailiff opened the door and we slipped through it. As we made our way down the marble corridor, I was listening to the sound of our shoes on the marble and it reminded me of getting off the train on my way to Ali's for the march and the porter playing the bongos on the luggage cart. Townes turned to me. "I don't want you to get your hopes up. The judge we got has a bad record when it comes to women, and he's already ruled there'll be no television cameras. I think that's a bad sign."

When we walked into the courtroom and around to the defense table, Razz and Elizabeth and Moore, Ali and David, Hank, Gigi and Tom were in the front row. Jinx, Savannah, Lynette, Suzanne and Lisa, Kimlee and Carl were in the second, then Sherry and Arthur and my friends from Sterling White in the third.

If I hadn't been so dehydrated, I would have cried, and if I'd had time I would have hugged every single friend, but Ali stopped me in my tracks with the news that Jake's brother had died that morning and the bailiff came in and said, "Ladies and gentlemen, please rise. The Honorable Herman Shower's court is in session."

I didn't have to rise because I was still standing and an ornate mahogany door opened and this dwarfy little man in a black robe ascended to the judge's throne. It was clear from the way he looked down on me that I was to be the surrogate for the legions of women who had, throughout his long and dwarfy life, done the exact same thing to him.

The bailiff read the charges and Herman peered down at me. "Do you understand these charges?"

"I do."

"How do you plead?"

"Not guilty."

"So noted. Mr. Duncan?"

Townes buttoned his coat and looked up. "Your Honor, my client is the dedicated and involved leader of over a hundred million people. She has shown an incredible commitment to both this community and this country and I ask that she be released on her own recognizance."

Herman didn't say anything for a long moment, then he closed his eyes like the burden of the decision weighed, oh so heavy, on his shoulders. He opened them. "Mr. Duncan, your client is no longer employed and is, I understand, being sued for custody of her child."

Then he looked at me and shook his head. "Ms. Fontaine, you have shown yourself to be volatile and unpredictable and I'm afraid to take a chance on your disappearing." Then he smiled at me like he was just doing this for my own good. "The court denies bail," he said and banged down his gavel. "Next case."

I didn't even look at Townes. I just turned around and walked the three steps to where my son stood and put my hand on the side of his face. "I love you," I said and kissed him, "and I'm holding you right here in my heart." And he didn't have a chance to say anything before the bailiff took my arm and led me away.

When all the arraignments were over and we were loaded back onto the prison bus, and the reporters were screaming questions through the reinforced glass, and the people who had come to protest were crying, I did the only thing I could do to survive the moment. I turned my back to the window.

Chapter 27

So anyway, this is where you came in. I'd been sitting in Tara, my lovely mobile home of the last seven weeks, three days and two hours, and things were not good. My world consisted of four tin walls and my meager belongings: a telephone that works from 9:00 in the morning to 9:00 at night, a Rolodex, a toothbrush and toothpaste, The Book of Common Prayer, an 8 x 10 photo of Razz, a small television, VCR, and Jane Fonda video, Razz's boom box and two tapes—*Little Richard Live at the O.K. Club* and *Edith Piaf / Little Sparrow*—a Sunday program from Ebenezer Baptist Church, and a purple hat with a wide polka-dot band and a tiny spray of white paper flowers.

I'd started having really frightening mood swings, waking up in a kind of manic euphoria that peaked around lunchtime and began to free-fall into an anthracitic depression that had me in bed by dark and bled into nightmares and night sweats and broke like a fever in the early hours of the morning. I even told Gigi not to come in the afternoons anymore.

Outside, things were worse. The Underwood impeachment hearings were still in limbo and the country continued to convulse in the throes of the strike. Without sex as the lubricant between the genders, the gears ground to a gritty and screeching halt. Statistics were showing violent crime at its highest level ever. But then so were the numbers of domestic abuse deaths, suicides and divorces. The only things down were productivity, morale and the lines of communication.

I was drinking iced tea, pacing around my living room, which is approximately the size of a pocketbook, and watching Oprah when the phone rang. It was Moore.

"Miss Lauren, are you busy?"

"Well, I'm throwing a little dinner dance tonight for the heads of all the Slavic countries, but other than that, I'm completely free. What's up?"

"Elizabeth and I want to come for a visit. We have a surprise for you."

I have come to detest surprises. "Good or bad? Bad or worse? Worse or nightmarish?"

"Good. No," he corrected himself, "great. A great surprise."

The happiness in his voice made me giddy. "You want to tell me what it is?"

"No. But we'll be there in about an hour."

"Well, hurry the hell up! I can't stand the suspense," I yelled into the phone.

It was late afternoon and I was sitting on the cement steps of Tara, making swirls in the dirt with my big toe, when Moore and Elizabeth showed up, escorted by the assistant warden, who seemed suspicious that these large, happy black people had come to see me. Elizabeth hugged me until I thought she might be causing me internal injuries, then Moore picked me up and kissed me on the top of the head while my feet dangled in the air.

"So, what's the surprise?"

They looked at each other. "Hold on," Elizabeth said and disappeared into my trailer.

"How's our boy?" I asked Moore.

"He misses you and he's dog tired of all this carrying-on. Other than that, he's fine."

"Good," I said and motioned back at the trailer door. "What is she doing?" Before he could answer, she was standing above me with the boom box that Razz had loaned me.

Moore beamed at her. "She's getting you out of jail, that's what she's doing."

I cupped my hand over my eyes to shield them from the glare of the setting sun and watched his burgundy lips give way to enormous alabaster teeth. I craned my neck around to look at her. "Elizabeth, how're you getting me out of jail?"

He didn't trust her to take the credit he thought she deserved. "Well, when she heard you tell your story to Mr. Duncan the day you went to jail, you said the reason the tape wasn't there for you to take to the meeting with Merrill Kennedy was because the power for the recorders had been knocked out. You'd been in Washington and the cabin on Chesapeake Bay all that week so that story made sense to you, but Elizabeth remembered that Atlanta hadn't gotten a drop of rain until the Fourth of July, the night you came home after you'd been fired, three days after you asked for the tapes."

I was trying to digest what he was telling me. I nodded for him to continue. "See, she remembered how she and Razz raced the rain that night in the kitchen and it came back to her how they talked about how long it had been since they played that game. From that she figured out that there hadn't been a power failure and that there would have been a tape made at your office on the day of the trade. That meant that somebody must have taken the tape, and since Merrill Kennedy knew the one you brought wasn't the real one, it meant that he had to know where the real one was."

He grinned like a drum majorette and I laughed and shook my head in amazement.

"So she found the number and called Merrill Kennedy's house and told his wife she knew the tape was there and that we needed it. But at first, Mrs. Kennedy wouldn't tell her that she knew where it was—but Elizabeth is so smart, she could tell she did. Mrs. Kennedy said she'd look for it and call Elizabeth if she found it."

Moore couldn't stop grinning. "But then we didn't hear from her for a long time—until this arrived about an hour ago. We were on our way out the door to go to the airport when the UPS truck pulls up."

"The airport?"

He laughed. "We were on our way up there to either convince her to give us the tape or find a way to get it. I know a bit about breaking and entering—"

I threw back my head and laughed at the sky.

Moore laughed too. "There are all kinds of ways of doing what needs doing. I learned this when I was a bodyguard. Elizabeth and I were going to get the tape one way or another."

I'd assumed that the tape had been destroyed. Louella turned it over? I was shaking my head, which was in my hands.

"Well, don't you want to hear it?" Elizabeth demanded, but she didn't give me a chance to respond. She popped the tape into the player and hit PLAY. They were watching me like children who have brought Mom breakfast in bed on Mother's Day, and "Mom" was pleased with the thought but waiting to see exactly what was under the napkin.

I closed my eyes to concentrate. The tape player made weird shimmying sounds like it was about to fall apart. And then it was me, backed by the sounds of traffic. "What's the bond market doing?"

And Vinnie. "Treasury intermediates are up 7/8ths. Long bonds up a point and a quarter."

"You get your ass on the goddamned phone and close those stupid positions or I am going to personally rip off your—"

"I closed 'em."

"What?"

"I closed the cocksucking positions!!"

"When?"

"At the fucking opening!"

"It's about damn time!"

Click.

I looked at them and smiled . . . scrambled eggs.

Then my voice again, but with more static on the line. "Who in the hell is it for?"

"Your old pal John Hollister," Ronnie says, sounding pleased.

"Swear to God?"

"Cross my heart and hope to die."

"How long has he been out of Menninger?"

"About eight months, I think."

"Hold on. I think I'll give the sex machine a call."

I could hear my recorded breathing and I opened my eyes and looked first into Elizabeth's, then Moore's. And John Hollister answers his phone and the two of us chat and I could feel my shoulders relax for the first time in months.

Hollister blurts his offer to buy me a cello so that I might stand naked on the equity trading desk and play for him, accompanied by the Philadelphia Orchestra, and I decline—and I usually hate to listen to myself on tape because I always sound like Jethro Bodine on Quaaludes but for the first time in my life I am loving the sound of my own voice.

The phone clicks and I'm saying to Ronnie, "Crazy as a possum on the freeway. I'll take the other side of that trade."

"The whole $100 million?"

"The whole thing. Call me back." Scrambled eggs *and* caviar.

I burst into tears and grabbed Elizabeth, who was in the process of saving my life, and she started crying and then even Moore got misty-eyed, so at first I didn't even notice that the tape was still going. It wasn't until I heard Merrill Kennedy's voice that I froze in midmovement.

"Did anyone see you come in?"

Then Vinnie Kovacevich growls, "Yeah, the night guard saw me. Did you think I could make myself fuckin' invisible?"

"What if someone comes back and asks—"

"I wrote Munroe's name on the sign-in sheet plus I gave the little freak at the desk a hundred bucks to keep his mouth shut. Listen, 'cause I don't want to hang around here all night. I found the ticket. She pulled $34 million and change out of a fucking currency trade."

"Too bad you can't trade that well, Mr. Kovacevich," Merrill sniped. "Then we wouldn't find ourselves in this unfortunate position."

"Yeah, who knows what I could do if I had $300 million in the market at one time," Vinnie shot back.

"Three hundred million. Are you sure?"

"I'm looking at the thing with my own goddamn eyeballs. Ronnie Wells did the trades in London."

"Trades? There was more than one?"

"Yeah, $200 million with Sumitomo and $100 million with Morgan Stanley, London. There's a notation on the ticket that it was John Hollister's account."

"I didn't even know that nutcase was back on the street," Merrill mused.

"Yeah, well he is and it looks like that bitch clipped him for $2 million."

"Interesting. Get the tape of that too. Hollister might be willing to work with us to unwind the trade."

"What do you mean?"

"I mean," Merrill huffed, "that if we offer to give him back a million, he'll help us teach Ms. Fontaine a valuable lesson. Oh, and for God's sake—make sure you pull the tape of this conversation."

The tape stopped, and I sat there with my mouth hanging open. I was so stunned I couldn't even speak—not because I didn't think that Merrill and Vinnie had framed me but because I'd assumed that I'd given them the idea by calling on Merrill to give the money back instead of continuing to criticize the trade. But they'd planned it from the beginning. Something bad had happened that wasn't my fault—a startling new concept.

Then we were all talking at the same time and nobody could understand a word anyone else was saying, because we were all crying and laughing and happier than I can describe.

Sometimes relief is the greatest ecstasy.

"Isn't she incredible!" Moore challenged. He'd asked the question at least twenty times in the hour that we'd been sitting on the steps.

"Incredible doesn't even begin to describe," I assured him, laughing. "Elizabeth, you are my fairy godmother. You know, I've been thinking about writing my memoirs and I've decided that instead of *sex, lies and videotape*, I'll have to call it *no sex, lies and audiotape*."

Moore reached over and took Elizabeth's hand at the same time a thought began to flower in the rich manure that is my mind.

I put my hand on Elizabeth's knee. "I need you to do me a favor as soon as you get back home."

She raised an eyebrow.

"I want you to call Louella Kennedy and convince her to disappear for a little while. It's really important. Make sure she understands how dead serious this is. I only need a couple of days, but she has got to be somewhere where he can't find her. OK?"

"What are you gonna do now?" She scowled.

"I got a plan."

She leaned in until she was close enough to kiss me, then she whispered, "I might remind you that it is your plans that got you here in jail to begin with. Now why in the hell can't we just turn this tape in to the police or the newspapers and get you out of here?"

"Because that won't solve the larger problem."

"Which is?"

I looked up at the fat guard in the tower who was watching us through binoculars and covered my mouth with the back of my hand. "Getting that sadistic prick off the Supreme Court so we can call off the sex strike."

I could see her mind turning that over. I knew if there was anything that would convince her to take one more step into the seventh ring of hell for me it was the thought that the strike might soon be over and she and Moore could be together.

The assistant warden appeared and started across the quad. Elizabeth looked at Moore, then at me. "OK," she growled. "But if you screw things up again I'm gonna let you rot in here. I'm gonna sell that big ol' house and take that boy and we three sane folks gonna disappear to the islands and you ain't never gonna hear from us again. You hear me?"

I nodded solemnly. Now the assistant warden stood, sweating profusely, at the foot of the steps.

"Sorry, folks," he said, little sweat drops beading his top lip and stains spreading under his arms. "Visiting time's over."

Moore nodded, standing up, and Elizabeth turned to me. "What else?"

"Would you mind bringing me a new tape player? I'm going to try to fix this one but I'm afraid it's on its last leg. Oh, and I need ten one-dollar bills." I turned to Barney Fife and gave him my most dazzling smile. "Do you mind if they drop those things off in the morning?"

He turned bright red and stammered that he thought that would be fine. With that, Elizabeth rose and dusted off her bottom.

I looked up and whispered, "Thanks."

She rolled her eyes and turned around, but not before I caught the beginnings of a grin.

"Merrill?"

"Yes?" He answered cheerfully, obviously not recognizing my voice.

"It's Lauren Fontaine."

"What do you want?"

"To invite you down here for a visit."

"Where? To your prison cell?" he sneered.

"Yeah, it's actually a prison trailer, or as we mobile-home folks like to say, a modular dwelling."

There was a long silence and his voice was tighter than the control panel of minimizer panty hose worn to a twenty-fifth high school re-union. "What do you want?"

"You know that tape Vinnie Kovacevich stole for you . . . well, guess who's got it now?"

A longer silence this time and then a much smaller voice, "I see. Well, what do you want?"

"Like I said, I want you for a little face-to-face. And guess what? I'm going to give you a chance to get the tape back."

"Why?" he croaked.

" 'Cause I'm such a nice person. But if I don't see you in the next, say twenty-four hours, I'm going to turn that tape over to the authorities. Oh, and Merrill, here's what you need to bring: a cashier's check made out to me for the money you owe me—which I believe comes to over $2.8 million and change, and you should bring a little cash . . . and if you've got a lucky charm, I suggest you bring that too. Ta-ta," I said and hung up. I've never said ta-ta to anyone before, but I thought if there was ever a situation that called for it, it was this one.

I couldn't get to sleep that night so I picked up the scrapbook Gigi had left on her last visit. I didn't read the articles. I know well enough what happened. Instead, I studied the photographs until way past midnight. Then I sat on my bed and stared outside my window where the only lights were the stars and the spotlight that swung from one gleaming razor-wire fence to the other. Around and around it shone on the proud and polished metal.

I could close my eyes and see the pictures; not the ones pressed between pages in the leather book, but the ones burned flawless in memory. The ones that made me cry, like the ones from Townes Duncan's car, of the people I love standing in Hank's yard, waving good-bye. Or the ones that made me laugh, like the one in the warden's office the afternoon after my arraignment, when over the warden's shoulder moved a shadow and next to it *he* was standing there. Standing there with outstretched arms, Jake Ward.

Those pictures and the others I'll forever remember; the heroes and the villains, the passion and the adventure and the love and the achievement . . . and the fury and the anguish and the terror and the cost.

I sat alone in the dark, remembering how I came to be there and praying that my plan would work and that I wouldn't have to stay.

Chapter 28

I had eaten my toast and was staring at the crumbs when the assistant warden brought the tape player and the dollar bills to the door of Tara. "Your friend said to tell you that Louella was going to the beach."

"Good. I think she needs some sun. She's looking awfully pale these days."

He nodded as if Louella's pallor had long been a mutual concern. "You expecting any visitors today?"

"Maybe. Why do you ask?"

"Got a call from a fellow in New York City. Kenny Merrill or somethin' like that. Said you invited him down for a visit. He'll be arriving around noon. That OK?"

"Couldn't be better," I said and took the tape player from him and set it on the floor. Then I smiled and held out my hand and he put the money in it. "Thanks for the cash. You a gambling man?"

"Not really," he confessed, blushing. "My daddy was a Baptist minister so I never played any betting games."

I tilted my head. "Ever wanted to learn?"

His face was crimson. "I better not. I'm not supposed to be in there, you know."

I looked at my watch. It was only 7:18 and it was going to be a very long morning. "I've got an idea," I said and batted my lashes. "Why don't you drop by around 11:30 to keep me company until my guest arrives. We can sit out here on the steps and I'll teach you how to play a famous Wall Street game called liar's poker."

"You've got a deal!" he squealed, rearranged himself and bounced down the steps on the balls of his feet.

I closed the door and rubbed my face hard. Then I sat down on the couch and got to work. I spread the dollar bills out on the floor and began to study the serial number of each one.

There was a knock on my door at 11:30 on the dot and the assistant warden presented himself. He had doused himself with enough Aqua Velva to clear the sinuses of a mummy and I was profoundly glad that our lesson was to take place outside.

I settled on the cement middle step and he stood facing me, with his back to the sun. "Got any cash?"

He nodded, pulled out his wallet and found eight singles.

"Keep those. Now have a seat and I'll explain how the game is played." He did and I pulled a dollar bill from the pocket of my lovely orange jumpsuit. "OK. Take one of those bills and look at it. On that dollar there's a serial number in bright green. See it?"

He nodded.

"All right. The serial number begins and ends with a letter but that's not important. The thing you need to pay attention to are the eight numbers in between. That is, for our purposes, your hand." I leaned over and pointed out that his dollar's serial number was L 59510551 C. "You have a pair of ones and four fives. That's a very good hand."

I showed him my bill. "Let's take a look at mine. My serial number is F 38282767 F. I have a pair of twos, a pair of sevens and a pair of eights. Now, liar's poker is like a lot of card games in that we bid. But instead of bidding on just what's in our hand, each one of us bids on what's contained in the total of our two hands, which in this case is sixteen numbers. The thing is that you can't see what's in my hand so you have to guess. And I can't see what's in your hand either. That's where the bluffing comes in—you try to fool me about what's in your hand.

"We take turns bidding, and each bid has to be higher than the last. So your first bid might be three ones. You know you have two and you're betting that I have at least one in my serial number. Now it's my turn. I can either raise your bid by saying four ones or I can raise it by bidding three twos. Now you know that you don't have any twos—so either I have three in my hand or I'm bluffing. Follow me?"

"So far."

"Good. If you challenge me then you'd win because there aren't but a pair of twos in our combined hands. If you don't challenge me then you have to come up with a higher bid, like four fives, which you know is safe. Or maybe you think I've got at least one five so you'd bid five fives.

"Here's where you're in danger—say you bid four fives; I know that I don't have any fives so you've got to convince me that you really do have five or I'm going to challenge you—in which case I would win 'cause in fact you only have four."

He nodded furiously. "This is just like I Doubt It."

"Yeah. Exactly. Now let's play." I pulled out another dollar and he picked up his next bill. I looked at mine, then pressed it against my chest. "I'll start the bidding with a pair of threes."

"I bid a pair of sixes," he said.

"Three sixes," I said.

"Four sixes." He smiled.

"I challenge," I said and his face fell.

I held out my dollar and he held out his. He had two sixes, I had none. "How did you know I only had two," he whined.

"Because you started out your bid with two and I didn't have any. So when you got to four, I figured you were bluffing. That's because I see you as a cautious guy. If you had started your bid at four sixes, I would have figured that's how many you actually had. But, for example, if you knew that I'm a big gambler then you might wait until I got pretty outrageous before you challenged me. Instead, you'd try to trick me into challenging you when you made a bid that you actually had in your hand. See, liar's poker is not just a game of luck and mathematics, it's really a game of psychology."

"Oh, OK. I see what you mean."

We played several hands and he wasn't too bad. It was even kind of fun to watch him enjoy himself and I must admit that it helped pass the time. When his walkie-talkie blared that I had a visitor at the front gate, we both just about jumped out of our skins.

"That was so much fun." He grinned, clapping his hands like a child. "Let's do this again soon."

"Sure thing," I said. He went to get Merrill and I stepped back into Tara and waited. I watched through the glass until the two figures came out the door to the administration building. When they were halfway across the quad, I turned on the tape and walked out onto the top step.

I stood there for about fifteen seconds until the two of them reached the bottom step. I don't want to sound melodramatic, but this guy scared the hell out of me. I looked at the assistant warden. "This won't be a very long visit. Do you mind waiting outside?"

"Not at all," my new best friend said and winked.

I motioned for Merrill to come up the stairs. When we were both standing at the door, I was close enough to see a patch of stubble he'd missed under his nose. I asked under my breath, "Did you bring the check?"

"I did. You have the tape here?"

I opened the door and we walked in to the sound of Vinnie Kovace-vich bellowing "*I closed the cocksucking positions!*"

I closed the door. "That would be the tape you're referring to?"

"Yes," he said, and I could see the vein at his left temple begin to pulse.

"OK," I said and crossed my arms in front of my chest. "I've proven I have the tape. Now where's the check?"

"In my pocket."

In the background, I'm snarling "*It's about damn time!*" to a dial tone. I held out my hand. "Let's see it."

He pulled it from his inside jacket pocket and held it just out of reach. It was close enough for me to see that it was authentic. A Citibank cashier's check made out to Lauren M. Fontaine for the sum of $2,982,439.62.

"Put it on the table," I ordered. He did, while John Hollister happily chatted about his cello on the tape. I don't know why it never hit me until that moment, but it was obvious from his breathing patterns that Hollister was playing with himself the whole time he's telling me about his plans for me and the Philadelphia Orchestra.

We stood there for a long minute just watching each other. "You said you were going to give me a chance to get the tape back." The vein in his temple was longer now and pulsing more visibly.

I pulled out a plastic chair and sat down. "Yes, Merrill, I did. But first, let's listen to you conspiring to frame me." And as if on cue, his voice came floating from the speakers of Razz's boom box. "Interesting. Get the tape of that too. Hollister might be willing to work with us to unwind the trade."

"Interesting, indeed," I said and walked over to the boom box, hit the EJECT button and removed the tape just as it finished playing. Then I walked back to the table and tossed it on top of the cashier's check. "You ready?"

"For what?"

"Liar's poker. Winner takes the pot."

He stood silent for a long time, first looking at the table, then studying me. My face gave away nothing; a pleasant smile and an eyebrow raised in challenge. I didn't hurry him, I just let him look . . . and think . . . and wonder what in the hell I was doing.

Finally he spoke. "Can I have some water?"

Did he want to snatch the tape? Did he think I'd let him out of there with it? Was he planning to slit my throat while I was at the sink? Or was he stalling for time? I looked at the cold and arrogant man who'd caused my life to unravel like a $6.00 sweater; the sleazemaster who'd used all his power to destroy me, to take everything that was mine and force me to rot in prison, giving a crack addict a chance to take my sweet son, this man who'd beaten and terrorized and tormented his wife and deserved a hundred eternities on his knees giving Satan himself a rim job. I stood back up, looked at him and smiled. "Sure, help yourself."

He stood at the sink for a long moment with his back to me. He drank one glassful, then another. Finally, he turned around and we stared into each other's faces.

I could feel my adrenal glands release their spicy product, and the thin drug shot through my arms straight into my fingertips, over and over, until I could feel the flash of heat that intensified into nausea then finally the infinitely small vibrations that felt like perfect clarity. I reached in my pocket and pulled out the dollar I had selected.

I signaled that I was waiting. This was the real gamble. What if he said no? And he read my mind. "What is this really about?"

I could have told him that I needed the money. But he'd know that after our conversation the day I called to apologize that I'd never admit to a vulnerability, not while I held the power to ruin him. I didn't want to spook him so I affected a little sneer. "I wanted to see if you'd have the balls to put it all on the line."

"I don't have much of a choice, do I?"

I shrugged. Finally, he opened his wallet and removed a hundred-dollar bill. I gave him a minute to look at his bill while I pretended to study mine. The serial number was T 72771437 B.

I looked up. He wasn't moving. "What's the real reason?"

It was my turn to bid. "I wanted to know why you did it—why you framed me, sent me to prison, ruined my life? I'm willing to give you a chance to win the tape back to find out why you'd do that to me when I never did anything to you."

"I never should have done that, Lauren. It was wrong and I'm deeply sorry." His response was as transparent and oily as mayonnaise left out in the July sun.

I called him and raised him. "Don't fuck with me or I'll open that door and both of our chances will disappear, mine to know and yours to save yourself. I said I want to know why you did it."

He folded. "I'm not a man who's ever had many close relationships and Lawrence Underwood is my oldest and probably only real friend. . . ." His voice trailed off. "I was just trying to protect him."

I kept my eyes on the filthy paper cupped in my hand and nodded slowly, as if understanding that somehow made me feel better. "I'll start the bidding with a pair of twos."

"A pair of fours," he said.

I looked up. "Would he do the same thing for you?"

His answer was immediate. "No. He wouldn't."

I lowered my eyes back to my dollar. "I see. Two sevens."

He was concentrating on his hundred-dollar bill. "Three fours."

I didn't hesitate. "Three sevens."

He took a breath and looked up. The vein on the side of his temple seemed more bunched up, almost varicose. "Three nines."

"Four sevens."

He blinked but said nothing, looked down at the bill cradled in his palm.

"You knew he needed protection because you knew he was guilty."

He looked up, his face suddenly silver with fury at my ignorance. "You don't know him. Nobody does," he spat. "You don't know the kind of terrible life he had as a child . . . that he was regularly beaten and burned and tortured by his mother, who was a whore and a sociopath. I knew him. I knew he had rages. I knew that he couldn't help himself," he said, hitting himself in the chest for emphasis every time he said the word *I*. "I knew that he couldn't even remember what he'd done after they were over."

His words came out slowly, each one distinctly enunciated. "When he was in one of his rages, he wasn't in control." He stopped and smiled, a fat prep school boy with a nasty surprise. "I'm the one who's known for forty years that he strangled his mother to death when he was twelve."

I didn't so much as blink.

He leaned in closer. "Betcha didn't know that, did you?"

I shook my head.

"It was our secret," he bragged. "Not even Lynn knew that."

"Yeah, but she certainly knew about the rages," I said.

He put his hand to his mouth and seemed to look right through me. "She knew firsthand about that. She could make him madder than anybody since his mother. It's really a miracle he didn't kill her."

My first thought was that of course he *had* killed her, but I didn't speak. I didn't even dare breathe.

He was off in his own little world now, his eyes completely unfocused. "He only beat her because he loved her so much. He didn't mean to hurt her, he just couldn't help it. Especially when he discovered that she was having an affair. He was terrified he was losing her."

"She was going to leave him?"

"No." He half smiled at the irony. "She was too afraid of him to actually leave. I told her if she ever even tried, he'd kill us both."

My stomach did a somersault. "Did he know she was having the affair with you?"

His eyes refocused and contempt stretched his thin lips into a self-satisfied smile. "I'm still alive. Therefore, the answer to that is obviously no."

"So you protected Larry Underwood because you were afraid of him."

"I prefer to think that my protection of Larry was an attempt at redemption."

I smiled. It was the single greatest act of will in my entire life. "Enough small talk. The last bid was mine at four sevens."

"Four nines."

"Five sevens."

"I challenge," he said and held out his bill. The serial number was D 29934993 A. No sevens.

I bit the inside of my lip and held out mine.

His laugh was loud and abrupt, like the bark of a seal. "Well, lookie here. The great Lauren Fontaine is bested by Merrill Kennedy." He picked up the tape and the check with great ceremony and walked to the door.

I looked over his shoulder and said through clenched teeth, "You win."

I watched him walk out and across the yard, escorted by the assistant warden. Then I removed the tape from the new tape player until he was completely out of sight.

They don't call it liar's poker for nothing.

Chapter 29

Peter Jennings looked into the camera and said, "We interrupt this broadcast to bring you some stunning news from New York," and he had that cute smile on his face and I sat down and there was a big SPECIAL REPORT banner at the bottom of the screen and he said, "Late last night, in yet another bizarre twist in what is surely one of the strangest chapters in this country's history, an audiotape was turned over to authorities which begins with what appears to be a recording of several conversations, one between Sterling White chairman Merrill Kennedy"—on the screen was a video clip of Merrill, a policeman's hand on his ugly head, being put into a car—"and famed arbitrageur John Hollister which proves a conspiracy to frame Lysistrata leader, Lauren Fontaine."

Then on the screen, there was John Hollister, crying like a baby. "The tape now in police hands also includes a full recording of the conversation between Fontaine and John Hollister that clearly shows the alleged securities parking scheme with which Ms. Fontaine was charged to be totally false."

I clapped my hands with joy as they showed film of Vinnie, who'd obviously been picked up at the office. The sound had been cut off because he was screaming what I'm certain were obscenities, but there are a bunch of the sales assistants and secretaries standing around, cheering.

"Authorities also say that the tape they received includes a recording of the disputed conversation between Lauren Fontaine and Vincent Kovacevich, proving that Kovacevich reported to her that he had closed the now infamous bond positions a full three days before they actually were closed.

"The recordings at the beginning of the tape turned over to authorities are also said to include conversations between Kovacevich and Sterling White chairman Merrill Kennedy, conspiring to retrieve the incriminating tape so that they might accuse Ms. Fontaine of securities fraud. Mr. Kennedy, Mr. Kovacevich and Mr. Hollister have all been charged with lying to the grand Jury. There are other charges pending.

"At this time, we're not sure exactly how all of this came to be, but it appears that jailed women's leader Lauren Fontaine was playing the damning tape for Merrill Kennedy inside the Hardwick Women's Correctional Facility, simultaneously recording his response. While that was surely surprising enough, it seems that during a card game that followed, Fontaine coaxed from Kennedy a stunning incrimination of Chief Justice Lawrence Underwood as both an insanely jealous wife beater and preteen murderer of his own mother."

Peter Jennings shook his head. "No Hollywood scriptwriter could have penned an uglier ending to a more bitterly fought battle. For in addition to pointing the finger at his prep school roommate, Kennedy confessed that he had been having an affair with the late Lynn Underwood and it was that affair that had precipitated Justice Underwood's violent abuse of his wife, causing her suicide.

"It is believed that Fontaine gained possession of the original tape and used the threat of exposure to lure Kennedy to the Georgia prison, then challenged him to game of cards with the tape and a cashier's check made out to Fontaine for almost $3 million as the ante.

"Merrill Kennedy had the cashier's check made out to Ms. Fontaine on his person when he was apprehended by authorities. The FBI is determining where the money came from before returning it to its rightful owner, but one source tells us that it may represent Ms. Fontaine's severance payment from Sterling White.

"While he is currently in FBI custody, there have been no charges brought as of yet against the chief justice. On Capitol Hill, Speaker of the House Don Gertchen has reconvened impeachment hearings for this afternoon at 1:00 P.M. Political commentators agree that the hearings will be swift and Lawrence Underwood stands no chance of remaining on the Supreme Court. Political fallout is expected to be severe for many of the players in this drama.

"While it is not known how Ms. Fontaine gained possession of the incriminating tape, there are rumors that it was given to her by Louella Kennedy, Merrill Kennedy's estranged wife. We will be reporting to you as events unfold in this deeply disturbing resolution of the country's battle over the Underwood case."

Then Savannah was on the screen, talking to a zillion reporters. "We expect Lauren to be back with us by this evening, working with us to bring Lawrence Underwood to justice."

I didn't know what else they said because I was on my feet, dancing. My heart was pounding and I was laughing and doing a combination Irish jig, rain dance and jitterbug.

The phone rang and I snatched it up, laughing. "Hello."

"Mom?"

"Hi, baby! Did ya see the TV?"

"Yeah, we just saw it." I could barely make out his words from all the yelling in the background. "Your lawyer just called and said to tell you he's on his way."

The things I remember most were the staccato of the helicopters and the heat. The gates were unlocked and thousands of screaming, chanting people rushed forward and police in riot gear formed a blockade and Townes motioned me to a bank of microphones that had been set up. I walked over to them and as soon as I started to speak, there was complete silence.

"Well, what can I say? I want to thank Louella Kennedy for giving me the tape. As soon as I get home, I'll be calling her personally to express my tremendous gratitude for her courage and her friendship. I want to thank all of you for your support. I'll be making a statement later today but right now I just want to be with my family.

"Oh, one more thing. I'd like to wish Mr. Kennedy, Mr. Hollister, Mr. Kovacevich and Mr. Underwood good luck in their new homes." Then I laughed and Townes and Moore and two FBI guys hustled me into a waiting limo and we took off for my house.

When we got through the mass of reporters and Hank and Razz opened the door, I yelled, "Hi, honey, I'm home!" and hugged Razz so hard I almost knocked him down and Hank didn't fare much better. Then Gigi came around the corner and we started crying and laughing and hugging and stuff. Elizabeth hugged me and then Moore hugged me again and then Elizabeth hugged Moore. Hank poured everybody champagne and Townes made a toast to me and then I held up my glass. "I propose a toast to my beloved friend and hero—Elizabeth," and everybody yelled, "Hear! hear!" and somebody asked how it all happened, so Elizabeth told the story again. Then we toasted her again and she was beaming and I was so happy I could cry—so I did.

Hank handed me his handkerchief and I blew my nose, then I remembered my promise and ran up to my room. There by the side of the bed was my Sterling White directory. I dialed the Kennedys' number. It was picked up on the second ring.

"Hello."

"Louella, this is Lauren Fontaine. I wanted to thank you for what you did—"

"You're welcome," she said, her voice warm as oatmeal on a January morning, "but you shouldn't be thanking me; I should be apologizing to you. I know now that I should have turned the tape over as soon as I found it."

I could hardly disagree. "When did you find it?"

"The same night Annie Moriarty called me in tears about seeing you with J.T. on that boat on TV, the same night J.T. told her about you two. Annie Moriarty's my best friend and she was devastated, which left me very disillusioned about you and the things you said about women sticking together. I didn't know what to do with the tape so I hid it and didn't say anything to anybody about having it. Then, when your friend Elizabeth called me, she said she knew I had the tape and that you needed it. She also told me that you'd been her best friend for over twelve years and that she'd do whatever she had to to help you. Then I started thinking that maybe you were sincere about the things you said. I called the Moriartys yesterday and told Annie about the tape and asked her what she wanted me to do. She told me to turn it in."

"Annie?"

"Annie. She said it was the right thing to do. She said that we women have to stop fighting each other and start standing together."

"Thank you both," I said before I replaced the receiver. So Slick had been right all along. Under different circumstances, Annie and I would have been great pals.

They played it over and over and over. The tape began with the former chief justice of the Supreme Court, Lawrence Underwood, being escorted from the Longworth Building after his impeachment. He was imperious even in defeat, his head held high, his posture erect. Then the back of someone's head appeared at the far left of the screen. It was a young woman reporter, thrusting a microphone in his face. She extended it farther than she meant to, and he jerked back to avoid being hit with it and the transformation was instantaneous. At that point, the tape was the same on all stations—shown in slow motion to make it all the more horrifying.

It is the first public glimpse ever of a very private terror, the terror that Louella knew all these years . . . and Gigi's best friend Sofia . . . and Lynn Underwood and every other woman who had ever come face to face with the shiny eyes of a cobra. He drew back and struck her, literally knocking her off the screen, and there was a moment of stunned silence before the crowd and the police reacted. And he could not help it, he was smiling.

Chapter 30

The press conference had been given and all the reporters were gone. The day's jubilant celebration had finally come to an end and the larger one, the one with Savannah and Ali and the rest of the gang, was planned for the next afternoon in Washington.

I dipped my finger in the empty champagne bucket and the water was warm, it was past midnight and I was finally alone. My speech was folded up on the coffee table. I retrieved it and reread the first few paragraphs.

"Good evening. I'm Lauren Fontaine. Before I make my statement, I'd like to speak for a moment from my heart to the American people. I want to thank you for the faxes and letters and e-mail and for the support that you've shown me and my family during my incarceration. It was a very difficult time for all of us, and your prayers and your messages of love and encouragement meant more to us than I could ever put into words.

"I've called this conference to express my pleasure and relief at this afternoon's impeachment of Lawrence Underwood. I hope that this difficult chapter in our history will be remembered for its satisfying outcome and that no man will ever again raise his hand to a woman without knowing that his share of the pain he is about to inflict will surely be commensurate. So, without further ado, I am calling for the end of the sex strike. Effective . . . immediately."

I refolded the piece of paper and smiled at the thought that if the eruption of cheers that came from my own living room was any indication of the nation's response, I was pretty sure that, at least that night, America was the happiest nation on earth.

The phone was off the hook and I was in my nightgown, barefoot and snuggled into my big chair, happier to be home than I could have possibly expressed. I was exhausted and just about to get up and go to bed when there was a soft knock at the door.

"Who is it?"

"Harold."

"Harold who?"

"Harold from Sparta."

I swung open the door and Jake Ward took me in his arms. He picked me up and carried me to my bedroom, then he locked the door and began to unbutton my nightgown.

"On the 23rd of June, at approximately midnight, in a room at the Four Seasons hotel in Washington, D.C., I made you a promise," he said, lifting the nightgown over my head. "I told you in detail what I intended to do to you when the sex strike was over."

"A lot has happened since then," I noted, backing away from him. I lay down on my bed, naked, and ever so slowly raised my hands above my head.

Then I smiled. "Refresh my memory."

Acknowledgments

I want to acknowledge and thank the people who made it possible for me to write *Holding Out:*

Allen McDaniel, George White, and Edwin Hines of Salomon Brothers for sharing their expertise in the field of currency trading.

Sally Brooks, Gary Fisketjon, and Morgan Entrekin for their early encouragement.

Dianne Lindsey, Tina Mash, and Earl Howell for all their hard work and support.

Lynnette Hart and my friends at Triangle and St. Anne's for their love.

I also want to express my gratitude to the people who turned my manuscript into this book:

My agent, Joni Evans, for things way too numerous to mention.

Her assistants, Sarah Rosen and Tiffany Ericksen, for their patience.

Amy Schiffman and Steven Bulka for their advice.

My editor Michael Korda, for his guidance and kindness, and all the wonderful people at Simon & Schuster.

And especially to Anita Wood and Jim Engelhardt, without whom this book would still be a stack of pages in my closet.

At last but certainly not least, a kiss for my friends who made the whole process of writing an adventure;

The Conti, Curly, King, Bops, T.F.B., David, Colleen, Raymond, Ned, Beverly, Garth, Mike, Tom, Scott, and Pauly.